Praise for the Christmas novels of Debbie Macomber

"Warm and sweet as Christmas cookies, this new Debbie Macomber romance is sure to be a hit this holiday season."

—*Bookreporter* on *Merry and Bright*

"Heartfelt, cheerful… Readers looking for a light and sweet holiday treat will find it here."

—*Publishers Weekly* on *Merry and Bright*

"Another heartwarming seasonal Macomber tale, which fans will find as bright and cozy as a blazing fire on Christmas Eve."

—*Kirkus Reviews* on *Twelve Days of Christmas*

"*Twelve Days of Christmas* is a delightful, charming read for anyone looking for an enjoyable Christmas novel…. Settle in with a warm blanket and a cup of hot chocolate, and curl up for some Christmas fun with Debbie Macomber's latest festive read."

—*Bookreporter*

"Feel-good… A dash of hilarity… The good, clean holiday fun should satisfy."

—*Publishers Weekly* on *The Christmas Basket*

"A delightful holiday story filled with romance, conflict and lots of humor."

—*Bookreporter* on *The Christmas Basket*

"Perfect for the holiday season, this little book is the perfect gift for the person you know who truly needs the Christmas spirit. Just don't forget to reward yourself with a copy as well."

—*RT Book Reviews* on *Shirley, Goodness and Mercy*

DEBBIE MACOMBER

Holiday Lights

Previously published as *The Forgetful Bride*, *Sugar and Spice*, and *Friends—and Then Some*

ISBN-13: 978-0-7783-8825-8

Holiday Lights

This edition published by arrangement with Harlequin Books S.A.

For questions and comments about the quality of this book, please contact us at CustomerService@Harlequin.com.

Mira
22 Adelaide St. West, 40th Floor
Toronto, Ontario M5H 4E3, Canada
BookClubbish.com

Printed in U.S.A.

Also available from
Debbie Macomber and MIRA

Blossom Street

The Shop on Blossom Street
A Good Yarn
Susannah's Garden
Back on Blossom Street
Twenty Wishes
Summer on Blossom Street
Hannah's List
"The Twenty-First Wish"
(in *The Knitting Diaries*)
A Turn in the Road

Cedar Cove

16 Lighthouse Road
204 Rosewood Lane
311 Pelican Court
44 Cranberry Point
50 Harbor Street
6 Rainier Drive
74 Seaside Avenue
8 Sandpiper Way
92 Pacific Boulevard
1022 Evergreen Place
Christmas in Cedar Cove
(*5-B Poppy Lane* and
A Cedar Cove Christmas)
1105 Yakima Street
1225 Christmas Tree Lane

The Dakota Series

Dakota Born
Dakota Home
Always Dakota
Buffalo Valley

The Manning Family

The Manning Sisters
(*The Cowboy's Lady* and
The Sheriff Takes a Wife)
The Manning Brides
(*Marriage of Inconvenience*
and *Stand-In Wife*)
The Manning Grooms
(*Bride on the Loose* and
Same Time, Next Year)

Christmas Books

A Gift to Last
On a Snowy Night
Home for the Holidays
Glad Tidings
Christmas Wishes
Small Town Christmas
When Christmas Comes
(now retitled *Trading Christmas*)
There's Something About Christmas
Christmas Letters
The Perfect Christmas
Choir of Angels
(*Shirley, Goodness and Mercy*,
Those Christmas Angels, and
Where Angels Go)
Call Me Mrs. Miracle

Heart of Texas

Texas Skies
(*Lonesome Cowboy*
and *Texas Two-Step*)
Texas Nights
(*Caroline's Child* and *Dr. Texas*)
Texas Home
(*Nell's Cowboy* and *Lone Star Baby*)
Promise, Texas
Return to Promise

Midnight Sons

Alaska Skies
(*Brides for Brothers* and
The Marriage Risk)
Alaska Nights
(*Daddy's Little Helper* and
Because of the Baby)
Alaska Home
(*Falling for Him*, *Ending in
Marriage*, and *Midnight Sons
and Daughters*)

This Matter of Marriage
Montana
Thursdays at Eight
Between Friends
Changing Habits
Married in Seattle
(*First Comes Marriage* and *Wanted: Perfect Partner*)
Right Next Door
(*Father's Day* and *The Courtship of Carol Sommars*)
Wyoming Brides
(*Denim and Diamonds* and *The Wyoming Kid*)
Fairy Tale Weddings
(*Cindy and the Prince* and *Some Kind of Wonderful*)
The Man You'll Marry
(*The First Man You Meet* and *The Man You'll Marry*)
Orchard Valley Grooms
(*Valerie* and *Stephanie*)
Orchard Valley Brides
(*Norah* and *Lone Star Lovin'*)
The Sooner the Better
An Engagement in Seattle
(*Groom Wanted* and *Bride Wanted*)
Out of the Rain
(*Marriage Wanted* and *Laughter in the Rain*)
Learning to Love
(*Sugar and Spice* and *Love by Degree*)
You...Again
(*Baby Blessed* and *Yesterday Once More*)
The Unexpected Husband
(*Jury of His Peers* and *Any Sunday*)
Three Brides, No Groom
Love in Plain Sight
(*Love 'n' Marriage* and *Almost an Angel*)
I Left My Heart
(*A Friend or Two* and *No Competition*)
Marriage Between Friends
(*White Lace and Promises* and *Friends—and Then Some*)
A Man's Heart
(*The Way to a Man's Heart* and *Hasty Wedding*)
North to Alaska
(*That Wintry Feeling* and *Borrowed Dreams*)
On a Clear Day
(*Starlight* and *Promise Me Forever*)
To Love and Protect
(*Shadow Chasing* and *For All My Tomorrows*)
Home in Seattle
(*The Playboy and the Widow* and *Fallen Angel*)
Together Again
(*The Trouble with Caasi* and *Reflections of Yesterday*)
The Reluctant Groom
(*All Things Considered* and *Almost Paradise*)
A Real Prince
(*The Bachelor Prince* and *Yesterday's Hero*)
Private Paradise
(in *That Summer Place*)

Debbie Macomber's Cedar Cove Cookbook
Debbie Macomber's Christmas Cookbook

CONTENTS

THE FORGETFUL BRIDE

For Karen Young and Rachel Hauck,
plotting partners and treasured friends.

PROLOGUE

"Not unless we're married."

Ten-year-old Martin Marshall slapped his hands against his thighs in disgust. "I told you she was going to be unreasonable about this."

Caitlin watched as her brother's best friend withdrew a second baseball card from his shirt pocket. If Joseph Rockwell wanted to kiss her, then he was going to have to do it the right way. She might be only eight, but Caitlin knew about these things. Glancing down at the doll held tightly in her arms, she realized instinctively that Barbie wouldn't approve of kissing a boy unless he married you first.

Martin approached her again. "Joe says he'll throw in his Don Drysdale baseball card."

"Not unless we're married," she repeated, smoothing the front of her sundress with a haughty air.

"All right, all right, I'll marry her," Joe muttered as he stalked across the backyard.

"How you gonna do that?" Martin demanded.

"Get your Bible."

For someone who wanted to kiss her so badly, Joseph didn't look very pleased. Caitlin decided to press her luck. "In the fort."

"The fort?" Joe exploded. "No girls are allowed in there!"

"I refuse to marry a boy who won't even let me into his fort."

"Call it off," Martin demanded. "She's asking too much."

"You don't have to give me the second baseball card," she said. The idea of being the first girl ever to view their precious fort had a certain appeal. And it meant she'd probably get invited to Betsy McDonald's birthday party.

The boys exchanged glances and started whispering to each other, but Caitlin heard only snatches of their conversation. Martin clearly wasn't thrilled with Joseph's concessions, and he kept shaking his head as though he couldn't believe his friend might actually go through with this. For her part, Caitlin didn't know whether to trust Joseph. He liked playing practical jokes and everyone in the neighborhood knew it.

"It's time to feed my baby," she announced, preparing to leave.

"All right, all right," Joseph said with obvious reluctance. "I'll marry you in the fort. Martin'll say the words, only you can't tell anyone about going inside, understand?"

"If you do," Martin threatened, glaring at his sister, "you'll be sorry."

"I won't tell," Caitlin promised. It would have to be a secret, but that was fine because she liked keeping secrets.

"You ready?" Joseph demanded. Now that the terms were set, he seemed to be in a rush, which rather annoyed Caitlin. The frown on his face didn't please her, either. A bridegroom should at least *look* happy. She was about to say so, but decided not to.

"You'll have to change clothes, of course. Maybe the suit you wore on Easter Sunday..."

"What?" Joseph shrieked. "I'm not wearing any suit. Listen, Caitlin, you've gone about as far as you can with this. I get married exactly the way I am or we call it off."

She sighed, rolling her eyes expressively. "Oh, all right, but I'll need to get a few things first."

"Just hurry up, would you?"

Martin followed her into the house, letting the screen door slam behind him. He took his Bible off the hallway table and rushed back outside.

Caitlin hurried up to her room, where she grabbed a brush to run through her hair and straightened the two pink ribbons tied around her pigtails. She always wore pink ribbons because pink was a color for girls. Boys were supposed to wear blue and brown and boring colors like that. Boys were okay sometimes, but mostly they did disgusting things.

Her four dolls accompanied her across the backyard and into the wooded acre behind. She hated getting her Mary Janes dusty, but that couldn't be avoided.

With a good deal of ceremony, she opened the rickety door and then slowly, the way she'd seen it done at her older cousin's wedding, Caitlin marched into the boys' packing-crate-and-cardboard fort.

Pausing inside the narrow entry, she glanced around. It wasn't anything to brag about. Martin had made it sound like a palace with marble floors and crystal chandeliers. She couldn't help feeling disillusioned. If she hadn't been so eager to see the fort, she would've insisted they do this properly, in church.

Her brother stood tall and proud on an upturned apple crate, the Bible clutched to his chest. His face was dutifully somber. Caitlin smiled approvingly. He, at least, was taking this seriously.

"You can't bring those dolls in here," Joseph said loudly.

"I most certainly can. Barbie and Ken and Paula and Jane are our children."

"Our children?"

"Naturally they haven't been born yet, so they're really just a glint in your eye." She'd heard her father say that once and it sounded special. "They're angels for now, but I thought they should be here so you could meet them." She was busily arranging her dolls in a tidy row behind Martin on another apple crate.

Joseph covered his face with his hands and it looked for a moment like he might change his mind.

"Are we going to get married or not?" she asked.

"All right, all right." Joseph sighed heavily and pulled her forward, a little more roughly than necessary, in Caitlin's opinion.

The two of them stood in front of Martin, who randomly opened his Bible. He gazed down at the leather-bound book and then at Caitlin and his best friend. "Do you, Joseph James Rockwell, take Caitlin Rose Marshall for your wife?"

"Lawfully wedded," Caitlin corrected. She remembered this part from a television show.

"Lawfully wedded wife," Martin amended grudgingly.

"I do." Caitlin noticed that he didn't say it with any real enthusiasm. "I think there's supposed to be something about richer or poorer and sickness and health," Joseph said, smirking at Caitlin as if to say she wasn't the only one who knew the proper words.

Martin nodded and continued. "Do you, Caitlin Rose Marshall, hereby take Joseph James Rockwell in sickness and health and in riches and in poorness?"

"I'm only going to marry a man who's healthy and rich."

"You can't go putting conditions on this now," Joseph argued. "We already agreed."

"Just say 'I do,'" Martin urged, his voice tight with annoyance. Caitlin suspected that only the seriousness of the occasion prevented him from adding, "You pest."

She wasn't sure if she should go through with this or not. She was old enough to know that she liked pretty things and when she married, her husband would build her a castle at the edge of the forest. He would love her so much, he'd bring home silk ribbons for her hair, and bottles and bottles of expensive perfume. So many that there wouldn't be room for all of them on her makeup table.

"Caitlin," Martin said through clenched teeth.

"I do," she finally answered.

"I hereby pronounce you married," Martin proclaimed, closing the Bible with a resounding thud. "You may kiss the bride."

Joseph turned to face Caitlin. He was several inches taller than she was. His eyes were a pretty shade of blue that reminded her of the way the sky looked the morning after a bad rainstorm. She liked Joseph's eyes.

"You ready?" he asked.

She nodded, closed her eyes and pressed her lips tightly together as she angled her head to the left. If the truth be known, she wasn't all that opposed to having Joseph kiss her, but she'd never let him know that because…well, because kissing wasn't something ladies talked about.

A long time passed before she felt his mouth touch hers. Actually his lips sort of bounced against hers. Gee, she thought. What a big fuss over nothing.

"Well?" Martin demanded of his friend.

Caitlin opened her eyes to discover Joseph frowning down

at her. "It wasn't anything like Pete said it would be," he grumbled.

"Caitlin might be doing it wrong," Martin offered, frowning accusingly at his sister.

"If anyone did anything wrong, it's Joseph." They were making it sound like she'd purposely cheated them. If anyone was being cheated, it was Caitlin, because she couldn't tell Betsy McDonald about going inside their precious fort.

Joseph didn't say anything for a long moment. Then he slowly withdrew his prized baseball cards from his shirt pocket. He gazed at them lovingly before he reluctantly held them out to her. "Here," he said, "these are yours now."

"You aren't going to *give* 'em to her, are you? Not when she messed up!" Martin cried. "Kissing a girl wasn't like Pete said, and that's got to be Caitlin's fault. I told you she's not really a girl, anyway. She's a pest."

"A deal's a deal," Joseph said sadly.

"You can keep your silly old baseball cards." Head held high, Caitlin gathered up her dolls in a huff, prepared to make a dignified exit.

"You won't tell anyone about us letting you into the fort, will you?" Martin shouted after her.

"No." She'd keep that promise.

But neither of them had said a word about telling everyone in school that she and Joseph Rockwell had gotten married.

1

For the third time that afternoon, Cait indignantly wiped sawdust from the top of her desk. If this remodeling mess got much worse, the particles were going to get into her computer, destroying her vital link with the New York Stock Exchange.

"We'll have to move her out," a gruff male voice said from behind her.

"I beg your pardon," Cait demanded, rising abruptly and whirling toward the doorway. She clapped the dust from her hands, preparing to do battle. So much for this being the season of peace and goodwill. All these men in hard hats strolling through the office, moving things around, was inconvenient enough. But at least she'd been able to close her door to reduce the noise. Now, it seemed, even that would be impossible.

"We're going to have to pull some electrical wires through there," the same brusque voice explained. She couldn't see the man's face, since he stood just outside her doorway, but she had an impression of broad-shouldered height. "We'll have everything back to normal within a week."

"A week!" She wouldn't be able to service her customers, let alone function, without her desk and phone. And exactly where did they intend to put her? Certainly not in a hallway! She wouldn't stand for it.

The mess this simple remodeling project had created was one thing, but transplanting her entire office as if she were nothing more than a…a tulip bulb was something else again.

"I'm sorry about this, Cait," Paul Jamison said, slipping past the crew foreman to her side.

The wind went out of her argument at the merest hint of his devastating smile. "Don't worry about it," she said, the picture of meekness and tolerance. "Things like this happen when a company grows as quickly as ours."

She glanced across the hallway to her best friend's office, shrugging as if to ask, *Is Paul ever going to notice me?* Lindy shot her a crooked grin and a quick nod that suggested Cait stop being so negative. Her friend's confidence didn't help. Paul was a wonderful district manager and she was fortunate to have the opportunity to work with him. He was both talented and resourceful. The brokerage firm of Webster, Rodale and Missen was an affiliate of the fastest-growing firm in the country. This branch had been open for less than two years and already they were breaking national sales records. Due mainly, Cait believed, to Paul's administrative skills.

Paul was slender, dark-haired and handsome in an urbane, sophisticated way—every woman's dream man. Certainly Cait's. But as far as she could determine, he didn't see her in a similar romantic light. He thought of her as an important team member. One of the staff. At most, a friend.

Cait knew that friendship was often fertile ground for romance, and she hoped for an opportunity to cultivate it.

Willingly surrendering her office to an irritating crew of carpenters and electricians was sure to gain her a few points with her boss.

"Where would you like me to set up my desk in the meantime?" she asked, smiling warmly at Paul. From habit, she lifted her hand to push back a stray lock of hair, forgetting she'd recently had it cut. That had been another futile attempt to attract Paul's affections—or at least his attention. Her shoulder-length chestnut-brown hair had been trimmed and permed into a pixie style with a halo of soft curls.

The difference from the tightly styled chignon she'd always worn to work was striking, or so everyone said. Everyone except Paul. The hairdresser had claimed it changed Cait's cooly polished look into one of warmth and enthusiasm. It was exactly the image Cait wanted Paul to have of her.

Unfortunately he didn't seem to detect the slightest difference in her appearance. At least not until Lindy had pointedly commented on the change within earshot of their absent-minded employer. Then, and only then, had Paul made a remark about noticing something different; he just hadn't been sure what it was, he'd said.

"I suppose we could move you…." Paul hesitated.

"Your office seems to be the best choice," the foreman said.

Cait resisted the urge to hug the man. He was tall, easily six three, and as solid as Mount Rainier, the majestic mountain she could see from her office window. She hadn't paid much attention to him until this moment and was surprised to note something vaguely familiar about him. She'd assumed he was the foreman, but she wasn't certain. He seemed to be around the office fairly often, although not on a predictable schedule. Every time he did show up, the level of activity rose dramatically.

"Ah… I suppose Cait could move in with me for the time

being," Paul agreed. In her daydreams, Cait would play back this moment; her version had Paul looking at her with surprise and wonder, his mouth moving toward hers and—

"Miss?"

Cait broke out of her reverie and glanced at the foreman—the man who'd suggested she share Paul's office. "Yes?"

"Would you show us what you need moved?"

"Of course," she returned crisply. This romantic heart of hers was always getting her into trouble. She'd look at Paul and her head would start to spin with hopes and fantasies and then she'd be lost....

Cait's arms were loaded with files as she followed the carpenters, who hauled her desk into a corner of Paul's much larger office. Her computer and phone came next, and within fifteen minutes she was back in business.

She was on the phone, talking with one of her most important clients, when the same man walked back, unannounced, into the room. At first Caitlin assumed he was looking for Paul, who'd stepped out of the office. The foreman—or whatever he was—hesitated for a few seconds. Then, scooping up her nameplate, he grinned at her as if he found something highly entertaining. Cait did her best to ignore him, flipping needlessly through the pages of the file.

Not taking the hint, he stepped forward and plunked the nameplate on the edge of her desk. As she looked up in annoyance, he boldly winked at her.

Cait was not amused. How dare this…this…redneck flirt with her!

She glared at him, hoping he'd have the good manners and good sense to leave—which, of course, he didn't. In fact, he seemed downright stubborn about staying and making her as uncomfortable as possible. Her phone conversation ran its natural course and after making several notations, she replaced the receiver.

"You wanted something?" she demanded, her eyes meeting his. Once more she noted his apparent amusement. She didn't understand it.

"No," he answered, grinning again. "Sorry to have bothered you."

For the second time, Cait was struck by a twinge of the familiar. He strolled out of her makeshift office as if he owned the building.

Cait waited a few minutes, then approached Lindy. "Did you happen to catch his name?"

"Whose name?"

"The…man who insisted I vacate my office. I don't know who he is. I thought he was the foreman, but…" She crossed her arms and furrowed her brow, trying to remember if she'd heard anyone say his name.

"I have no idea." Lindy pushed back her chair and rolled a pencil between her palms. "He is kinda cute, though, don't you think?"

A smile softened Cait's lips. "There's only one man for me and you know it."

"Then why are you asking questions about the construction crew?"

"I…don't know. That guy seems familiar for some reason, and he keeps grinning at me as if he knows something I don't. I hate it when men do that."

"Then ask one of the others what his name is. They'll tell you."

"I can't do that."

"Why not?"

"He might think I'm interested in him."

"And we both know how impossible that would be," Lindy said with mild sarcasm.

"Exactly." Lindy and probably everyone else in the office complex knew how Cait felt about Paul. The district manager himself, however, seemed to be completely oblivious. Other than throwing herself at him, which she'd seriously considered more than once, there was little she could do but be patient. One of these days Cupid was going to let fly an arrow and hit her lovable boss directly between the eyes.

When it happened—and it would!—Cait planned to be ready.

"You want to go for lunch now?" Lindy asked.

Cait nodded. It was nearly two and she hadn't eaten since breakfast, which had consisted of a banana and a cup of coffee. A West Coast stockbroker's day started before dawn. Cait was generally in the office by six and didn't stop work until the market closed at one-thirty, Seattle time. Only then did she break for something to eat.

Somewhere in the middle of her turkey on whole wheat, Cait convinced herself she was imagining things when it came to that construction worker. He'd probably been waiting around to ask her where Paul was and then changed his mind. He did say he was sorry for bothering her.

If only he hadn't winked.

He was back the following day, a tool pouch riding on his hip like a six-shooter, hard hat in place. He was issuing orders like a drill sergeant, and Cait found herself gazing after him with reluctant fascination. She'd heard he owned the construction company, and she wasn't surprised.

As she studied him, she realized once again how striking he was. Not because he was extraordinarily handsome, but because he was somehow commanding. He possessed an authority, a presence, that attracted attention wherever he went. Cait was as drawn to it as those around her. She observed how the crew instinctively turned to him for directions and approval.

The more she observed him, the more she recognized that he was a man who had an appetite for life. Which meant excitement, adventure and probably women, and that confused her even more because she couldn't recall ever knowing anyone quite like him. Then why did she find him so…familiar?

Cait herself had a quiet nature. She rarely ventured out of the comfortable, compact world she'd built. She had her job, a nice apartment in Seattle's university district, and a few close friends. Excitement to her was growing herbs and participating in nature walks.

The following day while she was studying the construction worker, he'd unexpectedly turned and smiled at something one of his men had said. His smile, she decided, intrigued her most. It was slightly off center and seemed to tease the corners of his mouth. He looked her way more than once and each time she thought she detected a touch of humor, an amused knowledge that lurked just beneath the surface.

"It's driving me crazy," Cait confessed to Lindy over lunch.

"What is?"

"That I can't place him."

Lindy set her elbows on the table, holding her sandwich poised in front of her mouth. She nodded slowly, her eyes distant. "When you figure it out, introduce me, will you? I could go for a guy this sexy."

So Lindy had noticed that earthy sensuality about him, too. Well, of course she had—any woman would.

After lunch, Cait returned to the office to make a few calls. He was there again.

No matter how hard she tried, she couldn't place him.

Work became a pretense as she continued to scrutinize him, racking her brain. Then, when she least expected it, he strolled past her and brazenly winked a second time.

As the color clawed up her neck, Cait flashed her attention back to her computer screen.

"His name is Joe," Lindy rushed in to tell her ten minutes later. "I heard one of the men call him that."

"Joe," Cait repeated slowly. She couldn't remember ever knowing anyone named Joe.

"Does that help?"

"No," Cait said, shaking her head regretfully. If she'd ever met this man, she wasn't likely to have overlooked the experience. He wasn't someone a woman easily forgot.

"Ask him," Lindy said. "It's ridiculous not to. It's driving you insane. Then," she added with infuriating logic, "when you find out, you can nonchalantly introduce me."

"I can't just waltz up and start quizzing him," Cait argued. The idea was preposterous. "He'll think I'm trying to pick him up."

"You'll go crazy if you don't."

Cait sighed. "You're right. I'm not going to sleep tonight if I don't settle this."

With Lindy waiting expectantly in her office, Cait approached him. He was talking to another member of the crew and once he'd finished, he turned to her with one of his devastating lazy smiles.

"Hello," she said, and her voice shook slightly. "Do I know you?"

"You mean you've forgotten?" he asked, sounding shocked and insulted.

"Apparently. Though I'll admit you look somewhat familiar."

"I should certainly hope so. We shared something very special a few years back."

"We did?" Cait was more confused than ever.

"Hey, Joe, there's a problem over here," a male voice shouted. "Could you come look at this?"

"I'll be with you in a minute," he answered brusquely over his shoulder. "Sorry, we'll have to talk later."

"But—"

"Say hello to Martin for me, would you?" he asked as he stalked past her and into the room that had once been Cait's office.

Martin, her brother. Cait hadn't a clue what her brother could possibly have to do with this. Mentally she ran through a list of his teenage friends and came up blank.

Then it hit her. Bull's-eye. Her heart started to pound until it roared like a tropical storm in her ears. Mechanically Cait made her way back to Lindy's office. She sank into a chair beside the desk and stared into space.

"Well?" Lindy pressed. "Don't keep me in suspense."

"Um, it's not that easy to explain."

"You remember him, then?"

She nodded. Oh, Lord, did she ever.

"Good grief, what's wrong? You've gone so pale!"

Cait tried to come up with an explanation that wouldn't sound…ridiculous.

"Tell me," Lindy said. "Don't just sit there wearing a foolish grin and looking like you're about to faint."

"Um, it goes back a few years."

"All right. Start there."

"Remember how kids sometimes do silly things? Like when you're young and foolish and don't know any better?"

"Me, yes, but not you," Lindy said calmly. "You're perfect. In all the time we've been friends, I haven't seen you do one impulsive thing. Not one. You analyze everything before you act. I can't imagine you ever doing anything silly."

"I did once," Cait told her, "but I was only eight."

"What could you have possibly done at age eight?"

"I… I got married."

"Married?" Lindy half rose from her chair. "You've got to be kidding."

"I wish I was."

"I'll bet a week's commissions that your husband's name is Joe." Lindy was smiling now, smiling widely.

Cait nodded and tried to smile in return.

"What's there to worry about? Good grief, kids do that sort of thing all the time! It doesn't mean anything."

"But I was a real brat about it. Joe and my brother, Martin, were best friends. Joe wanted to know what it felt like to kiss a girl, and I insisted he marry me first. If that wasn't bad enough, I pressured them into performing the ceremony inside their boys-only fort."

"So, you were a bit of pain—most eight-year-old girls are when it comes to dealing with their brothers. He got what he wanted, didn't he?"

Cait took a deep breath and nodded again.

"What was kissing him like?" Lindy asked in a curiously throaty voice.

"Good heavens, I don't remember," Cait answered shortly, then reconsidered. "I take that back. As I recall, it wasn't so bad, though obviously neither one of us had any idea what we were doing."

"Lindy, you're still here," Paul said as he strolled into the office. He inclined his head briefly in Cait's direction, but she had the impression he barely saw her. He'd hardly been around in the past couple of days—almost as if he was purposely avoiding her, she mused, but that thought was too painful to contemplate.

"I was just finishing up," Lindy said, glancing guiltily toward Cait. "We both were."

"Fine, fine, I didn't mean to disturb you. I'll see you two in the morning." A second later, he was gone.

Cait gazed after him with thinly disguised emotion. She waited until Paul was well out of range before she spoke. "He's so blind. What do I have to do, hit him over the head?"

"Quit being so negative," Lindy admonished. "You're going to be sharing an office with him for another five days. Do whatever you need to make darn sure he notices you."

"I've tried," Cait murmured, discouraged. And she had. She'd tried every trick known to woman, with little success.

Lindy left the office before her. Cait gathered up some stock reports to read that evening and stacked them neatly inside her leather briefcase. What Lindy had said about her being methodical and careful was true. It was also a source of pride; those traits had served her clients well.

To Cait's dismay, Joe followed her. "So," he said, smiling down at her, apparently oblivious to the other people clustering around the elevator. "Who have you been kissing these days?"

Hot color rose instantly to her face. Did he have to humiliate her in public?

"I could find myself jealous, you know."

"Would you kindly stop," she whispered furiously, scowling at him. Her hand tightened around the handle of her briefcase so hard her fingers ached.

"You figured it out?"

She nodded, her eyes darting to the lighted numbers above the elevator door, praying it would make its descent in record time instead of pausing on each floor.

"The years have been good to you."

"Thank you." *Please hurry,* she urged the elevator.

"I never would've believed Martin's little sister would turn out to be such a beauty."

If he was making fun of her, she didn't appreciate it. She was attractive, she knew that, but she certainly wasn't waiting for anyone to place a tiara on her head. "Thank you," she repeated grudgingly.

He gave an exaggerated sigh. "How are our children doing? What were their names again?" When she didn't answer right away, he added, "Don't tell me you've forgotten."

"Barbie and Ken," she muttered under her breath.

"That's right. I remember now."

If Joe hadn't drawn the attention of her co-workers before, he had now. Cait could have sworn every single person standing by the elevator turned to stare at her. The hope that no one was interested in their conversation was forever lost.

"Just how long do you intend to tease me about this?" she snapped.

"That depends," Joe responded with a chuckle Cait could only describe as sadistic. She gritted her teeth. He might have found the situation amusing, but she derived little enjoyment from being the office laughingstock.

Just then the elevator arrived, and not a moment too soon to suit Cait. The instant the doors slid open, she stepped toward it, determined to get as far away from this irritating man as possible.

He quickly caught up with her and she swung around to face him, her back ramrod stiff. "Is this really necessary?" she hissed, painfully conscious of the other people crowding into the elevator ahead of her.

He grinned. "I suppose not. I just wanted to see if I could

get a rise out of you. It never worked when we were kids, you know. You were always so prim and proper."

"Look, you didn't like me then and I see no reason for you to—"

"Not *like* you?" he countered loudly enough for everyone in the building to hear. "I married you, didn't I?"

2

Cait's heart seemed to stop. She realized that not only the people on the elevator but everyone left in the office was staring at her with unconcealed interest. The elevator was about to close and she quickly stepped forward, stretching out her arms to hold the doors open. She felt like Samson balanced between two marble columns.

"It's not the way it sounds," she felt obliged to explain in a loud voice, her gaze pleading.

No one made eye contact with her and, desperate, she turned to Joe, sending him a silent challenge to retract his words. His eyes were sparkling with mischief. If he did say anything, Cait thought in sudden horror, it was bound to make things even worse.

There didn't seem to be anything to do but tell the truth. "In case anyone has the wrong impression, this man and I are not married," she shouted. "Good grief, I was only eight!"

There was no reaction. It was as if she'd vanished into thin air. Defeated, she dropped her arms and stepped back, freeing the doors, which promptly closed.

Ignoring the other people on the elevator—who were carefully ignoring her—Cait clenched her hands into hard fists and glared up at Joe. Her face tightened with anger. "That was a rotten thing to do," she whispered hoarsely.

"What? It's true, isn't it?" he whispered back.

"You're being ridiculous to talk as though we're married!"

"We were once. It wounds me that you treat our marriage so lightly."

"I…it wasn't legal." The fact that they were even discussing this was preposterous. "You can't possibly hold me responsible for something that happened so long ago. To play this game now is…is infantile, and I refuse to be part of it."

The elevator finally came to a halt on the ground floor and, eager to make her escape, Cait rushed out. Straightening to keep her dignity intact, she headed through the crowded foyer toward the front doors. Although it was midafternoon, dusk was already setting in, casting dark shadows between the towering office buildings.

Cait reached the first intersection and sighed in relief as she glanced around her. Good. No sign of Joseph Rockwell. The light was red and she paused, although others hurried across the street after checking for traffic; Cait always felt obliged to obey the signal.

"What do you think Paul's going to say when he hears about this?" Joe asked from behind her.

Cait gave a start, then turned to look at her tormenter. She hadn't thought about Paul's reaction. Her throat seemed to constrict, rendering her speechless, otherwise she would have demanded Joe leave her alone. But he'd raised a question she dared not ignore. Paul might hear about her so-called former relationship with Joe and might even think there was something between them.

"You're in love with him, aren't you?"

She nodded. At the very mention of Paul's name, her knees went weak. He was everything she wanted in a man and more. She'd been crazy about him for months and now it was all about to be ruined by this irritating, unreasonable ghost from her past.

"Who told you?" Cait snapped. She couldn't imagine Lindy betraying her confidence, but Cait hadn't told anyone else.

"No one had to tell me," Joe said. "It's written all over you."

Shocked, Cait stared at Joe, her heart sinking. "Do...do you think Paul knows how I feel?"

Joe shrugged. "Maybe."

"But Lindy said..."

The light changed and, clasping her elbow, Joe urged her into the street. "What was it Lindy said?" he prompted when they'd crossed.

Cait looked up, about to tell him, when she realized exactly what she was doing—conversing with her antagonist. This was the very man who'd gone out of his way to embarrass and humiliate her in front of the entire office staff. Not to mention assorted clients and carpenters.

She stiffened. "Never mind what Lindy said. Now if you'll kindly excuse me..." With her head high, she marched down the sidewalk. She hadn't gone more than a few feet when the hearty sound of Joe's laughter caught up with her.

"You haven't changed in twenty years, Caitlin Marshall. Not a single bit."

Gritting her teeth, she marched on.

* * *

"Do you think Paul's heard?" Cait asked Lindy the instant she had a free moment the following afternoon. The New York Stock Exchange had closed for the day and Cait hadn't seen Paul since morning. It looked like he really *was* avoiding her.

"I wouldn't know," Lindy said as she typed some figures into her computer. "But the word about your childhood marriage has spread like wildfire everywhere else. It's the joke of the day. What did you and Joe do? Make a public announcement before you left the office yesterday afternoon?"

It was so nearly the truth that Cait guiltily lowered her eyes. "I didn't say a word," she defended herself. "Joe was the one."

"He told everyone you were married?" A suspicious tilt at the corner of her mouth betrayed Lindy's amusement.

"Not exactly. He started asking about our children in front of everyone."

"There were children?"

Cait resisted the urge to close her eyes and count to ten. "No. I brought my dolls to the wedding. Listen, I don't want to rehash a silly incident that happened years ago. I'm more afraid Paul's going to hear about it and put the wrong connotation on the whole thing. There's absolutely nothing between me and Joseph Rockwell. More than likely Paul won't give it a second thought, but I don't want there to be any… doubts between us, if you know what I mean."

"If you're so worried about it, talk to him," Lindy advised without lifting her eyes from the screen. "Honesty is the best policy, you know that."

"Yes, but it could prove to be a bit embarrassing, don't you think?"

"Paul will respect you for telling him the truth before he

hears the rumors from someone else. Frankly, Cait, I think you're making a fuss over nothing. It isn't like you've committed a felony, you know."

"I realize that."

"Paul will probably be amused, like everyone else. He's not going to say anything." She looked up quickly, as though she expected Cait to try yet another argument.

Cait didn't. Instead she mulled over her friend's advice, gnawing on her lower lip. "You might be right. Paul will respect me for explaining the situation myself, instead of ignoring everything." Telling him the truth could be helpful in other respects, too, now that she thought about it.

If Paul had any feeling for her whatsoever, and oh, how she prayed he did, then he might become just a little jealous of her relationship with Joseph Rockwell. After all, Joe was an attractive man in a rugged outdoor sort of way. He was tall and muscular and, well, good-looking. The kind of good-looking that appealed to women—not Cait, of course, but other women. Hadn't Lindy commented almost immediately on how attractive he was?

"You're right," Cait said, walking resolutely toward the office she was temporarily sharing with Paul. Although she'd felt annoyed at first about being shuffled out of her own space, she'd come to think of this inconvenience as a blessing in disguise. However, she had to admit she'd been disappointed thus far. She had assumed she'd be spending a lot of time alone with him. That hadn't happened yet.

The more Cait considered the idea of a heart-to-heart talk with her boss, the more appealing it became. As was her habit, she mentally rehearsed what she wanted to say to him, then gave herself a small pep talk.

"I don't remember that you talked to yourself." The male

voice booming behind her startled Cait. "But then there's a great deal I've missed over the years, isn't there, Caitlin?"

Cait was so rattled she nearly stumbled. "What are you doing here?" she demanded. "Why are you following me around? Can't you see I'm busy?" He was the last person she wanted to confront just now.

"Sorry." He raised both hands in a gesture of apology contradicted by his twinkling blue eyes. "How about lunch later?"

He was teasing. He had to be. Besides, it would be insane for her to have anything to do with Joseph Rockwell. Heaven only knew what would happen if she gave him the least bit of encouragement. He'd probably hire a skywriter and announce to the entire city that they'd married as children.

"It shouldn't be that difficult to agree to a luncheon date," he informed her coolly.

"You're serious about this?"

"Of course I'm serious. We have a lot of years to catch up on." His hand rested on his leather pouch, giving him a rakish air of indifference.

"I've got an appointment this afternoon..." She offered the first plausible excuse she could think of; it might be uninspired but it also happened to be true. She'd made plans to have lunch with Lindy.

"Dinner then. I'm anxious to hear what Martin's been up to."

"Martin," she repeated, stalling for time while she invented another excuse. This wasn't a situation she had much experience with. She did date, but infrequently.

"Listen, bright eyes, no need to look so concerned. This isn't an invitation to the senior prom. It's one friend to another. Strictly platonic."

"You won't mention…our wedding to the waiter? Or anyone else?"

"I promise." As if to offer proof of his intent, he licked the end of his index finger and crossed his heart. "That was Martin's and my secret pledge sign. If either of us broke our word, the other was entitled to come up with a punishment. We both understood it would be a fate worse than death."

"I don't need any broken pledge in order to torture you, Joseph Rockwell. In two days you've managed to turn my life into—" She paused midsentence as Paul Jamison casually strolled past. He waved in Cait's direction and smiled benignly.

"Hello, Paul," she called out, weakly raising her right hand. He looked exceptionally handsome this morning in a three-piece dark blue suit. The contrast between him and Joe, who was wearing dust-covered jeans, heavy boots and a tool pouch, was so striking that Cait had to force herself not to stare at her boss. If only Paul had been the one to invite her to dinner…

"If you'll excuse me," she said politely, edging her way around Joe and toward Paul, who'd gone into his office. Their office. The need to talk to him burned within her. Words of explanation began to form themselves in her mind.

Joe caught her by the shoulders, bringing her up short. Cait gasped and raised shocked eyes to his.

"Dinner," he reminded her.

She blinked, hardly knowing what to say. "All right," she mumbled distractedly and recited her address, eager to have him gone.

"Good. I'll pick you up tonight at six." With that he released her and stalked away.

After taking a couple of moments to compose herself, Cait

headed toward the office. "Hello, Paul," she said, standing just inside the doorway. "Do you have a moment to talk?"

He glanced up from a file on his desk. "Of course, Cait. Sit down and make yourself comfortable."

She moved into the room, closing the door behind her. When she looked back at Paul, he'd cocked his eyebrows in surprise. "Problems?" he asked.

"Not exactly." She pulled out the chair opposite his desk and slowly sat down. Now that she had his full attention, she was at a loss. All her prepared explanations and witticisms had flown out of her head. "The rate on municipal bonds has been extremely high lately," she said nervously.

Paul agreed with a quick nod. "They have been for several months now."

"Yes, I know. That's what makes them such excellent value." Cait had been selling bonds heavily in the past few weeks.

"You didn't close the door to talk to me about bonds," Paul said softly. "What's troubling you, Cait?"

She laughed uncomfortably, wondering how a man could be so astute in one area and so blind in another. If only he'd reveal some emotion toward her. Anything. All he did was sit across from her and wait. He was cordial enough, gracious even, but there was no hint of anything more. Nothing to give Cait any hope that he was starting to care for her.

"It's about Joseph Rockwell."

"The contractor who's handling the remodeling?"

Cait nodded. "I knew him years ago when we were just children." She glanced at Paul, whose face remained blank. "We were neighbors. In fact Joe and my brother, Martin, were best friends. Joe moved out to the suburbs when he and Martin were in the sixth grade and I hadn't heard anything from him since."

"It's a small world, isn't it?" Paul remarked affably.

"Joe and Martin were typical young boys," she said, rushing her words a little in her eagerness to have this out in the open. "Full of tomfoolery and pranks."

"Boys will be boys," Paul said without any real enthusiasm.

"Yes, I know. Once—" she forced a light laugh "—they actually involved me in one of their crazy schemes."

"What did they put you up to? Robbing a bank?"

She somehow managed a smile. "Not exactly. Joe—I always called him Joseph back then, because it irritated him. Anyway, Joe and Martin had this friend named Pete who was a year older and he'd spent part of his summer vacation visiting his aunt in Peoria. I think it was Peoria.... Anyway he came back bragging about having kissed a girl. Naturally Martin and Joe were jealous and as you said, boys will be boys, so they decided that one of them should test it out and see if kissing a girl was everything Pete claimed it was."

"I take it they decided to make you their guinea pig."

"Exactly." Cait slid to the edge of the chair, pleased that Paul was following this rather convoluted explanation. "I was eight and considered something of a...pest." She paused, hoping Paul would make some comment about how impossible that was. When he didn't, she continued, a little let down at his restraint. "Apparently I was more of one than I remembered," she said, with another forced laugh. "At eight, I didn't think kissing was something nice girls did, at least not without a wedding band on their finger."

"So you kissed Joseph Rockwell," Paul said absently.

"Yes, but there was a tiny bit more than that. I made him marry me."

Paul's eyebrows shot to the ceiling.

"Now, almost twenty years later, he's getting his revenge

by going around telling everyone that we're actually married. Which of course is ridiculous."

A couple of strained seconds followed her announcement.

"I'm not sure what to say," Paul murmured.

"Oh, I wasn't expecting you to say anything. I thought it was important to clear the air, that's all."

"I see."

"He's only doing it because…well, because that's Joe. Even when we were kids he enjoyed playing these little games. No one really minded, though, especially not the girls, because he was so cute." She certainly had Paul's attention now.

"I thought you should know," she added, "in case you happened to hear a rumor or something. I didn't want you thinking Joe and I were involved, or even considering a relationship. I was fairly certain you wouldn't, but one never knows and I'm a firm believer in being forthright and honest."

Paul blinked. Wanting to fill the awkward silence, Cait chattered on. "Apparently Joe recognized my name when he and his men moved my office in here with yours. He was delighted when I didn't recognize him. In fact, he caused a commotion by asking me about our children in front of everyone."

"Children?"

"My dolls," Cait was quick to explain.

"Joe Rockwell's an excellent man. I couldn't fault your taste, Cait."

"The two of us *aren't* involved," she protested. "Good grief, I haven't seen him in nearly twenty years."

"I see," Paul said slowly. He sounded…disappointed, Cait thought. But she must have misread his tone because there wasn't a single, solitary reason for him to be disappointed. Cait felt foolish now for even trying to explain this fiasco.

Paul was so oblivious about her feelings that there was nothing she could say or do to make him understand.

"I just wanted you to know," she repeated, "in case you heard the rumors and were wondering if there was anything between me and Joseph Rockwell. I wanted to assure you there isn't."

"I see," he said again. "Don't worry about it, Cait. What happened between you and Rockwell isn't going to affect your job."

She stood up to leave, praying she'd detect a suggestion of jealousy. A hint of rivalry. Anything to show he cared. There was nothing, so she tried again. "I agreed to have dinner with him, though."

Paul had returned his attention to the papers he'd been reading when she'd interrupted him.

"For old times' sake," she said in a reassuring voice—to fend off any violent display of resentment, she told herself. "I certainly don't have any intention of dating him on a regular basis."

Paul grinned. "Have a good time."

"Yes, I will, thanks." Her heart felt as heavy as a sinking battleship. Without knowing where she was headed or who she'd talk to, Cait wandered out of Paul's office, forgetting for a second that she had no office of her own. The area where her desk once sat was cluttered with wire reels, ladders and men. Joe must have left, a fact for which Cait was grateful.

She walked into Lindy's small office across the hall. Her friend glanced up. "So?" she murmured. "Did you talk to Paul?"

Cait nodded.

"How'd it go?"

"Fine, I guess." She perched on the corner of Lindy's desk, crossing her arms around her waist as her left leg swung rhythmically, keeping time with her discouraged heart. She should be accustomed to disappointment when it came to Paul, but somehow each rejection inflicted a fresh wound on her already battered ego. "I was hoping Paul might be jealous."

"And he wasn't?"

"Not that I could tell."

"It isn't as though you and Joe have anything to do with each other now," Lindy sensibly pointed out. "Marrying him was a childhood prank. It isn't likely to concern Paul."

"I even mentioned that I was going out to dinner with Joe," Cait said morosely.

"You are? When?" Lindy asked, her eyes lighting up. "Where?"

If only Paul had revealed half as much interest. "Tonight. And I don't know where."

"You are going, aren't you?"

"I guess. I can't see any way of avoiding it. Otherwise he'd pester me until I gave in. If I ever marry and have daughters, Lindy, I'm going to warn them about boys from the time they're old enough to understand."

"Don't you think you should follow your own advice?" Lindy asked, glancing pointedly in the direction of Paul's office.

"Not if I were to have Paul's children," Cait said, eager to defend her boss. "Our daughter would be so intelligent and perceptive she wouldn't need to be warned."

Lindy's smile was distracted. "Listen, I've got a few things to finish up here. Why don't you go over to the deli and grab us a table. I'll meet you there in fifteen minutes."

"Sure," Cait said. "Do you want me to order for you?"

"No. I don't know what I want yet."

"Okay, I'll see you in a few minutes."

They often ate at the deli across the street from their office complex. The food was good, the service fast, and generally by three in the afternoon, Cait was famished.

She was so wrapped up in her thoughts, which were muddled and gloomy after her talk with Paul, that she didn't notice how late Lindy was. Her friend rushed into the restaurant more than half an hour after Cait had arrived.

"I'm sorry," she said, sounding flustered and oddly shaken. "I had no idea those last few chores would take me so long. Oh, you must be starved. I hope you've ordered." Lindy removed her coat and stuffed it into the booth before sliding onto the red upholstered seat herself.

"Actually, no, I didn't." Cait sighed. "Just tea." Her spirits were at an all-time low. It was becoming painfully clear that Paul didn't harbor a single romantic feeling toward her. She was wasting her time and her emotional energy on him. If only she'd had more experience with the opposite sex. It seemed her whole love life had gone into neutral the moment she'd graduated from college. At the rate things were developing, she'd still be single by the time she turned thirty—a possibility too dismal to contemplate. She hadn't given much thought to marriage and children, always assuming they'd naturally become part of her life; now she wasn't so sure. Even as a child, she'd pictured her grown-up self with a career *and* a family. Behind the business exterior was a woman traditional enough to hunger for that most special of relationships.

She had to face the fact that marriage would never happen if she continued to love a man who didn't return her feelings. She gave a low groan, then noticed that Lindy was gazing at her in concern.

"Let's order something," Lindy said quickly, reaching for the menu tucked behind the napkin holder. "I'm starved."

"I was thinking I'd skip lunch today," Cait mumbled. She

sipped her lukewarm tea and frowned. "Joe will be taking me out to dinner soon. And frankly, I don't have much of an appetite."

"This is all my fault, isn't it?" Lindy asked, looking guilty.

"Of course not. I'm just being practical." If Cait was anything, it was practical—except about Paul. "Go ahead and order."

"You're sure you don't mind?"

Cait gestured nonchalantly. "Heavens, no."

"If you're sure, then I'll have the turkey on whole wheat," Lindy said after a moment. "You know how much I like turkey, though you'd think I'd have gotten enough over Thanksgiving."

"I'll just have a refill on my tea," Cait said.

"You're still flying to Minnesota for the holidays, aren't you?" Lindy asked, fidgeting with the menu.

"Mmm-hmm." Cait had purchased her ticket several months earlier. Martin and his family lived near Minneapolis. When their father had died several years earlier, Cait's mother moved to Minnesota, settling down in a new subdivision not far from Martin, his wife and their four children. Cait tried to visit at least once a year. However, she'd been there in August, stopping off on her way home from a business trip. Usually she made a point of visiting her brother and his family over the Christmas holidays. It was generally a slow week on the stock market, anyway. And if she was going to travel halfway across the country, she wanted to make it worth her while.

"When will you be leaving?" Lindy asked, although Cait was sure she'd already told her friend more than once.

"The twenty-third." For the past few years, Cait had used one week of her vacation at Christmas time, usually starting the weekend before.

But this year Paul was having a Christmas party and Cait didn't want to miss that, so she'd booked her flight closer to the holiday.

The waitress came to take Lindy's order and replenish the hot water for Cait's tea. The instant she moved away from their booth, Lindy launched into a lengthy tirade about how she hated Christmas shopping and how busy the malls were this time of year. Cait stared at her, bewildered. It wasn't like her friend to chat nonstop.

"Lindy," she interrupted, "is something wrong?"

"Wrong? What could possibly be wrong?"

"I don't know. You haven't stopped talking for the last ten minutes."

"I haven't?" There was an abrupt, uncomfortable silence.

Cait decided it was her turn to say something. "I think I'll wear my red velvet dress," she mused.

"To dinner with Joe?"

"No," she said, shaking her head. "To Paul's Christmas party."

Lindy sighed. "But what are you wearing tonight?"

The question took Cait by surprise. She didn't consider this dinner with Joe a real date. He just wanted to talk over old times, which was fine with Cait as long as he behaved himself. Suddenly she frowned, then closed her eyes. "Martin's a Methodist minister," she said softly.

"Yes, I know," Lindy reminded her. "I've known that since I first met you, which was what? Three years ago now."

"Four last month."

"So what does Martin's occupation have to do with anything?" Lindy asked.

"Joe Rockwell can't find out," Cait whispered.

"I didn't plan on telling him," Lindy whispered back.

"I've got to make up some other occupation like…"

"Counselor," Lindy suggested. "I'm curious, though. Why can't you tell Joe about Martin?"

"Think about it!"

"I am thinking. I really doubt Joe would care one way or the other."

"He might try to make something of it. You don't know Joe like I do. He'd razz me about it all evening, claiming the marriage was valid. You know, because Martin really *is* a minister, and since Martin performed the ceremony, we must really be married—that kind of nonsense."

"I didn't think about that."

But then, Lindy didn't seem to be thinking much about anything lately. It was as if she was walking around in a perpetual daydream. Cait couldn't remember Lindy's ever being so scatterbrained. If she didn't know better, she'd guess there was a man involved.

3

At ten to six, Cait was blow-drying her hair in a haphazard fashion, regretting that she'd ever had it cut. She was looking forward to this dinner date about as much as a trip to the dentist. All she wanted was to get it over with, come home and bury her head under a pillow while she sorted out how she was going to get Paul to notice her.

Restyling her hair hadn't done the trick. Putting in extra hours at the office hadn't impressed him, either. Cait was beginning to think she could stand on top of his desk naked and not attract his attention.

She walked into her compact living room and smoothed the bulky-knit sweater over her slim hips. She hadn't dressed for the occasion, although the sweater was new and expensive. Gray wool slacks and a powder-blue turtleneck with a silver heart-shaped necklace dangling from her neck were about as dressy as she cared to get with someone like Joe. He'd probably be wearing cowboy boots and jeans, if not his hard hat and tool pouch.

Oh, yes, Cait had recognized his type when she'd first seen him. Joe Rockwell was a man's man. He walked and talked macho. No doubt he drove a truck with tires so high off the ground she'd need a stepladder to climb inside. He was tough and gruff and liked his women meek and submissive. In that case, of course, she had nothing to worry about; he'd lose interest immediately.

He arrived right on time, which surprised Cait. Being prompt didn't fit the image she had of Joe Rockwell, redneck contractor. She sighed and painted on a smile, then walked slowly to the door.

The smile faded. Joe stood before her, tall and debonair, dressed in a dark gray pin-striped suit. His gray silk tie had *pink* stripes. He was the picture of smooth sophistication. She knew that Joe was the same man she'd seen earlier in dusty work clothes—yet he was different. He was nothing like Paul, of course. But Joseph Rockwell was a devastatingly handsome man. With a devastating charm. Rarely had she seen a man smile the way he did. His eyes twinkled with warmth and life and mischief. It wasn't difficult to imagine Joe with a little boy whose eyes mirrored his. Cait didn't know where that thought came from, but she pushed it aside before it could linger and take root.

"Hello," he said, flashing her that smile.

"Hi." She couldn't stop looking at him.

"May I come in?"

"Oh…of course. I'm sorry," she faltered, stumbling in her haste to step aside. He'd caught her completely off guard. "I was about to change clothes," she said quickly.

"You look fine."

"These old things?" She feigned a laugh. "If you'll excuse me, I'll only be a minute." She poured him a cup of coffee, then dashed into her bedroom, ripping the sweater over her head and closing the door with one foot. Her shoes went flying as she ran to her closet. Jerking aside the orderly row of business jackets and skirts, she pulled clothes off their hangers, considered them, then tossed them on the bed. Nearly everything she owned was more suitable for the office than a dinner date.

The only really special dress she owned was the red velvet one she'd purchased for Paul's Christmas party. The temptation to slip into that was strong but she resisted, wanting to save it for her boss, though heaven knew he probably wouldn't notice.

Deciding on a skirt and blazer, she hopped frantically around her bedroom as she pulled on her panty hose. Next she threw on a rose-colored silk blouse and managed to button it while stepping into her skirt. She tucked the blouse into the waistband and her feet into a pair of medium-heeled pumps. Finally, her velvet blazer and she was ready. Taking a deep breath, she returned to the living room in three minutes flat.

"That was fast," Joe commented, standing by the fireplace, hands clasped behind his back. He was examining a framed photograph that sat on the mantel. "Is this Martin's family?"

"Martin…why, yes, that's Martin, his wife and their children." She hoped he didn't detect the breathless catch in her voice.

"Four children."

"Yes, he and Rebecca wanted a large family." Her heartbeat was slowly returning to normal though Cait still felt light-headed. She had a sneaking suspicion that she was suffering from the effects of unleashed male charm.

She realized with surprise that Joe hadn't said or done anything to embarrass or fluster her. She'd expected him to arrive with a whole series of remarks designed to disconcert her.

"Timmy's ten, Kurt's eight, Jenny's six and Clay's four." She introduced the freckle-faced youngsters, pointing each one out.

"They're handsome children."

"They are, aren't they?"

Cait experienced a twinge of pride. The main reason she went to Minneapolis every year was Martin's children. They adored her and she was crazy about them. Christmas wouldn't be Christmas without Jenny and Clay snuggling on her lap while their father read the Nativity story. Christmas was singing carols in front of a crackling wood fire, accompanied by Martin's guitar. It meant stringing popcorn and cranberries for the seven-foot-tall tree that always adorned the living room. It was having the children take turns scraping fudge from the sides of the copper kettle, and supervising the decorating of sugar cookies with all four crowded around the kitchen table. Caitlin Marshall might be a dedicated stockbroker with an impressive clientele, but when it came to Martin's children, she was Auntie Cait.

"It's difficult to think of Martin with kids," Joe said, carefully placing the family photo back on the mantel.

"He met Rebecca his first year of college and the rest, as they say, is history."

"What about you?" Joe asked, turning unexpectedly to face her.

"What about me?"

"Why haven't you married?"

"Uh..." Cait wasn't sure how to answer him. She had a glib reply she usually gave when anyone asked, but somehow she knew Joe wouldn't accept that. "I... I've never really fallen in love."

"What about Paul?"

"Until Paul," she corrected, stunned that she'd forgotten

the strong feelings she held for her employer. She'd been so concerned with being honest that she'd overlooked the obvious. "I am deeply in love with Paul," she said defiantly, wanting there to be no misunderstanding.

"There's no need to convince me, Caitlin."

"I'm not trying to convince you of anything. I've been in love with Paul for nearly a year. Once he realizes he loves me, too, we'll be married."

Joe's mouth slanted in a wry line and he seemed about to argue with her. Cait waylaid any attempt by glancing pointedly at her watch. "Shouldn't we be leaving?"

After a long moment, Joe said, "Yes, I suppose we should," in a mild, neutral voice.

Cait went to the hall closet for her coat, aware with every step she took that Joe was watching her. She turned back to smile at him, but somehow the smile didn't materialize. His blue eyes met hers, and she found his look disturbing—caressing, somehow, and intimate.

Joe helped her on with her coat and led her to the parking lot, where he'd left his car. Another surprise awaited her. It wasn't a four-wheel-drive truck, but a late sixties black convertible in mint condition.

The restaurant was one of the most respected in Seattle, with a noted chef and a reputation for excellent seafood. Cait chose grilled salmon and Joe ordered Cajun shrimp.

"Do you remember the time Martin and I decided to open our own business?" Joe asked, as they sipped a predinner glass of wine.

Cait did indeed recall that summer. "You might have been a bit more ingenious. A lemonade stand wasn't the world's most creative enterprise."

"Perhaps not, but we were doing a brisk business until an annoying eight-year-old girl ruined everything."

Cait wasn't about to let that comment pass. "You were using moldy lemons and covering the taste with too much sugar. Besides, it's unhealthy to share paper cups."

Joe chuckled, the sound deep and rich. "I should've known then that you were nothing but trouble."

"It seems to me the whole mess was your own fault. You boys wouldn't listen to me. I had to do something before someone got sick on those lemons."

"Carrying a picket sign that read 'Talk to me before you buy this lemonade' was a bit drastic even for you, don't you think?"

"If anything, it brought you more business," Cait said dryly, recalling how her plan had backfired. "All the boys in the neighborhood wanted to see what contaminated lemonade tasted like."

"You were a damn nuisance, Cait. Own up to it." He smiled and Cait sincerely doubted that any woman could argue with him when he smiled full-force.

"I most certainly was not! If anything you two were—"

"Disgusting, I believe, was your favorite word for Martin and me."

"And you did your level best to live up to it," she said, struggling to hold back a smile. She reached for a breadstick and bit into it to disguise her amusement. She'd always enjoyed rankling Martin and Joe, though she'd never have admitted it, especially at the age of eight.

"Picketing our lemonade stand wasn't the worst trick you ever pulled, either," Joe said mischievously.

Cait had trouble swallowing. She should have been prepared for this. If he remembered her complaints about the lemonade stand, he was sure to remember what had happened once Betsy McDonald found out about the kissing incident.

"It wasn't a trick," Cait protested.

"But you told everyone at school that I'd kissed you—even though you'd promised not to."

"Not exactly." There was a small discrepancy that needed clarification. "If you think back you'll remember you said I couldn't tell anyone I'd been inside the fort. You didn't say anything about the kiss."

Joe frowned darkly as if attempting to jog his memory. "How can you remember details like that? All of this happened years ago."

"I remember everything," Cait said grandly—a gross exaggeration. She hadn't recognized Joe, after all. But on this one point she was absolutely clear. "You and Martin were far more concerned that I not tell anyone about going inside the fort. You didn't say a word about keeping the kiss a secret."

"But did you have to tell Betsy McDonald? That girl had been making eyes at me for weeks. As soon as she learned I'd kissed you instead of her, she was furious."

"Betsy was the most popular girl in school. I wanted her for my friend, so I told."

"And sold me down the river."

"Would an apology help?" Confident he was teasing her once again, Cait gave him her most charming smile.

"An apology just might do it." Joe grinned back, a grin that brightened his eyes to a deeper, more tantalizing shade of blue. It was with some difficulty that Cait pulled her gaze away from his.

"If Betsy liked you," she asked, smoothing the linen napkin across her lap, "then why didn't you kiss her? She'd probably have let you. You wouldn't have had to bribe her with your precious baseball cards, either."

"You're kidding. If I kissed Betsy McDonald I might as well have signed over my soul," Joe said, continuing the joke.

"Even as mere children, men are afraid of commitment," Cait said solemnly.

Joe ignored her remark.

"Your memory's not as sharp as you think," Cait felt obliged to tell him, enjoying herself more than she'd thought possible.

Once again, Joe overlooked her comment. "I can remember Martin complaining about how you'd line up your dolls in a row and teach them school. Once you even got him to come in as a guest lecturer. Heaven knew what you had to do to get him to play professor to a bunch of dolls."

"I found a pair of dirty jeans stuffed under the sofa with something dead in the pocket. Mom would have tanned his hide if she'd found them, so Martin owed me a favor. Then he got all bent out of shape when I collected it. He didn't seem the least bit appreciative that I'd saved him."

"Good old Martin," Joe said, shaking his head. "I swear he was as big on ceremony as you were. Marrying us was a turning point in his life. From that point on, he started carting a Bible around with him the way some kids do a slingshot. Right in his hip pocket. If he wasn't burying something, he was holding revival meetings. Remember how he got in a pack of trouble at school for writing 'God loves you, ask Martin' on the back wall of the school?"

"I remember."

"I sort of figured he might become a missionary."

"Martin?" She gave an abrupt laugh. "Never. He likes his conveniences. He doesn't even go camping. Martin's idea of roughing it is doing without valet service."

She expected Joe to chuckle. He did smile at her attempted joke, but that was all. He seemed to be studying her the same way she'd been studying him.

"You surprise me," Joe announced suddenly.

"I do? Am I a disappointment to you?"

"Not at all. I always thought you'd grow up and have a house full of children yourself. You used to haul those dolls of yours around with you everywhere. If Martin and I were too noisy, you'd shush us, saying the babies were asleep. If we wanted to play in the backyard, we couldn't because you were having a tea party with your dolls. It was enough to drive a ten-year-old boy crazy. But if we ever dared complain, you'd look at us serenely and with the sweetest smile tell us we had to be patient because it was for the children."

"I did get carried away with all that motherhood business, didn't I?" Joe's words stirred up uncomfortable memories, the same ones she'd entertained earlier that afternoon. She really did love children. Yet, somehow, without her quite knowing how, the years had passed and she'd buried the dream. Nowadays she didn't like to think too much about a husband and family—the life that hadn't happened. It haunted her at odd moments.

"I should have known you'd end up in construction," she said, switching the subject away from herself.

"How's that?" Joe asked.

"Wasn't it you who built the fort?"

"Martin helped."

"Sure, by staying out of the way." She grinned. "I know my brother. He's a marvel with people, but please don't ever give him a hammer."

Their dinner arrived, and it was as delicious as Cait had expected, although by then she was enjoying herself so much that even a plateful of dry toast would have tasted good. They drank two cups of cappuccino after their meal, and talked and laughed as the hours melted away. Cait couldn't remember the last time she'd laughed so much.

When at last she glanced at her watch, she was shocked to

realize it was well past ten. "I had no idea it was so late!" she said. "I should get home." She had to be up by five.

Joe took care of the bill and collected her coat. When they walked outside, the December night was clear and chilly, with a multitude of stars twinkling brightly above.

"Are you cold?" he asked as they waited for the valet to deliver the car.

"Not at all." Nevertheless, he placed his arm around her shoulders, drawing her close.

Cait didn't protest. It felt natural for this man to hold her close.

His car arrived and they drove back to her apartment building in silence. When he pulled into the parking lot, she considered inviting him in for coffee, then decided against it. They'd already drunk enough coffee, and besides, they both had to work the following morning. But more important, Joe might read something else into the invitation. He was an old friend. Nothing more. And she wanted to keep it that way.

She turned to him and smiled softly. "I had a lovely time. Thank you so much."

"You're welcome, Cait. We'll do it again."

Cait was astonished to realize how appealing another evening with Joseph Rockwell was. She'd underestimated him.

Or had she?

"There's something else I'd like to try again," he was saying, his eyes filled with devilry.

"Try again?" she repeated. "What?"

He slid his arm behind her and for a breathless moment they looked at each other. "I don't know if I've got a chance without trading a few baseball cards, though."

Cait swallowed. "You want to kiss me?"

He nodded. His eyes seemed to grow darker, more intense. "For old times' sake." His hand caressed the curve of her neck, his thumb moving slowly toward the scented hollow of her throat.

"Well, sure. For old times' sake." She was astonished at the way her heart was reacting to the thought of Joe holding her…kissing her.

His mouth began a slow descent toward hers, his warm breath nuzzling her skin.

"Just remember," she whispered when his mouth was about to settle over hers. Her hands gripped his lapels. "Old times'…"

"I'll remember," he said as his lips came down on hers.

She sighed and slid her hands up his solid chest to link her fingers at the base of his neck. The kiss was slow and thorough. When it was over, Cait's hands were clutching his collar.

Joe's fingers were in her hair, tangled in the short, soft curls, cradling the back of her head.

A sweet rush of joy coursed through her veins. Cait felt a bubbling excitement, a burst of warmth, unlike anything she'd ever known before.

Then he kissed her a second time…

"Just remember…" she repeated when he pulled his mouth from hers and buried it in the delicate curve of her neck.

He drew in several ragged breaths before asking, "What is it I'm supposed to remember?"

"Yes, oh, please, remember."

He lifted his head and rested his hands lightly on her shoulders, his face only inches from hers. "What's so important you don't want me to forget?" he whispered.

It wasn't Joe who was supposed to remember; it was Cait. She didn't realize she'd spoken out loud. She blinked, uncertain, then tilted her head to gaze down at her hands, anywhere but at him. "Oh…that I'm in love with Paul."

There was a moment of silence. An awkward moment. "Right," he answered shortly. "You're in love with Paul." His arms fell away and he released her.

Cait hesitated, uneasy. "Thanks again for a wonderful dinner." Her hand closed around the door handle. She was eager now to make her escape.

"Any time," he said flippantly. His own hands gripped the steering wheel.

"I'll see you soon."

"Soon," he echoed. She climbed out of the car, not giving Joe a chance to come around and open the door for her. She was aware of him sitting in the car, waiting until she'd unlocked the lobby door and stepped inside. She hurried down the first-floor hall and into her apartment, turning on the lights so he'd know she'd made it safely home.

Then she removed her coat and carefully hung it in the closet. When she peeked out the window, she saw that Joe had already left.

Lindy was at her desk working when Cait arrived the next morning. Cait smiled at her as she hurried past, but didn't stop to indulge in conversation.

Cait could feel Lindy's gaze trailing after her and she knew her friend was disappointed that she hadn't told her about the dinner date with Joe Rockwell.

Cait didn't want to talk about it. She was afraid that if she said anything to Lindy, she wouldn't be able to avoid mentioning the kiss, which was a subject she wanted to avoid at all costs. She wouldn't be able to delay her friend's questions forever, but Cait wanted to put them off until at least the end of the day. Longer, if possible.

What a fool she'd been to let Joe kiss her. It had seemed so right at the time, a natural conclusion to a delightful evening.

The fact that she'd let him do it without even making a token protest still confused her. If Paul happened to hear about it, he might think she really *was* interested in Joe. Which, of course, she wasn't.

Her boss was a man of principle and integrity—and altogether a frustrating person to fall in love with. Judging by his reaction to her dinner with Joe, he seemed immune to jealousy. Now if only she could discover a way of letting him know how she felt...and spark his interest in the process!

The morning was hectic. Out of the corner of her eye, Cait saw Joe arrive. Although she was speaking to an important client on the phone, she stared after him as he approached the burly foreman. She watched Joe remove a blueprint from a long, narrow tube and roll it open so two other men could study it. There seemed to be some discussion, then the foreman nodded and Joe left, without so much as glancing in Cait's direction.

That stung.

At least he could have waved hello. But if he wanted to ignore her, well, fine. She'd do the same.

The market closed on the up side, the Dow Jones industrial average at 2600 points after brisk trading. The day's work was over.

As Cait had predicted, Lindy sought her out almost immediately.

"So how'd your dinner date go?"

"It was fun."

"Where'd he take you? Sam's Bar and Grill as you thought?"

"Actually, no," she said, clearing her throat, feeling more than a little foolish for having suggested such a thing. "He took me to Henry's." She announced it louder than necessary, since Paul was strolling into the office just then. But for all the notice he gave her, she might as well have been fresh paint drying on the office wall.

"Henry's," Lindy echoed. "He took you to Henry's? Why, that's one of the best restaurants in town. It must have cost him a small fortune."

"I wouldn't know. My menu didn't list any prices."

"You're joking. No one's ever taken me anyplace so fancy. What did you order?"

"Grilled salmon." She continued to study Paul for some clue that he was listening in on her and Lindy's conversation. He was seated at his desk, reading a report on short-term partnerships as a tax advantage. Cait had read it earlier in the week and had recommended it to him.

"Was it wonderful?" Lindy pressed.

It took Cait a moment to realize her friend was quizzing her about the dinner. "Excellent. The best fish I've had in years."

"What did you do afterward?"

Cait looked back at her friend. "What makes you think we did anything? We had dinner, talked, and then he drove me home. Nothing more happened. Understand? Nothing."

"If you say so," Lindy said, eyeing her suspiciously. "But you're certainly defensive about it."

"I just want you to know that nothing happened. Joseph Rockwell is an old friend. That's all."

Paul glanced up from the report, but his gaze connected with Lindy's before slowly progressing to Cait.

"Hello, Paul," Cait greeted him cheerfully. "Are Lindy and I disturbing you? We'd be happy to go into the hallway if you'd like."

"No, no, you're fine. Don't worry about it." He looked past them to the doorway and got to his feet. "Hello, Rockwell."

"Am I interrupting a meeting?" Joe asked, stepping into

the office as if it didn't really matter whether he was or not. His hard hat was back in place, along with the dusty jeans and the tool pouch. And yet Cait had no difficulty remembering last night's sophisticated dinner companion when she looked at him.

"No, no," Paul answered, "we were just chatting. Come on in. Problems?"

"Not really. But there's something I'd like you to take a look at in the other room."

"I'll be right there."

Joe threw Cait a cool smile as he strolled past. "Hello, Cait."

"Joe." Her heart was pounding hard, and that was ridiculous. It must have been due to embarrassment, she told herself. Joe was a friend, a boy from the old neighborhood; just because she'd allowed him to kiss her didn't mean there was—or ever would be—anything romantic between them. The sooner she made him understand this, the better.

"Joe and Cait went out to dinner last night," Lindy said pointedly to Paul. "He took her to Henry's."

"How nice," Paul commented, clearly more interested in troubleshooting with Joe than discussing Cait's dating history.

"We had a good time, didn't we?" Joe asked Cait.

"Yes, very nice," she responded stiffly.

Joe waited until Paul was out of the room before he stepped back and dropped a kiss on her cheek. Then he announced loudly enough for everyone in the vicinity to hear, "You were incredible last night."

4

"I thought you said nothing happened," Lindy said, looking intently at a red-faced Cait.

"Nothing did happen." Cait was furious enough to kick Joe Rockwell in the shins the way he deserved. How dared he say something so…so embarrassing in front of Lindy! And probably within earshot of Paul!

"But then why would he say something like that?"

"How should I know?" Cait snapped. "One little kiss and he makes it sound like—"

"He kissed you?" Lindy asked sharply, her eyes narrowing. "You just got done telling me there's nothing between the two of you."

"Good grief, the kiss didn't mean anything. It was for old times' sake. Just a platonic little kiss." All right, she was exaggerating a bit, but it couldn't be helped.

While she was speaking, Cait gathered her things and shoved them in her briefcase. Then she slammed the lid closed and reached for her coat, thrusting her arms into the sleeves, her movements abrupt and ungraceful.

"Have a nice weekend," she said tightly, not completely understanding why she felt so annoyed with Lindy. "I'll see you Monday." She marched through the office, but paused in front of Joe.

"You wanted something, sweetheart?" he asked in a cajoling voice.

"You're despicable!"

Joe looked downright disappointed. "Not low and disgusting?"

"That, too."

He grinned from ear to ear just the way she knew he would. "I'm glad to hear it."

Cait bit back an angry retort. It wouldn't do any good to engage in a verbal battle with Joe Rockwell. He'd have a comeback for any insult she could hurl. Seething, Cait marched to the elevator and jabbed the button impatiently.

"I'll be by later tonight, darling," Joe called to her just as the doors were closing, effectively cutting off any protest.

He was joking. He had to be joking. No man in his right mind could possibly expect her to invite him into her home after this latest stunt. Not even the impertinent Joe Rockwell.

Once home, Cait took a long, soothing shower, dried her hair and changed into jeans and a sweater. Friday nights were generally quiet ones for her. She was munching on pretzels and surveying the bleak contents of her refrigerator when there was a knock on the door.

It couldn't possibly be Joe, she told herself.

It *was* Joe, balancing a large pizza on the palm of one hand and clutching a bottle of red wine in the other.

Cait stared at him, too dumbfounded at his audacity to speak.

"I come bearing gifts," he said, presenting the pizza to her with more than a little ceremony.

"Listen here, you…you fool, it's going to take a whole lot more than pizza to make up for that stunt you pulled this afternoon."

"Come on, Cait, lighten up a little."

"Lighten up! You…you…"

"I believe the word you're looking for is fool."

"You have your nerve." She dug her fists into her hips, knowing she should slam the door in his face. She would have, too, but the pizza smelled *so* good it was difficult to maintain her indignation.

"Okay, I'll admit it," Joe said, his deep blue eyes revealing genuine contrition. "I got carried away. You're right, I am an idiot. All I can do is ask your forgiveness." He lifted the lid of the pizza box and Cait was confronted by the thickest, most mouthwatering masterpiece she'd ever seen. The top was crowded with no less than ten tempting toppings, all covered with a thick layer of hot melted cheese.

"Do you accept my humble apology?" Joe pressed, waving the pizza under her nose.

"Are there any anchovies on that thing?"

"Only on half."

"You're forgiven." She took him by the elbow and dragged him inside her apartment.

Cait led the way into the kitchen. She got two plates from the cupboard and collected knives, forks and napkins as she mentally reviewed his crimes. "I couldn't believe you actually said that," she mumbled, shaking her head. She set the kitchen table, neatly positioning the napkins after shoving the day's mail to one side. "The least you can do is tell me why you found it necessary to say that in front of Paul. Lindy had already started grilling me. Can you imagine what she and Paul must think now?" She retrieved two wineglasses from the cupboard and set them by the plates. "I've never been more embarrassed in my life."

"Never?" he prompted, opening and closing her kitchen drawers until he located a corkscrew.

"Never," she repeated. "And don't think a pizza's going to ensure lasting peace."

"I wouldn't dream of it."

"It's a start, but you're going to owe me a long time for this prank, Joseph Rockwell."

"I'll be good," he promised, his eyes twinkling. He agilely removed the cork, tested the wine and then filled both glasses.

Cait jerked out a wicker-back chair and threw herself down. "Did Paul say anything after I left?"

"About what?" Joe slid out a chair and joined her.

Cait had already dished up a large slice for each of them, fastidiously using a knife to disconnect the strings of melted cheese that stretched from the box to their plates.

"About me, of course," she growled.

Joe handed her a glass of wine. "Not really."

Cait paused and lifted her eyes to his. "Not really? What does that mean?"

"Only that he didn't say much about you."

Joe was taunting her, dangling bits and pieces of information, waiting for her reaction. She should have known better than to trust him, but she was so anxious to find out what Paul had said that she ignored her pride. "Tell me everything he said," she demanded, "word for word."

Joe had a mouthful of pizza and Cait was left to wait several moments until he swallowed. "I seem to recall he said you explained that the two of us go a long way back."

Cait straightened, too curious to hide her interest. "Did he look concerned? Jealous?"

"Paul? No, if anything, he looked bored."

"Bored," Cait repeated. Her shoulders sagged with defeat. "I swear that man wouldn't notice me if I pranced around his office naked."

"That's a clever idea, and one that just might work. Maybe you should practice around the house first, get the hang of it. I'd be willing to help you out if you're serious about this." He sounded utterly nonchalant, as though she'd suggested subscribing to cable television. "This is what friends are for. Do you need help undressing?"

Cait took a sip of her wine to hide a smile. Joe hadn't changed in twenty years. He was still witty and fun-loving and a terrible tease. "Very funny."

"Hey, I wasn't kidding. I'll pretend I'm Paul and—"

"You promised you were going to be good."

He wiggled his eyebrows suggestively. "I will be. Just you wait."

Cait could feel the tide of color flow into her cheeks. She quickly lowered her eyes to her plate. "Joe, cut it out. You're making me blush and I hate to blush. It makes my face look like a ripe tomato." She lifted her slice of pizza and bit into it, chewing thoughtfully. "I don't understand you. Every time I think I have you figured out you do something to surprise me."

"Like what?"

"Like yesterday. You invited me to dinner, but I never dreamed you'd take me someplace as elegant as Henry's. You were the perfect gentleman all evening and then today, you were so…"

"Low and disgusting."

"Exactly." She nodded righteously. "One minute you're

the picture of charm and culture and the next you're badgering me with your wisecracks."

"I'm a tease, remember?"

"The problem is I can't deal with you when I don't know what to expect."

"That's my charm." He reached for a second piece of pizza. "Women are said to adore the unexpected in a man."

"Not this woman," she informed him promptly. "I need to know where I stand with you."

"A little to the left."

"Joe, please, I'm not joking. I can't have you pulling stunts like you did today. I've lived a good, clean life for the past twenty-eight years. Two days with you has ruined my reputation with the company. I can't walk into the office and hold my head up any longer. I hear people whispering and I know they're talking about me."

"Us," he corrected. "They're talking about us."

"That's even worse. If they want to talk about me and a man, I'd rather it was Paul. Just how much longer is this remodeling project going to take, anyway?" As far as Cait was concerned, the sooner Joe and his renegade crew were out of her office, the sooner her life would return to normal.

"Not too much longer."

"At the rate you're progressing, Webster, Rodale and Missen will have offices on the moon."

"Before the end of the year, I promise."

"Yes, but just how reliable are your promises?"

"I'm being good, aren't I?"

"I suppose," she conceded ungraciously, jerking a stack of mail away from Joe as he started to sort through it.

"What's this?" Joe asked, rescuing a single piece of paper before it fluttered to the floor.

"A Christmas list. I'm going shopping tomorrow."

"I should've known you'd be organized about that, too." He sounded vaguely insulting.

"I've been organized all my life. It isn't likely to change now."

"That's why I want you to lighten up a little." He continued studying her list. "What time are you going?"

"The stores open at eight and I plan to be there then."

"I suppose you've written down everything you need to buy so you won't forget anything."

"Of course."

"Sounds sensible." His remark surprised her. He scanned her list, then yelped, "Hey, I'm not on here!" He withdrew a pen from his shirt pocket and added his own name. "Do you want me to give you a few suggestions about what I'd like?"

"I already know what I'm getting you."

Joe arched his brows. "You do? And please don't say 'nothing.'"

"No, but it'll be something appropriate—like a muzzle."

"Oh, Caitlin, darling, you injure me." He gave her one of his devilish smiles, and Cait could feel herself weakening. Just what she didn't want! She had every right to be angry with Joe. If he hadn't brought that pizza, she'd have slammed the door in his face. Wouldn't she? Sure, she would! But she'd always been susceptible to Italian food. Her only other fault was Paul. She did love him. No one seemed to believe that, but she'd known almost from the moment they'd met that she was destined to spend the rest of her life loving Paul Jamison. Only she'd rather do it as his wife than his employee....

"Have you finished your shopping?" she asked idly, making small talk with Joe since he seemed determined to hang around.

"I haven't started. I have good intentions every year, you know, like I'll get a head start on finding the perfect gifts for my nieces and nephews, but they never work out. Usually panic sets in Christmas Eve and I tear around the stores like mad and buy everything in sight. Last year I forgot wrapping paper. My mother saved the day."

"I doubt it'd do any good to suggest you get organized."

"I haven't got the time."

"What are you doing right now? Write out your list, stick to it and make the time to go shopping."

"My darling Cait, is this an invitation for me to join you tomorrow?"

"Uh..." Cait hadn't intended it to be, but she supposed she couldn't object as long as he behaved himself. "You're welcome on one condition."

"Name it."

"No jokes, no stunts like you pulled today and absolutely no teasing. If you announce to even one person that we're married, I'm walking away from you and that's a promise."

"You've got it." He raised his hand, then ceremoniously crossed his heart.

"Lick your fingertips first," Cait demanded. The instant the words were out of her mouth, she realized how ridiculous she sounded, as if they were eight and ten all over again. "Forget I said that."

His eyes were twinkling as he stood to bring his plate to the sink. "I swear it's a shame you're so in love with Paul," he told her. "If I'm not careful, I could fall for you myself." With that, he kissed her on the cheek and let himself out the door.

Pressing her fingers to her cheek, Cait drew in a deep, shuddering breath and held it until she heard the door close. Then and only then did it seep out in ragged bursts, as if she'd forgotten how to breathe normally.

"Oh, Joe," she whispered. The last thing she wanted was for Joe to fall in love with her. Not that he wasn't handsome and sweet and wonderful. He was. He always had been. He just wasn't for her. Their personalities were poles apart. Joe was unpredictable, always doing the unexpected, whereas Cait's life ran like clockwork.

She liked Joe. She almost wished she didn't, but she couldn't help herself. However, a steady diet of his pranks would soon drive her into the nearest asylum.

Standing, Cait closed the pizza box and tucked the uneaten portion onto the top shelf of her refrigerator. She was putting the dirty plates in her dishwasher when the phone rang. She quickly washed her hands and reached for it.

"Hello."

"Cait, it's Paul."

Cait was so startled that the receiver slipped out of her hand. Grabbing for it, she nearly stumbled over the open dishwasher door, knocking her shin against the sharp edge. She yelped and swallowed a cry as she jerked the dangling phone cord toward her.

"Sorry, sorry," she cried, once she'd rescued the telephone receiver. "Paul? Are you still there?"

"Yes, I'm here. Is this a bad time? I could call back later if this is inconvenient. You don't have company, do you? I wouldn't want to interrupt a party or anything."

"Oh, no, now is perfect. I didn't realize you had my home number…but obviously you do. After all, we've been working together for nearly a year now." Eleven months and four days, not that she was counting or anything. "Naturally my number would be in the Human Resources file."

He hesitated and Cait bent over to rub her shin where it had collided with the dishwasher door. She was sure to have an ugly bruise, but a bruised leg was a small price to pay. Paul had phoned her!

"The reason I'm calling…"

"Yes, Paul," she prompted when he didn't immediately continue.

The silence lengthened before he blurted out, "I just wanted to thank you for passing on that article on the tax advantages of limited partnerships. It was thoughtful of you and I appreciate it."

"I've read quite a lot in that area, you know. There are several recent articles on the same subject. If you'd like, I could bring them in next week."

"Sure. That would be fine. Thanks again, Cait. Goodbye."

The line was disconnected before Cait could say anything else and she was left holding the receiver. A smile came, slow and confident, and with a small cry of triumph, she tossed the telephone receiver into the air, caught it behind her back and replaced it with a flourish.

Cait was dressed and waiting for Joe early the next morning. "Joe," she cried, throwing open her apartment door, "I could just kiss you."

He was dressed in faded jeans and a hip-length bronze-colored leather jacket. "Hey, I'm not stopping you," he said, opening his arms.

Cait ignored the invitation. "Paul phoned me last night." She didn't even try to contain her excitement; she felt like leaping and skipping and singing out loud.

"Paul did?" Joe sounded surprised.

"Yes. It was shortly after you left. He thanked me for giving him an interesting article I found in one of the business journals and—this is the good part—he asked if I was alone… as if it really mattered to him."

"If you were alone?" Joe repeated, and frowned. "What's that got to do with anything?"

"Don't you understand?" For all his intelligence Joe could

be pretty obtuse sometimes. "He wanted to know if *you* were here with me. It makes sense, doesn't it? Paul's jealous, only he doesn't realize it yet. Oh, Joe, I can't remember ever being this happy. Not in years and years and years."

"Because Paul Jamison phoned?"

"Don't sound so skeptical. It's exactly the break I've been waiting for all these months. Paul's finally noticed me, and it's thanks to you."

"At least you're willing to give credit where credit is due." But he still didn't seem particularly thrilled.

"It's just so incredible," she continued. "I don't think I slept a wink last night. There was something in his voice that I've never heard before. Something…deep and personal. I don't know how to explain it. For the first time in a whole year, Paul knows I'm alive!"

"Are we going Christmas shopping or not?" Joe demanded brusquely. "Damn it all, Cait, I never expected you to go soft over a stupid phone call."

"But this wasn't just any call," she reminded him. She reached for her purse and her coat in one sweeping motion. "It was was from *Paul*."

"You sound like a silly schoolgirl." Joe frowned, but Cait wasn't about to let his short temper destroy her mood. Paul had phoned her at home and she was sure that this was the beginning of a *real* relationship. Next he'd ask her out for lunch, and then…

They left her apartment and walked down the hall, Cait grinning all the way. Standing just outside the front doors was a huge truck with gigantic wheels. Just the type of vehicle she'd expected him to drive the night he'd taken her to Henry's.

"This is your truck?" she asked when they were outside. She couldn't keep the laughter out of her voice.

"Something wrong with it?"

"Not a single thing, but Joe, honestly, you are so predictable."

"That's not what you said yesterday."

She grinned again as he opened the truck door, set down a stool for her and helped her climb into the cab. The seat was cluttered, but so wide she was able to shove everything to one side. When she'd made room for herself, she fastened the seat belt, snapping it jauntily in place. She was so happy, the whole world seemed delightful this morning.

"Will you quit smiling before someone suggests you've been overdosing on vitamins?" Joe grumbled.

"My, aren't we testy this morning."

"Where to?" he asked, starting the engine.

"Any of the big malls will do. You decide. Do you have your list all made out?"

Joe patted his heart. "It's in my shirt pocket."

"Good."

"Have you decided what you're going to buy for whom?"

His smile was slightly off-kilter. "Not exactly. I thought I'd follow you around and buy whatever you did. Do you know what you're getting your mother? Mine's damn difficult to buy for. Last year I ended up getting her a dozen bags of cat food. She's got five cats of her own and God only knows how many strays she's feeding."

"At least your idea was practical."

"Well, there's that, and the fact that by the time I started my Christmas shopping the only store open was a supermarket."

Cait laughed. "Honestly, Joe!"

"Hey, I was desperate and before you get all righteous on me, Mom thought the cat food and the two rib roasts were great gifts."

"I'm sure she did," Cait returned, grinning. She found herself doing a lot of that when she was with Joe. Imagine buying his mother rib roasts for Christmas!

"Give me some ideas, would you? Mom's a hard case."

"To be honest, I'm not all that imaginative myself. I buy my mother the same thing every year."

"What is it?"

"Long-distance phone cards. That way she can phone her sister in Dubuque and her high-school friend in Kansas. Of course she calls me every now and then, too."

"Okay, that takes care of Mom. What about Martin? What are you buying him?"

"A bronze eagle." She'd decided on that gift last summer when she'd attended Sunday services at Martin's church. In the opening part of his sermon, Martin had used eagles to illustrate a point of faith.

"An eagle," Joe repeated. "Any special reason?"

"Y-yes," she said, not wanting to explain. "It's a long story, but I happen to be partial to eagles myself."

"Any other hints you'd care to pass on?"

"Buy wrapping paper in the after-Christmas sales. It's about half the price and it stores easily under the bed."

"Great idea. I'll have to remember that for next year."

Joe chose Northgate, the shopping mall closest to Cait's apartment. The parking lot was already beginning to fill up and it was only a few minutes after eight.

Joe managed to park fairly close to the entrance and came around to help Cait out of the truck. This time he didn't bother with the step stool, but clasped her around the waist to lift her down. "What did you mean when you said I was so predictable?" he asked, giving her a reproachful look.

With her hands resting on his shoulders and her feet dangling in midair, she felt vulnerable and small. "Nothing. It was just that I assumed you drove one of these Sherman-tank trucks, and I was right. I just hadn't seen it before."

"The kind of truck I drive bothers you?" His brow furrowed in a scowl.

"Not at all. What's the matter with you today, Joe? You're so touchy."

"I am not touchy," he snapped.

"Fine. Would you mind putting me down then?" His large hands were squeezing her waist almost painfully, though she doubted he was aware of it. She couldn't imagine what had angered him. Unless it was the fact that Paul had called her—which didn't make sense. Maybe, like most men, he just hated shopping.

He lowered her slowly to the asphalt and released her with seeming reluctance. "I need a coffee break," he announced grimly.

"But we just arrived."

Joe forcefully expelled his breath. "It doesn't matter. I need something to calm my nerves."

If he needed a caffeine fix so early in the day, Cait wondered how he'd manage during the next few hours. The stores quickly became crowded this time of year, especially on a Saturday. By ten it would be nearly impossible to get from one aisle to the next.

By twelve, she knew: Joe disliked Christmas shopping every bit as much as she'd expected.

"I've had it," Joe complained after making three separate trips back to the truck to deposit their spoils.

"Me, too," Cait agreed laughingly. "This place is turning into a madhouse."

"How about some lunch?" Joe suggested. "Someplace far away from here. Like Tibet."

Cait laughed again and tucked her arm in his. "That sounds like a great idea."

Outside, they noticed several cars circling the lot looking for a parking space and three of them rushed to fill the one Joe vacated. Two cars nearly collided in their eagerness. One man leapt out of his and shook an angry fist at the other driver.

"So much for peace and goodwill," Joe commented. "I swear Christmas brings out the worst in everyone."

"And the best," Cait reminded him.

"To be honest, I don't know what crammed shopping malls and fighting the crowds and all this commercialism have to do with Christmas in the first place," he grumbled. A car cut in front of him, and Joe blared his horn.

"Quite a lot when you think about it," Cait said softly. "Imagine the streets of Bethlehem, the crowds and the noise..." The Christmas before, fresh from a shopping expedition, Cait had asked herself the same question. Christmas seemed so commercial. The crowds had been unbearable. First at Northgate, where she did most of her shopping and then at the airport. Sea-Tac had been filled with activity and noise, everyone in a hurry to get someplace else. There seemed to be little peace or good cheer and a whole lot of selfish concern and rudeness. Then, in the tranquility of church on Christmas Eve, everything had come into perspective for Cait. There had been crowds and rudeness that first Christmas, too, she reasoned. Yet in the midst of that confusion had come joy and peace and love. For most people, it was still the same. Christmas gifts and decorations and dinners were, after all, expressions of the love you felt for your family and friends. And if the preparations sometimes got a bit chaotic, well, that no longer bothered Cait.

"Where should we go to eat?" Joe asked, breaking into her thoughts. They were barely moving, stuck in heavy traffic.

She looked over at him and smiled serenely. "Any place will do. There're several excellent restaurants close by. You choose, only let it be my treat this time."

"We'll talk about who pays later. Right now, I'm more concerned with getting out of this traffic sometime within my life span."

Still smiling, Cait said, "I don't think it'll take much longer."

He returned her smile. "I don't, either." His eyes held hers for what seemed an eternity—until someone behind them honked irritably. Joe glanced up and saw that traffic ahead of them had started to move. He immediately stepped on the gas.

Cait didn't know what Joe had found so fascinating about her unless it was her unruly hair. She hadn't combed it since leaving the house; it was probably a mass of tight, disorderly curls. She'd been so concerned with finding the right gift for her nephews and niece that she hadn't given it a thought.

"What's wrong?" she asked, feeling self-conscious.

"What makes you think anything's wrong?"

"The way you were looking at me a few minutes ago."

"Oh, that," he said, easing into a restaurant parking lot. "I don't think I've ever fully appreciated how lovely you are," he answered in a calm, matter-of-fact voice.

Cait blushed and glanced away. "I'm sure you're mistaken. I'm really not all that pretty. I sometimes wondered if Paul would have noticed me sooner if I was a little more attractive."

"Trust me, Bright Eyes," he said, turning off the engine. "You're pretty enough."

"For what?"

"For this." And he leaned across the seat and captured her mouth with his.

5

"I...wish you hadn't done that," Cait whispered, slowly opening her eyes in an effort to pull herself back to reality.

As far as kisses went, Joe's were good. Very good. He kissed better than just about anyone she'd ever kissed before—but that didn't alter the fact that she was in love with Paul.

"You're right," he muttered, opening the door and climbing out of the cab. "I shouldn't have done that." He walked around to her side and yanked the door open with more force than necessary.

Cait frowned, wondering at his strange mood. One minute he was holding her in his arms, kissing her tenderly; the next he was short-tempered and irritable.

"I'm hungry," he barked, lifting her abruptly down to the pavement. "I sometimes do irrational things when I haven't eaten."

"I see." The next time she went anywhere with Joseph Rockwell, she'd have to make sure he ate a good meal first.

The restaurant was crowded and Joe gave the hostess their names to add to the growing waiting list. Sitting on the last empty chair in the foyer, Cait set her large black leather purse on her lap and started rooting through it.

"What are you searching for? Uranium?" Joe teased, watching her.

"Crackers," she answered, shifting the bulky bag and handing him several items to hold while she continued digging.

"You're searching for crackers? Whatever for?"

She glanced up long enough to give him a look that questioned his intelligence. "For obvious reasons. If you're irrational when you're hungry, you might do something stupid while we're here. Frankly, I don't want you to embarrass me." She returned to the task with renewed vigor. "I can just see you standing on top of the table dancing."

"That's one way to get the waiter's attention. Thanks for suggesting it."

"Aha!" Triumphantly Cait pulled two miniature bread sticks wrapped in cellophane from the bottom of her purse. "Eat," she instructed. "Before you're overcome by some other craziness."

"You mean before I kiss you again," he said in a low voice, bending his head toward hers.

She leaned back quickly, not giving him any chance of following through on that. "Exactly. Or waltz with the waitress or any of the other loony things you do."

"You have to admit I've been good all morning."

"With one minor slip," she reminded him, pressing the bread sticks into his hand. "Now eat."

Before Joe had a chance to open the package, the hostess approached them with two menus tucked under her arm. "Mr. and Mrs. Rockwell. Your table is ready."

"Mr. and Mrs. Rockwell," Cait muttered under her breath, glaring at Joe. She should've known she couldn't trust him.

"Excuse me," Cait said, standing abruptly and raising her index finger. "His name is Rockwell, mine is Marshall," she explained patiently. She was not about to let Joe continue his silly games. "We're just friends here for lunch." Her narrowed eyes caught Joe's, which looked as innocent as freshly fallen snow. He shrugged as though to say any misunderstanding hadn't been *his* fault.

"I see," the hostess replied. "I'm sorry for the confusion."

"No problem." Cait hadn't wanted to make a big issue of this, but on the other hand she didn't want Joe to think he was going to get away with it, either.

The woman led them to a linen-covered table in the middle of the room. Joe held out Cait's chair for her, then whispered something to the hostess who immediately cast Cait a sympathetic glance. Joe's own gaze rested momentarily on Cait before he pulled out his chair and sat across from her.

"All right, what did you say to her?" she hissed.

The menu seemed to command his complete interest for a couple of minutes. "What makes you think I said anything?"

"I heard you whispering and then she gave me this pathetic look like she wanted to hug me and tell me everything was going to be all right."

"Then you know."

"Joe, don't play games with me," Cait warned.

"All right, if you must know, I explained that you'd suffered a head injury and developed amnesia."

"Amnesia," she repeated loudly enough to attract the attention of the diners at the next table. Gritting her teeth, Cait snatched up her menu, gripping it so tightly the edges curled. It didn't do any good to argue with Joe. The man was impossible. Every time she tried to reason with him, he did something to make her regret it.

"How else was I supposed to explain the fact that you'd forgotten our marriage?" he asked reasonably.

"I did not forget our marriage," she informed him from between clenched teeth, reviewing the menu and quickly making her selection. "Good grief, it wasn't even legal."

She realized that the waitress was standing by their table, pen and pad in hand. The woman's ready smile faded as she looked from Cait to Joe and back again. Her mouth tightened as if she suspected they really were involved in something illegal.

"Uh..." Cait hedged, feeling like even more of an idiot. The urge to explain was overwhelming, but every time she tried, she only made matters worse. "I'll have the club sandwich," she said, glaring across the table at Joe.

"That sounds good. I'll have the same," he said, closing his menu.

The woman scribbled down their order, then hurried away, pausing to glance over her shoulder as if she wanted to be able to identify them later in a police lineup.

"Now look what you've done," Cait whispered heatedly once the waitress was far enough away from their table not to overhear.

"Me?"

Maybe she was being unreasonable, but Joe was the one who'd started this nonsense in the first place. No one could rattle her as effectively as Joe did. And worse, she let him.

This shopping trip was a good example, and so was the pizza that led up to it. No woman in her right mind should've allowed Joe into her apartment after what he'd said to her in front of Lindy. Not only had she invited him inside her home, she'd agreed to let him accompany her Christmas shopping. She ought to have her head examined!

"What's wrong?" Joe asked, tearing open the package of bread sticks. Rather pointless in Cait's opinion, since their lunch would be served any minute.

"What's wrong?" she cried, dumbfounded that he had to ask. "You mean other than the hostess believing I've suffered a head injury and the waitress thinking we're drug dealers or something equally disgusting?"

"Here." He handed her one of the miniature bread sticks. "Eat this and you'll feel better."

Cait sincerely doubted that, but she took it, anyway, muttering under her breath.

"Relax," he urged.

"Relax," she mocked. "How can I possibly relax when you're doing and saying things I find excruciatingly embarrassing?"

"I'm sorry, Cait. Really, I am." To his credit, he did look contrite. "But you're so easy to fluster and I can't seem to stop myself."

Their sandwiches arrived, thick with slices of turkey, ham and a variety of cheeses. Cait was reluctant to admit how much better she felt after she'd eaten. Joe's spirits had apparently improved, as well.

"So," he said, his hands resting on his stomach. "What do you have planned for the rest of the afternoon?"

Cait hadn't given it much thought. "I suppose I should wrap the gifts I bought this morning." But that prospect didn't particularly excite her. Good grief, after the adventures she'd had with Joe, it wasn't any wonder.

"You mean you actually wrap gifts before Christmas Eve?" Joe asked. "Doesn't that take all the fun out of it? I mean, for me it's a game just to see if I can get the presents bought."

She grinned, trying to imagine herself in such a disorganized race to the deadline. Definitely not her style.

"How about a movie?" he suggested out of the blue. "I have the feeling you don't get out enough."

"A movie?" Cait ignored the comment about her social life, mainly because he was right. She rarely took the time to go to a show.

"We're both exhausted from fighting the crowds," Joe added. "There's a six-cinema theater next to the restaurant. I'll even let you choose."

"I suppose you'd object to a love story?"

"We can see one if you insist, only..."

"Only what?"

"Only promise me you won't ever expect a man to say the kinds of things those guys on the screen do."

"I beg your pardon?"

"You heard me. Women hear actors say this incredible drivel and then they're disappointed when real men don't."

"Real men like you, I suppose?"

"Right." He looked smug, then suddenly he frowned. "Does Paul like romances?"

Cait had no idea, since she'd never gone on a date with Paul and the subject wasn't one they'd ever discussed at the office. "I imagine he does," she said, dabbing her mouth with her napkin. "He isn't the type of man to be intimidated by such things."

Joe's deep blue eyes widened with surprise and a touch of respect. "Ouch. So Martin's little sister reveals her claws."

"I don't have claws. I just happen to have strong opinions on certain subjects." She reached for her purse while she was speaking and removed her wallet.

"What are you doing now?" Joe demanded.

"Paying for lunch." She sorted through the bills and withdrew a twenty. "It's my turn and I insist on paying…" She hesitated when she saw Joe's deepening frown. "Or don't real men allow women friends to buy their lunch?"

"Sure, go ahead," he returned flippantly.

It was all Cait could do to hide a smile. She guessed that her gesture in paying for their sandwiches would somehow be seen as compromising his male pride.

Apparently she was right. As they were walking toward the cashier, Joe stepped up his pace, grabbed the check from her hand and slapped some money on the counter. He glared at her as if he expected a drawn-out public argument. After the fuss they'd already caused in the restaurant, Cait was darned if she was going to let that happen.

"Joe," she argued the minute they were out the door. "What was *that* all about?"

"Fine, you win. Tell me my views are outdated, but when a woman goes out with me, I pick up the tab, no matter how liberated she is."

"But this isn't a real date. We're only friends, and even that's—"

"I don't give a damn. Consider it an apology for the embarrassment I caused you earlier."

"Isn't that kind of sexist?"

"No! I just have certain…standards."

"So I see." His attitude shouldn't have come as any big surprise. Just as Cait had told him earlier, he was shockingly predictable.

Hand at her elbow, Joe led the way across the car-filled lot toward the sprawling theater complex. The movies were geared toward a wide audience. There was a Disney classic, along with a horror flick and a couple of adventure movies and last but not least, a well-publicized love story.

As they stood in line, Cait caught Joe's gaze lingering on

the poster for one of the adventure films—yet another story about a law-and-order cop with renegade ideas.

"I suppose you're more interested in seeing that than the romance."

"I already promised you could choose the show, and I'm a man of my word. If, however, you were to pick another movie—" he buried his hands in his pockets as he grinned at her appealingly "—I wouldn't complain."

"I'm willing to pick another movie, but on one condition."

"Name it." His eyes lit up.

"I pay."

"Those claws of yours are out again."

She raised her hands and flexed her fingers in a catlike motion. "It's your decision."

"What about popcorn?"

"You can buy that if you insist."

"All right," he said, "you've got yourself a deal."

When it was Cait's turn at the ticket window, she purchased two for the Disney classic.

"Disney?" Joe yelped, shocked when Cait handed him his ticket.

"It seemed like a good compromise," she answered.

For a moment it looked as if he was going to argue with her, then a slow grin spread across his face. "Disney," he said again. "You're right, it does sound like fun. Only I hope we're not the only people there over the age of ten."

They sat toward the back of the theater, sharing a large bucket of buttered popcorn. The theater was crowded and several kids seemed to be taking turns running up and down the aisles. Joe needn't have worried; there were plenty of adults in attendance, but of course most of them were accompanying children.

The lights dimmed and Cait reached for a handful of popcorn, relaxing in her seat. "I love this movie."

"How many times have you seen it?"

"Five or six. But it's been a few years."

"Me, too." Joe relaxed beside her, crossing his long legs and leaning back.

The credits started to roll, but the noise level hadn't decreased much. "Will the kids bother you?" Joe wanted to know.

"Heavens, no. I love kids."

"You do?" The fact that he was so surprised seemed vaguely insulting and Cait frowned.

"We've already had this discussion," she responded, licking the salt from her fingertips.

"We did? When?"

"The other day. You commented on how much I used to enjoy playing with my dolls and how you'd expected me to be married with a house full of children." His words had troubled her then, because "a house full of children" was exactly what Cait would have liked, and she seemed a long way from realizing her dream.

"Ah, yes, I remember our conversation about that now." He scooped up a large handful of popcorn. "You'd be a very good mother, you know."

That Joe would say this was enough to bring an unexpected rush of tears to her eyes. She blinked them back, annoyed that she'd get weepy over something so silly.

The previews were over and the audience settled down as the movie started. Cait focused her attention on the screen, munching popcorn every now and then, reaching blindly for the bucket. Their hands collided more than once and almost before she was aware of it, their fingers were entwined. It was a peaceful sort of feeling, being linked to Joe in this way. There was a *rightness* about it that she didn't want to explore just yet. He hadn't really changed; he was still lovable and funny and fun. For that matter, she hadn't changed very much, either….

The movie was as good as Cait remembered, better, even—perhaps because Joe was there to share it with her. She half expected him to make the occasional wisecrack, but he seemed to respect the artistic value of the classic animation and, judging by his wholehearted laughter, he enjoyed the story.

When the show was over, he released Cait's hand. Hurriedly she gathered her purse and coat. As they walked out of the noisy, crowded theater, it seemed only natural to hold hands again.

Joe opened the truck, lifted down the step stool and helped her inside. Dusk came early these days, and bright, cheery lights were ablaze on every street. A vacant lot across the street was now filled with Christmas trees. A row of red lights was strung between two posts, sagging in the middle, and a portable CD player sent forth saccharine versions of better-known Christmas carols.

"Have you bought your tree yet?" Joe asked, nodding in the direction of the lot after he'd climbed into the driver's seat and started the engine.

"No. I don't usually put one up since I spend the holidays with Martin and his family."

"Ah."

"What about you? Or is that something else you save for Christmas Eve?" she joked. It warmed her a little to imagine Joe staying up past midnight to decorate a Christmas tree for his nieces and nephews.

"Finding time to do the shopping is bad enough," he said, not really answering her question.

"Your construction projects keep you that busy?" She hadn't given much thought to Joe's business. She knew from remarks Paul had made that Joe was very successful. It wasn't logical that she should feel pride in his accomplishments, but she did.

"Owning a business isn't like being in a nine-to-five job. I'm on call twenty-four hours a day, but I wouldn't have it any other way. I love what I do."

"I'm happy for you, Joe. I really am."

"Happy enough to decorate my Christmas tree with me?"

"When?"

"Next weekend."

"I'd like to," she told him, touched by the invitation, "but I'll have left for Minnesota by then."

"That's all right," Joe said, grinning at her. "Maybe next time."

She turned, frowning, to hide her blush.

They remained silent as he concentrated on easing the truck into the heavy late-afternoon traffic.

"I enjoyed the movie," she said some time later, resisting the urge to rest her head on his shoulder. The impulse to do that arose from her exhaustion, she told herself. Nothing else!

"So did I," he said softly. "Only next time, I'll be the one to pay. Understand?"

Next time. There it was again. She suspected Joe was beginning to take their relationship, such as it was, far too seriously. Already he was suggesting they'd be seeing each other soon, matter-of-factly discussing dates and plans as if they were longtime companions. Almost as if they were married…

She was mulling over this realization when Joe pulled into the parking area in front of her building. He climbed out and began to gather her packages, bundling them in his arms. She managed to scramble down by herself, not giving him a chance to help her, then she led the way into the building and unlocked her door.

Cait stood just inside the doorway and turned slightly to take a couple of the larger packages from Joe's arms.

"I had a great time," she told him briskly.

"Me, too." He nudged her, forcing her to enter the living room. He followed close behind and unloaded her remaining things onto the sofa. His presence seemed to reach out and fill every corner of the room.

Neither of them spoke for several minutes, but Cait sensed Joe wanted her to invite him to stay for coffee. The idea was tempting but dangerous. She mustn't let him think there might ever be anything romantic between them. Not when she was in love with Paul. For the first time in nearly a year, Paul was actually beginning to notice her. She refused to ruin everything now by becoming involved with Joe.

"Thank you for…today," she said, returning to the door, intending to open it for him. Instead, Joe caught her by the wrist and pulled her against him. She was in his arms before she could voice a protest.

"I'm going to kiss you," he told her, his voice rough yet strangely tender.

"You are?" She'd never been more aware of a man, of his hard, muscular body against hers, his clean, masculine scent. Her own body reacted in a chaotic scramble of mixed sensations. Above all, though, it felt *good* to be in his arms. She wasn't sure why and dared not examine the feeling.

Slowly, leisurely, he lowered his head. She made a soft weak sound as his mouth touched hers.

Cait sighed, forgetting for a moment that she meant to free herself before his kiss deepened. Before things went any further…

Joe must have sensed her resolve because his hands slid

down her spine in a gentle caress, drawing her even closer. His mouth began a sensuous journey along her jaw, and down her throat—

"Joe!" She moaned his name, uncertain of what she wanted to say.

"Hmm?"

"Are you hungry again?" She wondered desperately if there were any more bread sticks in the bottom of her purse. Maybe that would convince him to stop.

"Very hungry," he told her, his voice low and solemn. "I've never been hungrier."

"But you had lunch and then you ate nearly all the popcorn."

He slowly raised his head. "Cait, are we talking about the same things here? Oh, hell, what does it matter? The only thing that matters is this." He covered her parted lips with his.

Cait felt her knees go weak and sagged against him, her fingers gripping his jacket as though she expected to collapse any moment. Which was becoming a distinct possibility as he continued to kiss her....

"Joe, no more, please." But she was the one clinging to him. She had to do something, and fast, before her ability to reason was lost entirely.

He drew an unsteady breath and muttered something she couldn't decipher as his lips grazed the delicate line of her jaw.

"We...need to talk," she announced, keeping her eyes tightly closed. If she didn't look at Joe, then she could concentrate on what she had to do.

"All right," he agreed.

"I'll make a pot of coffee."

With a heavy sigh, Joe abruptly released her. Cait half fell against the sofa arm, requiring its support while she collected herself enough to walk into the kitchen. She unconsciously reached up and brushed her lips, as if she wasn't completely sure even now that he'd taken her in his arms and kissed her.

He hadn't been joking this time, or teasing. The kisses they'd shared were serious kisses. The type a man gives a woman he's strongly attracted to. A woman he's interested in developing a relationship with. Cait found herself shaking, unable to move.

"You want me to make that coffee?" he suggested.

She nodded and sank down on the couch. She could scarcely stand, let alone prepare a pot of coffee.

Joe returned a few minutes later, carrying two steaming mugs. Carefully he handed her one, then sat across from her on the blue velvet ottoman.

"You wanted to talk?"

Cait nodded. "Yes." Her throat felt thick, clogged with confused emotion, and forming coherent words suddenly seemed beyond her. She tried gesturing with her free hand, but that only served to frustrate Joe.

"Cait," he asked, "what's wrong?"

"Paul." The name came out in an eerie squeak.

"What about him?"

"He phoned me."

"Yes, I know. You already told me that."

"Don't you understand?" she cried, her throat unexpectedly clearing. "Paul is finally showing some interest in me and now you're kissing me and telling anyone who'll listen that the two of us are married and you're doing ridiculous things like..." She paused to draw in a deep breath. "Joe, oh, please, Joe, don't fall in love with me."

"Fall in love with you?" he echoed incredulously. "Caitlin, you can't be serious. It won't happen. No chance."

6

"No chance?" Cait repeated, convinced she'd misunderstood him. She blinked a couple of times as if that would correct her hearing. Either Joe was underestimating her intelligence, or he was more of a…a cad than she'd realized.

"You have nothing to worry about." He sipped coffee, his gaze steady and emotionless. "I'm not falling in love with you."

"In other words you make a habit of kissing unsuspecting women."

"It isn't a habit," he answered thoughtfully. "It's more of a pastime."

"You certainly seem to be making a habit of it with me." Her anger was quickly gaining momentum and she was at odds to understand why she found his casual attitude so offensive. He was telling her exactly what she wanted to hear. But she hadn't expected her ego to take such a beating in the process. The fact that he wasn't the least bit tempted to fall in love with her should have pleased her.

It didn't.

It was as if their brief kisses were little more than a pleasant interlude for him. Something to occupy his time and keep him from growing bored with her company.

"This may come as a shock to you," Joe continued indifferently, "but a man doesn't have to be in love with a woman to kiss her."

"I know that," Cait snapped, fighting to hold back her temper, which was threatening to break free at any moment. "But you don't have to be so…so casual about it, either. If I wasn't involved with Paul, I might have taken you seriously."

"I didn't know you were involved with Paul," he returned with mild sarcasm. He leaned forward and rested his elbows on his knees, his pose infuriatingly relaxed. "If that was true I'd never have taken you out. The way I see it, the involvement is all on your part. Am I wrong?"

"No," she admitted reluctantly. How like a man to bring up semantics in the middle of an argument!

"So," he said, leaning back again and crossing his legs. "Are you enjoying my kisses? I take it I've improved from the first go-around."

"You honestly want me to rate you?" she sputtered.

"Obviously I'm much better than I was as a kid, otherwise you wouldn't be so worried." He took another drink of his coffee, smiling pleasantly all the while.

"Believe me, I'm not worried."

He arched his brows. "Really?"

"I'm sure you expect me to fall at your feet, overcome by your masculine charm. Well, if that's what you're waiting for, you'll have one hell of a long wait!"

His grin was slightly off center, as if he was picturing her arrayed at his feet—and enjoying the sight. "I think the problem here is that *you* might be falling in love with *me* and just don't know it."

"Falling in love with you and not know it?" she repeated with a loud disbelieving snort. "You've gone completely out of your mind. There's no chance of that."

"Why not? Plenty of women have told me I'm a handsome son of a gun. Plus, I'm said to possess a certain charm. Heaven knows, I'm generous enough and rather—"

"Who told you that? Your mother?" She made it sound like the most ludicrous thing she'd heard in years.

"You might be surprised to learn that I do have admirers."

Why this news should add fuel to the fire of her temper was beyond Cait, but she was so furious with him she could barely sit still. "I don't doubt it, but if I fall in love with a man you can believe it won't be just because he's 'a handsome son of a gun,'" she quoted sarcastically. "Look at Paul— he's the type of man I'm attracted to. What's on the inside matters more than outward appearances."

"Then why are you so worried about falling in love with me?"

"I'm not worried! You've got it the wrong way around. The only reason I mentioned anything was because I thought *you* were beginning to take our times together too seriously."

"I already explained that wasn't a problem."

"So I heard." Cait set her coffee aside. Joe was upsetting her so much that her hand was shaking hard enough to spill it.

"Well," Joe murmured, glancing at her. "You never did answer my question."

"Which one?" she asked irritably.

"About how I rated as a kisser."

"You weren't serious!"

"On the contrary." He set his own coffee down and raised

himself off the ottoman far enough to clasp her by the waist and pull her into his lap.

Caught off balance, Cait fell onto his thighs, too astonished to struggle.

"Let's try it again," he whispered in a rough undertone.

"Ah..." A frightening excitement took hold of Cait. Her mind commanded her to leap away from this man, but some emotion, far stronger than common sense or prudence, urged the opposite.

Before she could form a protest, Joe bent toward her and covered her mouth with his. She'd hold herself stiff in his arms, that was what she'd do, teach him the lesson he deserved. How dared he assume she'd automatically fall in love with him. How dared he insinuate he was some...some Greek god all women adored. But the instant his lips met hers, Cait trembled with a mixture of shock and profound pleasure.

Everything within her longed to cry out at the unfairness of it all. It shouldn't be this good with Joe. They were friends, nothing more. This was the kind of response she expected when Paul kissed her. If he ever did.

She meant to pull away, but instead, Cait moaned softly. It felt so incredibly wonderful. So incredibly right. At that moment, there didn't seem to be anything to worry about—except the likelihood of dissolving in his arms then and there.

Suddenly Joe broke the contact. Her instinctive disappointment, even more than the unexpectedness of the action, sent her eyes flying open. Her own dark eyes met his blue ones, which now seemed almost aquamarine.

"So, how do I rate?" he murmured thickly, as though he was having trouble speaking.

"Good." A one-word reply was all she could manage, although she was furious with him for asking.

"Just good?"

She nodded forcefully.

"I thought we were better than that."

"We?"

"Naturally I'm only as good as my partner."

"Th-then how do you rate me?" She had to ask. Like a fool she handed him the ax and laid her neck on the chopping board. Joe was sure to use the opportunity to trample all over her ego, to turn the whole bewildering experience into a joke. She couldn't take that right now. She dropped her gaze, waiting for him to devastate her.

"Much improved."

She cocked one eyebrow in surprise. She had no idea what to say next.

They were both silent. Then he said softly, "You know, Cait, we're getting better at this. Much, much better." He pressed his forehead to hers. "If we're not careful, you just might fall in love with me, after all."

"Where were you all day Saturday?" Lindy asked early Monday morning, walking into Cait's office. The renovations to it had been completed late Friday and Cait had moved everything back into her office first thing this morning. "I must have tried calling you ten times."

"I told you I was going Christmas shopping. In fact, I bought some decorations for my office."

Lindy nodded. "But all day?" Her eyes narrowed suspiciously as she set down her briefcase and leaned against Cait's desk, crossing her arms. "You didn't happen to be with Joe Rockwell, did you?"

Cait could feel a telltale shade of pink creeping up her neck. She lowered her gaze to the list of current Dow Jones stock prices and took a moment to compose herself. She couldn't admit the truth. "I told you I was shopping," she said somewhat defensively. Then, in an effort to change the topic, she reached for a thick folder with Paul's name inked across the top and muttered, "You wouldn't happen to know Paul's schedule for the day, would you?"

"N-no, I haven't seen him yet. Why do you ask?"

Cait flashed her friend a bright smile. "He phoned me Friday night. Oh, Lindy, I was so excited I nearly fell all over myself." She dropped her voice as she glanced around to make sure none of the others could hear her. "I honestly think he intends to ask me out."

"Did he say so?"

"Not exactly." Cait frowned. Lindy wasn't revealing any of the enthusiasm she expected.

"Then why did he phone?"

Cait rolled her chair away from the desk and glanced around once again. "I think he might be jealous," she whispered.

"Really?" Lindy's eyes widened.

"Don't look so surprised." Cait, however, was much too excited recounting Paul's phone call to be offended by Lindy's attitude.

"What makes you think Paul would be jealous?" Lindy asked next.

"Maybe I'm magnifying everything in my own mind because it's what I so badly want to believe. But he did phone..."

"What did he say?" Lindy pressed, sounding more curious now. "It seems to me he must have had a reason."

"Oh, he did. He mentioned something about appreciating an article I'd given him, but we both know that was just an excuse. What clued me in to his jealousy was the way he kept asking if I was alone."

"But that could've been for several different reasons, don't you think?" Lindy suggested.

"Yes, but it made sense that he'd want to know if Joe was at the apartment or not."

"And was he?"

"Of course not," Cait said righteously. She didn't feel guilty about hiding the fact that he'd been there earlier, or that they'd spent nearly all of Saturday together. "I'm sure Joe's ridiculous remark when I left the office on Friday is what convinced Paul to phone me. If I wasn't so furious with Joe, I might even be grateful."

"What's that?" Lindy asked abruptly, pointing to the folder in front of Cait. Her lips had thinned slightly as if she was confused or annoyed—about what, Cait couldn't figure out.

"This, my friend," she began, holding up the folder, "is the key to my future with our dedicated manager."

Lindy didn't immediately respond and looked more puzzled than before. "How do you mean?"

Cait couldn't get over the feeling that things weren't quite right with her best friend; she seemed to be holding something back. But Cait realized Lindy would tell her when she was ready. Lindy always hated being pushed or prodded.

"The folder?" Lindy prompted when Cait didn't answer.

Cait flipped it open. "I spent all day Sunday reading through old business journals looking for articles that might interest Paul. I must've gone back five years. I copied the articles I consider the most valuable and included a brief analysis of my own. I was hoping to give it to him sometime today. That's why I was asking if you knew his schedule."

"Unfortunately I don't," Lindy murmured. She straightened, picked up her briefcase and made a show of checking her watch. Then she looked up to smile reassuringly at Cait. "I'd better get to work. I'll come by later to help you put up your decorations, okay?"

"Thanks," Cait said, then added, "Wish me luck with Paul."

"You know I do," Lindy mumbled on her way out the door.

Mondays were generally slow for the stock market—unless there was a crisis. World events and financial reports had a significant impact on the market. However, as the day progressed, everything ran smoothly.

Cait looked up every now and then, half expecting to see Joe lounging in her doorway. His men had started early that morning, but by noon, Joe still hadn't arrived.

Not until much later did she realize it was Paul she should be anticipating, not Joe. Paul was the romantic interest of her life and it annoyed her that Joe seemed to occupy her thoughts.

As it happened, Paul did stroll past her office shortly after the New York market closed. Grabbing the folder, Cait raced toward his office, not hesitating for an instant. This was her golden opportunity and she was taking hold of it with both hands.

"Good afternoon, Paul," she said cordially as she stood in his doorway, clutching the folder. "Do you have a moment or would you rather I came back later?"

He looked tired, as if the day had already been a grueling one. It was all Cait could do not to offer to massage away the stress and worry that complicated his life. Her heart swelled with a renewed wave of love. For a wild, impetuous moment, it was true, she'd suffered her doubts. Any woman would have when a man like Joe took her in his arms. He might be arrogant in the extreme and one of the worst pranksters she'd ever met; despite all that, he had a certain charm. But now that she was with Paul, Cait remembered sharply who it was she really loved.

"I don't want to be a bother," she told him softly.

He give her a listless smile. "Come in, Cait. Now is fine." He gestured toward a chair.

She hurried into the office, trying to keep the bounce out of her step. Knowing she'd be spending a few extra minutes alone with Paul, Cait had taken special care with her appearance that morning.

He glanced up and smiled at her again, but this time Cait thought she could see a glimmer of appreciation in his eyes. "What can I do for you? I hope you're pleased with your office." He frowned slightly.

For a second, she forgot what she was doing in Paul's office and stared at him blankly until his own gaze fell to the folder. "The office looks great," she said quickly. "Um, the reason I'm here…" She faltered, then gulped in a quick breath and continued, "I went through some of the business journals I have at home and found several articles I felt would interest you." She extended the folder to him, like a ceremonial offering.

He took it from her and opened it gingerly. "Gracious," he said, flipping through the pages and scanning her written comments, "you must've spent hours on this."

"It was…nothing." She'd willingly have done a good deal more to gain his appreciation and eventually his love.

"I won't have a chance to look at this for a few days," he said.

"Oh, please, there's no rush. You happened to mention you got some useful insights from the previous article I gave you. So I thought I'd share a few others that seem relevant to what's going on with the market now."

"It's very thoughtful of you."

"I was happy to do it. More than happy," she amended with her most brilliant smile. When he didn't say anything more, Cait rose reluctantly to her feet. "You must be swamped after being in meetings for most of the day, so I'll leave you now."

She was almost at the door when he spoke. "Actually I only dropped in to the office to collect a few things before heading out again. I've got an important date this evening."

Cait felt as if the floor had suddenly disappeared and she was plummeting through empty space. "Date?" she repeated before she could stop herself. It was a struggle to keep smiling.

Paul's grin was downright boyish. "Yes, I'm meeting her for dinner."

"In that case, have a good time."

"Thanks, I will," he returned confidently, his eyes alight with excitement. "Oh, and by the way," he added, indicating the folder she'd worked so hard on, "thanks for all the effort you put into this."

"You're...welcome."

By the time Cait got back to her office she felt numb. Paul had an important date. It wasn't as though she'd expected him to live the life of a hermit, but before today, he'd never mentioned going out with anyone. She might have suspected he'd thrown out the information hoping to make her jealous if it hadn't been for one thing. He seemed genuinely thrilled about this date. Besides, Paul wasn't the kind of man to resort to pretense.

"Cait, my goodness," Lindy said, strolling into her office a while later, "what's wrong? You look dreadful."

Cait tried to swallow the lump in her throat and managed a shaky smile. "I talked to Paul and gave him the research I'd done."

"He didn't appreciate it?" Lindy picked up the Christmas wreath that lay on Cait's desk and pinned it to the door.

"I'm sure he did," she replied. "What he doesn't appreciate is me. I might as well be invisible to that man." She pushed the hair away from her forehead and braced both elbows on her desk, feeling totally disheartened. Unless she acted quickly, she was going to lose Paul to some faceless, nameless woman.

"You've been invisible to him before. What's different about this time?" Lindy fastened a silver bell to the window as Cait abstractedly fingered her three ceramic wise men.

"Paul's got a date, and from the way he talked about it, this isn't with just any woman, either. Whoever she is must be important, otherwise he wouldn't have said anything. He looked like a little kid who's been given the keys to a candy store."

The information seemed to surprise Lindy as much as it had Cait. She was quiet for a few minutes before she asked, "What are you going to do about it?"

"I don't know," Cait cried, hiding her face in her hands. She'd once jokingly suggested to Joe that she parade around naked in an effort to gain Paul's attention. Of course she'd been exaggerating, but some form of drastic action was obviously needed. If only she knew what.

Lindy mumbled an excuse and left. It wasn't until Cait looked up that she realized her friend was gone. She sighed wearily. She'd arrived at work this morning with such bright expectations, and now everything had gone wrong. She felt more depressed than she'd been in a long time. She knew the best remedy would be to force herself into some physical activity. Anything. The worst possible thing she could do was sit home alone and mope. Maybe she should plan to buy herself a Christmas tree and some ornaments. Her spirits couldn't help being at least a little improved by that; it would get her out of the house, if nothing else. And then she'd have something to entertain herself with, instead of brooding about this unexpected turn of events. Getting out of the house had an added advantage. If Joe phoned, she wouldn't be there to answer.

No sooner had that thought passed through her mind when a large form filled her doorway.

Joe.

A bright orange hard hat was pushed back on his head, the way movie cowboys wore their Stetsons. His boots were dusty and his tool pouch rode low on his hip, completing the gunslinger image. Even the way he stood with his thumbs tucked in his belt suggested he was waiting for a showdown.

"Hi, beautiful," he drawled, giving her that lazy, intimate smile of his. The one designed, Cait swore, just to unnerve her. But it wasn't going to work, not in her present state of mind.

"Don't you have anyone else to pester?" she asked coldly.

"My, my," Joe said, shaking his head in mock chagrin. Disregarding her lack of welcome, he strode into the office and threw himself down in the chair beside her desk. "You're in a rare mood."

"You would be too after the day I've had. Listen, Joe. As you can see, I'm poor company. Go flirt with the receptionist if you're trying to make someone miserable."

"Those claws are certainly sharp this afternoon." He ran his hands down the front of his shirt, pretending to inspect the damage she'd inflicted. "What's wrong?" Some of the teasing light faded from his eyes as he studied her.

She sent him a look meant to blister his ego, but as always Joe seemed invincible against her practiced glares.

"How do you know I'm not here to invest fifty thousand dollars?" he demanded, making himself at home by reaching across her desk for a pen. He rolled it casually between his palms.

Cait wasn't about to fall for this little game. "Are you here to invest money?"

"Not exactly. I wanted to ask you to—"

"Then come back when you are." She grabbed a stack of papers and slapped them down on her desk. But being rude, even to Joe, went against her nature. She was battling tears and the growing need to explain her behavior, apologize for it, when he rose to his feet. He tossed the pen carelessly onto her desk.

"Have it your way. If asking you to join me to look for a Christmas tree is such a terrible crime, then—"

"You're going to buy a Christmas tree?"

"That's what I just said." He flung the words over his shoulder as he strode out the door.

In that moment, Cait felt as though the whole world was tumbling down around her shoulders. She felt like such a shrew. He'd come here wanting to include her in his Christmas preparations and she'd driven him away with a spiteful tongue and a haughty attitude.

Cait wasn't a woman easily given to tears, but she struggled with them now. Her lower lip started to quiver. She might have been eight years old all over again—this was like the day she'd found out she wasn't invited to Betsy McDonald's birthday party. Only now it was Paul doing the excluding. He and this important woman of his were going out to have the time of their lives while she stayed home in her lonely apartment, suffering from a serious case of self-pity.

Gathering up her things, Cait thrust the papers into her briefcase with uncharacteristic negligence. She put on her coat, buttoned it quickly and wrapped the scarf around her neck as though it were a hangman's noose.

Joe was talking to his foreman, who'd been unobtrusively working around the office all day. He hesitated when he saw her, halting the conversation. Cait's eyes briefly met his and although she tried to disguise how regretful she felt, she obviously did a poor job of it. He took a step toward her, but she raised her chin a notch, too proud to admit her feelings.

She had to walk directly past Joe on her way to the elevator and forced herself to look anywhere but at him.

The stocky foreman clearly wanted to resume the discussion, but Joe ignored him and stared at Cait instead, with narrowed, assessing eyes. She could feel his questioning concern as profoundly as if he'd touched her. When she could bear it no longer, she turned to face him, her lower lip quivering uncontrollably.

"Cait," he called out.

She raced for the elevator, fearing she'd burst into tears before she could make her grand exit. She didn't bother to respond, knowing that if she said anything she'd make a greater fool of herself than usual. She wasn't even sure what had prompted her to say the atrocious things to Joe that she had. He wasn't the one who'd upset her, yet she'd unfairly taken her frustrations out on him.

She should've known it would be impossible to make a clean getaway. She almost ran through the office, past the reception desk, toward the elevator.

"Aren't you going to answer me?" Joe demanded, following on her heels.

"No." She concentrated on the lighted numbers above the elevator, which moved with painstaking slowness. Three more floors and she could make her escape.

"What's so insulting about inviting you to go Christmas-tree shopping?" he asked.

Close to weeping, she waved her free hand, hoping he'd

understand that she was incapable of explaining just then. Her throat was clogged and it hurt to breathe, let alone talk. Her eyes filled with tears, and everything started to blur.

"Tell me," he commanded a second time.

Cait gulped at the tightness in her throat. "Y-you wouldn't understand." Why, oh, why, wouldn't that elevator hurry?

"Try me."

It was either give in and explain, or stand there and argue. The first choice was easier; frankly, Cait didn't have the energy to fight with him. Sighing deeply, she began, "It—it all started when I made up this folder of business articles for Paul…"

"I might've known Paul had something to do with this," Joe muttered under his breath.

"I spent hours putting it together, adding little comments, and…and… I don't know what I expected but it wasn't…"

"What happened? What did Paul do?"

Cait rubbed her eyes with the back of her hand. "If you're going to interrupt me, then I can't see any reason to explain."

"Boss?" the foreman called out, sounding impatient.

Just then the elevator arrived and the doors opened, revealing half a dozen men and women. They stared out at Cait and Joe as he blocked the entrance, gripping her by the elbow.

"Joseph," she hissed, "let me go!" Recognizing her advantage, she called out, "This man refuses to release my arm." If she expected a knight in shining armor to leap to her rescue, Cait was to be sorely disappointed. It was as if no one had heard her.

"Don't worry, folks, we're married." Joe charmed them with another of his lazy, lopsided grins.

"Boss?" the foreman pleaded again.

"Take the rest of the day off," Joe shouted. "Tell the crew to go out and buy Christmas gifts for their wives."

"You want me to do *what?*" the foreman shouted back. Joe moved into the elevator with Cait.

"You heard me."

"Let me make sure I understand you. You want the men to go Christmas shopping for their wives? I thought you just said we're on a tight schedule?"

"That's right," Joe said loudly as the elevator doors closed.

Cait had never felt more conspicuous in her life. Every eye was focused on her and Joe, and it was all she could do to keep her head high.

When the tension became intolerable, Cait turned to face her fellow passengers. "We are not married," she announced.

"Yes, we are," Joe insisted. "She's simply forgotten."

"I did not forget our marriage and don't you dare tell them that cock-and-bull story about amnesia."

"But, darling—"

"Stop it right now, Joseph Rockwell! No one believes you. I'm sure these people can figure out that I'm the one who's telling the truth."

The elevator finally stopped on the ground floor, a fact for which Cait was deeply grateful. The doors glided open and two women stepped out first, but not before pausing to get a good appreciative look at Joe.

"Does she do this often?" one of the men asked, directing his question to Joe, his amusement obvious.

"Unfortunately, yes," he answered, chuckling as he tucked his hand under Cait's elbow and led her into the foyer. She tried to jerk her arm away, but he wouldn't allow it. "You see, I married a forgetful bride."

7

Pacing the carpet in the living room, Cait nervously smoothed the front of her red satin dress, her heart pumping furiously while she waited for Joe to arrive. She'd spent hours preparing for this Christmas party, which was being held in Paul's home. Her stomach was in knots.

She, the mysterious woman Paul was dating, would surely be there. Cait would have her first opportunity to size up the competition. Cait had studied her reflection countless times, trying to be objective about her chances with Paul based on looks alone. The dress was gorgeous. Her hair flawless. Everything else was as perfect as she could make it.

The doorbell sounded and Cait hurried across the room, throwing open the door. "You know what you are, Joseph Rockwell?"

"Late?" he suggested.

Cait pretended not to hear him. "A bully," she said. "A badgering bully, no less. I'm sorry I ever agreed to let you take me to Paul's party. I don't know what I was thinking."

"You were probably hoping to corner me under the mistletoe," he remarked with a wink that implied he wouldn't be difficult to persuade.

"First you practically kidnap me into going Christmas-tree shopping with you," she raged. "Then—"

"Come on, Cait, admit it, you had fun." He lounged indolently on her sofa while she got her coat and purse.

She hesitated, her mouth twitching with a smile. "Who'd ever believe that a man who bought his mother a rib roast and a case of cat food for Christmas last year would be so particular about a silly tree?" Joe had dragged her to no fewer than four lots yesterday, searching for the perfect tree.

"I took you to dinner afterward, didn't I?" he reminded her.

Cait nodded. She had to admit it: Joe had gone out of his way to help her forget her troubles. Although she'd made the tree-shopping expedition sound like a chore, he'd turned the evening into an enjoyable and, yes, memorable one.

His good mood had been infectious and after a while she'd completely forgotten Paul was out with another woman—someone so special that his enthusiasm about her had overcome his normal restraint.

"I've changed my mind," Cait decided suddenly, clasping her hands over her stomach, which was in turmoil. "I don't want to go to this Christmas party, after all." The evening was already doomed. She couldn't possibly have a good time watching the man she loved entertain the woman *he* loved. Cait couldn't think of a single reason to expose herself to that kind of misery.

"Not go to the party?" Joe repeated. "But I thought you'd arranged your flight schedule just so you could."

"I did, but that was before." Cait stubbornly squared her shoulders and elevated her chin just enough to convince Joe she meant business. He might be able to bully her into going shopping with him for a Christmas tree, but this was entirely different. "*She'll* be there," Cait added as an explanation.

"She?" Joe repeated slowly, burying his hands in his suit pockets. He was exceptionally handsome in his dark blue suit and no doubt knew it. He was as comfortable in tailored slacks as he was in dirty jeans.

A lock of thick hair slanted across his forehead; Cait managed—it was an effort—to resist brushing it back. An effort not because it disrupted his polished appearance, but because she had the strangest desire to run her fingers through his hair. Why she'd think such a thing now was beyond her. She'd long since stopped trying to figure out her feelings for Joe. He was a friend and a confidant even if, at odd moments, he behaved like a lunatic. Just remembering some of the comments he'd made to embarrass her brought color to her cheeks.

"I'd imagine you'd want to meet her," Joe challenged. "That way you can size her up."

"I don't even want to know what she looks like," Cait countered sharply. She didn't need to. Cait already knew everything she cared to about Paul's hot date. "She's beautiful."

"So are you."

Cait gave a short, derisive laugh. She wasn't discounting her own homespun appeal. She was reasonably attractive, and never more so than this evening. Catching a glimpse of herself in the mirror, she was pleased to see how nice her hair looked, with the froth of curls circling her head. But she wasn't going to kid herself, either. Her allure wasn't extraordinary by any stretch of the imagination. Her eyes were a warm shade of brown, though, and her nose was kind of cute. Perky, Lindy had once called it. But none of that mattered. Measuring herself against Paul's sure-to-be-gorgeous, nameless date was like comparing bulky sweat socks with a silk stocking. She'd already spent hours picturing her as a classic beauty…tall…sophisticated.

"I've never taken you for a coward," Joe said in a flat tone as he headed toward the door.

Apparently he wasn't even going to argue with her. Cait almost wished he would, just so she could show him how strong her will was. Nothing he could say or do would convince her to attend this party. Besides, her feet hurt. She was wearing new heels and hadn't broken them in yet, and if she did go, she'd be limping for days afterward.

"I'm not a coward," she told him, schooling her face to remain as emotionless as possible. "All I'm doing is exercising a little common sense. Why depress myself over the holidays? This is the last time I'll see Paul before Christmas. I leave for Minnesota in the morning."

"Yes, I know." Joe frowned as he said it, hesitating before he opened her door. "You're sure about this?"

"Positive." She was mildly surprised Joe wasn't making more of a fuss. From past experience, she'd expected a full-scale verbal battle.

"The choice is yours of course," he granted, shrugging. "But if it was me, I know I'd spend the whole evening regretting it." He studied her when he'd finished, then gave her a smile Cait could only describe as crafty.

She groaned inwardly. If there was one thing that drove her crazy about Joe it was the way he made the most outrageous statements. Then every once in a while he'd say something so wise it caused her to doubt her own conclusions and beliefs. This was one of those times. He was right: if she didn't go to Paul's, she'd regret it. Since she was leaving for Minnesota the following day, she wouldn't be able to ask anyone about the party, either.

"Are you coming or not?" he demanded.

Grumbling under her breath, Cait let him help her on with her coat. "I'm coming, but I don't like it. Not one darn bit."

"You're going to do just fine."

"They probably said that to Joan of Arc, too."

Cait clutched the punch glass in both hands, as though terrified someone might try to take it back. Standing next to the fireplace, with its garlanded mantel and cheerful blaze, she hadn't moved since they'd arrived a half hour earlier.

"Is *she* here yet?" she whispered to Lindy when her friend walked past carrying a tray of canapés.

"Who?"

"Paul's woman friend," Cait said pointedly. Both Joe and Lindy were beginning to exasperate her. "I've been standing here for the past thirty minutes hoping to catch a glimpse of her."

Lindy looked away. "I… I don't know if she's here or not."

"Stay with me, for heaven's sake," Cait requested, feeling shaky inside and out. Joe had deserted her almost as soon as they got there. Oh, he'd stuck around long enough to bring her a cup of punch, but then he'd drifted away, leaving Cait to deal with the situation on her own. This was the very man who'd insisted she attend this Christmas party, claiming he'd be right by her side the entire evening in case she needed him.

"I'm helping Paul with the hors d'oeuvres," Lindy explained, "otherwise I'd be happy to stay and chat."

"See if you can find Joe for me, would you?" She'd do it herself, but her feet were killing her.

"Sure."

Once Lindy was gone, Cait scanned the crowded living room. Many of the guests were business associates and clients Paul had worked with over the years. Naturally everyone from the office was there, as well.

"You wanted to see me?" Joe asked, reaching her side.

"Thank you very much," she muttered, doing her best to sound sarcastic and keep a smile on her face at the same time.

"You're welcome." He leaned one elbow on the fireplace mantel and grinned at her boyishly. "Might I ask what you're thanking me for?"

"Don't play games with me, Joe. Not now, please." She shifted her weight from one foot to the other, drawing his attention to her shoes.

"Your feet hurt?" he asked, frowning.

"Walking across hot coals would be less painful than these stupid high heels."

"Then why did you wear them?"

"Because they go with the dress. Listen, would you mind very much if we got off the subject of my shoes and discussed the matter at hand?"

"Which is?"

Joe was being as obtuse as Lindy had been. She assumed he was doing it deliberately, just to get a rise out of her. Well, it was working.

"Did you see her?" she asked with exaggerated patience.

"Not yet," he whispered back as though they were exchanging top-secret information. "She doesn't seem to have arrived."

"Have you talked to Paul?"

"No. Have you?"

"Not really." Paul had greeted them at the door, but other than that, Cait hadn't had a chance to do anything but watch him mingle with his guests. The day at the office hadn't been any help, either. Paul had breezed in and out without giving Cait more than a friendly wave. Since they hadn't exchanged a single word, it was impossible for her to determine how his date had gone.

It must have been a busy day for Lindy, as well, because Cait hadn't had a chance to talk to her, either. They'd met on their way out the door late that afternoon and Lindy had hurried past, saying she'd see Cait at Paul's party.

"I think I'll go help Lindy with the hors d'oeuvres," Cait said now. "Do you want me to get you anything?"

"Nothing, thanks." He was grinning as he strolled away, leaving Cait to wonder what he found so amusing.

Cait limped into the kitchen, leaving the polished wooden door swinging in her wake. She stopped abruptly when she encountered Paul and Lindy in the middle of a heated discussion.

"Oh, sorry," Cait apologized automatically.

Paul's gaze darted to Cait's. "No problem," he said quickly. "I was just leaving." He stalked past her, shoving the door open with the palm of his hand. Once again the door swung back and forth.

"What was that all about?" Cait wanted to know.

Lindy continued transferring the small cheese-dotted crackers from the cookie sheet onto the serving platter. "Nothing."

"It sounded as if you and Paul were arguing."

Lindy straightened and bit her lip. She avoided looking at Cait, concentrating on her task as if it was of vital importance to properly arrange the crackers on the plate.

"You were arguing, weren't you?" Cait pressed.

"Yes."

As far as she knew, Lindy and Paul had always gotten along. The fact that they were at odds surprised her. "About what?"

"I—I gave Paul my two-week notice this afternoon."

Cait was so shocked, she pulled out a kitchen chair and sank down on it. "You did *what?*" Removing her high heels, she massaged her pinched toes.

"You heard me."

"But why? Good grief, Lindy, you never said a word to anyone. Not even me. The least you could've done was talk to me about it first." No wonder Paul was angry. If Lindy left, it would mean bringing in someone new when the office was already short-staffed. With Cait and a number of other people away for the holidays, the place would be a madhouse.

"Did you receive an offer you couldn't refuse?" Cait hadn't had any idea her friend was unhappy at Webster, Rodale and Missen. Still, that didn't shock her nearly as much as Lindy's remaining tight-lipped about it all.

"It wasn't exactly an offer—but it was something like that," Lindy replied vaguely. She set aside the cookie sheet, smiled at Cait and then carried the platter into the living room.

For the past couple of weeks Cait had noticed that something was troubling her friend. It hadn't been anything she could readily name. Just that Lindy hadn't been her usual high-spirited self. Cait had meant to ask her about it, but she'd been so busy herself, so involved with her own problems, that she'd never brought it up.

She was still sitting there rubbing her feet when Joe sauntered into the kitchen, nibbling on a cheese cracker. "I thought I'd find you in here." He pulled out the chair across from her and sat down.

"Has she arrived yet?"

"Apparently so."

Cait dropped her foot and frantically worked the shoe back and forth until she'd managed to squeeze her toes inside. Then she forced her other foot into its shoe. "Well, for heaven's sake, why didn't you say something sooner?" she chastised. She stood up, ran her hands down the satin skirt and drew a shaky breath. "How do I look?"

"Like your feet hurt."

She sent him a scalding frown. "Thank you very much," she said sarcastically for the second time in under ten minutes. Hobbling to the door, she opened it a crack and peeked out, hoping to catch sight of the mystery woman. From what she could see, there weren't any new arrivals.

"What does she look like?" Cait demanded and whirled around to discover Joe standing directly behind her. She nearly collided with him and gave a small cry of surprise. Joe caught her by the shoulders to keep her from stumbling. Eager to question him about Paul's date, she didn't take the time to analyze why her heartrate soared when his hands made contact with her bare skin.

"What does she look like?" Cait asked again.

"I don't know," Joe returned flippantly.

"What do you mean you don't know? You just said she'd arrived."

"Unfortunately she doesn't have a tattoo across her forehead announcing that she's the woman Paul's dating."

"Then how do you know she's here?" If Joe was playing games with her, she'd make damn sure he'd regret it. Her love for Paul was no joking matter.

"It's more a feeling I have."

"You had me stuff my feet back into these shoes for a stupid feeling?" It was all she could do not to slap him silly. "You are no friend of mine, Joseph Rockwell. No friend whatsoever." Having said that, she limped back into the living room.

Obviously unscathed by her remark, Joe wandered out of the kitchen behind her. He walked over to the tray of canapés and helped himself to three or four while Cait did her best to ignore him.

Since the punch bowl was close by, she poured herself a second glass. The taste was sweet and cold, but Cait noticed that she felt a bit light-headed afterward. Potent drinks didn't sit well on an empty stomach, so she scooped up a handful of mixed nuts.

"I remember a time when you used to line up all the Spanish peanuts and eat those first," Joe said from behind her. "Then it was the hazelnuts, followed by the—"

"Almonds." Leave it to him to bring up her foolish past. "I haven't done that since I was—"

"Twenty," he guessed.

"Twenty-five," she corrected.

Joe laughed, and despite her aching feet and the certainty that she should never have come to this party, Cait laughed, too.

Refilling her punch glass, she downed it all in a single drink. Once more, it tasted cool and refreshing.

"Cait," Joe warned, "how much punch have you had?"

"Not enough." She filled the crystal cup a third time—or was it the fourth?—squared her shoulders and gulped it down. When she'd finished, she wiped the back of her hand across her mouth and smiled bravely.

"Are you purposely trying to get drunk?" he demanded.

"No." She reached for another handful of nuts. "All I'm looking for is a little courage."

"Courage?"

"Yes," she said with a sigh. "The way I figure it…" She paused, smiling giddily, then whirled around in a full circle. "There *is* some mistletoe here, isn't there?"

"I think so," Joe said, frowning. "What makes you ask?"

"I'm going to kiss Paul," she said proudly. "All I have to do is wait until he walks past. Then I'll grab him by the hand, wish him a merry Christmas and give him a kiss he won't soon forget." If the fantasy fulfilled itself, Paul would immediately realize he'd met the woman of his dreams, and propose marriage on the spot….

"What is kissing Paul supposed to prove?"

She returned to reality. "Well, this is where you come in. I want you to look around and watch the faces of the other women. If one of them shows signs of jealousy, then we'll know who it is."

"I'm not sure this plan of yours is going to work."

"It's better than trusting those feelings of yours," she countered.

She saw the mistletoe hanging from the archway between the formal dining room and the living room. Slouched against the wall, hands tucked behind her back, Cait waited patiently for Paul to stroll past.

Ten minutes passed or maybe it was fifteen—Cait couldn't tell. Yawning, she covered her mouth. "I think we should leave," Joe suggested as he casually walked by. "You're ready to fall asleep on your feet."

"I haven't kissed Paul yet," she reminded him.

"He seems to be involved in a lengthy discussion. This could take a while."

"I'm in no hurry." Her throat felt unusually dry. She would have preferred something nonalcoholic, but the only drink nearby was the punch.

"Cait," Joe warned when he saw her helping herself to yet another glass.

"Don't worry, I know what I'm doing."

"So did the captain of the *Titanic*."

"Don't get cute with me, Joseph Rockwell. I'm in no mood to deal with someone amusing." Finding herself hilariously funny, she smothered a round of giggles.

"Oh, no," Joe groaned. "I was afraid of this."

"Afraid of what?"

"You're drunk!"

She gave him a sour look. "That's ridiculous. All I had is four little, bitty glasses of punch." To prove she knew exactly what she was doing, she held up three fingers, recognized her mistake and promptly corrected herself. At least she tried to do it promptly, but figuring out how many fingers equaled four seemed to take an inordinate amount of time. She finally held up two from each hand.

Expelling her breath, she leaned back against the wall and closed her eyes. That was her second mistake. The world took a sharp and unexpected nosedive. Snapping open her eyes, Cait looked to Joe as the anchor that would keep her afloat. He must have read the panic in her expression because he moved toward her and slowly shook his head.

"That does it, Ms. Singapore Sling. I'm getting you out of here."

"But I haven't been under the mistletoe yet."

"If you want anyone to kiss you, it'll be me."

The offer sounded tempting, but it was her stubborn boss Cait wanted to kiss, not Joe. "I'd rather dance with you."

"Unfortunately there isn't any music at the moment."

"You need music to dance?" It sounded like the saddest thing she'd ever heard, and her bottom lip began to tremble at the tragedy of it all. "Oh, dear, Joe," she whispered, clasping both hands to the sides of her head. "I think you might be right. The punch seems to be affecting me…."

"It's that bad, is it?"

"Uh, yes… The whole room's just started to pitch and heave. We're not having an earthquake, are we?"

"No." His hand was on her forearm, guiding her toward the front door.

"Wait," she said dramatically, raising her index finger. "I have a coat."

"I know. Stay here and I'll get it for you." He seemed worried about leaving her. Cait smiled at him, trying to reassure him she'd be perfectly fine, but she seemed unable to keep her balance. He urged her against the wall, stepped back a couple of paces as though he expected her to slip sideways, then hurriedly located her coat.

"What's wrong?" he asked when he returned.

"What makes you think anything's wrong?"

"Other than the fact that you're crying?"

"My feet hurt."

Joe rolled his eyes. "Why did you wear those stupid shoes in the first place?"

"I already told you," she whimpered. "Don't be mad at me." She held out her arms to him, needing his comfort. "Would you carry me to the car?"

Joe hesitated. "You want me to carry you?" He sounded as though it was a task of Herculean proportions.

"I can't walk." She'd taken the shoes off, and it would take God's own army to get them back on. She couldn't very well traipse outside in her stocking feet.

"If I carry you, we'd better find another way out of the house."

"All right." She agreed just to prove what an amicable person she actually was. When she was a child, she'd been a pest, but she wasn't anymore and she wanted to be sure Joe understood that.

Grasping Cait's hand, he led her into the kitchen.

"Don't you think we should make our farewells?" she asked. It seemed the polite thing to do.

"No," he answered sharply. "With the mood you're in you're likely to throw yourself into Paul's arms and demand that he make mad passionate love to you right then and there."

Cait's face went fire-engine red. "That's ridiculous."

Joe mumbled something she couldn't hear while he lifted her hand and slipped one arm, then the other, into the satin-lined sleeves of her full-length coat.

When he'd finished, Cait climbed on top of the kitchen chair, stretching out her arms to him. Joe stared at her as though she'd suddenly turned into a werewolf.

"What are you doing now?" he asked in an exasperated voice.

"You're going to carry me, aren't you?"

"I was considering it."

"I want a piggyback ride. You gave Betsy McDonald a piggyback ride once and not me."

"Cait," Joe groaned. He jerked his fingers through his hair, and offered her his hand, wanting her to climb down from the chair. "Get down before you fall. Good Lord, I swear you'd try the patience of a saint."

"I want you to carry me piggyback," she insisted. "Oh, please, Joe. My toes hurt so bad."

Once again her hero grumbled under his breath. She couldn't make out everything he said, but what she did hear was enough to curl her hair. With obvious reluctance, he walked to the chair, and giving a sigh of pure bliss, Cait wrapped her arms around his neck and hugged his lean hips with her legs. She laid her head on his shoulder and sighed again.

Still grumbling, Joe moved toward the back door.

Just then the kitchen door opened and Paul and Lindy walked in. Lindy gasped. Paul just stared.

"It's all right," Cait was quick to assure them. "Really it is. I was waiting under the mistletoe and you—"

"She downed four glasses of punch nonstop," Joe inserted before Cait could admit she'd been waiting there for Paul.

"Do you need any help?" Paul asked.

"None, thanks," Joe returned. "There's nothing to worry about."

"But..." Lindy looked concerned.

"She ain't heavy," Joe teased. "She's my wife."

★★★

The phone rang, waking Cait from a sound sleep. Her head began throbbing in time to the painful noise and she groped for the telephone receiver.

"Hello," she barked, instantly regretting that she'd spoken loudly.

"How are you feeling?" Joe asked.

"About like you'd expect," she whispered, keeping her eyes closed and gently massaging one temple. It felt as though tiny men with hammers had taken up residence in her head and were pounding away, hoping to attract her attention.

"What time does your flight leave?" he asked.

"It's okay. I'm not scheduled to leave until this afternoon."

"It is afternoon."

Her eyes flew open. "What?"

"Do you still need me to take you to the airport?"

"Yes...please." She tossed aside the covers and reached for her clock, stunned to realize Joe was right. "I'm already packed. I'll be dressed by the time you get here. Oh, thank goodness you phoned."

Cait didn't have time to listen to the pounding of the tiny men in her head. She showered and dressed as quickly as possible, swallowed a cup of coffee and a couple of aspirin, and was just shrugging into her coat when Joe arrived at the door. She let him in, despite the suspiciously wide grin he wore.

"What's so amusing?"

"What makes you think I'm amused?" He strolled into the room, hands behind his back, as if he owned the place.

"Joe, we don't have time for your little games. Come on, or I'm going to miss my plane. What's with you, anyway?"

"Nothing." He circled her living room, still wearing that silly grin. "I don't suppose you realize it, but liquor has a peculiar effect on you."

Cait stiffened. "It does?" She remembered most of the party with great clarity. Good thing Joe had taken her home when he had.

"Liquor loosens your tongue."

"So?" She picked up two shopping bags filled with wrapped packages, leaving the lone suitcase for him. "Did I say anything of interest?"

"Oh, my, yes."

"Joe!" She glanced quickly at her watch. They needed to get moving if she was to catch her flight. "Discount whatever I said—I'm sure I didn't mean it. If I insulted you, I apologize. If I told any family secrets, kindly forget I mentioned them."

He strolled to her side and tucked his finger under her chin. "This was a secret, all right," he informed her in a lazy drawl. "It was something you told me on the drive home."

"Are you sure it's true?"

"Relatively sure."

"What did I say? Did I declare my undying love for you? Because if I—"

"No, no, nothing like that."

"Just how long do you intend to torment me with this?" She was rapidly losing interest in his little guessing game.

"Not much longer." He looked exceptionally pleased with himself. "So Martin's a minister now. Funny you never thought to mention that before."

"Ah…" Cait set aside the two bags and lowered herself to the sofa. So he'd found out. Worse, she'd been the one to tell him.

"That may well have some interesting ramifications, my dear. Have you ever stopped to think about them?"

8

"This is exactly why I didn't tell you about Martin," Cait informed Joe as he tossed her suitcase into the back seat of his car. She checked her watch again and groaned. They had barely an hour and a half before her flight was scheduled to leave. Cait was never late. Never—at least not when it was her own fault.

"It seems to me," Joe continued, his face deadpan, "that there could very well be some legal grounds to our marriage."

Joe was saying that just to annoy her, and unfortunately it was working. "I've never heard anything more ludicrous in my life."

"Think about it, Cait," he said, ignoring her protest. "We could be celebrating our anniversary this spring. How many years is it now? Eighteen? How the years fly."

"Listen, Joe, I don't find this amusing." She glanced at her watch. If only she hadn't slept so late. Never again would she have any Christmas punch. Briefly she wondered what else she'd said to Joe, then decided it was better not to know.

"I heard a news report of a three-car pileup on the freeway, so we'll take the side streets."

"Just hurry," Cait urged in an anxious voice.

"I'll do the best I can," Joe said, "but worrying about it isn't going to get us there any faster."

She glared at him. She couldn't help it. He wasn't the one who'd been planning this trip for months. If she missed the flight, her nephews and niece wouldn't have their Christmas presents from their Auntie Cait. Nor would she share in the family traditions that were so much a part of her Christmas. She *had* to get to the airport on time.

Everyone else had apparently heard about the accident on the freeway, too, and the downtown area was crowded with the overflow. Cait and Joe were delayed at every intersection and twice were forced to sit through two changes of the traffic signal.

Cait was growing more panicky by the minute. She just had to make this flight. But it almost seemed that she'd get to the airport faster if she simply jumped out of the car and ran there.

Joe stopped for another red light, but when the signal turned green, they still couldn't move—a delivery truck in front of them had stalled. Furious, Cait rolled down the window and stuck out her head. "Listen here, buster, let's get this show on the road," she shouted at the top of her lungs.

Her head was pounding and she prayed the aspirin would soon take effect.

"Quite the Christmas spirit," Joe muttered dryly under his breath.

"I can't help it. I have to catch this plane."

"You'll be there in plenty of time."

"At this rate we won't make it to Sea-Tac before Easter!"

"Relax, will you?" Joe suggested gently. He turned on the

radio and a medley of Christmas carols filled the air. Normally the music would have calmed her, but she was suffering from a hangover, depression and severe anxiety, all at the same time. Her fingernails found their way into her mouth.

Suddenly she straightened. "Darn! I forgot to give you your Christmas gift. I left it at home."

"Don't worry about it."

"I didn't get you a gag gift the way I said." Actually she was pleased with the book she'd managed to find—an attractive coffee-table volume about the history of baseball.

Cait waited for Joe to mention *her* gift. Surely he'd bought her one. At least she fervently hoped he had, otherwise she'd feel like a fool. Though, admittedly, that was a feeling she'd grown accustomed to in the past few weeks.

"I think we might be able to get back on the freeway here," Joe said, as he made a sharp left-hand turn. They crossed the overpass, and from their vantage point, Cait could see that the freeway was unclogged and running smoothly.

"Thank God," she whispered, relaxing against the back of the seat as Joe drove quickly ahead.

Her chauffeur chuckled. "I seem to remember you lecturing me—"

"I never lecture," she said testily. "I may have a strong opinion on certain subjects, but let me assure you, I never lecture."

"You were right, though. The streets of Bethlehem must have been crowded and bustling with activity at the time of that first Christmas. I can see it all now, can't you? A rug dealer is held up by a shepherd driving his flock through the middle of town."

Cait smiled for the first time that morning, because she could easily picture the scene Joe was describing.

"Then some furious woman, impatient to make it to the

local camel merchant before closing, sticks her nose in the middle of everything and shouts at the rug dealer to get his show on the road." He paused to chuckle at his own wit. "I'm convinced she wouldn't have been so testy except that she was suffering from one heck of a hangover."

"Very funny," Cait grumbled, smiling despite herself.

He took the exit for the airport and Cait was gratified to note that her flight wasn't scheduled to leave for another thirty minutes. She was cutting it close, closer than she ever had before, but she'd confirmed her ticket two days earlier and had already been assigned her seat.

Joe pulled up at the drop-off point for her airline and gave Cait's suitcase to a skycap while she rummaged around in her purse for her ticket.

"I suppose this is goodbye for now," he said with an endearingly crooked grin that sent her pulses racing.

"I'll be back in less than two weeks," she reminded him, trying to keep her tone light and casual.

"You'll phone once you arrive?"

She nodded. For all her earlier panic, Cait now felt oddly unwilling to leave Joe. She should be rushing through the airport to her airline's check-in counter to get her boarding pass, but she lingered, her heart overflowing with emotions she couldn't identify.

"Have a safe trip," he said quietly.

"I will. Thanks so much…for everything."

"You're welcome." His expression sobered and the ever-ready mirth fled from his eyes. Cait wasn't sure who moved first. All she knew was that she was in Joe's arms, his thumb caressing the softness of her cheek as they gazed hungrily into each other's eyes.

He leaned forward to kiss her. Cait's eyes drifted shut as his mouth met hers.

At first Joe's kiss was tender but it quickly grew in fervor. The noise and activity around them seemed to fade into the distance. Cait could feel herself dissolving. She moaned and arched closer, not wanting to leave the protective haven of his arms. Joe shuddered and hugged her tight, as if he, too, found it difficult to part.

"Merry Christmas, love," he whispered, releasing her with a reluctance that made her feel…giddy. Confused. *Happy.*

"Merry Christmas," she echoed, but she didn't move.

Joe gave her the gentlest of nudges. "You'd better hurry, Cait."

"Oh, right," she said, momentarily forgetting why she was at the airport. Reaching for the bags filled with gaily wrapped Christmas packages, she took two steps backward. "I'll phone when I get there."

"Do. I'll be waiting to hear from you." He thrust his hands into his pockets and Cait had the distinct impression he did it to stop himself from reaching for her again. The thought was a romantic one, a certainty straight from her heart.

Her heart… Her heart was full of feeling for Joe. More than she'd ever realized. He'd dominated her life these past few weeks—taking her to dinner, bribing his way back into her good graces with pizza, taking her on a Christmas shopping expedition, escorting her to Paul's party. Joe had become her whole world. Joe, not Paul. Joe.

Given no other choice, Cait abruptly turned and hurried into the airport, where she checked in, then went through security and down the concourse to the proper gate.

The flight had already been called and only a handful of passengers had yet to board.

Cait dashed to the counter with her boarding pass. A young soldier stood just ahead of her. "But you don't understand," the tall marine was saying to the airline employee.

"I booked this flight over a month ago. I've got to be on that plane!"

"I'm so sorry," the woman apologized, her dark eyes regretful. "This sort of thing happens, especially during holidays, but your ticket's for standby. I wish I could do something for you, but there isn't a single seat available."

"But I haven't seen my family in over a year. My uncle Harvey's driving from Duluth to visit. He was in the marines, too. My mom's been baking for three weeks. Don't you see? I can't disappoint them now!"

Cait watched as the agent rechecked her computer. "If I could magically create a seat for you, I would," she said sympathetically. "But there just isn't one."

"But when I bought the ticket, the woman told me I wouldn't have a problem getting on the flight. She said there're always no-shows."

"I'm so sorry," the agent repeated, looking past the young marine to Cait.

"All right," he said, forcefully expelling his breath. "When's the next flight with available space? Any flight within a hundred miles of Minneapolis. I'll walk the rest of the way if I have to."

Once again, the woman consulted her computer. "We have space available the evening of the twenty-sixth."

"The twenty-sixth!" the young man shouted. "But that's after Christmas and eats up nearly all my leave. I'd be home for less than a week."

"May I help you?" the airline employee said to Cait. She looked almost as unhappy as the marine, but apparently there wasn't anything she could do to help him.

Cait stepped forward and handed the woman her boarding pass. The soldier gazed at it longingly, then moved dejectedly from the counter and lowered himself into one of the molded plastic chairs.

Cait hesitated, remembering how she'd stuck her head out the window of Joe's truck on their drive to the airport and shouted impatiently at the truck driver who was holding up traffic. A conversation she'd had with Joe earlier returned to haunt her. She'd argued that Christmas was a time filled with love and good cheer, the one holiday that brought out the very best in everyone. And sometimes, Joe had insisted, the very worst.

"Since you already have your seat assignment, you may board the flight now."

The urge to hurry nearly overwhelmed Cait, yet she hesitated once again.

"Excuse me," Cait said, drawing a deep breath and making her decision. She approached the soldier. He seemed impossibly young now that she had a good look at him. No more than eighteen, maybe nineteen. He'd probably joined the service right out of high school. His hair was cropped close to his head and his combat boots were so shiny Cait could see her reflection in them.

The marine glanced up at her, his face heavy with defeat. "Yes?"

"Did I hear you say you needed to be on this flight?"

"I have a ticket, ma'am. But it's standby and there aren't any seats."

"Listen," she said. "You can have mine."

The way his face lit up was enough to blot out her own disappointment at missing Christmas with Martin and her sister-in-law. The kids. Her mother… "My family's in Minneapolis, too, but I was there this summer."

"Ma'am, I can't let you do this."

"Don't cheat me out of the pleasure."

They approached the counter to effect the exchange. The marine stood, his eyes wide with disbelief. "I insist," Cait said. "Here." She handed him the two bags full of gifts for her nephews and nieces. "There'll be a man waiting at the other end. A tall minister—he'll have a collar on. Give him these. I'll phone so he'll know to look for you."

"Thank you for everything… I can't believe you're doing this."

Cait smiled. Impulsively the marine hugged her, then swinging his duffel bag over his shoulder, he picked up the two bags of gifts and jogged over to Security.

Cait waited for a couple of minutes, then wiped the tears from her eyes. She wasn't completely sure why she was crying. She'd never felt better in her life.

It was around six when she awoke. The apartment was dark and silent. Sighing, she picked up the phone, dragged it onto the bed with her and punched out Joe's number.

He answered on the first ring, as if he'd been waiting for her call. "How was the flight?" he asked immediately.

"I wouldn't know. I wasn't on it."

"You missed the plane!" he shouted incredulously. "But you were there in plenty of time."

"I know. It's a long story, but basically, I gave my seat to someone who needed it more than I did." She smiled dreamily, remembering how the young marine's face had lit up. "I'll tell you about it later."

"Where are you now?"

"Home."

He exhaled sharply, then said, "I'll be over in fifteen minutes."

Actually it took him twelve. By then Cait had brewed a pot of coffee and made herself a peanut-butter-and-jelly sandwich. She hadn't eaten all day and was starved. She'd just finished the sandwich when Joe arrived.

"What about your luggage?" Joe asked, looking concerned. He didn't give her a chance to respond. "Exactly what do you mean, you gave your seat away?"

Cait explained as best she could. Even now she found herself surprised by her actions. Cait rarely behaved spontaneously. But something about that young soldier had reached deep within her heart and she'd reacted instinctively.

"The airline is sending my suitcase back to Seattle on the next available flight, so there's no need to worry," Cait said. "I talked to Martin, who was quick to tell me the Lord would reward my generosity."

"Are you going to catch a later flight, then?" Joe asked. He helped himself to a cup of coffee and pulled out the chair across from hers.

"There aren't any seats," Cait said. She leaned back, yawning, and covered her mouth. Why she should be so tired after sleeping away most of the afternoon was beyond her. "Besides, the office is short-staffed. Lindy gave Paul her notice and a trainee is coming in, which makes everything even more difficult. They can use me."

Joe frowned. "Giving up your vacation is one way to impress Paul."

Words of explanation crowded her tongue. She realized Joe wasn't insulting her; he was only stating a fact. What he didn't understand was that Cait hadn't thought of Paul once the entire day. Her staying or leaving had absolutely nothing to do with him.

If she'd been thinking of anyone, it was Joe. She knew now that giving up her seat to the marine hadn't been entirely unselfish. When Joe kissed her goodbye, her heart had started telegraphing messages she had yet to fully decode. The plain and honest truth was that she hadn't wanted to leave him. It was as if she really did belong with him....

That perception had been with her from the moment they'd parted at the airport. It had followed her in the taxi on the ride back to the apartment. Joe was the last person she'd thought of when she'd fallen asleep, and the first person she'd remembered when she awoke.

It was the most unbelievable thing.

"What are you going to do for Christmas?" Joe asked, still frowning into his coffee cup. For someone who'd seemed downright regretful that she was flying halfway across the country, he didn't seem all that pleased to be sharing her company now.

"I...haven't decided yet. I suppose I'll spend a quiet day by myself." She'd wake up late, indulge in a lazy scented bath, find something sinful for breakfast. Ice cream, maybe. Then she'd paint her toenails and settle down with a good book. The day would be lonely, true, but certainly not wasted.

"It'll be anything but quiet," Joe challenged.

"Oh?"

"You'll be spending it with me and my family."

"This is the first time Joe has ever brought a girl to join us for Christmas," Virginia Rockwell said as she set a large tray of freshly baked cinnamon rolls in the center of the huge kitchen table. She wiped her hands clean on the apron that was secured around her thick waist.

Cait felt she should explain. She was a little uncomfortable arriving unannounced with Joe like this. "Joe and I are just friends."

Mrs. Rockwell shook her head, which set the white curls bobbing. "I saw my son's eyes when he brought you into the house." She grinned knowingly. "I remember you from the old neighborhood, with your starched dresses and the pigtails with those bright pink ribbons. You were a pretty girl then and you're even prettier now."

"The starched dresses were me, all right," Cait confirmed. She'd been the only girl for blocks around who always wore dresses to school.

Joe's mother chuckled again. "I remember the sensation you caused in the neighborhood when you said Joe had kissed you." She chuckled, her eyes shining. "His father and I got quite a kick out of that. I still remember how furious Joe was when he learned his secret was out."

"I only told one person," Cait protested. But Betsy had told plenty of others, and the news had spread with alarming speed. However, Cait figured she'd since paid for her sins tenfold. Joe had made sure of that in the past few weeks.

"It's so good to see you again, Caitlin. When we've got a minute I want you to sit down and tell me all about your mother. We lost contact years ago, but I always thought she was a darling."

"I think so, too," Cait agreed, carrying a platter of scrambled eggs to the table. She did miss being with her family, but Joe's mother made it almost as good as being home. "I know that's how Mom feels about you, too. She'll want to thank you for being kind enough to invite me into your home for Christmas."

"I wouldn't have it any other way."

"I know." She glanced into the other room where Joe was sitting with his brother and sister-in-law. Her heart throbbed at the sight of him with his family. But these newfound feelings for Joe left her at a complete loss. What she'd told Mrs. Rockwell was true. Joe was her friend. The very best friend she'd ever had. She was grateful for everything he'd done for her since they'd chanced upon each other, just weeks ago, really. But their friendship was developing into something much stronger. If only she didn't feel so…so ardent about Paul. If only she didn't feel so confused!

Joe laughed at something one of his nephews said and Cait couldn't help smiling. She loved the sound of his laughter. It was vigorous and robust and lively—just like his personality.

"Joe says you're working as a stockbroker right here in Seattle."

"Yes. I've been with Webster, Rodale and Missen for over a year now. My degree was in accounting but—"

"Accounting?" Mrs. Rockwell nodded approvingly. "My Joe has his own accountant now. Good thing, too. His books were in a terrible mess. He's a builder, not a pencil pusher, that boy."

"Are you telling tales on me, Mom?" Joe asked as he sauntered into the kitchen. He picked up a piece of bacon and bit off the end. "When are we going to open the gifts? The kids are getting restless."

"The kids, nothing. You're the one who's eager to tear into those packages," his mother admonished. "We'll open them after breakfast, the way we do every Christmas."

Joe winked at Cait and disappeared into the living room once more.

Mrs. Rockwell watched her son affectionately. "Last year he shows up on my doorstep bright and early Christmas morning needing gift wrap. Then, once he's got all his presents wrapped, he walks into my kitchen—" her face crinkled in a wide grin "—and he sticks all those presents in my refrigerator." She smiled at the memory. "For his brother, he bought two canned hams and three gallons of ice cream. For me it was cat food and a couple of rib roasts."

Breakfast was a bustling affair, with Joe's younger brother, his wife and their children gathered around the table. Joe sat next to Cait and held her hand while his mother offered the blessing. Although she wasn't home with her own family, Cait felt she had a good deal for which to be thankful.

Conversation was pleasant and relaxed, but foremost on the children's minds was opening the gifts. The table was cleared and plates and bowls arranged inside the dishwasher in record time.

Cait sat beside Joe, holding a cup of coffee, as the oldest grandchild handed out the presents. While Christmas music played softly in the background, the children tore into their packages. The youngest, a two-year-old girl, was more interested in the box than in the gift itself.

When Joe came to the square package Cait had given him, he shook it enthusiastically.

"Be careful, it might break," she warned, knowing there was no chance of that happening.

Carefully he removed the bows, then unwrapped his gift. Cait watched expectantly as he lifted the book from the layers of bright paper. "A book on baseball?"

Cait nodded, smiling. "As I recall, you used to collect baseball cards."

"I ended up trading away my two favorites."

"I'm sure it was for a very good reason."

"Of course."

Their eyes held until it became apparent that everyone in the room was watching them. Cait glanced self-consciously away.

Joe cleared his throat. "This is a great gift, Cait. Thank you very much."

"You're welcome very much."

He leaned over and kissed her as if it was the most natural thing in the world. It felt right, their kiss. If anything, Cait was sorry to stop at one.

"Surely you have something for Cait," Virginia Rockwell prompted her son.

"You bet I do."

"He's probably keeping it in the refrigerator," Cait suggested, to the delight of Joe's family.

"Oh, ye of little faith," he said, removing a box from his shirt pocket.

"I recognize that paper," Sally, Joe's sister-in-law, murmured to Cait. "It's from Stanley's."

Cait's eyes widened at the name of an expensive local jewelry store. "Joe?"

"Go ahead and open it," he urged.

Cait did, hands fumbling in her eagerness. She slipped off the ribbon and peeled away the gold textured wrap to reveal a white jeweler's box. It contained a second box, a small black velvet one, which she opened very slowly. She gasped at the lovely cameo brooch inside.

"Oh, Joe," she whispered. It was a lovely piece carved in onyx and overlaid with ivory. She'd longed for a cameo, a really nice one, for years and wondered how Joe could possibly have known.

"You gonna kiss Uncle Joe?" his nephew, Charlie, asked, "'Cause if you are, I'm not looking."

"Of course she's going to kiss me," Joe answered for her. "Only she can do it later when there aren't so many curious people around." He glanced swiftly at his mother. "Just the way Mom used to thank Dad for her Christmas gift. Isn't that right, Mom?"

"I'm sure Cait…will," Virginia answered, clearly flustered. She patted her hand against the side of her head as though she feared the pins had fallen from her hair, her eyes downcast.

Cait didn't blame the older woman for being embarrassed,

but one look at the cameo and she was willing to forgive Joe anything.

The day flew past. After the gifts were opened—with everyone exclaiming in surprised delight over the gifts Joe had bought, with Cait's help—the family gathered around the piano. Mrs. Rockwell played as they sang a variety of Christmas carols, their voices loud and cheerful. Joe's father had died several years earlier, but he was mentioned often throughout the day, with affection and love. Cait hadn't known him well, but the family obviously felt Andrew Rockwell's presence far more than his absence on this festive day.

Joe drove Cait back to her apartment late that night. Mrs. Rockwell had insisted on sending a plate of cookies home with her, and Cait swore it was enough goodies to last her a month of Sundays. Now she felt sleepy and warm; leaning her head against the seat, she closed her eyes.

"We're here," Joe whispered close to her ear.

Reluctantly Cait opened her eyes and sighed. "I had such a wonderful day. Thank you, Joe." She couldn't quite stifle a yawn as she reached for the door handle, thinking longingly of bed.

"That's it?" He sounded disappointed.

"What do you mean, that's it?"

"I seem to remember a certain promise you made this morning."

Cait frowned, not sure she understood what he meant. "When?"

"When we were opening the gifts," he reminded her.

"Oh," Cait said, straightening. "You mean when I opened your gift to me and saw the brooch."

Joe nodded with exaggerated emphasis. "Right. *Now* do you remember?"

"Of course." The kiss. He planned to claim the kiss she'd

promised him. She brushed her mouth quickly over his and grinned. "There."

"If that's the best you can do, you should've kissed me in front of Charlie."

"You're faulting my kissing ability?"

"Charlie's dog gives better kisses than that."

Cait felt more than a little insulted. "Is this a challenge, Joseph Rockwell?"

"Yes," he returned archly. "You're darn right it is."

"All right, then you're on." She set the plate of cookies aside, slid closer and slipped her arms around Joe's neck. Next she wove her fingers into his thick hair.

"This is more like it," Joe murmured contentedly.

Cait paused. She wasn't sure why. Perhaps because she'd suddenly lost all interest in making fun out of something that had always been so wonderful between them.

Joe's eyes met hers, and the laughter and fun in them seemed to disappear. Slowly he expelled his breath and brushed his lips along her jaw. The warmth of his breath was exciting as his mouth skimmed toward her temple. His arms closed around her waist and he pulled her tight against him.

Impatiently he began to kiss her, introducing her to a world of warm, thrilling sensations. His mouth then explored the curve of her neck. It felt so good that Cait closed her eyes and experienced a curious weightlessness she'd never known—a heightened awareness of physical longing.

"Oh, Cait..." He broke away from her, his breathing labored and heavy. She knew instinctively that he wanted to say more, but he changed his mind and buried his face in her hair, exhaling sharply.

"How am I doing?" she whispered once she found her voice.

"Just fine."

"Are you ready to retract your statement?"

He hesitated. "I don't know. Convince me again." So she did, her kiss moist and gentle, her heart fluttering against her ribs.

"Is that good enough?" she asked when she'd recovered her breath.

Joe nodded, as though he didn't quite trust his own voice. "Excellent."

"I had a wonderful day," she whispered. "I can't thank you enough for including me."

Joe shook his head lightly. There seemed to be so much more he wanted to say to her and couldn't. Cait slipped out of the car and walked into her building, turning on the lights when she entered her apartment. She slowly put away her things, wanting to wrap this feeling around her like a warm quilt. Minutes later, she glanced out her window to see Joe still sitting in his car, his hands gripping the steering wheel, his head bent. It looked to Cait as though he was battling with himself to keep from following her inside. She would have welcomed him if he had.

9

Cait stared at the computer screen for several minutes, blind to the information in front of her. Deep in thought, she released a long, slow breath.

Paul had been grateful to see her when she'd shown up at the office that morning. The week between Christmas and New Year's could be a harried one. Lindy had looked surprised, then quickly retreated into her own office after exchanging a brief good-morning and little else. Her friend's behavior continued to baffle Cait, but she couldn't concentrate on Lindy's problems just now, or even on her work.

No matter what she did, Cait couldn't stop thinking about Joe and the kisses they'd exchanged Christmas evening. Nor could she forget his tortured look as he'd sat in his car after she'd gone into her apartment. Even now she wasn't certain why she hadn't immediately run back outside. And by the time she'd decided to do that, he was gone.

Cait was so absorbed in her musings that she barely heard the knock at her office door. Guiltily she glanced up to find

Paul standing just inside her doorway, his hands in his pockets, his eyes weary.

"Paul!" Cait waited for her heart to trip into double time the way it usually did whenever she was anywhere near him. It didn't, which was a relief but no longer much of a surprise.

"Hello, Cait." His smile was uneven, his face tight. He seemed ill at ease and struggling to disguise it. "Have you got a moment?"

"Sure. Come on in." She stood and motioned toward her client chair. "What can I do for you?"

"Nothing much," he said vaguely, sitting down. "Uh, I just wanted you to know how pleased I am that you're here. I'm sorry you canceled your vacation, but I appreciate your coming in today. Especially in light of the fact that Lindy will be leaving." His mouth thinned briefly.

No one, other than Joe and Martin, was aware of the real reason Cait wasn't in Minnesota the way she'd planned. Nor had she suggested to Paul that she'd changed her plans to help him out because they'd be short-staffed; obviously he'd drawn his own conclusions.

"So Lindy's decided to follow through with her resignation?"

Paul nodded, then frowned anew. "Nothing I say will change her mind. That woman's got a stubborn streak as wide as a..." He shrugged, apparently unable to come up with an appropriate comparison.

"The construction project's nearly finished," Cait offered, making small talk rather than joining in his criticism of Lindy. Absently she stood up and wandered around her office, stopping to straighten the large Christmas wreath on her door, the one she and Lindy had put up earlier in the month. Lindy was her friend and she wasn't about to agree with Paul, or argue with him, for that matter. Actually she should've been pleased that Paul had sought her out, but she felt curiously indifferent. And she did have work she needed to do.

"Yes, I'm delighted with the way everything's turned out," Paul said, "Joe Rockwell's done a fine job. His reputation is excellent and I imagine he'll be one of the big-time contractors in the area within the next few years."

Cait nodded casually, hoping she'd concealed the thrill of excitement that had surged through her at the mention of Joe's name. She didn't need Paul to tell her Joe's future was bright; she could see that for herself. At Christmas, his mother had boasted freely about his success. Joe had recently received a contract for a large government project—his most important to date—and she was extremely proud of him. He might have trouble keeping his books straight, but he left his customers satisfied. If he worked as hard at satisfying them as he did at finding the right Christmas tree, Cait could well believe he was gaining a reputation for excellence.

"Well, listen," Paul said, drawing in a deep breath, "I won't keep you." His eyes were clouded as he stood and headed toward the door. He hesitated, turning back to face her. "I don't suppose you'd be free for dinner tonight, would you?"

"Dinner," Cait repeated as though she'd never heard the word before. Paul was inviting her to dinner? After all these months? Now, when she least expected it? Now, when it no longer mattered? After all the times she'd ached to the bottom of her heart for some attention from him, he was finally asking her out on a date? Now?

"That is, if you're free."

"Uh…yes, sure…that would be nice."

"Great. How about if I pick you up around five-thirty? Unless that's too early for you?"

"Five-thirty will be fine."

"I'll see you then."

"Thanks, Paul." Cait felt numb. There wasn't any other way to describe it. It was as if her dreams were finally beginning to play themselves out—too late. Paul, whom she'd loved from afar for so long, wanted to take her to dinner. She should be dancing around the office with glee, or at least feeling something other than this peculiar dull sensation in the pit of her stomach. If this was such a significant, exciting, hoped-for event, why didn't she feel any of the exhilaration she'd expected?

After taking a moment to collect her thoughts, Cait walked down the hallway to Lindy's office and found her friend on the phone. Lindy glanced up, smiled feebly in Cait's direction, then abruptly dropped her gaze as if the call demanded her full concentration.

Cait waited a couple of minutes, then decided to return later when Lindy wasn't so busy. She needed to talk to her friend, needed her counsel. Lindy had always encouraged Cait in her dreams of a relationship with Paul. When she was discouraged, it was Lindy who bolstered her sagging spirits. Yes, it was definitely time for a talk. She'd try to get Lindy to confide in her, too. Cait valued Lindy's friendship; true, she couldn't help being hurt that the person she considered one of her best friends would give notice to leave the firm without even discussing it with her. But Lindy must've had her reasons. And maybe she, too, needed some support right about now.

Hearing her own phone ring, Cait hurried back to her office. She was consistantly busy from then on. The New York Stock Exchange was due to close in a matter of minutes when Joe happened by.

"Hi," Cait greeted him, her smile wide and welcoming. Her gaze connected with Joe's and he returned her smile. Her heart reacted automatically, leaping with sheer happiness.

"Hi, yourself." He sauntered into her office and threw himself down in the same chair Paul had taken earlier, stretching his long legs in front of him and folding his hands over his stomach. "So how's the world of finance doing this fine day?"

"About as well as usual."

"Then we're in deep trouble," he joked.

His smile was infectious. It always had been, but Cait had initially resisted him. Her defenses had weakened, though, and she responded readily with a smile of her own.

"You done for the day?"

"Just about." She checked the time. In another five minutes, New York would be closing down. There were several items she needed to clear from her desk, but nothing pressing. "Why?"

"Why?" It was little short of astonishing how far Joe's eyebrows could reach, Cait noted, all but disappearing into his hairline.

"Can't a man ask a simple question?" Joe asked.

"Of course." The banter between them was like a well-rehearsed play. Never had Cait been more at ease with a man—or had more fun with a man. Or with anyone, really. "What I want to know is whether 'simple' refers to the question or to the man asking it."

"Ouch," Joe said, grinning broadly. "Those claws are sharp this afternoon."

"Actually today's been good." Or at least it had since he'd arrived.

"I'm glad to hear it. How about dinner?" He jumped to his feet and pretended to waltz around her office, playing a violin. "You and me. Wine and moonlight and music. Romance and roses." He wiggled his eyebrows at her suggestively. "You work too hard. You always have. I want you to enjoy life a little more. It would be good for both of us."

Joe didn't need to give her an incentive to go out with him. Cait was thrilled at the mere idea. Joe made her laugh, made her feel good about herself and the world. Of course, he possessed a remarkable talent for driving her crazy, too. But she supposed a little craziness was good for the spirit.

"Only promise me you won't wear those high heels of yours," he chided, pressing his hand to the small of his back. "I've suffered excruciating back pains ever since Paul's Christmas party."

Paul's name seemed to leap out and grab Cait by the throat. "Paul," she repeated, sagging against the back of her chair. "Oh, dear."

"I know you consider him a dear," Joe teased. "What has your stalwart employer done this time?"

"He asked me out to dinner," Cait admitted, frowning. "Out of the blue this morning he popped into my office and invited me to dinner as if we'd been dating for months. I was so stunned, I didn't know what to think."

"What did you tell him?" Joe seemed to consider the whole thing a huge joke. "Wait—" he held up his hand "—you don't need to answer that. I already know. You sprang at the offer."

"I didn't exactly spring," she said, somewhat offended by Joe's attitude. The least he could do was show a little concern. She'd spent Christmas with him, and according to his own mother this was the first time he'd ever brought a woman home for the holiday. Furthermore, despite his insisting to all and sundry that they were married, he certainly didn't seem to mind her seeing another man.

"I'll bet you nearly went into shock." A smile trembled at the edges of his mouth as if he was picturing her reaction to Paul's invitation and finding it all terribly entertaining.

"I did not go into shock." She defended herself heatedly. She'd been taken by surprise, that was all.

"Listen," he said, walking toward the door, "have a great time. I'll catch you later." With that he was gone.

Cait couldn't believe it. Her mouth dropped open and she paced frantically, clenching and unclenching her fists. It took her a full minute to recover enough to run after him.

Joe was talking to his foreman, the same stocky man he'd been with the day he followed Cait into the elevator.

"Excuse me," she said, interrupting their conversation, "but when you're finished I'd like a few words with you, Joe." Her back was ramrod stiff and she kept flexing her hands as though preparing for a fight.

Joe glanced at his watch. "It might be a while."

"Then might I have a few minutes of your time now?"

The foreman stepped away, his step cocky. "You want me to dismiss the crew again, boss? I can tell them to go out and buy New Year's presents for their wives, if you like."

The man was rewarded with a look that was hot enough to barbecue spareribs. "That won't be necessary, thanks, anyway, Harry."

"You're welcome, boss. We serve to please."

"Then please me by kindly shutting up."

Harry chuckled and returned to another section of the office.

"You wanted something?" Joe asked.

Boy, did she. "Is that all you're going to say?"

"About what?"

"About my going to dinner with Paul? I expected you to be… I don't know, upset."

"Why should I be upset? Is he going to have his way with you? I sincerely doubt it, but if you're worried, invite me along and I'll be more than happy to protect your honor."

"What's the matter with you?" she demanded, not bothering to disguise her fury and disappointment. She stared at Joe, waiting for him to mock her again, but once more he surprised her. His gaze sobered.

"You honestly expect me to be jealous?"

"Not jealous exactly," she said, although he wasn't far from the truth. "Concerned."

"I'm not. Paul's a good man."

"I know, but—"

"You've been in love with him for months—"

"I think it was more of an infatuation."

"True. But he's finally asked you out, and you've accepted."

"Yes, but—"

"We know each other well, Cait. We were married, remember?"

"I'm not likely to forget it." Especially when Joe took pains to point it out at every opportunity. "Shouldn't that mean…something?" Cait was embarrassed she'd said that. For weeks she'd suffered acute mortification every time Joe mentioned the childhood stunt. Now she was using it to suit her own purposes.

Joe took hold of her shoulders. "As a matter of fact, our marriage means a lot to me. Because I care about you, Cait."

Hearing Joe admit as much was gratifying.

"I want only the best for you," he continued. "It's what you deserve. All I can say is that I'd be more than pleased if everything worked out between you and Paul. Now if you'll excuse me, I need to talk something over with Harry."

"Oh, right, sure, go ahead." She couldn't seem to get the words out fast enough. When she'd called Martin to explain why she wouldn't be in Minnesota for Christmas, he'd claimed that God would reward her sacrifice. If Paul's invitation to dinner was God's reward, she wanted her airline ticket back.

The numb feeling returned as Cait returned to her office. She didn't know what to think. She'd believed…she'd hoped that she and Joe shared a very special feeling. Clearly their times together meant something entirely different to him than they had to her. Otherwise he wouldn't behave so casually about her going out with Paul. And he certainly wouldn't seem so pleased about it!

That was what hurt Cait the most, and yes, she was hurt. It had taken her several minutes to identify her feelings, but now she knew…

More by accident than design, Cait walked into Lindy's office. Her friend had already put on her coat and was closing her briefcase, ready to leave the office.

"Paul asked me to dinner," Cait blurted out.

"He did?" Lindy's eyes widened with astonishment. But she didn't turn it into a joke, the way Joe had.

Cait nodded. "He just strolled in as if it was nothing out of the ordinary and asked me to have dinner with him."

"Are you happy about it?"

"I don't know," Cait answered honestly. "I suppose I should be pleased. It's what I'd prayed would happen for months."

"Then what's the problem?" Lindy asked.

"Joe doesn't seem to care. He said he hopes everything works out the way I want it to."

"Which is?" Lindy pressed.

Cait had to think about that a moment, her heart in her throat. "Honest to heaven, Lindy, I don't know anymore."

"I understand the salmon here is superb," Paul was saying, reading over the Boathouse menu. It was a well-known restaurant on Lake Union.

Cait scanned the list of entrées, which featured fresh seafood, then chose the grilled salmon—the same dish she'd ordered that night with Joe. Tonight, though, she wasn't sure why she was even bothering. She wasn't hungry, and Paul was going to be wasting good money while she made a pretense of enjoying her meal.

"I understand you've been seeing a lot of Joe Rockwell," he said conversationally.

That Paul should mention Joe's name right now was ironic. Cait hadn't stopped thinking about him from the moment he'd dropped into her office earlier that afternoon. Their conversation had left a bitter taste in her mouth. She'd sincerely believed their relationship was developing into something…special. Yet Joe had gone out of his way to give her the opposite impression.

"Cait?" Paul stared at her.

"I'm sorry, what were you saying?"

"Simply that you and Joe Rockwell have been seeing a lot of each other recently."

"Uh, yes. As you know, we were childhood friends," she murmured. "Actually Joe and my older brother were best friends. Then Joe's family moved to the suburbs and our families lost contact."

"Yes, I remember you mentioned that."

The waitress came for their order, and Paul requested a bottle of white wine. Then he chatted amicably for several minutes, bringing up subjects of shared interest from the office.

Cait listened attentively, nodding from time to time or adding the occasional comment. Now that she had his undivided attention, Cait wondered what it was about Paul that she'd found so extraordinary. He was attractive, but not nearly as dynamic or exciting as she found Joe. True, Paul possessed a certain charm, but compared to Joe, he was subdued and perhaps even a little dull. Cait couldn't imagine her stalwart boss carrying her piggyback out the back door because her high heels were too tight. Nor could she see Paul bantering with her the way Joe did.

The waitress delivered the wine, opened the bottle and poured them each a glass, once Paul had given his approval. Their dinners followed shortly afterward. After taking a bite or two of her delicious salmon, Cait noticed that Paul hadn't touched his meal. If anything, he seemed restless.

He rolled the stem of the wineglass between his fingers, watching the wine swirl inside. Then he suddenly blurted out, "What do you think of Lindy's leaving the firm?"

Cait was taken aback by the fervor in his voice when he mentioned Lindy's name. "Frankly I was shocked," Cait said. "Lindy and I have been good friends for a couple of years now." There'd been a time when the two had done nearly everything together. The summer before, they'd vacationed in Mexico and returned to Seattle with enough handwoven baskets and bulky blankets to set up shop themselves.

"Lindy's resigning came as a surprise to you, then?"

"Yes, this whole thing caught me completely unawares. Lindy didn't even mention the other job offer to me. I always thought we were good friends."

"Lindy *is* your friend," Paul said with enough conviction to persuade the patrons at the nearby tables. "You wouldn't believe what a good friend she is."

"I...know that." But friends sometimes had surprises up their sleeves. Lindy was a good example of that, and apparently so was Joe.

"I find Lindy an exceptional woman," Paul commented, watching Cait closely.

"She's probably one of the best stockbrokers in the business," Cait said, taking a sip of her wine.

"My…admiration for her goes beyond her keen business mind."

"Oh, mine, too," Cait was quick to agree. Lindy was the kind of friend who would trudge through the blazing sun of Mexico looking for a conch shell because she knew Cait really wanted to take one home. And Lindy had listened to countless hours of Cait's bemoaning her sorry fate of unrequited love for Paul.

"She's a wonderful woman."

Joe was wonderful, too, Cait thought. So wonderful her heart ached at his indifference when she'd announced she would be dining with Paul.

"Lindy's the kind of woman a man could treasure all his life," Paul went on.

"I couldn't agree with you more," Cait said. Now, if only Joe would realize what a treasure *she* was. He'd married her once—well, sort of—and surely the possibility of spending their lives together had crossed his mind in the past few weeks.

Paul hesitated as though at a loss for words. "I don't suppose you've given any thought to the reason Lindy made this unexpected decision to resign?"

Frankly Cait hadn't. Her mind and her heart had been so full of Joe that deciphering her friend's actions had somehow escaped her. "She received a better offer, didn't she?" Which was understandable. Lindy would be an asset to any firm.

It was then that Cait understood. Paul hadn't asked her to dinner out of any desire to develop a romantic relationship with her. He saw her as a means of discovering what had prompted Lindy to resign. This new awareness came as a relief, a burden lifted from her shoulders. Paul wasn't interested in her. He never had been and probably never would be. A few weeks ago, that realization would have been a crushing defeat, but all Cait experienced now was an overwhelming sense of gratitude.

"I'm sure if you talk to Lindy, she might reconsider," Cait suggested.

"I've tried, trust me. But there's a problem."

"Oh?" Now that Cait had sampled the salmon, she discovered it to be truly delicious. She hadn't realized how hungry she was.

"Cait, look at me," Paul said, raising his voice slightly. His face was pinched, his eyes intense. "Damn, but you've made this nearly impossible."

She looked up at him, her face puzzled. "What is it, Paul?"

"You have no idea, do you? I swear you've got to be the most obtuse woman in the world." He pushed aside his plate and briefly closed his eyes, shaking his head. "I'm in love with Lindy. I have been for weeks…months. But for the life of me I couldn't get her to notice me. I swear I did everything but turn cartwheels in her office. It finally dawned on me why she wasn't responding."

"Me?" Cait asked in a feeble, mouselike squeak.

"Exactly. She didn't want to betray your friendship. Then one afternoon—I think it was the day you first recognized Joe—we, Lindy and I, were in my office and— Oh, hell, I don't know how it happened, but Lindy was looking something up for me and she stumbled over one of the cords the construction crew was using. Fortunately I was able to catch her before she fell to the floor. I know it wasn't her fault, but I was so angry, afraid she might have been hurt. Lindy was just as angry with me for being angry with her, and it seemed the only way to shut her up was to kiss her. That was the beginning and I swear to you everything exploded in our faces at that moment."

Cait swallowed, fascinated by the story. "Go on."

"I tried for days to get her to agree to go out with me. But she kept refusing until I demanded to know why."

"She told you…how I felt about you?" The thought was mortifying.

"Of course not. Lindy's too good a friend to divulge your confidence. Besides, she didn't need to tell me. I've known all along. Good grief, Cait, what did I have to do to discourage you? Hire a skywriter?"

"I don't think anything that drastic was necessary," she muttered, humiliated to her very bones.

"I repeatedly told Lindy I wasn't attracted to you, but she wouldn't listen. Finally she told me if I'd talk to you, explain everything myself, she'd agree to go out with me."

"The phone call," Cait said with sudden comprehension. "That was the reason you called me, wasn't it? You wanted to talk about Lindy, not that business article."

"Yes." He looked deeply grateful for her insight, late though it was.

"Well, for heaven's sake, why didn't you?"

"Believe me, I've kicked myself a dozen times since. I wish I knew. I suppose it seemed heartless to have such a frank discussion over the phone. Again and again, I promised myself I'd say something. Lord knows I dropped enough hints, but you weren't exactly receptive."

She winced. "But why is Lindy resigning?"

"Isn't it obvious?" Paul asked. "It was becoming increasingly difficult for us to work together. She didn't want to betray her best friend, but at the same time…"

"But at the same time you two were falling in love."

"Exactly. I can't lose her, Cait. I don't want to hurt your

feelings, and believe me, it's nothing personal—you're a trustworthy employee and a decent person—but I'm simply not attracted to you."

Paul didn't seem to be the only one. Other than treating their relationship like one big joke, Joe hadn't ever claimed any romantic feelings for her, either.

"I had to do something before I lost Lindy."

"I agree completely."

"You're not angry with her, are you?"

"Good heavens, no," Cait said, offering him a brave smile.

"We both thought something was developing between you and Joe Rockwell. Like I said, you seemed to be seeing quite a bit of each other, and then at the Christmas party—"

"Don't remind me," Cait said with a low groan.

Paul's face creased in a spontaneous smile. "Joe certainly has a wit about him, doesn't he?"

Cait gave a resigned nod.

Now that Paul had cleared the air, he seemed to develop an appetite. He reached for his dinner and ate heartily. By contrast, Cait's salmon had lost its appeal. She stared down at her plate, wondering how she could possibly make it through the rest of the evening.

She did, though, quite nicely. Paul didn't even seem to notice that anything was amiss. It wasn't that Cait was distressed by his confession. If anything, she was relieved at this turn of events and delighted that Lindy had fallen in love. Paul was obviously crazy about her; she'd never seen him more animated than when he was discussing Lindy. It still shocked Cait that she'd been so unperceptive about Lindy's real feelings. Not to mention Paul's…

Paul dropped her off at her building and saw her to the front door. "I can't thank you enough for understanding," he said, his voice warm. Impulsively he hugged her, then hurried back to his sports car.

Although she was certainly guilty of being obtuse, Cait knew exactly where Paul was headed. No doubt Lindy would be waiting for him, eager to hear the details of their conversation. Cait planned to talk to her friend herself, first thing in the morning.

Cait's apartment was dark and lonely. So lonely the silence seemed to echo off the walls. She hung up her coat before turning on the lights, her thoughts as dark as the room had been.

She made herself a cup of tea. Then she sat on the sofa, tucking her feet beneath her as she stared unseeing at the walls, assessing her options. They seemed terribly limited.

Paul was in love with Lindy. And Joe… Cait had no idea where she stood with him. For all she knew—

Her thoughts were interrupted by the phone. She answered on the second ring.

"Cait?" It was Joe and he seemed surprised to find her back so early. "When did you get in?"

"A few minutes ago."

"You don't sound like yourself. Is anything wrong?"

"No," she said, breaking into sobs. "What could possibly be wrong?"

10

The flow of emotion took Cait by storm. She'd had no intention of crying; in fact, the thought hadn't even entered her mind. One moment she was sitting there, contemplating the evening's revelations, and the next she was sobbing hysterically into the phone.

"Cait?"

"Oh," she wailed. "This is all your fault in the first place." Cait didn't know what made her say that. The words had slipped out before she'd realized it.

"What happened?"

"Nothing. I… I can't talk to you now. I'm going to bed." With that, she gently replaced the receiver. Part of her hoped Joe would call back, but the telephone remained stubbornly silent. She stared at it for several minutes. Apparently Joe didn't care if he talked to her or not.

The tears continued to flow. They remained a mystery to Cait. She wasn't a woman given to bouts of crying, but now that she'd started she couldn't seem to stop.

She changed out of her dress and into a pair of sweats, pausing halfway through to wash her face.

Sniffling and hiccuping, she sat on the end of her bed and dragged a shuddering breath through her lungs. Crying like this made no sense whatsoever.

Paul was in love with Lindy. At one time, the news would have devastated her, but not now. Cait felt a tingling happiness that her best friend had found a man to love. And the infatuation she'd held for Paul couldn't compare with the strength of her love for Joe.

Love.

There, she'd admitted it. She was in love with Joe. The man who told restaurant employees that she was suffering from amnesia. The man who walked into elevators and announced to total strangers that they were married. Yet this was the same man who hadn't revealed a minute's concern about her dating Paul Jamison.

Joe was also the man who'd gently held her hand through a children's movie. The man who made a practice of kissing her senseless. The man who'd held her in his arms Christmas night as though he never intended to let her go.

Joseph Rockwell was a fun-loving jokester who took delight in teasing her. He was also tender and thoughtful and loving—the man who'd captured her heart only to drop it so carelessly.

Her doorbell chimed and she didn't need to look in the peephole to know it was Joe. But she felt panicky all of a sudden, too confused and vulnerable to see him now.

She walked slowly to the door and opened it a crack.

"What the hell is going on?" Joe demanded, not waiting for an invitation to march inside.

Cait wiped her eyes on her sleeve and shut the door. "Nothing."

"Did Paul try anything?"

She rolled her eyes. "Of course not."

"Then why are you crying?" He stood in the middle of her living room, fists planted on his hips as if he'd welcome the opportunity to punch out her boss.

If Cait knew why she was crying nonstop like this, she would have answered him. She opened her mouth, hoping some intelligent reason would emerge, but the only thing that came out was a low-pitched moan. Joe was gazing at her in complete confusion. "I… Paul's in love."

"With *you?*" His voice rose half an octave with disbelief.

"Don't make it sound like such an impossibility," she said crossly. "I'm reasonably attractive, you know." If she was expecting Joe to list her myriad charms, Cait was disappointed.

Instead, his frown darkened. "So what's Paul being in love got to do with anything?"

"Absolutely nothing. I wished him and Lindy the very best."

"So it is Lindy?" Joe murmured as though he'd known it all along.

"You didn't honestly think it was me, did you?"

"Hell, how was I supposed to know? I *thought* it was Lindy, but it was you he was taking to dinner. Frankly it didn't make a whole lot of sense to me."

"Which is something else," Cait grumbled, standing so close to him, their faces were only inches apart. Her hands were on her hips, her pose mirroring his. It occurred to Cait that they resembled a pair of gunslingers ready for a shoot-out. "I want to know one thing. Every time I turn around, you're telling anyone and everyone who'll listen that we're married. But when it really matters you—"

"When did it really matter?"

Cait ignored the question, thinking the answer was obvious. "You casually turn me over to Paul as if you can't wait to be rid of me. Obviously you couldn't have cared less."

"I cared," he shouted.

"Oh, right," she shouted back, "but if that was the case, you certainly didn't bother to show it!"

"What was I supposed to do, challenge him to a duel?"

He was being ridiculous, Cait decided, and she refused to take the bait. The more they talked, the more unreasonable they were both becoming.

"I thought dating Paul was what you wanted," he complained. "You talked about it long enough. Paul this and Paul that. He'd walk past and you'd all but swoon."

"That's not the least bit true." Maybe it had been at one time, but not now and not for weeks. "If you'd taken the trouble to ask me, you might have learned the truth."

"You mean you don't love Paul?"

Cait rolled her eyes again. "Bingo."

"It isn't like you to be so sarcastic."

"It isn't like you to be so…awful."

He seemed to mull that over for a moment. "If we're going to be throwing out accusations," he said tightly, "then maybe you should take a look at yourself."

"What exactly do you mean by that?" As usual, no one could get a reaction out of Cait more effectively than Joe. "Never mind," she answered, walking to the door. "This discussion isn't getting us anywhere. All we seem capable of doing is hurling insults at each other."

"I disagree," Joe answered calmly. "I think it's time we cleared the air."

She took a deep breath, feeling physically and emotionally deflated.

"Joe, it'll have to wait. I'm in no condition to be rational right now and I don't want either of us saying things we'll regret." She held open her door for him. "Please?"

He seemed about to argue with her, then he sighed and dropped a quick kiss on her mouth. Wide-eyed, she watched him leave.

Lindy was waiting in Cait's office early the next morning, holding two cups of freshly brewed coffee. Her eyes were vulnerable as Cait entered the office. They stared at each other for a long moment.

"Are you angry with me?" Lindy whispered. She handed Cait one of the cups as an apparent peace offering.

"Of course not," Cait murmured. She put down her briefcase and accepted the cup, which she placed carefully on her desk. Then she gave Lindy a reassuring hug, and the two of them sat down for their much-postponed talk.

"Why didn't you tell me?" Cait burst out.

"I wanted to," Lindy said earnestly. "I had to stop myself a hundred times. The worst part of it was the guilt—knowing you were in love with Paul, and loving him myself."

Cait wasn't sure how she would have reacted to the truth, but she preferred to think she would've understood, and wished Lindy well. It wasn't as though Lindy had stolen Paul away from her.

"I don't think I realized how I felt," Lindy continued, "until one afternoon when I tripped over a stupid cord and fell into Paul's arms. From there, everything sort of snowballed."

"Paul told me."

"He…told you about that afternoon?"

Cait grinned and nodded. "I found the story wildly romantic."

"You don't mind?" Lindy watched her closely as if half-afraid of Cait's reaction even now.

"I think it's wonderful."

Lindy's smile was filled with warmth and excitement. "I never knew being in love could be so exciting, but at the same time cause so much pain."

"Amen to that," Cait stated emphatically.

Her words shot like live bullets into the room. If Cait could have reached out and pulled them back, she would have.

"Is it Joe Rockwell?" Lindy asked softly.

Cait nodded, then shook her head. "See how much he's confused me?" She made a sound that was half sob, half giggle. "Sometimes that man infuriates me so much I want to scream. Or cry." Cait had always thought of herself as a sane and sensible person. She lived a quiet life, worked hard at her job, enjoyed traveling and crossword puzzles. Then she'd bumped into Joe. Suddenly she found herself demanding piggyback rides, talking to strangers in elevators and seeking out phantom women at Christmas parties while downing spiked punch like it was soda pop.

"But then at other times?" Lindy prompted.

"At other times I love him so much I hurt all the way through. I love everything about him. Even those loony stunts of his. In fact, I usually laugh as hard as everyone else. Even if I don't always want him to know it."

"So what's going to happen with you two?" Lindy asked. She took a sip of coffee and as she did, Cait caught a flash of diamond.

"Lindy?" Cait demanded, jumping out of her seat. "What's that on your finger?"

Lindy's face broke into a smile so bright Cait was nearly blinded. "You noticed."

"Of course I did."

"It's from Paul. After he had dinner with you, he came over to my apartment. We talked for hours and then…he asked me to marry him. At first I didn't know what to say. It seems so soon. We…we hardly know each other."

"Good grief, you've worked together for ages."

"I know," Lindy said with a shy smile. "That's what Paul told me. It didn't take him long to convince me. He had the ring all picked out. Isn't it beautiful?"

"Oh, Lindy." The diamond was a lovely solitaire set in a wide band of gold. The style and shape were perfect for Lindy's long, elegant finger.

"I didn't know if I should wear it until you and I had talked, but I couldn't make myself take it off this morning."

"Of course you should wear it!" The fact that Paul had been carrying it around when he'd had dinner with her didn't exactly flatter Cait's ego, but she was so thrilled for Lindy that seemed a minor concern.

Lindy splayed her fingers out in front of her to better show off the ring. "When he slipped it on my finger, I swear it was the most romantic moment of my life. Before I knew it, tears were streaming down my face. I still don't understand why I started crying. I think Paul was as surprised as I was."

There must have been something in the air that reduced susceptible females to tears, Cait decided. Whatever it was had certainly affected her.

"Now you've sidetracked me," Lindy said, looking up from her diamond, her gaze dreamy. "You were telling me about you and Joe."

"I was?"

"Yes, you were," Lindy insisted.

"There's nothing to tell. If there was, you'd be the first person to hear. I know," she admitted before her friend could bring up the point, "we have seen a lot of each other recently, but I don't think it meant anything to Joe. When he found out Paul had invited me to dinner, he seemed downright delighted."

"I'm sure it was all an act."

Cait shrugged. She wished she could believe that. Oh, how she wished it.

"You're sure you're in love with him?" Lindy asked hesitantly.

Cait nodded and lowered her eyes. It hurt to think about Joe. Everything was a game to him—a big joke. Lindy had been right about one thing, though. Love was the most wonderful experience of her life. And the most painful.

The New York Stock Exchange had closed and Cait was punching some figures into her computer when Joe strode into her office and closed the door.

"Feel free to come in," she muttered, continuing her work. Her heart was pounding but she dared not let him know the effect he had on her.

"I will make myself at home, thank you," he answered cheerfully, ignoring her sarcasm. He pulled out a chair and sat down expansively, resting one ankle on the opposite knee and relaxing as if he was in a movie theater, waiting for the main feature to begin.

"If you're here to discuss business, might I suggest investing in blue-chip stocks? They're always a safe bet." Cait went on typing, doing her best to ignore Joe—which was nearly impossible, although she gave an Oscar-winning performance, if she did say so herself.

"I'm here to talk business, all right," Joe said, "but it has nothing to do with the stock market."

"What business could the two of us possibly have?" she asked, her voice deliberately ironic.

"I want to resume the discussion we were having last night."

"Perhaps you do, but unfortunately that was last night and this is now." How confident she sounded, Cait thought, mildly pleased with herself. "I can do without hearing you list my no doubt numerous flaws."

"Your being my wife is what I want to talk about."

"Your wife?" She wished he'd quit throwing the subject at her as if it meant something to him. Something other than a joke.

"Yes, my wife." He gave a short laugh. "Believe me, it isn't your flaws I'm here to discuss."

Despite everything, Cait's heart raced. She reached for a stack of papers and switched them from one basket to another. Her entire filing system was probably in jeopardy, but she needed some activity to occupy her hands before she stood up and reached out to Joe. She did stand then, but it was to remove a large silver bell strung from a red velvet ribbon hanging in her office window.

"Paul and Lindy are getting married," he said next.

"Yes, I know. Lindy and I had a long talk this morning." She took the wreath off her door next.

"I take it the two of you are friends again?"

"We were never not friends," Cait answered stiffly, stuffing the wreath, the bell and the three ceramic wise men into the bottom drawer of her filing cabinet. Hard as she tried to prevent it, she could feel her defenses crumbling. "Lindy's asked me to be her maid of honor and I've agreed."

"Will you return the favor?"

It took a moment for the implication to sink in, and even then Cait wasn't sure she should follow the trail Joe seemed to be forging through this conversation. She leaned forward and rested her hands on the edge of the desk.

"I'm destined to be an old maid," she said flippantly, although she couldn't help feeling a sliver of real hope.

"You'll never be that."

Cait was hoping he'd say her beauty would make her irresistible, or that her warmth and wit and intelligence were sure to attract a dozen suitors. Instead he said the very thing she could have predicted. "We're already married, so you don't need to worry about being a spinster."

Cait released a sigh of impatience. "I wish you'd give up on that, Joe. It's growing increasingly old."

"As I recall, we celebrated our eighteenth anniversary not long ago."

"Don't be ridiculous. All right," she said, straightening abruptly. If he wanted to play games, then she'd respond in kind. "Since we're married, I want a family."

"Hey, sweetheart," he cried, throwing his arms in the air, "that's music to my ears. I'm willing."

Cait prepared to leave the office, if not the building. "Somehow I knew you would be."

"Two or three," he interjected, then chuckled and added, "I suppose we should name the first two Ken and Barbie."

Cait's scowl made him chuckle even louder.

"If you prefer, we'll leave the names open to negotiation," he said.

"Of all the colossal nerve..." Cait muttered, moving to the window and gazing out.

"If you want daughters, I've got no objection, but from what I understand that's not really up to us."

Cait turned around, crossing her arms. "Correct me if I'm wrong," she said coldly, certain he'd delight in doing so. "But you did just ask me to marry you. Could you confirm that?"

"All I want is to make legal what's already been done."

Cait sighed in exasperation. Was he serious, or wasn't he? He was talking about marriage, about joining their lives, as if he were planning a bid on a construction project.

"When Paul asked Lindy to marry him, he had a diamond ring."

"I was going to buy you a ring," Joe said emphatically. "I still am. But I thought you'd want to pick it out yourself. If you wanted a diamond, why didn't you say so? I'll buy you the whole store if that'll make you happy."

"One ring will suffice, thank you."

"Pick out two or three. I understand diamonds are an excellent investment."

"Not so fast," she said, holding out her arm. It was vital she maintain some distance between them. If Joe kissed her or started talking about having children again, they might never get the facts clear.

"Not so fast?" he repeated incredulously. "Honey, I've been waiting eighteen years to discuss this. You're not going to ruin everything now, are you?" He advanced a couple of steps toward her.

"I'm not agreeing to anything until you explain yourself." For every step he took toward her, Cait retreated two.

"About what?" Joe was frowning, which wasn't a good sign.

"Paul."

His eyelids slammed shut, then slowly rose. "I don't understand why that man's name has to come into every conversation you and I have."

Cait decided it was better to ignore that comment. "You haven't even told me you love me."

"I love you." He actually sounded annoyed, as if she'd insisted on having the obvious reiterated.

"You might say it with a little more feeling," Cait suggested.

"If you want feeling, come here and let me kiss you."

"No."

"Why not?" By now they'd completely circled her desk. "We're talking serious things here. Trust me, sweetheart, a man doesn't bring up marriage and babies with just any woman. I love you. I've loved you for years, only I didn't know it."

"Then why did you let Paul take me out to dinner?"

"You mean I could've stopped you?"

"Of course. I didn't want to go out with him! I was sick about having to turn you down for dinner. Not only that, you didn't even seem to care that I was going out with another man. And as far as you were concerned, he was your main competition."

"I wasn't worried."

"That wasn't the impression I got later."

"All right, all right," Joe said, drawing his fingers through his hair. "I didn't think Paul was interested in you. I saw him and Lindy together one night at the office and the electricity between them was so thick it could've lit up Seattle."

"You knew about Lindy and Paul?"

Joe shrugged. "Let me put it this way. I had a sneaking suspicion. But when you started talking about Paul as though you were in love with him, I got worried."

"You should have been." Which was a bold-faced lie.

Somehow, without her being quite sure how it happened, Joe maneuvered himself so only a few inches separated them.

"Are you ever going to kiss me?" he demanded.

Meekly Cait nodded and stepped into his arms like a child opening the gate and skipping up the walkway to home. This was the place she belonged. With Joe. This was home and she need never doubt his love again.

With a sigh that seemed to come from the deepest part of him, Joe swept her close. For a breathless moment they looked into each other's eyes. He was about to kiss her when there was a knock at the door.

Harry, Joe's foreman, walked in without waiting for a response. "I don't suppose you've seen Joe—" He stopped abruptly. "Oh, sorry," he said, flustered and eager to make his escape.

"No problem," Cait assured him. "We're married. We have been for years and years."

Joe was chuckling as his mouth settled over hers, and in a single kiss he wiped out all the doubts and misgivings, replacing them with promises and thrills.

EPILOGUE

The robust sound of organ music surged through the Seattle church as Cait walked slowly down the center aisle, her feet moving in time to the traditional music. As the maid of honor, Lindy stood to one side of the altar while Joe and his brother, who was serving as best man, waited on the other. The church was decorated with poinsettias and Christmas greenery, accented by white roses.

Cait's brother, Martin, stood directly ahead of her. He smiled at Cait as the assembly rose and she came down the aisle, her heart overflowing with happiness.

Cait and Joe had planned this day, their Christmas wedding, for months. If there'd been any lingering doubts that Joe really loved her, they were long gone. He wasn't the type of man who expressed his love with flowery words and gifts. But Cait had known that from the first. He'd insisted on building their home before the wedding and they'd spent countless hours going over the architect's plans. Cait was helping Joe with his accounting and would be taking over the task full-time when they started their family. Which would be soon. The way Cait figured it, she'd be pregnant by next Christmas.

But before they began their real life together, they'd enjoy a perfect honeymoon in New Zealand. He'd wanted to surprise her with the trip, but Cait had needed a passport. They'd only be gone two weeks, which was all the time Joe could afford to take, since he had several large projects coming up.

As the organ concluded the "Wedding March," Cait handed her bouquet to Lindy and placed her hands in Joe's. He smiled down on her as if he'd never seen a more beautiful woman in his life. Judging by the look on his face, Cait knew he could hardly keep from kissing her right then and there.

"Dearly beloved," Martin said, stepping forward, "we are gathered here today in the sight of God and man to celebrate the love of Joseph James Rockwell and Caitlin Rose Marshall."

Cait's eyes locked with Joe's. She did love him, so much that her heart felt close to bursting. After all these months of waiting for this moment, Cait was sure she'd be so nervous her voice would falter. That didn't happen. She'd never felt more confident of anything than her feelings for Joe and his for her. Cait's voice rang out strong and clear, as did Joe's.

As they exchanged the rings, Cait could hear her mother and Joe's weeping softly in the background. But these were tears of shared happiness. The two women had renewed their friendship and were excited about the prospect of grandchildren.

Cait waited for the moment when Martin would tell Joe he could kiss his bride. Instead he closed his Bible, reverently set it aside, and said, "Joseph James Rockwell, do you have the baseball cards with you?"

"I do."

Cait looked at the two men as if they'd both lost their minds. Joe reached inside his tuxedo jacket and produced two flashy baseball cards.

"You may give them to your bride."

With a dramatic flourish, Joe did as Martin instructed. Cait stared down at the two cards and grinned broadly.

"You may now kiss the bride," Martin declared.

Joe was more than happy to comply.

★ ★ ★ ★ ★

SUGAR AND SPICE

To the girls of Saint Joseph Academy—class of 1966

1

"You're going, aren't you?" Gloria Bailey asked for the third time.

And for the third time Jayne Gilbert stalled, taking a small bite of her egg-salad sandwich. She always ate egg salad on Tuesdays. "I don't know."

The invitation to her class reunion lay in the bottom of Jayne's purse, taunting her with memories she'd just as soon forget. The day was much too glorious to think about anything unpleasant. It was now mid-May, and the weather was finally warm enough to sit outside as they had lunch at a small café near the downtown Portland library.

"You'll regret it if you don't go," Gloria continued with a knowing look.

"You don't understand," Jayne said, pushing her glasses onto the bridge of her nose. She set aside the whole-wheat sandwich. "I was probably the only girl to graduate from St. Mary's in a state of grace."

Gloria tried unsuccessfully to swallow a chuckle.

"My whole senior year I had to listen while my classmates told marvelous stories about their backseat adventures," she said wryly. "I never had any adventures like that."

"And ten years later you still have no tales to tell?"

She nodded. "What's worse, all those years have slipped by, and I've turned out exactly as my classmates predicted. I'm a librarian and living alone—*alone* being the operative word."

Jayne even looked the same. The frames of her glasses were more fashionable now, but her hair was the same shade of brown—the color of cedar chips, just a tad too dark to be termed mousy. She'd kept it the same length, too, although she preferred it clasped at the base of her neck these days. She no longer wore the school's uniform of red blazer jacket and navy pleated skirt, but she wore another one, of sorts. The straight black skirt or tailored pants, white silk blouse and business jacket were her daily attire.

Her romantic dreams had remained dreams, and the love in her heart was showered generously upon the children who visited her regularly in the library. Jayne was the head of the children's department, while Gloria was a reference librarian. Both of them enjoyed their jobs.

"That's easy to fix," Gloria returned with a confidence Jayne lacked. "Go to the reunion looking different. Go dressed to the teeth, and bring along a gorgeous male who'll make you the envy of every girl in your class."

"I can't be something I'm not." Jayne didn't bother to mention the man. If she hadn't found a suitable male in ten years, what made Gloria think she could come up with one in two months?

"For one night you can be anything you want."

"It's *not* that easy," Jayne felt obliged to argue.

Until yesterday, before she'd sorted through her mail, she'd been content with her matter-of-fact existence. She liked her apartment and was proud of her accomplishments, however minor. Her life was uncomplicated, and frankly, she liked it that way.

But the last thing Jayne wanted was to go back and prove to her classmates that they'd been right. The thought was too humiliating. When she was a teenager, they'd taunted her as the girl most likely to succeed—behind the pages of a book. All her life, Jayne had been teased about her love for reading. Books were everything to her. She was the only child of doting parents who'd given up the hope of ever having children. Although her parents had been thrilled at her late arrival, Jayne often wondered if they'd actually known what to do with her. Both were English professors at a Seattle college and it seemed natural to introduce her to their beloved world of literature at an early age. So Jayne had spent her childhood reading the classics when other girls were watching TV, playing outside and going to birthday parties. It wasn't until she reached her teens that she realized how much of a misfit she'd become. Oh, she had friends, lots of friends… Unfortunately the majority of them lived between the covers of well-loved books.

"You need a man like the one across the street," Gloria said.

"What man?" Jayne squinted.

"The one in the raincoat."

"Him?" The tall man resembled the mystery guy who lived in her apartment building. Jayne thought of him that way because he seemed to work the oddest hours. Twice she'd seen him in the apartment parking lot making some kind of transaction with another man. At the time she'd wondered if he was a drug dealer. She'd immediately discounted the idea as the result of an overactive imagination.

"*Look* at him, Jayne. He's a perfect male specimen. He's

got that lean hardness women adore, and he walks as if he owns the street. A lot of women would go for him."

Watching the man her friend had pointed out, Jayne was even more convinced he was her neighbor. They'd met a few times in the elevator, but they'd just exchanged nods; they'd never spoken. He lived on the same floor, three apartments down from hers. Jayne had been living near him for months and never really noticed the blatantly masculine features Gloria was describing.

"His jaw has that chiseled quality that drives women wild," Gloria was saying.

"I suppose," Jayne concluded, losing interest. She forced her attention back to her lunch. There was something about that man she didn't trust.

"Well, you aren't going to find someone to take to your class reunion by sitting around your apartment," Gloria muttered.

"I haven't decided if I'm going yet." But deep down, Jayne wanted to attend. No doubt it was some deep-seated masochistic tendency she had yet to analyze.

"You should go. I think you'd be surprised to see how everyone's changed."

That was the problem; Jayne *hadn't* changed. She still loved her books, and her life was even more organized now than it had been when she was in high school. Ten years after her graduation, she'd still be the object of their ridicule. "I don't know what I'm going to do," she announced, hoping to put an end to the discussion.

Hours later, at her apartment, Jayne sat holding a cup of green tea while she fantasized walking into the class reunion with a tall, strikingly handsome man. He would gaze into her eyes and bathe her in the warm glow of his love. And the girls of St. Mary's would sigh with envy.

The problem was where to find such a man. Not any man, but that special one who'd turn women's heads and make their hearts pound wildly.

Stretching out her legs and crossing her bare feet at the ankle, Jayne released a steady breath and conjured up her image of the perfect male. She'd read so many romances in her life, from the great classics to contemporary titles, that the vision of the ideal man—nothing like the one Gloria found so fascinating—appeared instantly in her mind. He would be tall, with thick, curly black hair and eyes of piercing blue. A man with sensitivity, desires and goals. Someone who'd accept her as she was…who'd think she was a special person. She wanted a man who could look past her imperfections and discover the woman inside.

A troubled frown creased her brow. She knew that for too many years, she'd buried herself in books, living her life vicariously through the escapades of others. The time had come to abandon her sedentary life and form a plan of action. Gloria was right—she wasn't going to find a man like that while sitting in her apartment. Drastic needs demanded drastic measures.

Rising to her feet Jayne took off her glasses and pulled the clasp from her hair. The curls cascaded over her shoulder, and she shook her head, freeing them. Plowing her fingers through her hair, she vowed to change. Or at least to try. Yes, she felt content with her life, but she had to admit there was something—or rather *someone*—missing.

Not until Jayne had left her apartment and was inside the elevator did it occur to her that she hadn't the slightest idea of where to meet men. Mentally she eliminated the spots she knew they congregated—places like taverns, pool halls and sports arenas. Her hero wasn't any of those types. A singles bar? Did people even use that term anymore? She'd never gone to one, but it sounded like just the place for a woman on a man-finding mission. Gloria would approve.

Jayne walked out of her building and ten minutes later, she sat in the corner of a cocktail lounge several blocks away. It had the rather obscure name of Soft Sam's. An embarrassed flush heated her face as she wondered what had possessed her to enter this place. Each time an eligible-looking man sauntered her way, she slid farther down into her chair, until she was so low her eyes were practically level with the table. The men in this bar were not the ones of which dreams were made. Thank goodness the room was as dark as a theater, with candles flickering atop the small round tables. The pulsing music, surly bartender and raised voices made her uncomfortable. Repeatedly she berated herself for doing anything as naive as coming here. Her parents would be aghast if they knew their sweet little girl was sitting in what they'd probably call a den of iniquity.

Forcing herself to straighten, Jayne's fingers coiled around her icy drink, and the chill extended halfway up her arm. According to what everyone said, the internet and a bar were the best ways to meet men. She was wary of resorting to online dating services, but she might have to consider it. And as for the bars… What her friends hadn't told her was the *type* of man who frequented such places. A glance around her confirmed that this was not where she belonged. Still, her goal was important. When she returned to Seattle, she was going to hold her head up high. There would be an incredible man on her arm, and she'd be the envy of every girl in her high school class. But if she had to lower her standards to this level, she'd rather not go back at all.

Her shoulders sagged with defeat. She'd been a fool to listen to Gloria. In her enthusiasm, Jayne had gone about this all wrong. A bar wasn't the place to begin her search; she should've realized that. *Books* would tell her what she needed to know. They'd never failed her yet, and she was astonished now that she could've forgotten something so basic.

Jayne squinted as she studied the men lined up at the polished bar. Even without her glasses, she could see that there wasn't a single man she'd consider taking to her reunion. The various women all seemed overdressed and desperate. The atmosphere in the bar was artificial, the surface gaiety forced and frenetic.

Coming here tonight had been a mistake. She felt embarrassed about letting down her hair and hiding her glasses in her purse—acting like someone she wasn't. The best thing to do now was to stand up and walk out of this place before someone actually approached her. But if it had taken courage to walk in, Jayne discovered that it took nearly as much to leave.

Unexpectedly the door of the lounge opened, dispersing a shaft of late-afternoon sunlight into the dim interior. Jayne pursed her lips, determined to escape. Turning to look at the latest arrival, she couldn't help staring. The situation was going from bad to intolerable. This man, whose imposing height was framed by the doorway, was the very one Gloria had been so excited about this afternoon. He quickly surveyed the room, and Jayne recognized him; he was definitely her neighbor. The few times they'd met in the elevator, Jayne had sensed his disapproval. She didn't know what she'd done to offend him, but he seemed singularly unimpressed by her, and Jayne had no idea why. On second thought, Jayne told herself, he'd probably never given her a moment's notice. In fact, he'd probably paid as much attention to her as she had to him—almost none.

His large physique intimidated her, and the sharp glance he gave her was just short of unfriendly. He was more intriguing than good-looking. Though she knew that some women, like Gloria, found him attractive, his blunt features were far too rugged to classify as handsome. His hair was black and thick, and he was well over six feet tall. He walked with a hint of aggression in every stride. Jayne doubted he'd back down from a confrontation. She didn't know anything about him—not even his name—but she would've thought this was the last place he'd look for a date. But then, anyone who glanced at her would assume she didn't belong here, either. And she didn't.

Standing up, Jayne squared her shoulders and pushed back her chair while she studied the pattern on the carpet. Without raising her eyes, she fastened her raincoat and tucked her purse strap over her shoulder. The sooner she got out of this regrettable place, the better. She'd prefer to make her escape without attracting his attention, although with her hair down and without her glasses, it was unlikely that he'd recognize her.

Unfortunately her action caught his eye and he paused just inside the bar, watching her. Jayne hated the superior glare that burned straight through her. Blazing color moved up her neck and into her pale cheeks, but she refused to give him the satisfaction of lowering her gaze.

Jayne walked decisively toward the exit, which he was partially blocking. Something danced briefly in his dark blue eyes and she swallowed nervously. Slowly he stepped aside, but not enough to allow her to pass. The hard set of his mouth drew her attention. Her determined eyes met his. Brows as richly dark as his ebony hair rose slightly, and she saw a glimmer of arrogant amusement on his face.

"Well, well. If it isn't Miss Prim and Proper."

Jayne knew her expression must be horrified—he *had* recognized her—but she gritted her teeth, unwilling to acknowledge him. "If you'll excuse me, please."

"Of course," he murmured. He grinned as he gave her the necessary room. Jayne felt like running, her heart pounding as if she already had.

Humiliated, she hurried past him and stopped outside to hold her hand over her heart. As fast as her fingers would cooperate, she took her glasses from her purse. What on earth would he think of her being in a place like this? She didn't look like her normal self, but that hadn't fooled this sharp-eyed man. If he said something to her when they met again, she'd have an excuse planned.

She brushed the hair from her face and trekked down the sidewalk. He wouldn't say anything, she told herself. To imagine he'd even give her a second's thought would be overreacting. The only words he'd ever said to her had been that one taunting remark in the bar. It was unlikely that he'd strike up a conversation with her now. Especially since he so obviously found her laughable…

The following day at lunch, Jayne ordered Wednesday's roast-beef sandwich while Gloria chatted happily. "I've got the books on my desk."

"I only hope no one saw you take them."

"Not a soul," her friend said. "They look promising, particularly the one called *Eight Easy Steps to Meeting a Man.*"

"If you want, I'll pass it to you when I'm finished," Jayne offered.

"I just might take you up on that," Gloria surprised her by saying. Divorced for several years, she dated even less than Jayne did. "Don't act so shocked. I've been feeling the maternal urge lately. It would be nice to find a man and start a family."

The roast beef felt like a lead weight in the pit of Jayne's stomach. "Yes, it would," she agreed with a sigh. The worst thing about the lack of a husband was not having children. She always enjoyed them, and as the children's librarian she spent her days with other people's kids.

"I take it you've reconsidered my idea," Gloria continued.

"It might be worth a try." Jayne was much too embarrassed by her misadventure at the bar to say anything to her friend about it.

"You know, if that *was* your neighbor yesterday, you don't need to look too hard."

As far as Jayne was concerned, she never wanted to see *him* again.

"I suppose," she mumbled. "But I'd like to find a man with more…culture."

"Up to you," Gloria said, shaking her head.

The same afternoon, her arms loaded with borrowed books on meeting men, Jayne stepped onto the elevator—and came face-to-face with her neighbor. Her first instinct was to turn around and dash out again. His eyes darkened with challenge as they met hers, and she refused to give him the satisfaction of letting him know how much he unnerved her. With all the dignity she could muster, Jayne moved to the rear of the elevator, feeling unreasonably angry with Gloria.

His eyes flickered over her flushed face. Reaction more than need prompted her to push up her glasses, and she struggled to disguise her nervousness with deep breaths.

"Ninth floor, right?" he murmured.

"Yes." Her voice came out sounding like a frog with laryngitis. She'd been so flustered she hadn't even punched in her floor number. Hugging the books to her chest, she kept her eyes on the orange light that indicated the numbers above the elevator door.

"I have to admit it was a surprise seeing you last night," he said smoothly, clearly enjoying her discomfort.

Hot color flashed from her face like a neon light. "I beg your pardon?" If she could have gotten away with it, she would have given him a frown of utter bewilderment, as if to say she had no idea what he was talking about. But Jayne had never been a good liar. Her eye would twitch and her upper lip quiver. Fooling her parents had been impossible; she wouldn't dream of trying to deceive this way-too-perceptive man.

"I didn't know prim and proper little girls went into bars like that."

Clearing her throat, she sent him a look of practiced disdain usually reserved for teenagers she caught necking in the upstairs portion of the library. "Let me assure you, I am not the type of woman who frequents such places." She wished she didn't sound quite so stilted, and for the twentieth time in as many hours, she lamented her foolishness. Her back and shoulders ached with the effort to stand there rigidly. If he knew anything about body language, he'd get her message.

"You're telling me," he said and chuckled softly. Mischief glimmered in his eyes, and with an effort Jayne looked away.

"You must have mistaken me for someone else," she told him sternly, disgusted with herself for lying. Immediately her right eye started to twitch, and her grip on the books tightened. The elevator had never made its ascent more slowly. She finally relaxed when it came to a grinding halt on her floor. The minute the door opened she rushed out. In her haste, her shoe snagged on the thick carpet and propelled her forward. With a cry of alarm she went staggering into the wide hallway, the books flying from her arms. The wall opposite the elevator halted her progress when she was catapulted into it, catching herself with open palms.

"Are you okay?" A gentle hand touched her shoulder. She turned and gave a convulsive jerk of her head as humiliation robbed her of speech. The dark eyes that had been probing hers were now filled with concern.

"I—I'm fine," she managed, wiping a shaking hand over her eyes, hoping to wake and find that this entire episode was a nightmare.

"Let me help you with your books."

"No!" she cried breathlessly and scrambled to gather up her collection. The last thing she wanted was his pity. He'd made his feelings known. He didn't think much of her, but he was entitled to his opinion—and his fun. "I'm fine. Just leave. Please. That's all I want." She was only getting what she deserved for behaving so irrationally and going into that stupid bar in the first place. Now she'd made everything worse. Never had she felt more embarrassed, and it was all her own fault.

Her hands shook as she fumbled with the clasp of her purse and took out her apartment key. She didn't turn around, but she could feel his eyes on her. Her whole body was trembling by the time she entered the apartment. She shut the door and leaned against it, closing her eyes.

Several minutes passed before she was able to remove her coat and pile the books on her kitchen table. She hung her coat in the hall closet, went into her bedroom and set her purse on the dresser. Organization gave guidance and balance to Jayne's life, and there was never a time she'd needed it more.

The teapot was filled and heating on the stove. Trying to put the unfortunate encounter in the elevator out of her mind, she looked through the books she'd brought home.

Finding a Man in Thirty Days or Less was the first book in the stack. That one sounded helpful. She glanced at the next one, *How to Get a Man Interested in You*. These self-help books would provide all the advice she needed, Jayne mused. And if they worked for her, she'd pass them on to Gloria later. As always, Jayne would find the answer in books. The next title made her smile. *How to Convince a Man to Fall in Love with You Forever.* Nice thought, but all she really cared about right now was the one night of her class reunion.

She heard knocking and lifted her head abruptly, then slowly moved to the door, her legs weighted by reluctance. She was acquainted with only a few people in Portland. There was no one, other than Gloria, whom she'd call a good friend.

"Who is it?" she asked.

"Riley Chambers."

"Who?"

"Your neighbor."

Groaning inwardly, Jayne closed her eyes, dreading the thought of seeing him again for any reason. Hesitantly she turned the lock. "I'm perfectly fine," she said, opening the door.

"I thought you might be looking for this." He leaned against the doorjamb, leafing indolently through the pages of a hardcover book.

Jayne's breath jammed in her throat as she struggled not to grab it from his hands. Noting the title, *How to Pick Up a Man*, she felt her face redden.

Brilliant little flecks of light showed in his eyes, which glinted with humor. "Listen, Ms. Gilbert, if you're so interested in finding yourself a man, I'd advise you to stay away from bars like Soft Sam's. They're not good places for little girls like you."

She frowned. "How do you know my name? Oh—the building directory."

He nodded.

"Well, *Mr. Chambers,* if you've come to make fun of me..."

"I haven't." The expression in his eyes hardened. "I don't want to ever see you there again."

"You have no business telling me where I can and cannot go." Her hands knotted at her sides in outrage. He was right, of course, but she had no intention of letting him know that. She jerked the book from his hand and when he stepped away, she slammed the door.

2

Riley dropped his arms and grinned at the door that had closed in his face. So prim little Ms. Gilbert had a fiery temper. She might act like a shy country mouse, but his opinion of her went up several notches. With that well-tamed hair and those glasses, she hadn't left much of an impression the few times he'd seen her in the elevator. Her air of blind trust and hopeful expectation made her look as though she'd stepped out of the pages of a Victorian novel. She'd better watch out, or she'd be wolves' prey. He'd wanted to tell her to open her eyes and look around her. She was too vulnerable for this day and age. This was the twenty-first century, not some romantic daydream.

It'd surprised him to see her in Soft Sam's. Admittedly, she'd been a fish out of water. She was absolutely correct; it was none of his business where she went, but he felt oddly protective of her.

Ms. J. Gilbert—he didn't even know her first name—was as untouched and naive as they come. All sugar and spice and everything nice. Rubbing a hand over the back of his neck, Riley sighed impatiently. He didn't have time to think about a woman—any woman. But a smile formed as he recalled the fire that had flared in her eyes when she'd grabbed that book from his hands. She had spunk. Briefly he wondered what other treasures were waiting to be discovered in her. Riley gave himself a mental shake. Years of following his instincts told him that women like this could be trouble for men like him. Besides, his days were filled with enough conflict. He didn't need a woman distracting him from the problems at hand. Maybe when this business with Priestly was over, he'd have the time— No! The best thing he could do was forget Ms. Sugar and Spice.

If she was in the market for a husband—which she obviously was—there were better men. She was far too wide-eyed and innocent for him. In the end he'd only hurt her. She deserved someone who hadn't become cynical, who wasn't hardened by life.

Jayne stared out at the rain that rolled down the side of the grimy bus window. A low gray fog hovered over the street. After five years in Portland, she was accustomed to gloomy springs. The paper lay folded in her lap; the headlines were the same day after day, although the names and places changed. War, death, disease and destruction. She saw that a prominent state official had been questioned by the FBI about ties to the underworld. Jayne wondered if Senator Priestly was one of the officials who'd visited the library recently. She'd been impressed with the group on the tour; there had been a number of men Gloria would have approved of. But then, that could mean neither Gloria nor Jayne was a good judge of character.

Riley Chambers was a perfect example of their poor judgment. He might not have been impressed with her, but from the first she'd thought he was...intriguing. A man of mystery. Despite the fact that they'd barely glanced at each other whenever they'd met in the elevator, she *might* have been interested in getting to know him. Her current opinion was decidedly different. He had a lot of nerve telling her not to go back to Soft Sam's! If it was such a terrible place, what was he doing there? The next time she saw him, she'd make a point of asking him exactly that.

Agitated, she pulled the cord to indicate that she wanted to get off at the next stop. She tucked the newspaper under her arm and hurried to the rear of the bus.

Avoiding a puddle, she leapt from the bottom step to the sidewalk and paused to open her umbrella. Riley Chambers didn't deserve another minute of her consideration. He'd made his views of her obvious. He'd called her a little girl. She had a good mind to inform him that at five-seven she could hardly be described as *little.* Even now his taunting comment rankled. Jayne had the feeling that he'd said it just to get a reaction out of her. Well, he'd succeeded, and that should please him.

Gloria was waiting for her when Jayne arrived at the library.

"Well, what did the books say?" her friend asked as soon as Jayne had put her bag inside her desk.

"Plenty. Did you know one of the best places to meet men is in the supermarket? Can you see me sauntering up to someone in the frozen-food section and suggesting we have children together?"

Gloria's laughter floated around the room. "That may be worth a try. What other place did they suggest?"

"The art gallery."

"That's perfect for you!"

Jayne sighed and tucked a stray curl into her tightly coiled chignon. "I suppose."

"You've got to show more enthusiasm than this, m'dear." Opening the paper on Jayne's desk, Gloria ran down a list of current city events.

"The Portland Art Gallery is showing work by one of your favorite artists—Delacroix. I bet you were planning on attending, anyway. Now all you need to do is keep your eyes peeled for any handsome, eligible men."

"I don't know, Gloria. I can't even catch a cold, let alone a man. Especially a handsome one."

"You can do it."

"Now you sound like a cheerleader," Jayne moaned, not sure she wanted any of this.

"You need me," Gloria insisted. "Look upon me as your own personal cheering section. All I ask is that you think of God, country and your best friend as you stroll through that gallery."

"What?"

"Well, if this works for you, then I may give it a try."

Jayne had her doubts. Over the past several years, she'd visited a variety of galleries and had yet to see a single attractive man. However, she hadn't actually been on the lookout.

"Well?" Gloria stared at her with her hands positioned challengingly on her hips. "Are you or are you not going to the Delacroix show?"

"Gloria…" Jayne said, hedging.

"Jayne!"

"Fine, I'll go."

"When?"

"Tomorrow afternoon."

Although she might have agreed to Gloria's suggestion, Jayne wasn't sure she was doing the right thing. All day she fretted about the coming art show. By five she was a nervous wreck. Feeling that she needed the confidence a new outfit would give her, Jayne decided to go shopping after work. This was no easy decision. She equated clothes-shopping with trauma. Nothing ever seemed to fit well, and she dreaded standing in front of those three-way mirrors that revealed every imperfection.

At the end of the day, Jayne walked down the library steps, balking at the thought of this expedition. Sheer force of will led her into The Galleria, the downtown shopping center, where she found a navy wool dress with side pockets and long sleeves. The dress didn't do much for her, but it was the first one that fit without looking like a burlap bag flung over her head. Feeling somewhat relieved, she paid the saleslady and headed for the escalator that would take her to the transit mall. On her way out Jayne noticed a young woman draped on the arm of a much older man. She batted her long lashes and paused at an expensive jeweler's window display.

"Last month's emerald is so, so lonely," Jayne heard the woman's soft voice purr.

"We can't have that, can we, darling," the older man murmured as he steered the blonde inside the store.

The episode left a bad taste in Jayne's mouth, and she wondered if the woman had met her sugar daddy in Safeway. It was beyond her imagination that men would be attracted to women so shallow. If this was the type of behavior men sought, Jayne simply couldn't do it.

Saturday afternoon, wearing her new dress, Jayne strolled bravely through the Portland Art Gallery. Wandering around, she saw a man standing against a wall; he seemed to be more interested in the patrons than the art. Gathering her nerve and her resolve, she stood in front of a Delacroix painting,

Horse Frightened by a Storm, the most famous of the paintings on loan from the Seattle Art Museum. Jayne had long been an admirer of Delacroix's work and knew it well. He was, in her opinion, the greatest of the Romantic painters.

Again she studied the man, sizing him up without, she hoped, being too obvious. He was attractive, although it was difficult to tell for sure without her glasses. From what she could see, he looked approachable. Her hands felt clammy, and she resisted the urge to wipe them dry on the sides of her dress. Clearly she didn't know much about luring a man. But neither was she totally ignorant. She *had* dated before and had even felt the faint stirrings of desire. But her relationships usually died a natural death from lack of nourishment. Sad as it seemed, Jayne preferred her books.

She moved across the marble floor toward the man. Coming closer, she confirmed that he was attractive in a slender, refined way—not like Riley Chambers. Just the thought of *that* arrogant man brought a flash of hot color to her cheeks.

Trying to ignore the tension that knotted her stomach, Jayne mentally reviewed the books she'd read. Each had repeatedly stated that she couldn't wait for the man to take the initiative. One book had gone so far as to list ways of starting a conversation with a prospective love interest. Fumbling her purse clasp, Jayne pulled out the list of ideas she'd jotted down. She could ask for change for the parking meter, but she didn't own a car and lying would make her eye twitch. She discarded that plan. Next on the list was pretending not to notice the targeted male and accidentally-on-purpose walking straight into him. Too clichéd, Jayne decided. She wanted to be more original. The book had suggested asking him what time it was. Okay, she could try that.

Dropping the list in her purse, she took three strides toward the blonde man and did an abrupt about-face. She was wearing a watch! How could she ask the time when there was a watch on her wrist? She'd look like an idiot!

Jayne's heart felt as though it was pounding right out of her chest. Who would've supposed that anything this simple could be so difficult? Sighing, she remembered the look Gloria had given her as she hustled her out the door of the library. If she didn't make her move, Gloria would never let her live it down.

Eyes closed, she took slow, even breaths until calm reason returned. This whole idea was ludicrous. Dressing up and loitering around an art gallery hoping to meet men was so contrary to her painfully shy personality that she could hardly believe she was doing it. The girls of St. Mary's wouldn't be impressed by such desperate measures. Who did Jayne think she was going to fool? She'd turned out exactly as they'd predicted, and there was nothing she could do to change that.

"Excuse me." A male voice interrupted her thoughts. "Do you happen to have the time?"

Jayne's eyes flew open. "The time," she repeated.

The man Jayne had noticed came to stand beside her. Instantly her eyes went to her wrist. He must have read the same book!

"I'm afraid I forgot to replace the battery in my watch," he said with a sheepish smile, dispelling that notion.

"It's nearly three," she stammered, holding out her arm so he could examine her watch.

"I saw you were looking at the Delacroix painting of the horse."

"Yes," Jayne murmured. It'd worked! It had really worked. She smiled up at him brightly, remembering the adoring look on the young woman's face as she'd stared into the eyes of her sugar daddy.

"By the way, my name's Mark Bauer."

"Jayne Gilbert," she said and offered him her hand. Recalling "darling's" reactions, Jayne lowered her lashes alluringly so that they brushed the arch of her cheek.

"He's my favorite artist—Eugene Delacroix." Mark gestured at the painting with one hand.

Ferdinand Victor Eugene Delacroix, Jayne added mentally.

"When Delacroix died in 1863 he left behind a legacy of eight hundred oil paintings," Mark lectured.

And twice as many watercolors, Jayne said—but only to herself. "Is that a fact?" she simpered.

Warming to his subject, Mark continued by explaining the familiar painting, pointing out the colors chosen by the artist to establish mood. He went on to describe how particular lines in the work expressed certain feelings. Jayne batted her lashes at Mark and pretended to be impressed by his knowledge. She wished she had her glasses on so she could see more clearly what he looked like. From a distance he'd appeared attractive enough; close up he was a little blurry.

By the time Jayne was on the bus for the return trip to her apartment, she was thoroughly disgusted with herself. She wasn't any better than that syrupy blonde clinging to the arm of her generous benefactor. She was sure she knew much more about art than Mark did and yet she'd played dumb. He'd apparently done a quick search on Google to collect some basic facts, then spun them into the art history lecture she'd just heard. And she'd pretended to be awed....

Something was definitely wrong with her. She'd always been such a sensible woman. It astonished her that Mark hadn't seen through her act. She wasn't convinced she even liked the man. He spoke for half an hour on a subject he obviously knew very little about while Jayne continued to play dumb and batted her lashes every ten seconds. She supposed he was hoping to impress her, but, in fact, had accomplished just the opposite. The whole production had been pointless—for both of them. He'd asked for her phone number, but she figured she'd never hear from him again.

A walk in the park helped her clear away the confusion that clouded her perspective. She'd thought she'd known what she wanted. Suddenly she was unsure. Knights riding around on white horses, looking for women to escort to class reunions, seemed to be few and far between these days. But then, she didn't know much about knights and even less about men. Quite possibly, each and every one of them would turn out to be like Riley Chambers. The thought caused a shiver of apprehension to race over her skin and she realized for the first time that a slow drizzling rain had begun to fall. Of course, she'd left her umbrella at home. And of course there were no cabs in sight.

Burying her hands deep in her pockets, she quickened her pace. She was three blocks from her building when the clouds burst open in sheets of rain that pelted the sidewalk relentlessly. Jayne was drenched within seconds. Rivulets of water ran down the back of her neck until her hair fell in limp strands. When she stepped into the lobby, her glasses fogged, and her new dress was plastered to her. She felt the overwhelming desire to sneeze. This had been the most miserable day of her life. Not only had she behaved like an idiot over the first man to fall in with her schemes, but she'd been foolish enough to get caught in a downpour. The only thing worse would be to run into Riley Chambers.

No sooner had the thought formed than the man materialized.

Jayne groaned inwardly and stepped into the open elevator, praying he'd take another. The way her luck was going, Jayne should have known better.

★ ★ ★

Riley followed her inside and stared blatantly at the half-drowned country mouse, a small puddle of water forming at her feet. He couldn't resist a tiny smile as he studied her. Ms. J. Gilbert was badly in need of someone to watch over her. He hadn't seen her in the past couple of days, and it hadn't taken long to realize she was avoiding him. That was fine. She brought out his protective instincts with those wide, innocent eyes, which was something he couldn't really afford. She disturbed him, and innumerable times in the past two days thoughts of her had flitted through his head. Casually he'd tossed them aside, chalking up his curiosity to concern that she might go back to Soft Sam's.

Jayne turned her head away. "Go ahead and laugh," she told him as they began their slow ascent. "I know you're dying to make fun of me."

Riley scowled briefly. Suddenly she reminded him of a cat backed into a corner, its fur bristling and claws unsheathed. Riley had no desire to antagonize her. Instead, he felt the urge to comfort her—and that astonished him. "Are you still angry because I saw the title of your book?" he asked.

"Furious." She slipped her steamed glasses to the end of her nose so she could see him above the frames.

"I didn't mean to make fun of you." She looked vulnerable, and he ignored the impulse to ask her first name. He didn't see her as a Jessica or a Jennifer. Possibly a Jacqueline.

"Why not make fun of me?" she flared. "Everyone else has…all my life. People have always thought I'm some kind of weirdo. I like books. I like to read." He saw tears in her eyes, and she twisted around so he couldn't look at her.

The instant the elevator doors parted, she escaped, her shoulders back, her head held high, and glided down the hall to her apartment.

Riley went to his own door, walking slowly. He withdrew the keys from his pocket with a frown, then wearily turned the lock and stepped into his dark apartment. A flick of the wall switch flooded the room with cheerless light. He threw his raincoat over the back of a chair and went into the kitchen to put a frozen dinner in the microwave.

Once again the little mouse, as he still thought of her, had fired to life, turning on him. Even cold and miserable, she'd walked out of the elevator with her chin raised. Her back was ramrod straight, and she moved with as much dignity as any princess. He smiled as he recalled the way her wet dress had clung to her, revealing full breasts, round hips and a trim waist. She had long legs, nicely shaped. He couldn't imagine why she chose to hide behind those generic business suits. The dress she wore today was the first he could remember seeing her in. The dark navy color wasn't right for her. With that chestnut hair and those large honey-brown eyes she should wear lighter shades. At least she'd had her hair down, which was a definite improvement. Although it had been wet and clinging, he just knew it was soft. Silky. He wanted to lift it in his fingers and—

Slumping into a chair, Riley shook his head. He didn't like the things Ms. J. Gilbert brought to the surface in him. It had been a lot of years since he'd given a woman this much thought. What he felt was pity, he assured himself. She was lonely. For that matter, so was he.

The microwave made its annoying sound, and he removed the tray, wondering what the country mouse was having for her dinner.

Holding a tissue to her nose, Jayne sneezed loudly. Her eyes itched, and her throat felt scratchy. A glance at her watch told her it would be another three long hours before she could go home and soak in a hot tub. Thankfully Gloria had offered to handle storytime today. While the preschoolers huddled around her friend, Jayne sat at her desk and cut out brightly colored letters for the June bulletin board. Her class reunion was only seven weeks away. Like the ominous approach of a thunderstorm, defeat settled over her. She wouldn't go. It was as simple as that.

"Could you tell me where you keep the biographies?"

She raised her eyes, and they met a familiar blue gaze. Riley Chambers… She clutched the scissors so hard that her thumb ached. "Pardon?" Stunned, she couldn't remember what he'd asked.

"The biographies."

In an effort to stall for time, she put the scissors down. Riley Chambers was on her turf now. "They're directly to your left."

"Could you show me where they are?"

"Yes, of course, but you look like a man who knows his way around."

"Not in this library," he mumbled.

She stood, pausing to push the glasses up onto her nose, then led him to the section he'd requested. "The area to the right is the children's fiction department for ages three to six. If you like, we'll stop here so you can browse."

Riley ignored that. He'd had one heck of a time finding out where she worked. Their apartment manager had to have the most closed mouth of anyone he'd ever known. Generally speaking, he approved of that, but with a lie about undefined but urgent "legal matters," he'd managed to get his answer. "The name Jayne suits you," he said. He'd seen the nameplate on her desk.

"As long as you aren't Tarzan."

"I don't live in a jungle."

"But you obviously speak the language." A smile tugged at the corner of her mouth.

After delivering Riley to the section he'd requested, Jayne watched as he took down several volumes and flipped through the pages. She studied him with helpless fascination. Riley Chambers was a cynical man who looked at the world through wary eyes. Nonetheless, she had a glimmer—more than a glimmer—of his sensuality. Horrified at her thoughts, Jayne quickly returned to her desk. She resumed her task, doing her best to pretend he wasn't anywhere around.

"I'd like to check these out," Riley said, setting two thick volumes on the corner of her desk.

"Do you have a library card?"

"Yeah. It's tricky borrowing books without one."

"You don't need me for that." Jayne didn't know why he'd come. He probably wanted to throw her off guard. That wasn't going to work. Not in the library.

"I assumed that as a public employee you'd be willing to help me."

"Books are checked out at the front desk."

"I want you to do it."

"Why?"

"Why not?"

"I'm the children's librarian."

"That doesn't surprise me. You look like someone who'd prefer the world of make-believe and happy ever after."

"Is that so wrong?" she replied, her temper flaring.

"Just as long as you don't expect to find your heroes in a sleazy bar."

Color heated Jayne's already flushed face, and she glanced around, wondering if Gloria had heard him. Gloria raised her head long enough to wink encouragingly. "Why are you here?" Jayne whispered.

"You confuse me," he admitted after a minute. "Or maybe *disturb* would be a better word."

"Why?"

"I don't know. Probably because you look like an accident waiting to happen."

"I don't need a fairy godfather." Not when Gloria insisted on waving a magic wand over her head every morning.

"I know what you're after," he whispered back. "I saw the book, remember?"

Jayne bit her lip. Riley was playing with her, amusing himself at her expense. "I'm not looking for a husband. I… only need a man for one night."

"So that's it." The corner of his mouth edged up.

"No!" she cried at his knowing look. Her cry attracted the attention of the entire room. The library went silent as heads turned toward them. Embarrassed half to death, Jayne lowered her chin and pleaded, "Would you please just go away?"

Riley abandoned his books and stalked outside, berating himself with every step. Talk about stupid! What kind of game did he think he was playing? Earlier that afternoon the workload had gotten to him, and when he couldn't tolerate it anymore, he'd leaned back in his chair and closed his eyes. A picture of the alluring Jayne Gilbert, all sugar and spice, had immediately entered his mind. He didn't know why she fascinated him so much. Maybe it was because of her innocence, her gentle beauty and the goodness he sensed in her.

After a day like this one, he needed some of that innocence. It'd taken him the better part of an hour to get the information about her job out of the building manager. Discovering she was a librarian hadn't come as any surprise. It fit his image of her. But showing up here hadn't been one of his more brilliant ideas. He hadn't meant to browbeat Jayne and he'd been amused by her witty comebacks. She'd held her own.

Feeling angry and frustrated with himself, Riley went back to the office. He'd apologize to her later. Ms. Gilbert deserved that much.

By the time all the paperwork had been cleared from his desk, it was close to eight. He rubbed a hand over his face, feeling more tired than he'd been in years. He was getting too old for this work. Grabbing his jacket from the back of his chair, Riley tossed his empty paper cup into the garbage can. He hadn't had anything but coffee since early afternoon. The way things were going in this madhouse, it was a miracle he didn't have an ulcer.

Once he'd parked in the apartment lot and headed across the street to the building, thoughts of Jayne flooded his mind. He sighed, unable to disperse them.

The elevator stopped on the ninth floor. He stood for a full minute outside her door before deciding it would be better to get this apology over with. He knocked once, loudly.

Jayne was miserable. Her throat felt like fire every time she swallowed. Her head ached, and the last thing she wanted was company. Housecoat cinched tight around her waist, she unlocked the door.

"You again?" she whispered, hardly caring. "What's the matter, didn't you have enough fun earlier?"

Riley disregarded her comment. "You look awful."

"Thanks."

"Are you sick?"

"No," she answered hoarsely and coughed. "I enjoy looking like this."

Without an invitation, Riley walked into her apartment and demanded, "Have you seen a doctor?"

Jayne stood by the door, holding it open and staring pointedly into the empty hallway. "Make yourself at home," she said with heavy sarcasm. As it was, she'd spent a good part of the afternoon explaining Riley's visit to Gloria. Somehow her friend refused to believe it was a coincidence that he'd come into the library. According to Gloria, Riley was definitely interested in Jayne. That suggestion only made her laugh.

"You might have a fever. Have you taken your temperature?"

"I was about to do that." The man appeared oblivious to her lack of welcome. She closed the door and turned around, leaning against it.

"Sit down," he said.

"Are you always this bossy?"

"Always."

Too weak to argue, Jayne did as he said.

"Where's your thermometer?"

She pointed to the kitchen counter and tucked her bare feet underneath her. "Why do you keep pestering me?"

He didn't respond, seemingly intent on reading the thermometer. Impatiently he shook it.

"Open your mouth," he ordered, and when she complied, he gently inserted it under her tongue.

Curious, Jayne followed his progress as he paced the carpet in front of her, checking his watch every fifteen seconds. He picked up a book from the coffee table, read the title and arched his brows. Replacing the book, he resumed his pacing.

"I came because I wanted to apologize for this afternoon. I had no business, uh, pestering you."

"Then why did you?" she mumbled, holding the thermometer in her mouth as she spoke.

"I don't know." His hand sliced the air. "Probably for the reason I mentioned earlier. You…disturb me."

"Why?" she asked again.

"If I knew the answer to that, I wouldn't be here."

"Then go away."

"I thought misery loved company."

"Not this misery."

"Too bad." Carefully he withdrew the thermometer and examined it.

"Well? What does it say? Will I live?"

"A little over ninety-nine. Got any aspirin?"

Jayne shook her head. "I'm never sick."

He studied her skeptically, and Jayne waited for a harangue that never came.

"I'll be back." He left her door slightly ajar, and Jayne felt too miserable to get up and lock him out.

Riley returned a couple of minutes later, his arms loaded with a variety of objects: soup can, a box of tissues, bottle of aspirin, frozen lemonade and the paper.

"Are you moving in?" she asked irritably. The other day she'd assumed that she couldn't meet a man in her own living room. Riley was proving her wrong.

He scowled and stalked wordlessly into her tiny kitchen. What an odd man he was, Jayne thought. He obviously felt *something* for her if he was going to all this trouble, and yet he didn't seem to want her company.

After a moment Jayne decided to investigate. Struggling to her feet, she paused in the middle of the room to sneeze and blow her nose.

Riley stuck his head around the corner. "Sit," he ordered, giving her a ferocious glare.

Jayne glared back at him. "What are you doing in my kitchen?"

"Making dinner. Don't be ungrateful."

"I'm not hungry," she said, advancing a step. Riley would never be able to figure out her organizational methods. He'd look in her cupboards and claim that even her groceries were filed under the Dewey decimal system.

"Is it feed a cold and starve a fever or the other way around?" Riley asked next.

He made quite a sight with his white shirtsleeves rolled halfway up his arms and an apron tied high around his waist. The top two buttons of his shirt were opened to reveal dark curling hair. Jayne couldn't help smiling.

"Now what's so funny?" His own smile was lazy.

"You."

"What?" He glanced down at his flowered apron. "What's the matter, haven't you ever seen a man working in the kitchen?"

"Not in mine."

"Then it's time you did." He turned away from her and took a saucepan from the top of the stove, then opened and closed her cupboard doors until he located glasses and bowls. "You should smile more often," he said casually as he worked, pouring equal amounts of soup into the wide bowls.

"I've got a cold. My head hurts, my throat feels raw, and there's a crazy man in my kitchen, ordering me around. Give me a day or two, and I'll find the humor in all of this." She didn't add that she had seven weeks to come up with a man who'd make heads turn when he walked into a room.

"Sit."

"Again? See what I mean?" she complained, but she did as he asked, pulling out the high-backed oak chair.

Riley brought her a bowl of hot soup, a steaming mug and two aspirin. Jerking the apron from around his waist, he took the chair across from her.

"What is it?" she asked, staring at the steaming bowl.

"Chicken noodle soup." He pointed to the bowl, then the mug. "And hot lemonade."

"Couldn't you be more original than that?"

"Not on short notice."

"Are you eating here, too?"

"What's the matter? Do you expect the help to eat in the kitchen?"

Jayne smiled again. "Why are you doing this?"

Riley shrugged. "Because I owe you. I didn't mean to make fun of you earlier."

"When?" To her way of thinking, he'd done it more than once.

"This afternoon. I shouldn't have come in and given you a hard time. I want to apologize."

"If you're in the mood to make amends, you might mention the other night, as well."

"No." He scowled briefly, letting his eyes drop to her lips. "You brought that on yourself."

Jayne set her spoon aside. "I don't know if I like you. I've never met anyone who confuses me the way you do."

"Then that makes two of us. Listen, I've lived most of my life without women, and I don't want a prim little country mouse messing things up at this late date." The words were harsher than he'd intended, but Jayne was stronger than her soft, vulnerable manner had led him to believe. She had an inner strength he was only beginning to recognize.

Jayne bristled, her hand gripping the spoon tightly. "I didn't invite you here." She'd have a heck of a time explaining this to Gloria if her friend ever found out.

"I'm aware of that."

The phone rang, jerking Jayne's attention across the room.

"Do you want me to answer it?" Riley asked.

"No," she answered, rising from her chair. "I will." She reached the phone on the fourth ring and grabbed it. "Hello," she said, slightly out of breath.

"Jayne, it's Mark Bauer. Do you remember me? We met at the art gallery last Saturday."

3

"Hello, Mark, of course I remember you." Jayne leaned against the chair, trying to ignore Riley, who was standing behind her.

"You don't sound the same," Mark continued.

"I've got a cold." That had to be the understatement of the year.

"Not a bad one, I hope."

"Oh, no, I'll be fine in a day or two." Muffled sounds coming from behind Jayne made her tense. Riley was either pacing or fooling around in her kitchen. She wondered if he'd discovered how organized she was. Even her soup cans were stored in alphabetical order.

"Do you think you'd be well enough to go to a movie with me Friday night?" Mark asked.

Jayne was stunned. After behaving in such a ridiculous way, she hadn't expected to hear from Mark again. Least of all to have him ask her out. "I'd like that, thank you."

"Shall we say seven, then?"

"Seven will be fine."

Jayne replaced the receiver and stared at the phone, dumbfounded. A prickly feeling attacked the base of her neck and slithered down her spine. The dumb act had worked once, but she doubted she could maintain it for any length of time. Keeping it up for the seven weeks until her class reunion would be impossible. And once they were in Seattle, she couldn't suddenly tell him: *Surprise! It was all an act. I'm really brilliant.* "I shouldn't have agreed to go." Jayne was shocked to realize she'd spoken aloud.

"Why not?"

Feeling a bit sick to her stomach, Jayne turned to face Riley, who was standing beside the kitchen table. One large hand rested over the back of the polished oak chair. Their eyes met. "I...don't know exactly what he looks like," she admitted honestly, but that wasn't the reason for her hesitancy. Someone like Riley would have instantly seen through her act. Unfortunately—or fortunately—Mark wasn't Riley.

"What do you mean?"

"When we met, I wasn't wearing my glasses." Jayne vowed that if Riley so much as snickered, she'd ask him to leave.

"If wearing glasses bothers you, why don't you get contacts?" he asked matter-of-factly, reaching for his spoon. That night at Soft Sam's she hadn't worn her glasses, he remembered and stiffened.

"I've tried but I can't. My eye doctor recommended a book on how to use them, but..."

"It didn't help you?"

Jayne lowered her hands to her lap. "Sadly, no."

"Where did you meet this Mark guy?" He struggled to keep his voice calm and disinterested. He'd been trained not to reveal interest or emotion. It should come easy, but with Jayne, for some reason, it didn't.

"At the art gallery last Saturday." She caught a sneeze with her napkin just in time. "One of those books said that was a good place to meet men."

Relaxing, Riley tried his first spoonful of lukewarm chicken noodle soup. He might not be an inventive chef, but this meager meal would take the edge off his hunger. The fact that Jayne was sitting across from him with her quiet wit and seductive eyes made even soup more appealing.

They ate in silence, but it was a companionable one as if they were at ease with each other for the first time. Jayne wasn't hungry, but she managed to finish her soup. Riley insisted on doing the dishes, and she didn't argue too strenuously. There were only a couple of bowls and a saucepan that he rinsed and tucked in the dishwasher.

"Is there anything else I can do for you?" Riley asked, standing by the door.

Jayne smiled shyly and shook her head. "No, you've been very kind. Thank you." He was an attractive man, and she didn't know why he was paying her so much attention. His concern was so unexpected that she didn't know how to categorize it. They were neighbors, and it would be good to have a friend in the apartment complex. Riley was probably thinking the same thing, Jayne mused. Their relationship was mutually beneficial.

"I'll see you later," he said.

"Later," she agreed.

The next morning, Jayne woke feeling a hundred percent better. The ache in her throat was gone, as was the stiffness in her arms and legs. Declaring herself cured, she dressed for work, humming as she moved around the bedroom. For several days she'd been dreading the approach of summer and her class reunion, but this morning things looked brighter.

Mark had asked her out, and she was determined to keep his interest in her alive. That shouldn't be difficult with Gloria's coaching.

Although the day was predicted to be pleasantly warm, Jayne reached for her jacket on the way out the door. She half looked for Riley as she waited for the elevator, but she'd only seen him a few times in the mornings. Their paths didn't cross often. She would like to have told him how much better she felt and thank him again for his help.

Standing at the bus stop, she noticed that the clouds were breaking up. The air smelled fresh and springlike. Jayne had to remember that this was June, yet it felt more like April or early May. School would be out soon, and her section of the library would be busier than usual.

When a sleek black car pulled up by the curb, Jayne instinctively stepped back, then experienced a flush of pleasure when she recognized the driver.

Riley leaned across the front seat and opened the side door. "It might not be a good idea for you to stand out in the cold. I'll give you a ride downtown."

"I feel great this morning," she told him. "Thanks for the offer," she felt obliged to say, "but the bus will be here any minute."

Riley's grip tightened on the door handle. "I'll give you a ride if you want. The choice is yours." He said it without looking at her.

Jayne still didn't understand why he was so concerned about her health, but now wasn't the time to question his solicitude. She slid into the front seat, closed the door and fastened her seat belt. "You're going to spoil me, Mr. Chambers."

"I don't work far from you," he said, checking the side mirror before merging with the snarled traffic.

That explained why she and Gloria had seen him at lunchtime. Jayne studied him as he maneuvered the car. He might have offered her a ride, but he certainly didn't seem happy about it. His lips were pursed, and his forehead creased in a frown. Although traffic was heavy and sluggish, that didn't seem to be the reason for his impatience. She assumed it had something to do with her.

Jayne folded her hands in her lap, regretting that she'd accepted his invitation. She couldn't understand why he'd offer her a ride when her presence was clearly upsetting to him.

"You're quiet this morning," Riley commented, glancing her way.

"I was afraid to say anything." Jayne focused her gaze on her laced fingers. "You looked like you'd bite my head off if I did."

"When has that ever stopped you?"

"Today."

Riley's frown grew, if anything, fiercer. "What made you think I was angry?"

"You look like you ate rattlesnakes for breakfast," she replied.

"I do? Now?"

A quick movement—what Jayne termed an "almost smile"—touched his mouth.

"Your face was all scrunched up," she said, "and your expression was terribly intense. I was wondering why you're giving me a ride when it's clear you don't want me in the car with you."

"Not want you in the car?" he repeated. "That's not it at all. I was just thinking about a problem…at the office."

"Then your thoughts must be deep and dark."

"They have been lately." His face softened as he averted his eyes from the traffic to briefly look at her. "Don't worry,

I've never been one to do anything unless it's exactly what I want."

Pleased by his response, Jayne relaxed and smiled. Riley was different from anyone she'd known before. Yet in certain ways they were alike. He was at ease with her quiet manner. In the past Jayne had felt it necessary to make small talk with men. Doing that had been contrary to her nature; finding things to talk about was always difficult, even with Gloria. Mark would expect it, and she'd make the effort for his benefit.

Riley stopped at a red light, and Jayne watched as his fingers loosened their grip on the steering wheel. He turned to her. "You're looking better this morning."

"Like I said, I feel wonderful. It was probably the soup."

"Undoubtedly," Riley agreed with a crooked grin.

"Thank you again," she said shyly, astonished by how much a smile could alter a man's appearance. The glow in his blue eyes warmed Jayne as effectively as a ray of sunlight. "You mentioned an office. What do you do?"

The hesitation was so slight that Jayne thought she must have imagined it.

"I'm an inspector."

"For the city?" Somehow his words didn't ring entirely true, but Jayne attributed that notion to reading too many thrillers and suspense novels.

"Yeah, for the city. I'll let you off at the next corner." Not waiting for her response, he switched lanes and stopped at the curb.

"I'm in your debt again," she murmured. Her hand closed over the door handle. "Thank you."

"Have a good day, Miss Prim and Proper."

Jayne flashed angry eyes at him. When she clenched her hands and stalked away, Riley grinned. Jayne Gilbert was easy to bait. Her reaction to teasing suggested she was an only child. That would also account for her quiet, independent nature. He appreciated that quality in her. Without realizing it, Riley smiled, his troubled thoughts vanishing in the face of a simple display of emotion. Who would've guessed a shy librarian could have that effect on him?

Jayne was watching the evening news two days later while a casserole baked in the oven, when Riley's image flitted into her restless mind. The news story relayed the unsavory details of a prostitution ring that had recently been broken. The blonde woman on the screen looked vaguely familiar, and Jayne wondered if she'd seen her that night in Soft Sam's, the night she met Riley. But she hadn't been wearing her glasses, and it was difficult to tell.

Jayne didn't know what made her think of Riley. She hadn't seen him for a few days. In fact, she'd been half looking for him. At first he'd made his views of her plain. Now she wasn't sure what he thought of her. Not that she expected to bowl him over with her natural beauty and charm. She didn't expect that from any man. She liked Riley, enjoyed his company, and that was rare. The fact was, Jayne didn't know what to make of her relationship with him. Perhaps it was premature to even call it a relationship. Friends—she hoped so. But nothing more. Riley wasn't the type of man she pictured walking into her class reunion. No, she'd reserve Mark for her classmates' inspection. Riley was too…rough-edged. Mark seemed smoother. More sociable.

Shaking her head, Jayne felt guilty that her thoughts about Riley—and Mark, for that matter—could be so self-serving. After all, Riley had gone out of his way for her.

On impulse, she pulled the steaming casserole from the oven and divided it into two equal portions. With giant oven mitts protecting her hands, she carried the steaming dish down the hallway to Riley's apartment. She knocked at the door, balancing the casserole in one hand, and waited impatiently for him to answer.

The door was jerked open in an angry motion, but his frown disappeared as soon as he saw her. "Jayne?"

"Hi." Now that she was there, she felt like an idiot, but she'd been behaving a lot like one lately. "The library got a new cookbook this week. I read through it and decided to try this recipe."

"And you're looking for a guinea pig?"

"No." The comment offended her. "I wanted to thank you for fixing me dinner the other night and for the ride to work."

"It isn't necessary to repay me."

Jayne sighed. "I know that. But I wanted to do this. Now are you going to let me in, or do I have to stand here while we argue?"

"I don't know—you look kind of appealing like that."

"I didn't think men found 'prim and proper' appealing." She loved turning his own words back on him.

Riley grinned, and his whole face relaxed with the movement. The dark blue eyes sparkled, and Jayne was reminded that he could be devastatingly attractive when he wanted to be.

"Prim and proper women can be fascinating," he said softly.

Jayne sucked in her breath. "Don't play with me, Riley. I'm not good at games. The only reason I'm here is to thank you."

"I should be thanking you—this smells delicious." He stepped aside, and Jayne brought the dish to his kitchen. Riley's apartment was similar to her own, although Riley possessed none of her sense of orderliness. His raincoat had been carelessly tossed over the back of a living room chair, and three days' worth of newspapers littered the carpet.

"It's chicken tamale pie," she told him, feeling awkward without the dish in her hands.

"Will you join me?"

Jayne was convinced the invitation wasn't sincere until she remembered his claim that he never said or did anything without meaning it.

"No, my dinner is waiting for me. I just wanted—"

"—to thank me," he finished for her.

"No," she said mischievously. "I came to prove that prim and proper girls have talents you might not expect."

"Given half a chance, I'd say they'd take over the world."

"According to what I remember from Sunday school class, we're supposed to inherit it." She gave him a comical glance. "Or is that the meek and mild?"

"Never meek, Ms. Gilbert." Chuckling, Riley closed the door after her and sighed thoughtfully. He wasn't so sure Jayne was going to control the world as he'd teased, but he was genuinely concerned that he could be falling for her. And then, without much trouble, she'd end up ruling his heart and his life.

He swept a hand across his face, trying to wipe out the memory of her standing in his apartment. Instead, he realized how *right* it had felt to be with her, even if it was only for those few minutes. This woman was entering his life when he was least prepared to deal with it. He was in his thirties and cynical about the world. She was *much* too innocent for him, yet he found himself attracted to her. She touched a vulnerable part of him that Riley hadn't known existed, a softness he thought had vanished long ago.

For both their sakes, it would be best to avoid her.

★★★

Several times before her date with Mark, Jayne studied her dating advice books. With Gloria choosing her outfit, Jayne dressed casually, or what was casual for her—a plaid skirt and light sweater. She used lots of mascara and left her hair down. It fell in gentle waves to her shoulders and shone from repeated brushing. Rereading *How to Get a Man Interested in You* while she waited, Jayne mentally reviewed the discussion topics Gloria had given her and recalled her friend's tips on how to keep a conversation going. She hoped Mark would do most of the talking and all that would be required of her was to smile and bat her eyelashes. Granted, that felt a bit false, but she was starting to believe that social interactions, especially male-female ones, often were.

Mark arrived precisely when he said he would. Their evening together went surprisingly well. And fortunately she was farsighted so she had no trouble seeing the screen, even without her glasses. The movie was a comedy with slapstick humor.

After the movie, Mark suggested a cup of coffee.

Jayne agreed, and her hand slid automatically inside her pocket to the list of conversation ideas. But she didn't need them. Mark was a nice man with a huge ego. He spoke in astonishing detail about his position as an office manager. She didn't know why he felt the need to impress her with his importance, but as the books suggested, she fawned over every word, exhausting though that was.

In return she told him she worked for the city, but not in what capacity. Librarians were stereotyped. It didn't matter that she fit that stereotype perfectly. Later, as they went back to her apartment, Jayne thought wryly that Gloria needn't have worried about making up a list of topics to discuss. As she'd originally hoped, Mark had done most of the talking.

She should've been relieved, even pleased, but she wasn't. With Mark she felt like…like an accessory.

Outside her apartment door, clenching her keys, Jayne looked up at him. "I had a lovely time. Thank you, Mark."

He placed his hand on the wall behind her and lowered his head. Jayne felt a second of apprehension. She wasn't sure she wanted him to kiss her. Nonetheless, she closed her eyes as his mouth settled over hers for a gentle kiss. Pleasant, but not earth-shattering. "Can I see you again?" he asked, his breath fanning her temple.

"Ah…sure."

"How about dinner Wednesday night? Do you like to dance?"

"Love to," she told him, wondering how quickly a book and CD could teach her. She had about as much rhythm as a piece of lint. The class reunion was bound to have some kind of dancing, and she'd need to learn sooner or later, anyway. She'd check out an instruction book and CD on Monday. Her motto should be *By the Book,* she decided with a satisfied grin.

Monday afternoon, when she was walking home from the bus stop, she heard Riley call her from the parking lot across the street.

"Hello," Jayne called and waved back, feeling unreasonably pleased at seeing him again. He carried his raincoat over his arm, and she wondered if he ever wore the silly thing. She'd only seen it on him once or twice, yet he had it with him constantly.

Checking both sides of the street before jogging across, Riley joined her in front of the apartment building and smiled roguishly when he noted the CDs poking out of her bag. "Don't tell me the books on manhunting didn't help and you're advancing to audio?"

Jayne studied the sidewalk between her shoes. "No, Mark asked me to go dancing, and… I'm not very good at it."

"Two left feet aren't uncommon." Riley resisted the urge to fit his hand under her chin and lift her gaze to his. He wanted to pull her hair free of that confining clasp and run his fingers through it. The thought irritated him. He didn't want to feel these things. This woman was like a red light flashing *trouble.* She didn't hide her desire to get married, or at least find a man, while Riley had no intention of settling down. Yet he was like a moth fluttering dangerously close to that very same light. The light warning there was trouble ahead…

"I went to a few dances in high school, but that was years ago," Jayne said. "Ten, to be exact, and I don't remember much. I don't think just shuffling my feet around will work this time."

"Do you want any help?" The offer slid from his mouth before he could censor it. Silently he cursed himself.

"Help?" Jayne repeated, surprised. "You'd do that?"

He nodded. Yes, he'd do that, just so she'd marry this Mark guy and get out of his life. He sighed. Who was he trying to kid? He'd do it so he could stop wondering how she'd feel in his arms.

"It *would* be easier with a partner," Jayne murmured. She saw Riley's eyebrows drawn together in a dark glower as if he already regretted making the offer. "If you're sure."

"I'll be at your place in an hour."

"Let me cook dinner, then…as a means of thanking you," she added hurriedly.

This cozy scene was going to be difficult enough as it was. "Another time," he said, putting her off gently.

Calling himself every kind of fool, Riley knocked on Jayne's apartment door precisely one hour later. He'd never felt more mixed up in his life. His arms ached for the warm feel of this woman, and yet at the same time he dreaded what that sensation would do to him.

Jayne opened the door, and Riley mumbled something under his breath as he stalked past. She couldn't understand what he was saying. She'd changed out of her "uniform" and into linen pants the color of summer wheat and a soft cashmere sweater. The instruction book that came with the CD was open on the coffee table.

"You ready?" Riley's voice had a definite edge to it.

"Yes, of course," she said too quickly, turning on the CD player. "The first part is a guide to waltzing. The book says..." Feeling ridiculous, Jayne placed her hands on her hips and boldly met his scowl. "Listen, Riley, I appreciate the offer, but you don't have to do this."

"I thought you wanted to learn how to dance."

"I do, but with a willing partner. From the looks you're giving me, one would assume you're furious about the whole idea."

Indecision showed in every weather-beaten feature of his face. "I don't want you to get the wrong impression, Jayne. I'm rotten husband material."

She valued his honesty. He wasn't interested in her, not romantically. They hadn't even gone out on a date. He didn't think of her in those terms, yet he'd made an effort to seek her out, talk to her, be with her. If he wanted to be just friends, it was fine with her. In fact, wasn't friendship what *she* preferred, too? "I think I realized that from the first time I saw you in the elevator. You'd make some poor girl a terrible husband, Riley Chambers. What I don't understand is why you've appointed yourself my fairy godfather."

A slow smile crept into his eyes. "If you turned into a pumpkin at midnight, that might be the best thing all the way around."

"You don't know your fairy tales very well, Mr. Chambers. The coach turned back into a pumpkin. Not Cinderella."

The sweet sounds of a Viennese waltz swirled around them. An instructor's voice rang out. "Gentlemen. Place one hand on the lady's waist..."

Riley bowed elegantly. "Shall we?"

Pretending to fan her face, Jayne batted her lashes and gave him a demure look. "Why, Rhett, you have the most charmin' manner."

Loosely Riley took Jayne in his arms. She followed his lead, and he could tell by the concentration on her face that this was difficult for her. "*One,* two, three. *One,* two, three," the instructor's voice chanted.

"Pretend you're enjoying yourself," he told her, "otherwise Mark's going to think you're in pain."

Jayne laughed involuntarily. She *was* trying too hard. "Don't be so anxious for me to step on your toes."

"I'm not!" Riley positioned his hands so the need to touch her was at a minimum. He adjusted his fingers at her shoulder and then at her hip, all to no avail. Each time his hands shifted, he became aware of the warmth that lay just beneath his fingertips. He tried desperately not to notice.

Swallowing, he concentrated on moving to the music and held his breath. Fairy godfather indeed! He should be arrested for the thoughts that were racing at breakneck speed through his head. This entire situation was ridiculous. Riley had held women far more intimately than he was embracing Jayne, and yet he was acting like a teenage boy on his first date. Briefly he wondered if she had any suspicion of what she was doing to him. He doubted it; knowing Jayne, she'd have to read about it first. Or maybe she had. Maybe this whole thing was an experiment, just like her visit to Soft Sam's. Gritting his teeth, Riley did his utmost to ignore the feel and the flowery scent of the woman in his arms—to ignore the texture of her soft skin, the way her body moved in perfect rhythm with his.

Jayne nodded happily to the music. *One,* two, three... This was going so much better than she'd imagined. Riley was obviously a good dancer, moving confidently with a grace she wouldn't have expected in a man his size. She felt a warmth where he positioned his hands at her waist, and forced her body to relax.

"How am I doing?" she asked after a while.

"Fine," he muttered. He was more convinced than ever that Jayne had no idea what she was doing to him. He had to endure this torture, so he'd do it with a smile. "When you go out with Mark, do you plan to leave your hair up?" He inched back to put some distance between them.

"Probably not."

"Then maybe you should let it down now. You know, to... uh, practice." He couldn't believe he was suggesting this, well aware that he was only making things worse.

"Okay." She reached up and took off the clasp; the dark length fell free.

"What about your glasses?" he asked next, resisting the urge to lift a strand of hair and feel its texture.

"Mark has never seen me in glasses."

"Then take them off."

"All right." She laid her glasses beside the hair clasp on the end table. A fuzzy, blurred Riley smiled down at her.

"No squinting."

"I can't see you close up."

"You won't see Mark, either, so it shouldn't make any difference."

"True," she agreed. But it *did* make a difference. She didn't need her glasses or anything else to know it was Riley's arms around her. When she slid into his embrace once again, it felt completely natural. His hold on her tightened ever so slightly, and when he pressed his jaw against the side of her neck, Jayne's eyes slowly closed. They danced, and she observed that they fit together perfectly.

Riley drew her closer, and Jayne's mind whirled with a confused mixture of emotions. She shouldn't be feeling this. Not with Riley. But she didn't want to question it, not now....

"This feels good," she whispered, fighting the impulse to trace the rugged line of his jaw. He smelled wonderful, a blend of spicy aftershave and—what? Himself, she decided.

Riley smoothed her hair, letting his hand glide down the silky length from the crown of her head to her shoulder. Reluctantly he stopped when the last notes of the waltz faded away.

"Yes, it does feel good," Riley said, his voice husky. *Too good,* his mind added.

He dropped his arms, and Jayne thrilled at his hesitancy when he stepped back. "I don't think you'll have any problems with the waltz."

"I shouldn't have," she said. "Anyway, with Mark all I need to do is look at him with adoring eyes and bat my lashes, and he's happy."

Riley didn't like the idea of Jayne flirting with another man. He knew that didn't make sense, since he was helping her prepare for a date with this Mark guy. "That won't satisfy a man for long," he muttered.

"It'll satisfy Mark," she countered. "I'm not exactly a flirt, you know. I'm not even sure how most women do it."

"It seems to me you're doing a good job learning."

"What do you mean?"

"Just now—dancing. You were practically throwing yourself at me."

"I was not!"

"You sure were."

Jayne was too humiliated to argue. She vaulted across the room and removed the CD. Her hands shook as she returned it to the plastic case. "That was an awful thing to say."

"It's about time you woke up and realized what men are like."

"I've already told you I don't need a fairy godfather."

"You need *someone* to tell you the score."

Jayne glared at him angrily. "And I suppose you're the one to enlighten me."

"Yup. Someone has to. You can't go flaunting yourself the way you just did with me."

"Flaunting?" Jayne almost choked on the word.

"That's right—flaunting." Riley hated himself for the things he was saying. He was both furious and unreasonable—a bad combination.

"*You* were the one who offered to show me how to dance. I… I even told you—"

"You can't tease a man, Jayne," he interrupted, coming to grips with his emotions. "Not me, not Mark, not any man."

"And how many times do I have to tell you I'm not a tease? Honestly, look at me!"

"That's the problem. I *am* looking."

"And?" she whispered, shocked at the tightness of his voice.

"And…" He hesitated. "All I can think about is doing

this." He reached for her, taking her in his arms and covering her mouth with his.

Jayne was too stunned to react. The kiss had the sweetest, most tantalizing effect, momentarily causing her to forget the angry censure in his voice.

Regaining her composure—or pretending to—she broke away. "What made you do that?"

The look he was giving her told Jayne he wasn't pleased about that kiss. "I don't know. It was a mistake."

"I…yes." And yet Jayne didn't want to think of it that way.

"You go out with Mark, and we'll leave it at that."

"But—"

"Just go out with him, Jayne."

She dropped her gaze to the carpet. "All right."

4

After she'd buzzed Gloria in, Jayne jerked open the apartment door. "What took you so long? Mark's due any minute."

Flustered, Gloria shook her head. "If you weren't so afraid to wear your glasses, you'd see exactly what he looks like."

Being the good friend she was, Gloria had volunteered to be there when Mark arrived so she could tell Jayne if he'd be an acceptable date for the high school reunion. Mark's image remained a bit fuzzy in her mind, but as the day of her reunion drew closer, Jayne discovered how badly she wanted to go. But she'd decided early on not to attend without a handsome man at her side. The problem was that Mark was her only likely prospect. And she didn't even know if he'd be interested!

"You look fantastic," Gloria commented, stepping back to examine Jayne's outfit. "Are you sure you can dance in that?"

Jayne had wondered the same thing. The silk blouse was new, pale blue with a pleated front. The black skirt was standard straight fare, part of her everyday uniform. She'd spent what seemed like hours on her hair, but to no avail. It was too straight and thick to manage. In the end, she'd tied it at the base of her neck with a chiffon scarf that was a shade deeper than her blouse.

"I shouldn't have any trouble dancing." But then she hadn't graduated beyond the waltzing stage. Riley had left soon after their kissing fiasco, and she hadn't seen him since. Every time Jayne thought about what had happened, she grew angry… not with Riley, but with herself. She hadn't meant to flirt with him, but she wasn't so naive that she didn't know what was happening. Pride had demanded that she pretend otherwise. But she regretted the kiss. It had been so wonderful that four days later the warm taste of his mouth still lingered on hers. Nor could she erase the sensation of being held in his arms.

"You're sure I look okay?" Jayne raised questioning eyes to her friend. As it was, she had to drum up enthusiasm for this date.

"You look fine."

"Before, it was fantastic."

"Fantastic, then."

Straightening the chiffon scarf at her neck, Jayne closed her eyes. She had a bad feeling about tonight. If she was honest, she'd admit she'd rather be going with Riley. She felt comfortable with him. Except, of course, for that kiss. And it'd been…not comfortable but exciting. Memorable. However, Riley hadn't spoken to her in days. She wasn't entirely sure he even liked her; the signals she'd received from him were conflicting. It was almost as though he didn't want to be attracted to her but couldn't resist.

The buzzer went, and she cast a frantic glance in Gloria's direction and quickly tucked her glasses inside her purse.

"Calm down," Gloria said. "You're going to have a wonderful time."

"Tell me why I don't believe that," Jayne mumbled on her way to the door.

Riley Chambers pressed the button on his remote control to change channels. He'd seen fifteen-second segments of no fewer than ten shows. Nothing held his interest, and there was no point trying to distract himself. Jayne was on his mind again. Only she didn't flit in and out of his thoughts the way she had before. Tonight she was a constant presence, taunting him. Television wasn't going to help; neither was reading or the internet or any other diversion he could invent.

Standing, Riley paced to the window to stare at the rain-soaked street. He buried his hands in his pockets. So she was going out with this Mark character. Dinner and dancing. He shouldn't care. But he did. The idea of another man with his arms around Jayne disturbed him. It more than disturbed him, it made him completely crazy.

She'd felt so good in his arms. Far better than she had any right to. Days later, he still couldn't banish the feel, the taste, the smell of her from his mind. Avoiding her hadn't worked. Nothing had. She lived three doors down from him, yet she might as well have packed her bags and moved into his apartment. She was there every minute of every night and he didn't like it. What he really wanted to do was exorcise her from his life. Cast those honey-brown eyes from his memory and go about his business the way he was paid to do. *No.* He turned. What he really wanted to do was find out what Mark was like.

Before he could analyze this insanity, he grabbed his raincoat and stormed out the door.

★★★

"Hello, Mark." Jayne greeted him with a warm smile. "I'd like to introduce my friend Gloria."

"Hello, Gloria." Mark stepped forward to shake Gloria's hand, then held it far longer than necessary. His eyes caressed her face until Jayne noticed the pink color in her friend's cheeks.

"It's nice meeting you." Gloria pulled her hand free. "But I have to be going."

"No," Jayne objected. "Really, Gloria, stay."

Gloria threw her a look that could have boiled water. "No. You and Mark are going out. Remember?" The last word was issued through clenched teeth.

"The more the merrier, I always say." Mark was staring at Gloria with obvious interest, or what Jayne assumed was interest. She couldn't really tell without her glasses.

"No, I have to go," Gloria insisted.

"That's a shame," Mark said.

There was another knock at the door, and three faces glared at it.

"I'll get that," Jayne said, excusing herself. The few steps across the floor had never seemed so far. It could only be a neighbor, yet she wasn't expecting anyone. Least of all Riley.

"Riley." She breathed his name in a rush of excitement.

His gaze flew past her to Mark and Gloria. "I stopped by—" he paused, suddenly realizing he had to come up with a plausible excuse for his unexpected arrival "—to get the recipe for the casserole you made the other night. It was delicious," he said.

"Of course. Come in, please." Jayne stepped aside, trying to disguise her reaction, and Riley strolled past her.

"Riley Chambers, this is Mark Bauer and Gloria Bailey."

Somehow she made it through the introductions without revealing her pleasure at Riley's unexpected visit.

"Pleased to meet you," Mark said stiffly, and the two men shook hands.

"Gloria." Riley nodded in the direction of Jayne's friend.

"Riley lives down the hall from me," Jayne felt obliged to add. "Gloria and I work together," she explained.

Riley nodded.

"I'll get you that recipe," Jayne told him.

"I'll help," Gloria said hurriedly, following her into the kitchen. "What's going on?" Gloria whispered the minute they were out of sight.

"I don't know."

"You don't really think he cares about that stupid recipe, do you?"

Jayne thought back to all the times she'd been with Riley. He bewildered her. He'd come to the library intent on harassing her, then had looked after her when she was ill. Most surprising had been his willingness to teach her to dance—which had turned into a scene that wouldn't soon be forgotten by either of them. "With Riley, I never know."

"He's here to check out Mark."

Jayne's eyes widened with doubt. "I have trouble believing that."

"Trust me, kiddo, the guy's interested."

"Two men at the same time? The girls of St. Mary's would keel over if they knew." Two men interested in her was a slight exaggeration. The minute Mark had met Gloria he couldn't stop looking at her.

"What are you going to do?" Gloria wanted to know.

"What do you mean?"

"From the look of things, Riley isn't leaving."

Jayne bit her bottom lip. "What should I do, invite him along?"

"Invite us both."

"But what will Mark think?"

"It won't matter. The way Riley's giving him the evil eye, Mark's not likely to risk life and limb by asking you out again."

"Oh, I can't believe this."

"Where's that cookbook?" Gloria whispered, glancing into the living room.

There wasn't any point in looking. "I returned it last week."

"Then tell him that, for heaven's sake!"

Back in the living room, Jayne found the two men sitting on the sofa, staring at each other like angry bears. It was as if one had invaded the other's territory.

Riley stood. Slowly Mark followed suit.

"I'm sorry, Riley, but I returned that book to the library. I'll see if I can pick it up for you, if you'd like."

"Please."

Gloria stepped forward, linking her hands together. "Jayne and I were just thinking that since the four of us are all here maybe we could go out together."

Jayne nodded. "Right," she said boldly. "We were."

"Not dancing." Riley categorically dismissed that.

"There's a new movie at the Lloyd Center," Gloria suggested.

"A movie would be fun." Jayne nodded, looking at Mark. After all, he was supposed to be her date. "We could always eat later."

"That sounds fine," Mark agreed with little enthusiasm.

For that matter, eagerness for this impromptu double date was remarkably absent. The silence in Mark's car as they drove to the shopping complex grated on Jayne's fragile nerves. But she knew better than to even attempt a conversation.

At the theater Mark and Riley bought the popcorn while

the two women found seats. The place was crowded and they ended up far closer to the front than Jayne liked.

"This isn't working," she whispered.

"You're telling me. The temperature in that car was below freezing."

"I know. What should I do?" Jayne could hear the desperate appeal in her own voice.

"Nothing. Things will take care of themselves." Gloria sounded far more confident than Jayne felt.

The two men returned, and to her delighted surprise, Riley claimed the seat beside her. Mark took the one next to Gloria. The women glanced at each other and shared a sigh of relief. Apparently Mark and Riley had settled things in the theater lobby.

For his part, Riley wasn't pleased. His instincts told him Jayne was going to be hurt by this guy. He'd seen the looks Mark was giving Gloria. Three minutes in the lobby, and the two men had come to an agreement. Riley would sit with Jayne, Mark with Gloria. If Jayne was out to find herself a decent man, he thought grimly, Mark Bauer wasn't the one. She should look elsewhere.

The theater darkened, and after the previews the credits started to roll. Jayne squinted, then pulled her glasses out of her purse. It was ridiculous to pretend any longer. She doubted Mark had even noticed.

Before they'd entered the theater, Jayne hadn't paid much attention to the movie they were about to see. She soon realized it was going to be filled with blood and gore. She swallowed uncomfortably.

"What's wrong?" Riley whispered and grinned when he noticed she'd put her glasses back on.

"Nothing." She couldn't think of a way to tell him that any form of violence greatly upset her. She detested movies like this where men treated life cheaply, and grotesque horror was all part of an intriguing plot.

At the first gory scene, Jayne clutched the armrests until her fingers ached and closed her eyes, praying no one was aware of her odd behavior.

"Jayne?"

Riley's voice was so low she wasn't even sure she'd heard him. Opening her eyes, she turned to look at him. "Are you all right?" he asked solicitously.

With a weak smile, she nodded. A blast of gunfire rang from the screen, and she winced and shook her head.

"Do you want to leave?"

"No."

Watching her, Riley wasn't surprised that she was troubled by violence. It fit with what he knew of her—all part of the innocence he'd come to like so much, the goodness he'd come to count on. He didn't want to fall for her, but he knew the signs.

His interest in the movie waned. Her hand still clenched the armrest in a death grip, and with a gentleness he hardly knew he possessed, Riley pried her fingers loose and tucked her hand in his, offering her comfort. She turned to him with a look of such gratitude that it took years of hard-won self-control not to lean forward and kiss her. He didn't like this feeling. Now wasn't the time to get involved with a woman, especially *this* woman. It was too dangerous. For him and possibly for her.

Thursday morning, Gloria was waiting for Jayne on the front steps of the library.

"Morning," Jayne muttered, feeling defeated. She'd been standing at the bus stop when Riley drove past. He hadn't even looked in her direction, and she'd felt as though a little part of her had died at the disappointment. "How did everything go with Mark?" Jayne's original date had taken Gloria home.

"Fine… I guess."

"Did he ask you out?"

"Yeah, but I'm not interested." Gloria wrapped her arms around her waist and shook her head. "I finally figured out what's wrong. Mark reminds me too much of my ex."

"Mark's off my list, as well."

"I would think so. Riley would probably skin him alive if he showed up at your door again."

"I don't understand Riley," Jayne murmured. "He barely even said good-night when he dropped me off. He wouldn't even look at me." And men claimed they didn't understand women! For all her intelligence, all the reading she'd done, Jayne was at a loss to explain Riley's strange behavior. She had thought they'd shared something special during that horrible movie, and then the minute they got outside, he treated her as though she had some contagious disease.

"Who would you rather go to the reunion with? Riley or Mark?"

Jayne didn't need to mull that over. "Riley."

"Then you need to change tactics."

"Oh, Gloria, I don't know. You make this sound like some kind of game."

"Do you want to attend the reunion or not?"

"I do, but…"

"So, form your plan and choose your weapons."

Jayne might not have needed to ponder which man interested her most, but tactics were something else. She liked Riley, and she sensed that her feelings for him could grow a lot more intense. But the opposite side of the coin was the reality that if she chose to pursue a relationship with this man, she could be hurt.

That evening, still undecided about what to do, Jayne was surprised to receive a call from Mark, asking her out again. Apparently the man didn't scare off as easily as Gloria and Riley seemed to think. Or it could be that Mark had noticed Riley's lack of interest following the movie. It didn't matter; she politely declined.

When she didn't see Riley the following day, either, Jayne was convinced he was avoiding her again. Only this time she was armed with ammunition and reinforcement from Gloria.

That evening, Jayne made another casserole from the Mexican cookbook—which she'd taken out again—and delivered it to Riley's door.

Surprise etched fine lines around his eyes when Riley answered her knock.

"Hello." Jayne forced a bright smile.

He frowned, obviously not pleased to see her.

"I brought you dinner." It had all sounded so simple when she'd discussed her plans with Gloria earlier in the day. Now her stomach felt as though a weight had settled there, and her resolve was weakening more every minute. "It's another casserole from the same cookbook you asked about the other night."

His hand remained on the door. "You didn't need to do that."

"I wanted to." Her smile was about to crumple. "You mentioned it the night Mark was by.... You do remember, don't you?" He still hadn't asked her into his apartment. She wasn't any good at this flirting business. Chagrined, she dropped her gaze to the floor. "I can see you're busy, so I'll just leave this with you."

Reluctantly he stepped aside.

Rarely had Jayne been more miserable. Things weren't supposed to happen like this. According to Gloria, Riley would appreciate her efforts and gratefully ask her to join him.

She moved into his kitchen and saw the box from a frozen microwave dinner sitting on the counter.

After setting the casserole on the stove she removed her oven mitts. "Don't worry about returning the baking dish." She didn't want him thinking she was looking for more excuses to see him. She had been, but that didn't matter anymore. Embarrassed and ill at ease, she gave him a weak smile. "Enjoy your dinner."

"Jayne." His hand on her shoulder stopped her, and when she raised her eyes to his, he pulled away, thrusting his fingers into his hair. "I wish you hadn't done this."

"I know," she said and swallowed miserably. "I won't again. I… I don't know what I did to make you so upset with me, but your message is coming through loud and clear."

"Jayne, listen. I saw those books you're reading. I'm not the man for you. I told you already—I'd make a terrible husband." He took a step toward her.

"Husband!" she spat. "I'm not looking for a husband."

"Then what *do* you want?" He knew his voice was raised, he couldn't help it. Jayne did that to him. He saw the tears in her eyes and watched as she tried to blink them away. "Then why are you reading those ridiculous books?" he asked.

With her fists clenched, Jayne met his glare. "I have my reasons."

"No doubt." The proud tilt of her chin tore at his heart. He didn't know what Jayne thought she was doing, but if she was serious about a relationship with him, the timing couldn't be worse. The dangers of this undercover assignment were many and real. He had enough to worry about without having his head messed up by a woman. But Jayne wasn't an ordinary woman. He'd known it the first time she'd flared back at him. She was genuine and sweet and, yes, naive. She was also smart and he sensed the passion beneath her demure exterior.

"What you think of me is irrelevant," she said, flexing her hands at her sides. "If you must know, all I really want is to attend my high school reunion. And I'm going even if I have to hire a man to go with me." Her voice rose with every word. "And furthermore, I'm going to learn to dance, and if you won't help me, fine. I'll find someone else who will."

"So *that's* what this is all about? And the casserole is in exchange for dancing lessons?" No way was he addressing the issue of a hired companion. But at least she hadn't mentioned Mark Bauer.

"Yes."

"Fine." He walked across the room and flipped on the radio. Soft music filled the apartment. "Come on, let's dance, if that's all you want."

The invitation held as much welcome as cold charity. Jayne's first response was to throw his offer back in his face, but she managed to swallow her pride. After all, finding a way into his arms was exactly the reason she'd come here tonight.

When she walked into his embrace, he held her stiffly. His tense muscles kept her away from him, so there was only minimal contact.

"You didn't hold me like this the other day," she protested.

Gritting his teeth, Riley brought her closer into his arms. Eyes shut, he breathed in the scent of her hair. She reminded him of springtime, fresh and eager and so unbelievably trusting that it frightened him.

His hands sought her hair. Silky, glorious, just as he'd

known it would be. He removed the clasp and let it fall to the floor. His fingers tangled with her hair as a tenderness for the woman enveloped him.

The music changed to an upbeat song with a bubbly rhythm, but their steps remained unchanged. Dancing was only an excuse to hold each other, and they both knew it.

Riley wrapped his arms around her. Their feet barely shifted as the pretense lost its purpose.

Jayne's arms were tight around his neck. She didn't dare move for fear her actions would break this magical spell. There was something strong and powerful about Riley that she couldn't resist. Her mouth found his neck, and her warm breath left a film of moisture against his skin. Lightly she kissed him there.

Riley stiffened, his whole body tensing at her seemingly playful kiss. "Jayne," he breathed. "What are you trying to do to me?"

"The same thing you're doing to me," she answered. Her own voice was weak. "I've never felt like this before…."

The only response he seemed capable of was a groan.

"Riley, kiss me," she said urgently. "Please kiss me."

He angled her head to one side and slanted his mouth over hers with a desperate hunger that burned in him like a raging fire.

He kissed her again with an intensity that drove him beyond his will. His mouth sought hers until they were both weak and trembling.

"Jayne," he whispered harshly, "tell me to leave you alone. Tell me to stop."

"But I like it."

"Don't say that."

"But, Riley, it feels so good. *You* feel so good."

"Jayne," he pleaded, wanting her to stop him. Instead she arched into him, her mouth on his.

"I want to kiss you forever," she whispered.

"Don't tell me that," he said, fighting with everything that was in him and losing the battle with every breath he took.

Instinctively she moved against him, and Riley thought he'd die with the pleasure and pain. He lowered his hands to her waist. "No more of that. Understand?"

"I don't think I do. I never dreamed anything could feel this wonderful."

Riley didn't even hear her as he pressed his mouth to her cheek, her ear, her hair, anyplace but her lips.

"Jayne," he said a moment later. "We have to stop." He pressed his cheek to hers. His eyes were closed, and his breathing was labored as he struggled within himself.

Jayne moved so that her mouth found his, tasting, licking and kissing him until Riley feared she'd drive him mad.

"No more," he said harshly, breaking the contact. He held her away at arm's length, clasping her shoulder. "What's the matter with you?"

Jayne blinked.

"You're acting like a child with a new toy you've just discovered."

"But it feels so good." How flimsy that sounded, even to her.

"And just where did you think this kissing and touching would end?"

"I thought…" She didn't know what she thought.

Riley looked down into Jayne's bewildered face and cursed the anger in his voice. "Listen, maybe you'd better find someone else for these lessons you're so keen to learn."

Jayne swallowed down the hurt. She didn't consider Riley

her teacher. She'd believed they were exploring those exquisite sensations together. Her face felt hot with shame.

"Maybe I should!" she cried. "I'm sure Mark would be willing."

"Oh, no, you don't. Not with Mark."

"Who then? It isn't like I've got hordes of admirers lined up, dying to go out with me." Dramatically, she flung out her arm.

"That's not my problem." He attempted a show of indifference. "Find whoever you want. Just stay away from me."

"Don't worry." After this humiliation, she had no intention of ever seeing him again.

She couldn't get out of his apartment fast enough. Once inside her own, she felt tears of hurt and anger burning for release. They rolled down her face, despite all her efforts to hold them back.

Sinking into the soft cushion of her sofa, she buried her face in her hands. She was a twenty-seven-year-old virgin, hurrying to catch up with life, and it had backfired. She'd behaved like an irresponsible idiot just as Riley had claimed.

A loud knock sounded on the apartment door.

Aghast, she stared at it. There wasn't anyone in the world she wanted to see right now.

"Jayne!" Riley shouted. "Open up. I know you're in there."

She was too shocked to move. Riley was the last person she expected to come to her now.

Riley gave a disgusted sigh. "The choice is yours. Either open that door, or I'll kick it down."

His threat was convincing enough to prompt her to unlatch the lock and open the door.

Riley stood in front of her and handed her the oven mitts. "You forgot these."

Wordlessly she took them.

The guilt he felt at the sight of her red eyes knotted his stomach. "I think we'd better talk."

Like a robot, she moved aside. Riley stalked past her and into the apartment. "You want to attend that reunion? Fine. I'll take you."

"Why?"

"Haven't you ever heard that expression about not looking a gift horse in the mouth?"

"But why?"

"Because!" he shouted.

"That's not a reason."

"Well, it'll have to do."

5

The glorious June sunshine splashed over the street, silhouetting the Burnside Bridge that towered above Riverside Park. The Saturday market was in full swing, and noisy crowds wandered down the busy street. Some gathered to watch a banjo player while others strolled past, their arms heavy with a variety of newly discovered treasures.

Jayne nibbled on a cinnamon-covered "elephant ear" pastry as she strolled from one booth to the next. Riley was at her side, carrying the shopping bag that grew increasingly heavy with every stop.

"I can't believe you've lived in Portland all these months and you didn't know about the Saturday market," she remarked.

"You do most of your shopping here?"

"Just the produce." Jayne offered him a bite of her elephant ear. "They're good, aren't they?"

Chewing, Riley nodded. "Delicious."

Finishing it off, Jayne brushed the sugar from her fingers

and dumped the napkin in the garbage. Riley took her hand and smiled. "Where to next?"

"The fish market. I want to try a new salmon recipe." They strolled down the wide street to the vendor who displayed fresh fish laid out on a bed of crushed ice.

"I didn't know it was legal to catch salmon this small," Riley commented as the vendor wrapped up Jayne's choice.

"That's a rainbow trout," she said and laughed.

"I thought you said you were buying salmon."

"I changed my mind. The trout looked too good to resist."

"At the moment, so do you."

His lazy voice reached through the noisy crowd to touch her heart. Tears filled her eyes, and she quickly looked away, not wanting him to see the effect his words had on her.

The stout vendor handed Riley the fish, and he tucked it in the brown shopping bag. Before his attention returned to her, Jayne brushed the tears from her cheek.

"Jayne." Concern was evident in his tone. "What's wrong?"

She smiled up at him through her happiness. "No one's ever said things like that to me."

"Like what?" His brow compressed.

"That I'm irresistible."

"My sweet little librarian," he said, placing an arm around her shoulders, drawing her close to his side. "You tie me up in knots a sailor couldn't undo."

"Oh, Riley, do I really?" She felt excruciatingly pleased. "I owe you so much."

Despite his efforts not to, Riley frowned. He was grateful that Jayne didn't seem to notice. He wondered how this virtuous librarian, whom he'd once thought of as a prim and proper young woman, could inspire such desire in him. Over the years, he'd been with a number of women. None of them compared to her. None of them had meant to him what she did. At night, unable to sleep, he often lay awake imagining Jayne. This woman tugged, like a swift undercurrent, at his senses. Jayne in bed, soft and mussed, her hair spilling over the pillow. The image of her was so strong that it was a constant battle not to make it real. The intensity of his feelings for her shocked him even now, weeks after having accepted her into his life. This wasn't the time to be caught up with a woman. Losing sight of his assignment could be dangerous. It could cost him his life. But if he hadn't acted when he did, he could have lost *her,* and that thought was intolerable. As soon as this job was over, he was getting out. The time had come to think about settling down. Jayne had done that to him, and he realized for the first time how much he wanted the very lifestyle he'd previously shunned.

Therein lay the problem. Being with her had placed a burden on him. She made him ache with need; at the same time, he experienced the overpowering urge to protect her. This was a dilemma—because there was no one to protect her from him but his own conscience. The weight of that responsibility fell heavily on his shoulders.

"You're very quiet," Jayne commented when they reached the parked car. "Is something wrong?"

"No." He smiled down on her and was instantly drawn into those warm brown eyes.

"I'm glad you came with me."

Riley had to admit he looked for excuses to be with her. Carrying her bags was one, offering her a ride was another. Simple things to do, but they brought him pleasure out of all proportion to the effort they entailed.

They drove back to the apartment building in companionable silence. After parking in his assigned spot, Riley carried her purchases into the building.

"Will you come in?" she asked outside her door.

"Only for a minute."

Setting the shopping bags on the kitchen counter, Riley watched the subtle grace with which she moved around her small kitchen. "I'll have a surprise for you later," she announced.

"Dinner?"

"No. Not that." Every time Riley kissed her, he ended up pulling the clasp from her hair. Her surprise was an appointment with the hairdresser to restyle her hair so that when Riley held her again, he could do whatever he liked with it. "You'll have to come by this evening and see."

"I'll do that."

"Riley?" She turned to him and leaned against the counter, hands behind her back.

He looked at her intent face. "Hmm?"

"May I kiss you?"

"Now?" He swallowed; she didn't make keeping his hands off her easy.

"Please."

"Jayne, listen…"

"Okay." She moved to his side and slipped her arms over his chest to link her fingers behind his neck. Her soft body conformed to the hardness of his.

Riley groaned, finding it nearly impossible to maintain his resolve. He was convinced that she had no idea of the powerful effect she had on him.

"Do you like this?" She pressed her lips to his, and Riley felt his legs weaken. He was grateful for the support of the kitchen counter.

"Yes," he groaned.

She began to kiss him again, straining upward on her toes,

but Riley quickly took charge. He kissed her with the hunger that ate at his insides.

Jayne moved restlessly against him, but he broke away.

"No," he said abruptly, his chest heaving. "That's enough."

Jayne hung her head as the heat of embarrassment colored her cheeks. "I'm sorry, Riley."

"Think next time, will you? I'm not some high school kid for you to experiment with. I told you that before." He hated to see the hurt he was inflicting on her, but she didn't seem to understand the stress she was putting him under.

Jayne took a step backward.

He plowed his fingers through his hair. "I'll talk to you later. Okay?"

"Sure."

The door closed, and Jayne winced. Oh, dear, she was doing everything wrong. Riley wanted to cool things down just when she wanted to really heat them up for the first time in her life. Several men had kissed her over the years, but she'd never responded to any of them the way she did to Riley. He didn't merely light a spark; Riley Chambers ignited a bonfire within her. Jayne was as surprised as anyone. She'd thought she was too refined, too shy, trapped with too many hang-ups to experience the very physical desires Riley evoked in her. He'd taught her differently, and now she was riding a roller coaster, speeding downhill ahead of him. If it wasn't so ironic, she'd laugh.

Listening to the radio, Jayne finished putting away the morning's purchases. She changed clothes for her hair appointment and left the apartment soon after one. The beauty salon was a good mile away, but the day was gloriously warm, and she decided to walk instead of taking the bus. She wanted time to think.

As she strolled along, it seemed as if the whole world was

alive. She saw and heard things that had passed her notice only weeks before. Birdsong filled the air, as did the laughter of children in the park.

Jayne cut a path through the lush green boulevard, pausing to watch several children swooping high on the park swings. She recognized a little girl from the library's story hour and waved as she continued down the meandering walkway.

Looking both ways before crossing the street, Jayne's gaze fell on Soft Sam's. She gave an involuntary shudder as she remembered the desperation of that first visit. She'd been so naive, thinking that because the place was in her neighborhood it would fulfill her requirements. Now she couldn't believe she'd even gone inside. She could just imagine what Riley had thought when he first saw her there. He'd warned her about the bar several times since, but he needn't have bothered. People went into Soft Sam's with one thing on their minds, and it wasn't companionship.

Jayne started across the street, and as she stepped off the curb, Riley came into view. He was standing in the doorway of Soft Sam's. She raised her arm, then paused, not knowing if she should call out to him or not. Before she could decide, a tall blonde woman joined him, slipping an arm through his and smiling boldly up at him. Her face was familiar, and it took Jayne several troubled seconds to realize the woman was the same one she'd seen on the evening news.

The hand she'd raised fell lifelessly to her side. Jayne felt as though someone had kicked her in the stomach. The numbing sensation of shock and disbelief moved up her arms and legs, paralyzing her for a moment.

A car horn blared, and she saw that she was standing in the middle of the street. Hurriedly she moved to the other side. Pausing to still her frantically beating heart, she rested her trembling hand on a fire hydrant for support.

Hadn't she just admitted the reason men and women went to a place like Soft Sam's? Riley was there now, and it wasn't his first visit. He could even be a regular customer. And from the looks that...that woman was giving him, they knew each other well.

The pain that went through her was white-hot, and her eyelids fluttered downward.

"Are you all right, miss?"

Jayne opened her eyes to find a police officer studying her, his face concerned.

"I'm fine. I...just felt dizzy for a minute."

The young man smiled knowingly. "You might want to check with a doctor."

"I will. Thank you, officer."

He touched the tip of his hat with his index finger. "No problem. You sure you'll be okay?"

"I'm sure."

With a determination that surprised even her, Jayne squared her shoulders and walked in the direction of the beauty salon. She'd read about men like Riley. If there was a blessing to be found in this, it was learning early on that there was another side to him. One that sought cheap thrills.

Her hand was on the glass door of the salon when she hesitated. She wasn't having her hair done for Riley, she told herself; she was doing it for the reunion. She wanted to go back looking different, didn't she? *None* of this was for Riley. None of it. It was for her.

Three hours later the reflection that greeted her in the salon mirror was hardly recognizable. Instead of thick, straight hair, soft, bouncy curls framed her face. Jayne stared back at her reflection and blinked. She looked almost pretty.

"What a difference," the hairdresser was saying.

"Yes," Jayne agreed. She paid the stylist and left a hefty

tip. Anyone who could create the transformation this young woman had deserved a reward.

Jayne took the bus home. She sat staring out the side window, absorbed in what she'd witnessed earlier. For days she'd been planning this small surprise for Riley. Now she didn't care if she ever saw him again.

But perhaps that was a bit rash. If she was going to break things off, she'd wait until after the reunion. She knew she should be grateful to learn this about him, only she wasn't. The experience of undiluted love had been pure bliss.

Back inside her apartment, Jayne felt the need to talk to someone. She wouldn't mention what she'd seen. For that matter, she doubted she could put words to the emotions that simmered in her heart. She needed human contact so she wouldn't go crazy sitting here alone, thinking. She reached for the phone and called Gloria.

"Jayne, I'm so glad to hear from you," Gloria's voice boomed over the wire.

"Oh. Did something exciting happen?"

"I cannot believe my luck."

"You won the lottery!" It took effort to force some energy into her flat voice.

"Remember when you returned those how-to books about meeting men to the library?"

Of course she did. When Riley had said he'd attend the reunion with her, she hadn't seen any reason to keep them.

"Well, guess who checked them out?"

"Who?" The answer was obvious.

"Me. And, Jayne, guess what? They work! I met this fantastic man in the Albertsons store today."

"At the grocery store?"

"Sure," Gloria said. "Remember how that one book says

the supermarket on Saturdays is a great place to meet men? I met Lance in the frozen-food section."

"Congratulations."

"We're going to dinner tonight."

"That's great."

"I have a feeling about this man. He's everything I want. We even like the same things. Looking through our grocery carts, we discovered that we have identical tastes."

"I hate to rain on your parade," Jayne said, smiling for the first time. "But there's more to a compatible relationship than both of you liking broccoli."

"It's not only broccoli, but fish sticks and frozen orange juice. We even bought the same brand of microwave dinners."

The thought of cardboard meals reminded Jayne of Riley's haphazard eating patterns. She did her best to dispel all thoughts of him, with little success.

"I didn't mean to jabber on. You must've called for a reason."

"I just wanted to tell you about my hair."

"Oh, goodness, I was so excited about meeting Lance that I forgot. What does Riley think?"

"He hasn't seen it yet."

"All right, how do *you* feel about it?"

"It's…different."

"I knew it would be," Gloria said with a laugh.

"Listen, I've got to go. I'll talk to you Monday, and you can tell me all about your hot date." On second thought, it had been a mistake to phone Gloria. Jayne's mind was in turmoil, and she wondered if she'd made any sense at all.

"Okay, see you then."

After a few words of farewell, Jayne hung up.

Riley—she assumed it was him—knocked on her door at

about seven. Jayne had known he'd come by, but she didn't have the nerve to confront him with what she'd seen. There wasn't anything she could say. The hurt was still too fresh and too poignant.

Careful not to make any noise, she sat reading a new mystery novel. She could immerse herself in fiction and forget for a time.

After three loud knocks he'd left, and she'd breathed easier.

Sunday morning she went out early and returned late. She couldn't avoid him forever, but she needed to put distance between them until she'd dealt with her emotions. When they did meet, she didn't want what she'd learned to taint her reactions.

Early Monday afternoon Riley tossed an empty paper cup in the metal garbage can beside his desk. Jayne was avoiding him. He didn't blame her; he'd hurt her feelings by abruptly putting an end to their kissing. Someday, God willing, there wouldn't be any reason to stop. For now, he had to be in control and for more than the obvious reasons.

The report on his desk made him frown. He didn't like the sound of this. For that matter, he didn't like anything to do with Max Priestly. The man was a slimeball; Riley always felt as though he needed a shower after being around him. How anyone like Priestly had been elected to public office was beyond Riley.

Standing, he reached for his coat. He'd dealt with enough mud this weekend. He needed a break. Only he wasn't going to get it. He missed Jayne, missed her fresh, sweet scent and the way he felt about himself when he was with her. She brought out the best in him. For the first time in recent memory, he was being noble. Twice now he could have taken what she was so freely offering, and he hadn't. She didn't know or even appreciate his self-control, but in time she would. And he could wait.

A glance at his watch confirmed that he could probably catch her at the library. He'd take her to lunch and ease her embarrassment. There was always the possibility that Priestly would see them together, but it was a relatively small risk and one worth taking. Pulling on his raincoat, he walked out of the office.

His steps echoed on the floor of the main library as Riley made his way to the children's department. He stopped when he found Jayne. At first he didn't recognize her. She looked fabulous. A beauty. She was holding up a picture book to the children gathered around her on the floor.

One small boy raised his hand and said something Riley couldn't hear. Jayne reacted by laughing softly and shaking her head. Leaning forward, she spoke to the group of intent young faces.

Just watching her with those children made Riley's heart constrict. He loved this woman with a depth that astonished him. *Loved her.* The acknowledgment felt right and true. Jayne closed the book, and the kids got up and surged closer, all chattering happily. Seeing her with these children created such intense desire in Riley that for a minute he couldn't breathe. Jayne was everything he could ever want. And a lot more than he deserved.

Gloria moved to Jayne's side and whispered in her ear. Instantly Jayne's gaze darted in Riley's direction. For a moment her eyes held a stricken look but that was quickly disguised. She stood, put the picture book down and said goodbye to the children, then walked over to him.

"Hello, Riley." Her voice held a note of hesitancy.

"Can I take you to lunch?"

She opened her mouth to tell him she'd already made other

plans, when Gloria intervened. "Go ahead," Gloria urged. "You haven't had lunch yet. And if you're a few minutes late, I'll cover for you."

There was nothing left for Jayne to do but agree.

Riley's gaze held hers. He wasn't sure he understood the message he found there. Jayne looked almost as though she was afraid of him, but he couldn't imagine why. "I like your hair."

Self-consciously she lifted her hand to the soft curls. "Thank you."

"Where would you like to eat?"

"Anywhere."

Her lack of enthusiasm was obvious. "Jayne, is something wrong?"

Her stricken eyes clashed with his. "No...how could there be?" Immediately her right eye began to twitch.

Riley argued with himself and decided not to pursue whatever was troubling her. Given time, she'd tell him, anyway.

"There's a little restaurant on Fourth. A hole in the wall, but the food's excellent."

"That'll be fine," she said formally.

She knew that his hand at her elbow was meant to guide her. Today it was a stimulation she didn't want or need. It wasn't fair that the only man she'd ever really fallen for preferred women who frequented a sleazy bar—and worse. Remembering the type of people at Soft Sam's, Jayne knew she could never be as worldly and sophisticated as they were. There was no point in even pretending. She wasn't that good an actress.

"You're quiet today." Riley led the way outside to his parked car and in a few minutes pulled into the busy afternoon traffic.

She managed a smile. "I sent in my money for the reunion this morning. It's less than a month away now."

"I'm looking forward to it." Riley studied her, growing

more confused by the minute. Whatever was bothering her was more serious than he'd first believed. He forced himself not to pressure her to talk.

"So am I."

"I missed seeing you Saturday evening. You said you had a surprise for me." He found a parking space and pulled into it. "The restaurant's over there. I hope you like Creole cooking."

"That sounds fine."

He noted that she'd avoided responding to his first statement. "I recommend the shrimp-stuffed eggplant."

"That's what I'll order then." It would be a miracle if she could choke down any lunch.

They were seated almost immediately and handed menus. The selection wasn't large, but judging by the spicy smells wafting from the kitchen, Jayne guessed that the food would be as good as Riley claimed.

"I tried to call you Sunday," he told her, setting his menu aside. "I didn't leave a message."

"I rented a car and drove to Seaside for the day."

Riley knitted his brow. She'd left the apartment to get away from him. He would have sworn that was the reason. "You should've said something. I would have taken you."

Jayne lowered her eyes. "I didn't want to trouble you."

"It wouldn't have been any trouble. The trip could have been interesting. I've heard a lot about the Oregon coastline, but haven't had the chance to see it yet."

"It's lovely."

The waitress came, and they placed their order.

Jayne twisted the paper napkin in her lap, staring down at it, not looking at him.

"What did you do in Seaside all day?"

"Walked. And thought." She hadn't meant to admit that.

"And what were you thinking about?"

"You." No point in lying. Her eye would twitch, and he'd know, anyway.

"What did you decide?"

"That I wasn't going to let you hurt me," she whispered fervently.

He'd hurt her in the past and had discovered that any pain she suffered mirrored his own at having done something to upset her. "I would never purposely hurt you, Jayne."

He already had. Her napkin was shredded in half. "I'm different from other women you know, Riley. But being…inexperienced shouldn't be a fault."

"I consider your lack of experience a virtue." He didn't know where all this was leading, but they were on the right path.

A virtue! Jayne almost laughed. He'd gone from her arms to those of that…other woman without so much as a hint of conscience.

Their lunch arrived, and Jayne stared at the large pink shrimp that filled the crispy fried eggplant. She had no appetite.

"Why'd you change your hair?"

Jayne picked up her fork, refusing to meet his probing gaze. "For the reunion."

"Is that the only reason?"

"Should there be another one?"

"You said you had a surprise for me," he coaxed.

"Not exactly *for* you."

"I see." He didn't, but it shouldn't matter.

Tasting a shrimp, Jayne marveled at the wonderful flavors. "This is good."

"I thought you'd enjoy it."

They ate in silence for several minutes. Riley's appetite was quickly satisfied. He'd finished his meal before Jayne was one-third done. He saw the way she toyed with the shrimp, eating only a couple before laying her fork on the plate and pushing it aside.

"I guess I'm not very hungry," she murmured.

Riley crumpled his paper napkin. "Why is it so important for you to go to that reunion?" he asked bluntly.

Jayne had asked herself the same question over and over. Her hand went around the water glass. The condensation on the outside wet her hand, and she wiped her fingers dry on a fresh napkin.

"I'm not sure," she finally said. "I'd like to see everyone again. It's been a long time."

"You've kept in contact with them?"

"A few. Mainly a girl named Judy Thomas. She was the closest friend I had there."

"What about the boys?" They were the ones who worried Riley. Once her male classmates realized what an unspoiled beauty she'd turned out to be, they might give him a run for his money. He wouldn't relinquish this woman easily. He'd waited a lifetime for her.

"There weren't any. I attended a private girls' school."

Riley smiled at the unexpected relief that went through him. "That must have been tough."

"Not really. I attended a women's college, as well."

"So that's where you got your case of repressed relationship development." He tried to make a joke of it but saw quickly that his humor had fallen flat. Riley was baffled at the ready tears that sprang to her eyes.

"Jayne, I didn't mean that the way it sounded." His hand reached for hers.

Jayne jerked her fingers away. "Did you enjoy her, Riley?"

The question was asked in such a small, broken voice that his face tightened with alarm. "Who?"

"The blonde from Soft Sam's."

"I want to trust you." Indecision played across her face.

"Can you believe that I didn't touch her?" he asked.

In response, her eyes delved into his. "I believe you," she murmured. She had to trust Riley or go crazy picturing him in the arms of another woman. The image would destroy her.

"There's only one woman who interests me."

"Oh?"

"One exceptionally lovely woman with honey-brown eyes and a heart so full of love she can't help giving it away." He remembered finding her with the children in the library and again felt such overwhelming desire for her that he ached with it. As he watched her, he could picture her with their child. Until recently, Riley hadn't given much thought to a family. Because of his job, he lived hard, often encountering danger, even when he least expected it. No, that wasn't true; he *always* expected it. He'd seen other men, men with families, attempt to balance their two worlds, and the results could be disastrous. In an effort to avoid that, Riley had pushed any hope of a permanent relationship from his mind, and succeeded. Until he met Jayne.

"Come on," he said, standing. "Let's get out of here." He pulled his wallet from his back pocket and tossed a few bills on the table before waving to someone in the back kitchen. Then he led her outside.

When Jayne moved toward his car, Riley stopped her and directed her to a dark alley.

"I know this isn't the right time or place," he whispered, pressing her against the building's brick wall. His hands were on both sides of her face. "But I need this."

He kissed her hungrily, and Jayne responded the same way. She couldn't get enough of him. She could feel his kiss in every part of her. Sensations tingled along her nerves. The doubts that had weighed on her mind dissolved and with them the pain of the past two days. Lifting her arms, she slid them around his middle and arched toward him.

"Oh, my sweet Jayne." His voice was raspy and filled with emotion. "Trust me, for just a little longer."

"Forever," she whispered in return. "Forever and ever."

Riley closed his eyes. With his current case he was going to demand a lot more of her trust. He wanted to protect her and himself and walk away from this part of his life and start anew. His prayer was that they could hold on to this moment for all time, but he already knew that was impossible.

When Jayne got back to the library, she was ten minutes late. Her lips were devoid of lipstick and her hair was mussed.

"Sorry I'm late," she said, taking her seat and avoiding Gloria's probing gaze.

"Where'd you go?"

"I...don't recall the name of the restaurant, but they serve Creole food. It's on Fourth."

"They must've been busy."

"Why?" Jayne's eyes flew to her friend.

"Because you're late."

"As a matter of fact, we were lucky to find a table." Her right eye gave one convulsive jerk, and she quickly changed the subject. "Have you heard from Lance?"

"I already told you we're going out again tonight."

"So you did," Jayne mumbled, having momentarily forgotten.

"He's wonderful."

"I'm really happy for you." Who would have believed that after months of searching, Gloria would finally meet someone in the frozen-food section of Albertsons?

"Don't be in too much of a hurry to congratulate me," Gloria said. "It's too soon to tell if he's a keeper. So far, I like him quite a bit, and we seem to have several common interests—besides groceries. But then that's not always good, either."

"Why not?" The more time Jayne spent with Riley, the more she discovered that they enjoyed many of the same things. They were alike and yet completely different.

"Boring."

Jayne blinked. "I beg your pardon?"

Gloria took a chair beside her and crossed her legs. "Sometimes people are so much alike that they end up boring each other to death."

"That won't be a problem with Riley and me. In fact, I was thinking that although we're alike in some ways, we're quite different in others." Smiling, she looked at Gloria. "I like him, you know. I may even love him."

Gloria smiled back. "I know."

"I'm trying a new recipe for spaghetti sauce, if you'd like to come over for dinner," Jayne told Riley on Friday morning. He gave her a ride downtown most days now and phoned whenever he couldn't. His working hours often extended beyond hers, so she still took the bus home in the evenings. But things had worked out well. Since she arrived home first, she started preparing supper, taking pleasure in creating meals because it gave her an excuse to invite Riley over.

"I'll bring the wine."

"Okay." She smiled up at him with little of her former shyness.

"Jayne—" he paused, taking her hand "—you don't have to lure me to your place with wonderful meals."

Her eyes dropped. She hadn't thought her methods were quite that transparent. "I enjoy cooking," she said lamely.

"I just don't want you going to all this trouble for me. I

want to be with you, whether you feed me or not. It's you I'm attracted to. Not your cooking. Well, not *just* your cooking."

"I like being with you, too."

Since their lunch on Monday, they'd spent every available minute in each other's company. Often they didn't do anything more exciting than watch television. One night they'd sat together, each engrossed in a good book, and shared a bottle of excellent white wine. That whole evening they hadn't spoken more than a dozen times. But Jayne had never felt closer to another human being.

Riley kissed her and touched her often. It wasn't uncommon for him to sneak up behind her when she was standing at the stove or rinsing dishes. But he never let their kissing get out of control. Jayne wasn't half as eager to restrain their lovemaking as Riley seemed to be.

That evening Jayne had the sauce simmering on the stove and was ready to add the dry spaghetti to the boiling water when Riley called.

"I'm going to be late," he said gruffly.

"That's fine. I can hold dinner."

"I don't think you should." His voice tightened. "In fact, maybe you'd better eat without me."

"I don't want to." She'd been having her meals alone almost every night of her adult life, and suddenly the thought held no appeal.

"This can't be helped, Jayne."

The city worked its inspectors harder than necessary, in Jayne's opinion. "I understand." She didn't really, but asking a flurry of questions wouldn't help. As it was, his responses were clipped and impatient.

He sighed into the phone, and Jayne thought she heard a car honk in the background. "I'll talk to you in the morning," he said.

"Sure, the morning will be fine. I'll save some dinner for you, and you can have it for lunch. Spaghetti's always better the next day."

"Great," he said. She heard a loud shout. "I've got to go," he said hurriedly.

"See you tomorrow."

"Right, tomorrow," Riley said with an earnestness that caused a cold chill to race up Jayne's spine. She held on to the phone longer than necessary, her fingers tightening around the receiver. As she hung up, a feeling of dread settled in the pit of her stomach. Riley hadn't been calling her from his office. The sounds in the background were street noises. And he was with someone. A male. Something was wrong. She could feel it. Something was very, very wrong.

Jayne didn't sleep well that night, tossing and turning while her short conversation with Riley played back in her mind. She went over every detail. He'd sounded impatient, angry. His voice was hard and flat, reminding her of the first few times she'd talked to him.

When she finally did drift off to sleep, her dreams were troubled. Visions of Riley with that woman from Soft Sam's drifted into her mind until she woke with an abrupt start. The dream had been so real that goose bumps broke out on her arms, and she hugged her blankets closer.

The following morning, Saturday, Riley was at her door early. Jayne had barely dressed and had just finished her breakfast.

"Morning." She smiled, not quite meeting his gaze.

"Morning." He leaned forward and brushed his mouth over hers. "I'm sorry about last night." He gently pressed his hands against the sides of her neck, forcing her to meet his eyes.

"That's okay. I understand. There are times I need to work late, as well." All her fears seemed trivial now. He was a city inspector, so naturally he didn't spend all his time in an office or on his own. She'd overacted. Her niggling worries about why he'd canceled melted away under the warmth of his gaze.

He broke away from her and walked to the other side of her living room. "This next week is going to be busy, so maybe we shouldn't make any dinner plans."

Jayne rubbed her hands together. "If that's what you want."

"It isn't."

He said it with such honesty that Jayne could find no reason to doubt him.

After a cup of coffee, they left for Riverside Park. Together they did the shopping for the week, making several stops. When they returned to the apartment building, their arms were filled with packages.

"I want to stop off at the manager's," Riley announced as they stepped into the elevator.

"I'll go on up to my place and put these things away." She didn't want the ice cream to melt while Riley paid his rent.

"I'll be up shortly."

The elevator doors closed, and Jayne watched the light that indicated the floor numbers. She smiled at Riley, recalling similar rides in times past and how she'd dreaded being caught alone with him. Now she savored the moment.

Riley smiled back. Their morning had been marvelous, he thought. It seemed natural to have Jayne at his side, and he'd enjoyed going shopping together like a long-married couple. He experienced a surge of tenderness that was so powerful it was akin to pain. He'd been waiting for this woman for years. He was deeply grateful to have her in his life, especially after the unsavory people he'd been dealing with these past few years. He loved her wry wit. Her sense of humor was subtle and quick. Thinking about it now made him chuckle lightly.

"Is something funny?" She raised wide inquisitive eyes to him.

"No, just thinking about you."

"I'm so glad I amuse you." She shifted her shopping bag from one hand to the other.

"Here." Deliberately he took her bag and set it on the elevator floor. Before she could realize what he was doing, he turned her in his embrace and slid his arms around her waist. "You're the most beautiful woman I've ever met, Jayne Gilbert."

"Oh, Riley." She lowered her gaze, not knowing how to respond. No man had ever said anything so wonderful to her. From someone else it would have sounded like a well-worn line, but she could see the sincerity in his eyes. That told her *he* believed it, even if she couldn't.

"Do you doubt me?"

She answered him with a short nod. "I've seen myself in plenty of mirrors. I know what I look like."

"An angel. Pure, good, innocent." With each word, he drew closer to her. Sweeping her hair aside, he brushed her neck with his mouth. She tilted her head, and the brown curls fell to one side. When his lips moved up her jawline, Jayne felt her legs grow weak. She leaned against the back of the elevator for support. Finally his mouth found hers in a long, slow kiss that left her weak and clinging to him.

The elevator stopped then, and Riley released her for a few seconds, closing the door again.

"Riley, that was our floor," she objected.

"I know." His eyes blazed into hers, and he leaned forward and kissed her again.

Jayne clung to him, awed that this man could be attracted to her. "I can't believe this," she murmured, and tears clogged her throat.

"What? That we're kissing in an elevator?"

"No," she breathed. "That you're holding me like this. I know it's silly, but I'm afraid of waking up and discovering that this is all a dream. It's too good to be true."

"You'd have a hard time convincing me that this isn't real. You feel too right in my arms."

"You do, too."

Her heart swelled with love. Riley hadn't said he loved her, but he didn't need to. With every action he took and every word he spoke, he was constantly showing her his feelings. For that matter, she hadn't told him how she felt, either. It was unnecessary.

Reluctantly he let her go and pushed the button that would open the elevator doors. "I'll be back in a couple of minutes." He grinned. "I need to go all the way down again."

"I'll start the spaghetti."

"Okay." He caressed her cheek. "I'll see you soon."

She stepped out of the elevator and instantly caught sight of a tall man. She didn't recognize him as anyone from her building and certainly not from the ninth floor. Judging by his age, as well as the leather he wore, he could have been a member of some gang. Jayne swallowed uncomfortably and glanced back at Riley. The elevator doors were closing, and she doubted he saw her panicked look.

Squaring her shoulders, Jayne secured her small purse under her arm and moved the shopping bag to her left hand. Remembering a book she'd read about self-defense, she paused to remove her keys from her purse and held the one for her apartment between her index and middle fingers. If this creep tried to attack she'd be ready. Watching him, Jayne walked to her apartment, which was in the middle of the long corridor. Her breath felt tight in her lungs. With every step she took, the young man advanced toward her.

His eyes were dark, his pupils wide. Fear coated the inside of her mouth. Whoever this was appeared to be high on some sort of drug. All the headlines she'd read about drug-crazed criminals flashed through her mind. Getting into her apartment no longer seemed the safest alternative. What if he forced his way in?

Jayne whirled around and hurried back to the elevator, urgently pushing the button.

"You aren't going to run away, are you?" The man's words were slurred.

In a panic, Jayne pushed the button again. Nothing.

He was so close now that all he had to do was reach out and touch her. Lifting one hand, he pulled her hair and laughed when she winced at the slight pain.

"What do you want?" she demanded, backing away.

"Give me your money."

Jayne had no intention of arguing with him and held out her purse. "I don't have much." Almost all the cash she carried with her had been spent on groceries, and she hadn't brought any credit cards. Or her cell phone…

He grabbed her purse and started pawing through it. When he discovered the truth of her statement, he'd be furious, and there was no telling what he'd do next. If she was going to escape, her chance was now.

Raising the bag of groceries, she shoved it into his chest with all her strength and took off running. The stairwell was at the other end of the corridor, and she sprinted toward it. Fear and adrenaline pumped through her, but she wasn't fast enough to beat the young man. He got to the door before she did and blocked her only exit.

Jayne came to an abrupt halt and, with her hands at her sides, moved slowly backward.

She heard the elevator door opening behind her and swung

around. Riley stepped out. Jayne's relief was so great she felt like weeping. "Riley!" she called out.

Instantly her attacker straightened.

Riley saw the fear sketched so vividly on her face and felt an overwhelming instinct to protect. Wordlessly he moved toward her pursuer.

The man took one step toward Riley. "Give me your money."

Riley didn't say a word.

In her gratitude at seeing Riley, Jayne hadn't stopped to notice the lack of fear in him. With her back against the wall, her legs gave out, and she slumped helplessly against it.

Riley's face was as hard as granite and so intense that Jayne's breath caught in her lungs. The man who'd kissed her and held her in the elevator wasn't the same man who stood in the hallway now. This Riley was a stranger.

"Hey, buddy, it was just a joke," the young man said, reaching for the doorknob.

Jayne had never seen a man as fierce as Riley was at that moment. She hardly recognized him. Deadly fury blazed from his eyes, and Jayne felt cold shivers racing over her arms.

From there, everything seemed to happen in slow motion. Riley advanced on the young man and knocked him to the ground with one powerful punch.

The man let out a yelp of pain. Riley raised his fist to hit him again. Hand connected with jaw in a sickening thud.

Jayne screamed. "Riley! No more. No more."

As if he'd forgotten she was there, Riley turned back to her. Taking this unexpected opportunity to escape, the man propelled himself through the stairwell door and was gone.

Jayne forced back a tiny sobbing breath and stumbled to his side. She threw her arms around him as tears rained from her eyes. "Oh, Riley," she cried weakly.

Riley's body was rigid against hers for several minutes until the tension eased from his limbs and he wrapped his arms around her. "Did he hurt you?"

"No," she sobbed. "No. He was after my money, but I didn't have much."

His arms went around her with crushing force, driving the air from her lungs.

"If he'd hurt you—"

"He didn't, he didn't." No more words could make it past the constriction in her throat. Jayne realized it wasn't fear that had prompted this sudden paralysis, but the knowledge that Riley was capable of such violence. She didn't want to know what he might've done if she hadn't stopped him.

His hold gradually relaxed. "Tell me what happened," he said, leading her toward her apartment door.

"He wanted my money."

"You didn't do anything stupid like argue with him, did you?"

"No… I read in this self-defense book that—"

"You and your books."

She could almost laugh, but not quite. "I'm so grateful you got here when you did." She was thinking of her own safety, but also of the would-be mugger and what Riley would have done to him had he actually hurt her.

"I've never seen anyone fight like that," she murmured, stooping to pick up her purse and the groceries that littered the hallway.

"It's something I learned when I was in the military." Riley strove to make light of what he'd done. The last thing he wanted to do now was to fabricate stories to appease Jayne's curiosity.

He bent down to gather up some of the spilled groceries. Her hands trembled as she deposited one item after another in her bag.

"Are you sure you're all right?" Doubt echoed in his husky voice.

"Yes. I was more scared than anything."

"I don't blame you."

Her returning smile was wooden. "I surprised myself by how quickly I could move."

Getting to his feet, Riley brought the bag with him. "Let's get these things put away. I'll bet the ice cream is starting to melt."

Rushing ahead of him to unlock the apartment door, Jayne had the freezer open by the time he arrived in her kitchen. He handed the carton of vanilla ice cream to her; she shoved it inside and closed the door.

"Do you think we should call the police?" she asked, still shaking.

"No. He won't be back."

"How do you know?" His confidence was unnerving.

"I just do. But if it'll make you feel better, go ahead and call them."

"I might." She watched for his reaction, but he gave none. Maybe it was her imagination, but she had the distinct feeling that Riley didn't want her to contact the authorities.

Riley paced the floor. "Jayne, listen, I've got something to tell you."

"Yes?" She raised expectant eyes to him.

"I'm going away for a while."

"Away?"

"On vacation. A fishing trip. I'm leaving tonight."

7

"A fishing trip?" Jayne asked incredulously. Riley didn't know the difference between a salmon and a trout. "Isn't this rather sudden?"

"Not really. The timing looked good, so we decided to go now, instead of waiting until later in the summer." Riley opened the refrigerator and took out the bowl of spaghetti sauce, setting it on the counter.

Jayne moved to the cupboard and got a saucepan. She worked for the city, too, and knew from experience that vacation times were often planned a year in advance. One didn't simply decide "the timing looked good" and head off on vacation. "How long will you be gone?"

His eyes softened. "Don't worry. I'll be back in time for your reunion."

Jayne was apprehensive, but it wasn't over her high school reunion. This so-called vacation of Riley's had a fishy odor that had nothing to do with trout. Busy at the sink, she kept her back to him, swallowing down her doubts. "You must have had this planned for quite a while."

"Not really. It was a spur-of-the-moment decision." He didn't elaborate, and she didn't ask. Quizzing him about the particulars would only put a strain on these last few hours together.

She *should* ask him about these spur-of-the-moment vacation plans and how he'd arranged it with the city. From what he'd told her, Riley was a city inspector. But Jayne had doubts about that; she couldn't help it. Although he seemed to keep regular hours, he often needed to meet someone at night. She'd watched him several times from her living room window, seeing him in the parking lot below. She'd never questioned him about his late hours, though, afraid of what she'd discover if she pursued the subject.

She bit her bottom lip, angry with herself for being so complacent.

"You've got that look on your face," Riley said when she set the pan of water on the stove to boil.

"What look?"

"The one that tells me you disapprove."

"How could I possibly object to you taking a well-deserved vacation? You've been working long hours. You need a break. Right?"

"Right."

But he didn't sound as though he was excited about this trip. And from little things he'd let drop, Jayne suspected he didn't even know what a fishing pole looked like. He certainly didn't know anything about fish!

Standing behind her, Riley slipped his arms around her waist and pressed his mouth to the side of her neck. "A watched pot never boils," he murmured. "Jayne, listen—

I shouldn't be gone any more than ten days. Two weeks at the most."

"Two weeks!" The reunion was in three. Turning, she hugged him with all the pent-up love in her heart. "I'll miss you," she whispered.

"I'll miss you, too." Tenderly, he kissed her temple, then tilted her head so that his mouth could claim hers.

Jayne marveled that he could be so loving and gentle only minutes after punching out a mugger. The whole incident had frightened her. There were depths to this man that she had yet to glimpse, dangerous depths. But perhaps it was better not to see that side of his nature. An icy sensation ran down her arms, and she shivered.

"You're cold."

"No," she said. "Afraid."

"Why?" He tightened his hold. "What do you have to fear?"

"I don't know."

"That mugger won't be back."

"I know." After what Riley had done to him, Jayne was confident the man wouldn't dare return.

Forcing down her apprehension, she smiled and raised her fingers to his thick dark hair, then arched up and kissed his mouth. She was being unnecessarily silly, she told herself. Riley was going on a fishing trip. He'd return before her reunion, and everything would be wonderful again.

Reluctantly breaking away from him, she sighed. "I'll get lunch started. You probably have a hundred things you need to do this afternoon."

"What things?"

"What about getting all your gear together?" She added the dry noodles to the rapidly boiling water, wanting to believe with all her heart that Riley was doing exactly as he'd said.

"The other guy is bringing everything."

"But surely you've got stuff you need to do."

"Perhaps, but I decided I'd rather spend the day with you."

"When are you leaving?" One of her uncles was an avid sportsman, and from what Jayne remembered, he was emphatic that early morning was the best time for fishing.

"Tonight."

"Where will you be? Are you camping?"

He shrugged. "I don't know. I've left all the arrangements to my friend."

That sounded highly questionable, and her manufactured confidence quickly crumpled. Under the weight of her uncertainty, Jayne bowed her head.

"Honey." He tucked a finger beneath her chin, and her eyes lifted to his. "I'll be back in no time."

Despite her fears, Jayne laughed. "I sincerely doubt that." He hadn't even gone, and she already felt an empty void in her life.

"I know how important your reunion is to you."

Riley was more important to her than a hundred high school reunions. A thought went crashing through her mind with such searing impact that for a moment she was stunned. She wondered if she'd finally figured out why Riley paid her so much attention. "You seem awfully worried about my reunion."

"Only because I know how much you want to go."

With trembling hands she brought down two dinner plates from the cupboard. "I don't need your charity or your pity, Riley Chambers."

"What are you talking about?" His jaw sagged open in astonished disbelief.

Jayne's brown eyes burned with the fiery light of outrage. "It just dawned on me that...that all this attention you've been giving me lately could be attributed to precisely those reasons."

"Charity?" he demanded. "Pity? You don't honestly believe that!"

"I don't know what to think anymore. Why else would someone as…as worldly as you have anything to do with someone as plain and ordinary as me?"

Riley stared at her in shock. Jayne, plain and ordinary! Vivacious and outgoing she wasn't. But Jayne was special—more than any woman he'd ever known. He opened his mouth to speak, closed it and stalked across the room. What had gotten into her? He'd never known Jayne to be illogical. From her reaction, he could tell she wasn't falling for this fishing story of his. Telling her had been difficult enough. He hadn't wanted to do it, but there was no other option. He couldn't tell her the real reason for this unexpected "vacation," but he was lying to her for her own protection. The fewer people who were in on it, the better.

Jayne carried the plates to the table, feeling angry, hurt and confused; most of all, she was suspicious. How easily she'd been swayed by his charm and his kisses. She'd been a pushover for a man of Riley's experience. From the beginning she'd known that he wasn't everything he appeared to be. But she'd preferred to overlook the obvious. Riley was up to no good. She told herself she had a right to know what he was doing, and yet in the same breath, she had no desire to venture into the unknown mysteries he'd been hiding from her.

"Jayne, please look at me," he said quietly. "You can't accuse me of something as ridiculous as pitying you, then walk away."

"I didn't walk away… I'm setting the table." She turned to face him, her expression defiant.

"Charity, Jayne? Pity? I think you need to explain yourself."

"What's there to explain? I've always been a joke to people like you. Except that for a woman who's supposed to be smart, I've been incredibly stupid."

Riley was at a complete loss. His past dealings with women had been brief. In his line of work, it had been preferable to avoid any emotional ties. Now he discovered that he didn't know how to reassure Jayne, the first woman who'd touched his heart. He couldn't be entirely honest, but perhaps a bit of logic wouldn't be amiss....

"Even if you're right and everything I feel for you is of a charitable nature," he began, "what's my motive?"

"I don't know. But then I wouldn't, would I?"

He took a step toward her and paused. He couldn't rush her, although every instinct urged him to take her in his arms and comfort her. "That's not what's really bothering you, is it?"

Tears clouded her eyes as she shook her head. "No."

He reached for her, but Jayne avoided him. "Honey..." he murmured.

She blanched and pointed a shaking finger in his direction. "Don't call me *honey.* I'm not important to you."

"I love you, Jayne." He didn't know any other way to tell her. The flowery words she deserved and probably expected just weren't in him. He could only hope she trusted him—and that she'd give him time.

Jayne's reaction was to place her hand over her mouth and shake her head from side to side.

"Well?" he said impatiently. "Don't you have anything to say?"

Jayne stared at him, her eyes wet. "You *love* me?"

"It can't have been any big secret. You must've known, for heaven's sake."

"Riley…"

"No, it's your turn to listen. I've gone about this all wrong. Women like moonlight, roses, the whole deal." He paced the kitchen and ran a hand through his hair. "I'm no good at this. With you, I wanted to do everything right, and already I can see it's backfiring."

"Riley, I love you, too."

"Women need romance. I realize that and I feel like a jerk because you're entitled to all of it. Unfortunately, I don't know the right words to tell you about everything inside me."

"Riley." She said his name again, her voice gaining volume. "Did you hear what I said?"

"I know you love me," he muttered almost angrily. "You aren't exactly one to disguise your feelings."

She crossed her arms over her chest with an exasperated sigh. "Well, excuse me."

"I'm not good enough for you," he continued, barely acknowledging her response. "Someone as honorable and kind as you deserves a man who's a heck of a lot better than me. I've lived hard these past few years and I've done more than one thing I regret."

Jayne started to respond but wasn't given the opportunity.

"There hasn't been room in my life for a woman. But I can't wait any longer. I didn't realize how much I need you. I want to change, but that's going to take time and patience."

"I'm patient," Jayne told him shyly, her anger forgotten under the sweet balm of his words. "Gloria says I'm the most patient person she's ever known. In fact, my father gets angry with me because he feels I'm too meek…not that meekness and patience are the same thing, you understand. It's just that—"

"Are you going to chatter all day, or are you going to come over here and let me kiss you?" His eyes took on a fierce possessive light.

"Oh, Riley, I love you so much." She walked into his waiting arms, surrendering everything—her heart, her soul, her life. And her doubts.

They kissed, lightly at first, testing their freshly revealed emotions. Then their lips stayed together, gradually parting as their mouths moved, slanting, tasting, probing.

Jayne whimpered. She couldn't help herself. There was so much more she longed to discover....

His kisses deepened until he raised his head and whispered hoarsely. "Jayne. Oh, my sweet, sweet, Jayne."

"I love you," she said again and kissed him softly.

Riley tunneled his fingers through her hair and buried his face in the slope of her neck. But he didn't push her away as he had in the past. Nor did he bring her closer. His breath was rushed as he struggled with indecision.

"Riley..."

"Shhh, don't move. Okay?"

"Okay," she agreed, loving him more and more.

Gradually the tension eased from him, and he relaxed. But his hold didn't loosen, and he held her for what seemed like hours rather than minutes.

They spent the rest of the day together. After lunch they walked in the park, holding hands, making excuses to touch each other. Riley brought along a chessboard and set it up on the picnic table, and they played a long involved game. When Jayne won the match, Riley applauded her skill and reset the board. He won the second game. They decided against a third.

At dinnertime they ate Chinese food at a small hole-in-the-wall restaurant and brought the leftovers home.

Standing just inside her apartment door, Jayne asked, "Do you want to come in for coffee?"

"I've got to pack and get ready."

She nodded. "I understand. Thank you for today."

"No, thank *you.*" He laid his hand against her cheek, and when he spoke, his voice was warm and filled with emotion. "You'll take care of yourself while I'm gone, won't you?"

"Of course I will." She couldn't resist smiling. "I've been doing a fairly good job of that for several years now."

"I don't feel right leaving you." He studied her. He wished this case was over so he could give her all the things she had a right to ask for.

"You're coming back."

The words stung his conscience. There was always the possibility that he wouldn't. The risks and dangers of his job had been a stimulant before he'd fallen in love with Jayne. Now he experienced the first real taste of dread.

Fear shot through Jayne at the expression on Riley's face. She saw the way his eyes narrowed, the way his mouth tightened. "You *are* coming back, aren't you?" She repeated her question, louder and stronger this time.

"I'll be back." His voice vibrated with emotion. "I love you, Jayne. I'm coming back to you, don't worry."

Not worry! One glimpse at the intense look in his eyes, and she was terrified. From the way Riley was behaving, one would assume that he was going off on a suicide mission.

Riley smiled and brought his hand to her face. He touched her cheek, then her forehead, easing the frown between her brows. "I'll be back. I promise you that."

"I'll be waiting."

"I won't be able to contact you."

She nodded.

The story about his fishing trip was forgotten. Jayne didn't know where he was headed or why. For now, she didn't want to know. He said he was coming back, and that was all that mattered.

"Goodbye, my love," he said with a final kiss.

"Goodbye, Riley."

He turned and walked out the door, and Jayne was left with an aching void of uncertainty.

The library was busy on Monday morning. Jayne was sitting at the information desk in the children's department when the chief librarian approached, carrying a huge bouquet of red roses in a lovely ceramic vase.

"How beautiful," Jayne said, looking up.

"They just arrived for you." Her boss placed them on the desk.

"For me?" No one had ever sent her flowers at work.

Gloria walked across the room and joined her. "Who are they from?" she asked, then answered her own question. "It must be Riley."

"Must be." Jayne unpinned the small card and pulled it from the envelope.

"What's it say?" Gloria wanted to know.

"Just that he'll be home by the time these wilt."

"He must have sent them from out of town."

Jayne frowned. "Right." Except that the card was scrawled in Riley's own unmistakable handwriting. He could have ordered them before he went, or…or maybe he hadn't left Portland yet.

She squelched the doubts and possibilities that raced through her mind. She loved Riley and he loved her, and that was all that mattered. Not where he was or what he was doing. Or even whether he was fishing.

Without him, the days passed slowly. Jayne was astonished

that a man she'd known and loved for such a short time could so effectively fill her life. Now her days lacked purpose. She went to work, came home and plopped down in front of the television. During the first week that he was gone, Jayne ate more microwave dinners than she'd eaten the whole previous month. It was simpler that way.

"You look like you could do with some cheering up," Gloria commented Friday afternoon.

"I could," Jayne murmured.

"How about if we go shopping tomorrow for a dress to wear to your reunion? I know just the place."

Jayne would need something special for the reunion, but she didn't feel like shopping. Still, it had to be done sooner or later. "All right," she found herself agreeing.

"And in exchange for my expert advice, you can take me to the Creole restaurant where you and Riley had lunch."

"Sure. If I can remember where it is. We only went there once." That day had been so miserable for Jayne that she hadn't paid much attention to the place or the food.

"You said it was on Fourth."

"Right." She remembered now, and she also recalled why she'd been so miserable. That was when she'd seen Riley with the blonde.

Gloria showed up at her apartment early Saturday morning. Jayne had no enthusiasm for this shopping expedition.

Gloria got a carton of orange juice from the refrigerator and poured herself a glass. "I checked out this new boutique, and it's expensive, but worth it."

"Gloria." Jayne sighed. The longer Riley was away, the more unsure she felt about the reunion. "I've probably got something adequate in my closet."

"You don't." Gloria opened the fridge again and peeked inside. "I'm starved. Have you had breakfast yet?"

Jayne hadn't. "I'm not hungry, but help yourself."

"Thanks." Pulling out a loaf of bread, Gloria stuck a piece in the toaster. "When you walk in the grand ballroom of the Seattle Westin, I want every eye to be on you."

"I'll see what I can do to arrange a spotlight," Jayne said.

"I mean it. You're going to be a hit."

"Right." In twenty-seven years, she hadn't made an impression on anything except her mattress.

"Hey, where's your confidence? You can't back down now. You've got the man, kiddo. It's all downhill from here."

"I suppose," Jayne said.

"I thought you should get something in red."

"Red?" Jayne echoed with a small laugh. "I was thinking more along the lines of brown or beige."

"Nope." The toast popped up, and Gloria buttered it. "You want to stand out in the crowd, not blend in."

"Blending in is what I do."

"Nope." Gloria shook her head. "For one night, m'dear, you're going to be a knockout."

"Gloria." Jayne hesitated. "I don't know."

"Trust me. I've gotten you this far."

"But…"

"Trust me."

Two hours later, Jayne was pleased that she'd had faith in her friend's judgment. After seeing the inside of more stores than she'd visited in a year, she found the perfect dress. Or rather, Gloria did—and not in the new boutique she'd been so excited about, either. This was a classic women's wear shop Jayne would never have ventured into on her own. The dress was a lavender color, and Gloria insisted Jayne try it on. At first, Jayne had scoffed; in two hours, she'd dressed and undressed at least twenty times. She was about to throw up her arms and surrender—nothing fit right, or if it did fit, the color was wrong. Even Gloria showed signs of frustration.

Everything about this full-length gown was perfect. Jayne stood in front of the three-way mirror and blinked in disbelief.

"You look stunning," Gloria breathed in awe.

Jayne couldn't stop staring at herself. This one gown made up for every prom she'd ever missed. The off-the-shoulder style and close-fitting bodice accentuated her full breasts and tiny waist to exquisite advantage. The full side-shirred skirt and double lace ruffle danced about her feet. She couldn't have hoped to find a dress more beautiful.

"Do we dare look at the price?" Gloria murmured, searching for the tag.

"It's lovely, but can I afford it?" Jayne hesitated, expecting to discover some reason she couldn't have this perfect gown.

"You can't afford not to buy it," Gloria stated emphatically. "This is *the* dress for you. Besides, it's a lot more reasonable than I figured." She read the price to her, and Jayne couldn't believe it was so low; she'd assumed it would be twice as much.

"You're buying it, aren't you?" The look Gloria gave her said that if Jayne didn't, she'd never speak to her again.

"Naturally I'm buying it," Jayne responded with a wide grin. Excitement flowed through her, and she felt like singing and dancing. Riley would love how she looked in this dress. Everything was working out so well. She'd shock her former classmates. They'd take one look at her in that gown with Riley at her side, and their jaws would fall open with utter astonishment. And yet…that didn't matter the way it once did.

"Now are you going to feed me?" Gloria fluttered her

long lashes dramatically as though to say she was about to faint from hunger.

"Do you still want to try that place Riley took me to?"

"Only if we can get there quickly."

Smiling at her friend's humor, Jayne paid for the dress and made arrangements to have it delivered to her apartment later in the day.

She and Gloria chatted easily as they walked out to the street. Gloria drove, and with Jayne acting as navigator, they made their way down the freeway and across the Willamette River to the heart of downtown.

"There it is," Jayne announced as Gloria pulled onto Fourth Avenue. "To your left, about halfway down the block."

"Great." Gloria backed into a parking space. A flash of black attracted Jayne's attention. She glanced into the alley beside the restaurant and saw a sports car similar to Riley's. She immediately decided it wasn't his. There was no reason he'd be here—was there?

"I don't mind telling you I'm starved," Gloria said as she turned off the ignition.

"What's with you lately? I've never known you to show such an interest in food."

"Yes, well, you see…" Gloria paused to clear her throat. "I tend to eat when something's bothering me."

"What's bothering you?" Jayne instantly felt guilty. She'd been so involved with her own problems that she hadn't noticed her friend's.

"Well…"

"Is it Lance?" It had to be. Gloria hadn't talked about him all week, although the week before she'd been bubbling over about her newfound soul mate. "He's not turning out to be everything you thought?"

"I wish." Gloria reached for her purse and stepped out of the car door.

"What do you wish?"

"That he wasn't so wonderful. Jayne, I'm scared. Look at me." She held out her hand and purposely shook it. "I'm shaking all over."

"But if you like him so much, what's wrong?"

They crossed the street together and entered the restaurant, taking the first available booth. "I've been married once," Gloria told her unnecessarily. "And when that didn't work out, I was sure I'd never recover. I know it sounds melodramatic to anyone who hasn't been through a divorce, but it's true."

Gloria was right; Jayne probably couldn't fully understand, but she thought about Riley and how devastated she'd be if they ever stopped loving each other.

"Now I'm falling for another man and, Jayne, I'm so tied up in knots I can't think straight. Being with you today is an excuse not to be with Lance. Every time we're together, the attraction grows stronger and stronger. We're already talking about marriage."

"I guess it works that way sometimes," Jayne murmured, thinking she'd marry Riley in a minute. Gloria had met Lance only a couple of weeks after Jayne had started seeing Riley.

"We both want a family and we believe strongly in the same things."

"Are you going to marry him?"

Gloria shrugged. "Not yet. It's too serious a decision to make so quickly. Remember the old saying? Marry in haste and repent at leisure."

"And..."

"And I haven't told Lance. I know him, or at least I think I know him. He's just like a man."

"I should hope so." Jayne chuckled.

"Once he decides on something, he wants it *now.* I have

this horrible feeling that I'm going to tell him I want to wait, and he's going to argue with me and wear me down. He may even tell me to take a hike. There aren't many men around as good as Lance. I could be walking away from the last opportunity I have to meet a decent man."

"If he loves you, he'll agree. And if he's too impatient, you'll have your answer, won't you?"

"No, because knowing me, I'll want him even more."

The waitress came with glasses of water and a menu. They ordered, ate lunch and chatted over several cups of coffee and cheesecake.

Glancing at her watch, Gloria said, "Listen, I've got to get back. Lance is picking me up in an hour."

Drinking the last of her coffee, Jayne stood. "Then let's get going."

Outside the restaurant, Jayne idly checked the alley for the black car as she crossed the street. It was still there. She could have sworn it was Riley's. But it couldn't be. Could it?

8

There had to be a thousand black sports cars in Oregon like the one Riley drove, Jayne told herself repeatedly over the next twenty-four hours. Probably more than a thousand. She was being absurd in even wondering if Riley's car was the one in the alley beside the Creole restaurant. He was fishing with friends. Right?

Wrong, said a little voice in the back of her mind. He'd lied about that; Jayne was sure of it. He'd never introduced her to any of his friends. He was new in Portland, having lived in the city for only a few months. He'd admitted there were things in his life he regretted. He'd said he wanted to change and that he wasn't good enough for her.

All weekend, Jayne's thoughts vacillated. Even if he'd lied about the fishing trip, it didn't automatically mean he was doing anything illegal, although those mysterious meetings in the parking lot weren't encouraging. And if he was doing something underhanded, she didn't want to know about it. Ignorance truly was bliss. If she inadvertently found anything out… She simply preferred not to know because then she might be required to act on it.

Monday morning on the bus ride into town, Jayne sat looking out the window, the newspaper resting in her lap. She hadn't heard anything from Riley, but then she hadn't expected to.

She glanced at the headlines. The state senator whom she'd met several months earlier had been arrested and released on a large bail. Apparently Senator Max Priestly, who'd lobbied heavily for legalized gambling in Oregon, had ties to the Mafia. She skimmed the article, not particularly interested in the details. His court date had already been set. Jayne felt a grimace of distaste at the thought that a public official would willingly sell out the welfare of his state.

Setting aside the front-page section, she turned to the advice column. Maybe reading about someone else's troubles would lighten her own. It didn't.

At lunchtime Jayne decided not to fight her uncertainty any longer. She'd take a cab to the Creole restaurant and satisfy her curiosity. The black sports car would be gone, and she'd be reassured, calling herself a fool for being so suspicious.

Only she wasn't reassured. Even when she discovered that the car was nowhere to be seen, she didn't relax. Instead she instructed the driver to take her to Soft Sam's.

The minute she climbed out of the taxi, Jayne saw the familiar black car parked on a nearby side street. Her heart pounded against her ribs as dread crept up her spine. Absently she handed the driver his fare.

Just because the car was there didn't mean anything, she told herself calmly. It might not even be his.

But Jayne took one glance at the interior, with Riley's raincoat slung over the seat, and realized it *was* his car.

Stomach churning, Jayne ran her hand over the back fender, confused and unsure. From the beginning of this so-called fishing trip, she'd suspected Riley was lying. She didn't know what he was hiding from her or why—she just knew he was.

Her appetite gone, Jayne backed away from the car and returned to the library without eating lunch.

That evening when she arrived at her apartment, Jayne turned on the TV to drown out her fears. The first time she'd ever seen Riley, she'd thought he looked like…well, like a criminal. Some underworld gang member. He wore that silly raincoat as if he were carrying something he wanted to conceal—like a gun.

Slumping onto the sofa, Jayne buried her face in her hands. *Could* he be hiding a weapon? The very idea was ridiculous. Of course he wasn't! She'd know if he carried a gun. He'd held her enough for her to have felt it.

The local news blared from the TV. The evening broadcast featured the arrest of Senator Max Priestly, who'd been caught in a sting operation. This was the same story she'd read in the morning paper.

Jayne stared at the screen and at the outrage that showed on Priestly's face. He shouted that he'd been framed and he'd prove his innocence in court. The commentator came back to say that the state's case had been damaged by the mysterious disappearance of vital evidence.

Deciding she'd had enough unsavory news, Jayne stood and turned off the TV.

In bed that night, she kept changing positions. Nothing felt comfortable. She couldn't vanquish her niggling doubts, couldn't relax. When she did drift into a light sleep, her dreams were filled with Riley and Senator Max Priestly.

Waking in a cold sweat, Jayne lay staring at the dark ceiling, wondering why her mind had connected the two men.

Pounding her pillow, she rolled onto her side and forced her eyes to close. A burning sensation went through her, and her eyes opened with sudden alarm. She'd connected the two men because she'd seen Riley *with* Max Priestly. She hadn't met the state senator at the library, as she'd assumed. She'd seen him with Riley. But when? Weeks ago, she recalled, before she'd started dating Riley. Where? Closing her eyes again, she tried to drag up the details of the meeting. It must have been at the apartment. Yes, he was the man in the parking lot. She'd seen Priestly hand Riley a briefcase. At the time, Jayne remembered that Senator Priestly had looked vaguely familiar. Later, she'd associated him with the group of state legislators that had toured the library. But Max Priestly hadn't been one of them.

And Riley wasn't on any fishing trip. If he was somehow linked with this man—and he appeared to be—then he probably knew that Priestly had been arrested. Riley could very well have spent this "vacation" of his awaiting Priestly's bail hearing. No wonder he hadn't been able to give her the exact date of his return.

The first thing Jayne did the next morning was to rip through the paper, eagerly searching for more information. She didn't need to look far. Again Max Priestly dominated the front page. An interview with his secretary reported that the important missing evidence was telephone logs and copies of letters Max had dictated to her. They'd simply disappeared from her computer. When questioned about how long they'd been missing, the secretary claimed that their absence had been discovered only recently. After that, Jayne stopped reading.

The morning passed in a fog of regret. Jayne didn't know

what her coworkers must think of her. She felt like a robot, programmed to act and do certain assignments without thought or question, and that was what she'd done.

When Gloria started talking about her relationship with Lance during their coffee break, Jayne didn't hear a word. She nodded and smiled at the appropriate times and prayed her friend wouldn't notice.

"Isn't it terrible, all this stuff that's coming out about Senator Priestly?"

Jayne's coffee sloshed over the rim of her cup. "Yes," she mumbled, avoiding Gloria's eyes.

"The news this morning said he has connections to the underworld. Apparently he was hoping to promote prostitution rings along with legalized gambling."

"Prostitution," Jayne echoed, vividly recalling the bleached blonde on Riley's arm that afternoon. She'd refused to believe he had anything to do with the woman, even though she knew what the woman was. Somehow she'd even managed to overcome the pain of seeing Riley with her. Now she realized that Soft Sam's was more than simply a bar. Riley had repeatedly warned her to stay away from it. She hadn't needed his caution; Jayne had felt so out of place during her one visit that she wouldn't have returned under any circumstances.

After her coffee break with Gloria, Jayne's day went from bad to worse. Nothing seemed to go right for the rest of the afternoon.

That evening, stepping off the bus, she saw Riley's car parked in his spot across the street. He was back. A chill went through her. She wouldn't tell him what she knew but prayed that he loved her enough to be honest with her.

She hadn't been inside the apartment for more than five minutes when Riley was at her door. Jayne froze at the sound of his knock. Squaring her shoulders, she forced a smile on her lips.

"Welcome back," she said, pulling open the door.

Riley took one look at her pale features and walked into the apartment. For nearly two weeks, he'd tried to put Jayne out of his mind and concentrate on his assignment. A mistake could have been disastrous, even deadly. Yet he hadn't been able to forget her. She'd been with him every minute. All he'd needed to do was close his eyes and she'd be there. Her image, her memory, comforted him and brought him joy. *So this was love.* He'd avoided it for years, but now he realized the way he felt was beyond description.

"I've missed you," he whispered, reaching for her.

Willingly Jayne went into his arms. She couldn't doubt the sincerity in his low voice.

"Oh, Riley." His name became an aching sigh as she wound her arms around his neck and buried her face in his chest.

Her tense muscles immediately communicated to Riley that something was wrong. "Honey," he breathed into her hair. "What is it?" His hand curved around the side of her neck, his fingers tangling with her soft curls. He raised her head the fraction of an inch needed for her lips to meet his descending mouth. He'd dreamed of kissing her for days....

Jayne moaned softly. She loved this man. It didn't matter what he'd done or who he knew. Riley had said he wanted to change. Jayne's love would be the bridge that would link him to a clean, honest life. Together they'd work to undo any wrong Riley had been involved in before he met her. She'd help him. She'd do nothing, absolutely nothing, to destroy this blissful happiness they shared.

Their gentle exploratory kiss grew more intense. Riley lifted his head.

"Oh, my love," he moaned raggedly into the hollow of her throat. "I've missed you so much."

"I missed you, too," she whispered in return.

He buried his hands deep in her hair and didn't breathe. Then he mumbled something she couldn't hear and reluctantly broke the contact.

For days he'd dreamed about the feel of her in his arms, yet his imagination fell short of reality. Her lips were warm and swollen from his kisses, and he could hardly believe that this shy, gentle woman could raise such havoc with his senses. "Has anything interesting happened around here?" he asked, trying to distract himself.

"Not really." She shook her head, glancing down so her twitching eye wouldn't be so noticeable. "What about you?" She approached the subject cautiously. "Did you catch lots of fish?"

"Only one."

"Did you bring it back? I can fry up a great trout."

Riley hated lying to her and pursed his lips. He swore that after this case he never would again. "I gave it to…a friend."

"I didn't think you had many friends in Portland." Her voice quavered slightly.

"I have plenty of friends." He raked his hand through his hair as he stalked to the other side of the room. He'd broken the cardinal rule in this business; the line between his professional life and his personal one had been crossed. He'd seen it happen to others and swore it wouldn't happen to him. But it was too late. He'd fallen for Jayne with his eyes wide open and wouldn't change a thing. "So, nothing new came up while I was away?"

Sheer nerve was the only thing that prevented Jayne from collapsing into a blubbering mass of tears. She wanted to shout at him not to lie to her—that she *knew*. Maybe not everything, but enough to doubt him, and it was killing her. She loved him, but she expected honesty. Their love would never last without it.

"While you were gone, I bought a dress for the reunion."

His eyes softened. "Can I see it?"

"I'd like to keep it a surprise."

Unable to help himself, he leaned forward and pressed a lingering kiss to her lips. "That's fine, but you aren't going to surprise me with how beautiful you are. I've known that from the beginning."

Despite her efforts to the contrary, Jayne blushed. "You won't have any problem attending the reunion, will you?" If Riley was mixed up with Senator Priestly, then he probably wouldn't be able to leave the state.

Riley gave her an odd look. "No, why should I?"

"I don't know."

His eyebrows arched. "There's no problem, Jayne, and if there was, I'd do anything possible to deal with it." He wouldn't disappoint her. Not for the world. They were going to walk into that reunion together, and he was going to show her the time of her life.

The phone rang, and Jayne shrugged. "It's probably Gloria," she said as she hurried into the kitchen to answer it.

"I'm going down to collect my mail," Riley told her. "I'll be back in a minute."

"Okay."

Jayne was off the phone by the time Riley returned. He started to sort through a variety of envelopes, automatically tossing the majority of them. "What did Gloria have to say?" he asked with a preoccupied frown.

Jayne poured water into the coffeepot. "It…wasn't Gloria."

"Oh?" He raised his eyes to meet hers. "Who was it?"

"Mark Bauer." She had no reason to feel guilty about Mark's call, but she did, incredibly so.

"Mark Bauer," Riley repeated, lowering his mail to the counter. "Has he made a habit of calling you since I've been gone?"

"No," she said. "Of course not."

Riley responded with a snort. He'd recognized Mark's type immediately. The guy wasn't all bad, just seeking a little companionship. The problem with Mark was that he had the mistaken notion that he was a lady-killer. He kept the lines of communication open with a dozen different women so that if one fell through there was always another. Only this time Mark had picked the wrong woman. Riley wasn't about to let that second-rate would-be player anywhere near Jayne.

"It's true, Riley," Jayne protested. Mark hadn't contacted her in weeks.

"What did he want?"

"He suggested a movie next Saturday."

"And?"

"And I told him I wasn't interested."

"Good." Reassured, Riley resumed sorting through ten days' worth of junk mail.

"But… I'd go out with him if I wanted. It just so happens that I didn't feel like a movie, that's all." If he could lie to her so blithely, she could do the same. Jayne wouldn't have gone out with Mark again, but she didn't need to admit that to Riley.

Swiftly, she retreated into the living room, grabbing the remote and flicking on the TV, hoping to catch the evening news. If the early broadcast gave more details about the Max Priestly case, she could judge Riley's reaction to it.

Riley stiffened as he watched Jayne walk away, her spine

straight and defiant. So she'd go out with other men if the mood struck her? Fine. "Go ahead," he announced.

Jayne turned around. "What do you mean?"

"You want to go out with other men, then do so with my blessing." Anger quivered in his voice. He didn't know what game Jayne was playing, but he wanted no part of it.

"I don't need your blessing."

"You're right. You don't." His teeth hurt from clenching them so tightly. "Listen, we're both tired. Let's call it a night. I'll talk to you in the morning."

"Fine." Primly, she crossed her arms and refused to meet his gaze.

But when the door closed, Jayne's confidence dissolved. Their meeting hadn't worked out the way she'd wanted. Instead of confronting Riley with what she'd learned, Jayne had tried to test his love.

After ten minutes of wearing a path in her carpet, Jayne decided that she was doomed to another sleepless night unless they settled this. She'd go to him and tell him she'd seen his car parked at Soft Sam's when he was supposedly fishing with friends. She'd also tell him she remembered seeing him and Senator Priestly in the apartment parking lot. Once she confronted Riley with the truth, he'd open up to her. And they were desperately in need of some honesty.

Standing outside his door, Jayne felt like a fool. Riley didn't answer her first tentative knock. She tried again, more loudly.

"Just a minute," she heard him shout.

Angrily Riley threw open the front door. His quickly donned bathrobe clung to his wet body. Droplets of water dripped from his wet hair.

"Jayne," he breathed, surprised to see her. "I was in the shower."

She stepped into the apartment, nervously clasping her hands. "Riley, I'm sorry about what I said earlier."

His smile brightened his dark face. "I know, love."

Awkwardly she began pacing. "We need to talk." They couldn't skirt the truth anymore. It had to come out, and it had to be now.

"Give me a minute to dress." He paused long enough to kiss her before disappearing into the bedroom.

Feeling a little out of place, Jayne moved into the living room. "Would you mind if I turned on the television?" she called out. The evening newscast could help her lead into the facts she'd unwittingly discovered.

"Sure, go ahead" came Riley's reply. "Remote's on top of the TV."

As she walked across the room, Jayne caught sight of a reddish leather briefcase sticking out from under the TV. She froze. This was the case she'd seen Senator Priestly hand over to Riley that afternoon so long ago. At least it appeared to be. She hadn't seen many of this color and this particular design.

Trembling, Jayne sank to her knees on the carpet and pulled out the briefcase. Her heart felt as though it was about to explode as she pressed open the two spring locks. The sound of the clasp opening seemed to reverberate around the room. For a panicked second she waited for Riley to rush in and demand to know what she was doing.

When nothing happened, Jayne pushed her glasses higher on her nose and carefully raised the lid. The briefcase was empty except for one file folder and one computer flash drive. Her heart pounding, Jayne opened the file. What she saw caused her breath to jam in her throat. She lifted the sheet that was a telephone log—Senator Priestly's calls. Sorting through the other papers, Jayne discovered copies of the incriminating letters that were said to be missing. Riley had in his possession the evidence necessary to convict Priestly. The very evidence that the police needed.

Feeling numb with shock and disbelief, Jayne quietly closed the case and returned it to its position under the TV.

She was sitting with her hands folded in her lap while Riley hummed cheerfully in the background. She couldn't confront Riley with what she'd found. At least not yet. Nor could she let him know what else she'd learned. If she was going to fall in love, why, oh why, did it have to be with a money-hungry felon?

Hurriedly Riley dressed, pleased that Jayne had come to him. He didn't understand why she'd started acting so silly. It was obvious that they were in love, and two people in love don't talk about dating others. His hands froze on his buttons. Maybe Jayne had seen him with Mimi again. No, he thought and expelled his breath. Jayne wouldn't have been able to hide it this well. He'd known almost instantly that there was something drastically wrong the first time she'd been upset. Something was bothering Jayne now, but it couldn't be anything as major as seeing him with that woman.

Walking into the living room, Riley paused. Jayne's spine was ramrod straight, and tears streamed down her ashen face.

"Jayne," he whispered. "What is it?"

She came to him then, linking her arms around him. "I love you, Riley."

"I know, and I love you, too."

She sobbed once and buried her face in his shoulder.

"Honey, has someone hurt you?" he asked urgently.

She shook her head. "No." Breaking free, she wiped her cheeks. "I'm sorry. I'm being ridiculous. I...don't know what came over me." Immediately her right eye started twitching, and she stared down at the floor. "I just wanted to tell you I regret what happened earlier," she said in a low voice.

"I understand." But he didn't. Riley had never seen Jayne like this. "Are you hungry? Would you like to go out for dinner?" Showing himself in a public restaurant wouldn't be the smartest move, but they could find an out-of-the-way place.

"No," she said quickly, too quickly. "I'm not hungry. In fact, I've got this terrible headache. I should probably make it an early night."

Riley was skeptical. "If you want."

She backed away from him, inching toward the door. "Good night, Riley."

"Night, love. I'll see you in the morning."

Turning, she scurried across the room and out the door like a frightened mouse. More confused than ever, Riley rubbed his jaw. From the way Jayne was behaving, he could almost believe she knew something. But that was impossible. He'd gone to extreme measures to keep her out of this thing with Priestly.

Back inside her apartment, Jayne discovered that she couldn't stop shaking. The Riley Chambers she'd fallen in love with didn't seem to be the same man who'd returned from the fishing trip. Riley might believe he loved her, but secretly Jayne wondered how deep his love would be if he was aware of how much she knew.

Ignorance had been bliss, but her eyes were open now, and she had to take some kind of action. But *what* kind?

She'd refused to believe what the evidence told her about Riley; now she had to accept it. She didn't have any choice. No matter what the consequences, she had to act.

A sob escaped as she thought about that stupid class reunion, which had gotten her into this predicament in the first place. At this point, going back to St. Mary's was the last thing she wanted to do.

Tears squeezed past her tightly closed eyes, and Jayne gave

up the effort to restrain them. She let them fall, needing the release they gave her. No one had ever told her that loving someone could be so painful. In all the books she'd read over the years, love had been a precious gift, something beyond price. Instead she'd found it to be painful, intense and ever so confusing.

Jayne didn't bother to go to bed. She sat in the darkened room, staring blankly at the walls, feeling wretched. More than wretched. The bitter disappointment cut through her. She didn't know what would happen to Riley once she talked to the police. If he hadn't already been arrested, they'd probably come for him after that.

Once again she entertained the idea of confronting him with what she'd discovered and asking him to do the honorable thing. And again she realized the impossibility of that request. Riley had lied to her several times. She couldn't trust him. And yet, she still loved him....

As the sky lightened with early morning, Jayne noticed that the clouds were heavy and gray. It seemed like an omen, a premonition of what was to come.

Knowing what she had to do, Jayne waited until she guessed Riley was awake before phoning him.

"I won't be going to work today," she told him, unable to keep the anguish out of her voice.

Riley hesitated. It sounded as if Jayne was ready to burst into tears. "Jayne," he said, unsure of how much to pressure her right now, "honey, tell me what's wrong."

"I've...still got this horrible headache," she said on a rush of emotion. "I'm fine, really. Don't worry about me. And, Riley, I want you to know something important."

"What is it?" Momentarily he tensed.

"I care about you. I'll probably never love anyone more than I love you."

"Jayne..."

"I've got to call the library and tell them I won't be in."

"I'll talk to you this evening."

"Okay," she said hoarsely.

Ten minutes later, she heard him leave. She waited another fifteen and made two brief phone calls. One to Gloria at the library and another to a local cab company, requesting a taxi.

The cab arrived in a few minutes, and Jayne walked out of the lobby and into the car.

"Where to, miss?" the balding driver asked.

She reached for a fresh tissue. She hadn't put on her glasses because she kept having to take them off to mop up the tears. "The downtown police station," she whispered, hardly recognizing her own voice. "And hurry, please."

9

Lieutenant Hal Powers brought Jayne a cup of coffee and sat down at the table across from her. She supposed this little room was normally used for the interrogation of suspects. This morning she felt like a criminal herself, reporting the man she loved to the police.

"Now, Ms. Gilbert, would you like to start again?"

"I'm sorry," she murmured, brushing away the tears. "I told myself I wouldn't get emotional, and then I end up like this."

Lieutenant Powers gave her an encouraging smile. Jayne had liked him immediately. He was a sensitive man, and she hadn't expected that. From various mysteries she'd read, Jayne had assumed that the police often became cynical and callous. Lieutenant Powers displayed neither of those characteristics.

She gripped the foam cup with both hands and stared into it blindly. "I live in the Marlia Apartments, and I…have this neighbor. I suspect he may be involved in something that could get him into a great deal of trouble."

"What has your neighbor been doing?" the lieutenant asked gently.

"I think highly of this neighbor, and I… I don't want to say anything until I know what would happen to him."

Lieutenant Powers frowned. "That depends on what he's done."

Jayne took another sip of coffee in an effort to stall for time and clear her thoughts. "To be honest, I can't say for sure that…my neighbor's done anything unlawful. But he's holding something that he shouldn't. Something of value."

"Does it belong to him?"

Jayne's eyes fell to the smooth tabletop. "Not exactly."

"Do you know who it does belong to?"

With dismay in her heart, she nodded.

"Who?"

Jayne was silent. There'd never been a darker moment in her life.

"Ms. Gilbert?"

"What I found," she said as tears once again crept down the side of her face, "belongs to Senator Max Priestly."

The lieutenant straightened. "Do you know how your neighbor got this—whatever it is?"

"It's a briefcase with telephone logs and incriminating letters." Now that she'd finally spilled it out, she didn't feel any better. In fact, she felt worse.

"How did your neighbor get this briefcase?"

"I saw the senator give it to Ril—my neighbor." She hurried on to add, "He, my neighbor, doesn't realize that I saw the exchange or that I know what's inside."

"How *do* you know?"

Jayne's gaze locked with his. "I looked."

"I see." The lieutenant rose and walked to the other side of the room. "Ms. Gilbert—"

"Could you tell me what will happen to him?"

One side of his mouth lifted in a half smile. "I'm not sure...." He appeared preoccupied as he moved toward the door. "Could you excuse me for a minute?"

"Of course."

Lieutenant Powers left the room, and Jayne covered her face with both hands. This was so much worse than she'd imagined. Her deepest fear was that the police would insist she lead them to Riley. She felt enough like an informer. A betrayer... If only she'd been able to talk to Riley, confront him—but that would've been impossible. Loving him the way she did, she would've been eager to believe anything he told her. Jayne couldn't trust herself around Riley. So she'd done the unthinkable. She'd gone to the police to turn in the only man she'd ever loved.

The door opened, and Lieutenant Powers returned. "I think you two have something you need to discuss."

Jayne suddenly noticed that the lieutenant wasn't alone. Behind him stood Riley.

Jayne's mouth sagged open in utter disbelief.

"I'll wait for you outside," Powers added.

"Thanks, Hal," Riley said as the lieutenant walked out the door.

"Oh, Riley!" Jayne leapt to her feet. "I'm so sorry I had to do this!" she cried through her tears.

"Jayne..."

"No." She held up her hand to stop him. "Please, don't say anything. Just listen. I told you this morning that I love you, and I meant that with all my heart. We're going to get through this together. I promise you that I'll be by your side no matter how long you're in prison. I'll come and visit you and write every day until...until you're free again. You can turn your life around if you want. I believe in you." She spoke with all the fervency of her love.

Riley's mouth narrowed into a hard line.

"You told me once that you wanted to change," Jayne reminded him. "Let me help you. I want to do everything I can."

"Jayne—"

Her hand gripped his. "Riley, I beg you, please, please tell them everything."

He pulled his hand free. "Jayne, honestly, would you stop being so melodramatic!"

Melodramatic? She blinked, unsure that she'd heard him correctly. "What do you mean?"

"There's no need for you to write me in prison."

"But..."

"Jayne, I'm with the FBI. I've been working undercover for six months." Witnessing her distress, Riley cursed himself for not having told her sooner. He also realized that he *couldn't* have told her. Doing so could have put the entire operation in jeopardy. Breaking cover went against everything that had been ingrained in him from the time he was a rookie. But seeing the anguish Jayne had suffered was enough to persuade him that he had to explain.

"Honey, I couldn't tell you."

Stunned, Jayne managed to nod.

"I would've put you in danger if I had."

She continued staring at him. Riley, her Riley, worked for the FBI. She waited for the surge of relief to fill her. None came.

"Why do you have the evidence needed to convict Senator Priestly?" Her voice sounded frail and quavering.

"I'm working undercover, Jayne. I can't really say any more than that."

She didn't understand what being undercover had to do with anything. Then it dawned on her. "You're trying to catch someone else?"

Riley nodded.

"Doesn't that put you in a dangerous position?"

He shrugged nonchalantly. "It could."

Hal Powers stuck his head inside the door. "You two got everything straightened out yet?"

"Not quite," Riley answered for them.

"You want a refill on that coffee?" Powers asked Jayne.

She looked down at the half-full cup. "No, thanks."

"What about you, Riley?"

Riley shook his head, but Jayne noticed the look of respect and admiration the other man gave him.

"This isn't the first time you've done something like this, is it?" she asked.

"She doesn't know about Boston?" Hal stepped into the room, his voice enthusiastic. He paused to glance at Riley. "You've got yourself a famous neighbor, Ms. Gilbert. We even heard about that case out here. Folks call it the second French Connection."

Riley didn't look pleased to have the lieutenant reveal quite so much about his past.

"If you're working undercover, what are you doing here, in the police station?"

"He came to talk to you," Powers inserted.

Riley tossed him an angry glare. "I said I wasn't interested in coffee," he stated flatly.

Powers didn't have to be told twice. "Sure. If you need me, give me a call."

"Right." Riley crossed the room and closed the door behind the other man.

Given a moment's respite Jayne blew her nose and stuffed

the tissue inside her purse. Her hand shook as she secured the clasp. She'd made a complete fool of herself.

"How did you know about the briefcase?" Riley asked, turning back to her.

"You were careless, Riley," she said in a small voice. "The corner was poking out from under your TV."

Riley didn't bother to correct her. The briefcase was exactly where it was supposed to be.

"What made you check the contents?" Jayne wasn't the meddling type. She must have suspected something to have taken it upon herself to peek inside that briefcase.

"I saw Max Priestly give it to you weeks ago…before I knew you. It was late one Saturday afternoon, in the parking lot."

Riley frowned. "Since you seem to have figured out that much, you're probably aware that my fishing trip—"

She gave a tiny half sob, half laugh. "I know. You don't need to explain."

Riley doubted she really knew, but he wasn't at liberty to elaborate. "I didn't want to lie to you. When this is over, I'll never do it again."

Jayne stood up. All she wanted to do now was escape. "I was obtuse. If I hadn't been so melodramatic, as you put it, I would have guessed sooner."

"You did the right thing. I know how difficult coming here must have been."

Jayne didn't deny it. She was sure there'd never be anything more physically or mentally draining—except telling Riley goodbye. Her hand tightened around the strap of her purse as she prepared to leave. "I…"

"Let's get out of here." Riley took her hand and raised it to his lips. "I'm sorry for having put you through this."

She quickly shook her head. "I put myself through it."

"We're done in here," Riley told Lieutenant Powers on the way out the door. He slipped his arm around Jayne's waist. "Where do you want me to drop you off?"

"But…you don't want to be seen coming out of here, do you?"

"Having you with me would make an explanation easier if the wrong person happens to see me. Do you want to go home?"

"Yes, please. I didn't sleep well last night."

Again Riley felt the bitterness of regret. Unwittingly he'd involved Jayne in this situation and put her through emotional distress. Once he was through with the Priestly case, he planned to accept a management position in law enforcement and work at a desk. He'd had enough risk and subterfuge. More than enough. He wanted Jayne as his wife, and he wanted children. He pictured a son and daughter and felt an emotion so strong that it seemed as though his heart had constricted. Jayne was everything honest and good, and he desperately needed her in his life.

The ride back to the apartment building was completed in silence. Although she'd been awake all the night, Jayne didn't think she'd be able to sleep now. Her mind had shifted into double time, spinning furiously as she sorted through the facts she'd recently learned.

When Riley parked the car and walked her into the building, Jayne was mildly surprised. She hadn't expected him to be so solicitous. Besides, she'd prefer to be alone, for the next few hours anyway.

She paused outside her apartment door, not wanting him to come in. "I'm fine. You don't have to stay."

She didn't look fine. In fact, he couldn't remember ever seeing her this pale. "Do you need an aspirin?" he asked, following her inside.

"No." Jayne couldn't believe that he hadn't noticed her lack of welcome. Too much had happened, and she needed time alone to find her place in the scheme of things—if she had a place. Everything was different now. Nothing about her relationship with Riley would remain the same.

"There's aspirin in my apartment if you need some."

"I'm fine," she said again. "Really."

He helped her out of her jacket and glanced at the heap of discarded tissues on the coffee table. The evidence that Jayne had spent a sleepless night crying lay before him. "Honey, why didn't you say something when you found the briefcase?"

She shrugged, not answering.

"You must've been frantic." He picked up the wadded tissues and dumped them in the kitchen garbage. The fact that Jayne had left a mess in her neatly organized apartment told him how great her distress had been. Riley wanted to kick himself for having put her through this.

"I was a little worried," was all she'd admit.

"I can't understand why you wouldn't confront me with what you knew." He'd raised his voice, but his irritation was directed more at himself than at Jayne. Riley didn't know what his response would have been had she come to him, but at least he could have prevented this night of anxious tears.

"I couldn't!" she cried angrily. She pulled another tissue from the box.

Riley frowned tiredly. "Why not?"

"It's obvious that you don't know anything about love," she said sharply. "When you love someone, it's so easy to believe the excuses he or she gives you—because you want to trust that person so badly. You've lied to me repeatedly, Riley.... You've had to. I understand that now. But...but—" She paused to inhale a deep breath. "I couldn't tell you *before*

I knew that. I couldn't have counted on you telling me the truth, and worse, I couldn't have trusted my own response."

"Oh, my love." Riley wrapped her in his arms, fully appreciating her dilemma for the first time.

The pressure of his hands molded her against him, and her hands slipped around his neck. Her pulse thundered in her ears when he raised her chin and then she felt the warmth of his mouth on hers. His kiss melted away the frost that had enclosed her heart.

When the kiss was over, Jayne reeled slightly. His hands steadied her. "I've got to get back," he said.

She took a step away from him, breaking all physical contact, trying to put distance between them. It was far too easy to fall into his arms and accept the comfort of his kiss. "I understand. Don't worry about me, Riley. I'll go to bed and probably sleep all day." At least she hoped she would, but something told her differently.

"I'll call you this afternoon."

"Okay," she told him and walked him to the door. He kissed her again briefly and was gone.

Standing in the hallway, Riley felt like ramming his fist through the wall. He would've given anything to have avoided this. She looked so small and lost, her face drained, her expression shocked. He'd thought Priestly and his accomplice would've made their move by now. He'd been waiting days for this thing to be over. Jayne's reunion was this coming weekend; he'd make sure all the loose ends were tied up by then.

Putting on her glasses, Jayne wandered over to the living room window and watched from nine floors above as Riley, carrying the briefcase, approached his car. He got in and pulled out of the lot and onto the street. Still standing at the window, Jayne saw another car pull out almost immediately after and follow him. Her heart jumped into her throat when she realized that he was being tailed.

Craning her neck, she saw the blue sedan behind him turn at the same intersection. Nervously she rubbed her palms together, wondering what she should do. She had no way of contacting Riley. The only phone number she had was for his apartment, not his cell.

Running into the kitchen, she called the police and asked for Lieutenant Powers, saying it was an emergency.

"Powers here," she heard a moment later.

"Lieutenant," Jayne said, fighting down her panic. "This is Jayne Gilbert. Riley dropped me off at my apartment, and I saw someone follow him."

"Listen, Ms. Gilbert, I wouldn't worry. Riley's been working undercover a lot of years. He can take care of himself."

"But…"

"I doubt anyone would tail Riley Chambers without him knowing about it."

"But he's concerned about me. He may not be paying attention the way he should. Could you please contact him and let him know?" She raised her voice, trying to impress the urgency of her request on him.

"Ms. Gilbert, I don't think—"

"Riley's life could be in danger!"

She could hear the lieutenant's sigh of resignation. "If it'll reassure you, then I'll contact him."

"Thank you." But Jayne wasn't completely mollified; she was also worried about how Riley would react. He wouldn't appreciate her warning. He might even be insulted. As Powers had claimed, Riley had been around a long time. He knew how to take care of himself.

Sagging onto the sofa, Jayne found that her knees were trembling. She couldn't help imagining Riley caught in a trap from which he couldn't escape. Forcefully she dispelled the images from her mind. This wasn't Riley's first case, she reminded herself, and it probably wouldn't be his last. That knowledge wasn't comforting. Not in the least. Loving Riley Chambers wasn't going to work. Could he really change the way he lived? He'd tasted adventure, lived with excitement; a house with a white picket fence would be so mundane to someone like him.

Jayne woke hours later, shocked that she'd managed to sleep. She rubbed a hand along the back of her neck to ease the crick she'd gotten from sleeping with her head propped against the sofa arm. Brilliant sunlight splashed in through her open drapes, and a glance at her watch said it was after five. She suddenly realized that Riley hadn't called. She wouldn't have slept through the ringing of the phone.

Pushing the hair away from her face, she swallowed down the fear that threatened to overtake her. Fleetingly she wondered if Powers had warned him about the blue sedan. She doubted it. It was obvious from their conversation that the lieutenant thought she was overreacting. Maybe she was.

In an effort to calm her fears, Jayne looked out her window. His parking space was empty, she noted sadly, and then felt a surge of relief when his car made a left-hand turn a block away. She also took consolation from the knowledge that there wasn't a blue car anywhere near Riley's.

But her relief quickly died when Jayne noticed a blue sedan parked on the side street. It might not have been the same one, but the resemblance was close enough to alarm her. Jayne was undecided—should she do anything?—until she saw a man climb out of the car. He paused and looked both ways before crossing the street to head in Riley's direction.

Jayne's heart flew into her throat when she watched him step behind a parked car, apparently to wait. It occurred to her that he could be planning to ambush Riley. Instantly she knew she was right. Jayne could sense it, could feel the threat. She had to get to Riley and warn him.

Without another thought, she raced out of her apartment and down the hall. For once, the elevator appeared immediately. By the time the wide doors opened into the lobby, Jayne was frantic.

She ran outside and came to an abrupt halt. She couldn't run up to Riley. She might be putting him in even greater danger if she intervened now. The thing to do was remain calm and see what the man planned to do—if anything.

Walking into the lot, Jayne saw Riley standing beside his car with the briefcase. He wasn't moving. The other man faced him and had his back to her. Approaching the pair at an angle, Jayne caught a flash of metal. The man had a gun trained on Riley.

Tension momentarily froze her, but she knew what she had to do. She broke into a run.

Riley saw her move, and terror burned through him. A scream rose in his throat as he called out, "Jayne…no!"

10

Jayne saw the way Riley's face had become drawn and white as she'd started to run. She didn't know much about martial arts, but after the incident with the mugger, she'd read a wonderfully simple book filled with illustrations. When she'd finished the book, Jayne had felt fairly confident that she could defend herself, if need be. Seeing a gun pointed at Riley's heart was all the incentive she needed to apply the lessons she'd learned.

Unfortunately her skill wasn't quite up to what she'd hoped it would be, and her aim fell far below his chest, possibly because she wasn't wearing her glasses. But where her foot struck caused enough pain to double the man over and send him slumping to the pavement. The gun went flying.

Riley recovered it. His face was pinched and drawn. "For crying out loud, Jayne. I don't believe you." He rubbed a hand over his face. "You idiot! Couldn't you see he had a gun?"

Feeling undeniably proud of herself, Jayne smiled shyly. "Of course I saw the gun."

"Did it ever occur to you that you might've been shot?" he shouted.

She shrugged. "To be honest, I didn't really think of that. I just…acted."

The man she'd felled remained on the ground, moaning. From seemingly nowhere, a uniformed officer appeared and forced him to stand before handcuffing his wrists.

Riley paced back and forth, and for the first time Jayne noticed how furious he was. The self-satisfied grin faded from her face. The least Riley could do was show a little appreciation. "I saved your life, for heaven's sake."

"Saved it?" He shook his head, momentarily closing his eyes. "You nearly cost us both our lives."

"But…"

"Do you think I'm stupid? I knew that Simpson—Priestly's campaign manager and accomplice—was in the parking lot. We were surrounded by three teams of plainclothes detectives. In addition, a squad car was parked on the other side of the building."

"Oh," Jayne replied in a small voice.

"You scared me half to death." He groaned. "And you're the one who hides her eyes during movies." He raked his fingers through his hair. "How do you think I'd feel if something happened to you?" Some of the harsh anger drained from his voice.

"I did what I thought I had to," Jayne returned, feeling faintly indignant.

Riley shook his head again. "I don't think my system could take another one of your acts of heroism. Where did you learn to leap through the air like that?"

"In a book…"

"You mean to tell me you learned that crippling move from something you read?"

"The illustrations were excellent, but I have to admit I was off a bit. I was actually aiming for his chest."

Riley just rolled his eyes.

"Under the circumstances," she said, trying to maintain her dignity, "I thought I did rather well."

Briefly his gaze met hers, and a reluctant grin lifted his mouth. "You did fine, but promise me you'll never, *ever* interfere again."

"I promise." Now that everything was over, reaction set in, and Jayne began to tremble. She'd seen Riley in terrible danger and responded without a thought for her own welfare. Riley was as incredulous as the policemen who milled around, shaking their heads in wonder at this woman who'd downed an armed man.

"Are you all right?" he asked, draping an arm around her shoulders and pulling her close. He savored the warmth of her body next to his.

"I'm fine." She wasn't, but she couldn't very well break down now.

"I've got to go downtown and debrief, write my report. But I'll be back in a couple of hours. Will you be all right until I return?"

"Of course."

Riley hesitated. Jayne was putting on a brave front, but he could tell that she was frightened now that she'd realized what could have happened. He didn't want to leave her, but it was unavoidable.

"I'll walk you to your apartment," he said, wanting to reassure her that everything was under control.

"I'm fine," she insisted in a shaky voice. "You're needed at the station."

"Jayne," he said, then paused.

"Go on," she urged. "I'll be waiting here. I'm not going anyplace."

He dropped a quick kiss on her mouth. "I love you, Jayne." And he did love her—so much that he doubted he could have survived if anything had happened to her.

As he left, Jayne went back to her apartment, telling herself Riley was safe, and that was what mattered most.

An hour later, Jayne reached her decision. It wasn't so difficult, really. She'd known it would come to this sooner or later, and she'd prefer it to be sooner. Again, as she had in the parking lot, she was only doing what she had to.

By the time Riley appeared, she was composed and confident. She opened her door and stepped aside as he entered her apartment. He bent to kiss her, and she let him, savoring the moment.

"We need to talk." She spoke first, not giving him a chance to say anything.

"You're telling me," Riley said with a grin. "I still can't get over you." If he lived for another century, Riley doubted he would forget those few seconds when Jayne had come running toward Simpson. And she'd done it to protect *him*—Riley Chambers. Naturally, she'd been unaware that he wasn't in any danger. All the way back from the jail, Riley was lost in the memory of those brief moments. He'd found himself an exceptional woman. And he wasn't going to lose her. He'd already started looking at diamond rings. On the night of her reunion he was going to ask her to marry him.

"Riley, about the reunion."

"What about it?"

"I've asked Mark to take me."

"What?"

"I want you to know I appreciate the fact that you were willing to attend it with me, but—"

"Jayne, you're not thinking straight," Riley countered, still not believing what she'd said.

She forced out a light laugh. "Actually, I've been giving it some thought over the past few days. This wasn't a sudden decision. When I went to the police this morning, I knew there was every likelihood that you wouldn't be able to go to Seattle with me."

Riley frowned. "So you asked Mark?"

"Yes." Her right eye remained still. Riley had taught her several things, and one of those was how to lie. The smoothness with which she told him this one was shocking. What a sad commentary on their relationship, Jayne mused unhappily. She'd love Riley forever, and years from now, when the hurt went away, she'd be able to look back on their weeks together and be glad she'd known and loved him—however briefly.

Riley clenched his fists. "Something's not right here. You're lying."

"I'm not the expert in that department. You are." She stalked into the kitchen. "Here," she said, handing him the telephone receiver. "If you don't believe me, call Mark."

Riley stared at the phone in utter astonishment. "Jayne... don't do this." His gut instinct told him she was lying.

"How was I supposed to know you weren't some crook? I couldn't take that chance. So... I asked Mark."

"Then unask him."

"I won't do that."

"Why not?" Riley was becoming angrier with every breath.

"Because I'm not sure you're the type of man I'd want to go with—the type of man I want to be with." The pain of what she was doing was so powerful that Jayne reached out to hold on to the kitchen counter. "I'm sorry, Riley, I am. I've known for some time that things weren't working out."

"Not sorry enough." Abruptly he swiveled around. "I'd suggest you have fun, but I doubt you will with Mark Bauer."

"I'm sure I'll have a perfectly good time," she lied, but the effort to hold back her tears made the words unintelligible.

"Jayne, darling, let me look at you." Dorothy Gilbert held her daughter by the shoulders and shook her gray head. Jayne's parents had met her at the train station. "You look fabulous."

Jayne smiled absently. The train had arrived on time. She was afraid to fly, but she beamed proudly at the thought of the one shining moment in her life when she'd ignored her fear and attacked a gunman. Such ironies were common with her.

"The new hairstyle suits you."

"Thank you, Mom." But the happiness she felt at seeing her parents didn't compensate for the emptiness inside her after that last confrontation with Riley. From her mother's arm, Jayne moved forward to receive her father's gruff embrace.

"Good to see you, sweetie," Howard Gilbert said.

"Thank you, Daddy."

Slowly they walked toward the terminal where Jayne was to collect her luggage.

"That Thomas girl arrived this morning from California. You might want to call her at her parents' house," Dorothy told Jayne as she put an arm around her waist. "She's already called to ask about you."

"I… I'd like to talk to her."

"She's married and has two daughters."

"How nice." Jayne wasn't married. Nor did she have children. She was the prim and proper woman Riley had accused her of being. It was what she'd been destined to be from the time she'd graduated from high school. She had been a fool to believe otherwise. Angry with herself for the self-pitying thoughts, Jayne smiled brightly at her mother.

"Judy said the reception at the Westin starts about eight."

"They mailed me a program, Mom." Jayne had decided she'd attend the reunion alone. Her dream had been to arrive with Riley at her side, but that was out of the question. So, as she'd done most of her life, Jayne would pretend. She'd walk into the reception with her head held high and imagine everyone turning toward her and sighing with envy.

She hadn't seen Riley. Not once since that fateful afternoon. For all she knew he could have moved out of the building. She was grateful he'd accepted her lies, making it unnecessary to fabricate others. She'd purposely hurt him to be kind. She wasn't the right woman for him, and his life was too different from hers.

She'd read about the charges against Priestly and Simpson. The articles and news reports gave an abbreviated version of Riley's part in all this, mentioning only that an FBI agent had worked with police departments statewide to destroy Priestly's organization.

Her father collected her suitcase, and then the three of them walked to the car parked across from the King Street Station.

"I have a lovely new dress," Jayne said.

"I'm so pleased you're attending this reunion, Jayne. I'd been worried you might not want to go." She stared intently at Jayne.

"I wouldn't miss it, Mom."

"Those girls never appreciated you," her father commented, placing Jayne's suitcase in the trunk of the car.

"Nonsense, Dad, I had some good friends."

"She did, Howard."

They chatted companionably on the drive toward Jayne's childhood home on Queen Anne Hill.

Once she got home, Jayne phoned her high school friend, Judy Thomas, and they chatted for nearly an hour.

"It's so good to talk to you again," Judy said. "I can hardly wait to see you."

"Me, too."

"I think I'd better get off the phone. Dad's giving me disapproving looks just like he did ten years ago."

"I guess we'll always be teenagers to our parents."

"Unfortunately." Judy giggled.

Jayne smiled when her mother stuck her head around the corner. "Don't you think you should start to get ready?"

Jayne contained a smile. Judy was right. They would always be teenagers to their parents. "Okay, Mom, I'll be off in a minute."

"See what I mean?" Judy said.

"Oh, yes. Listen, I'll see you tonight."

"See you then."

Jayne spent most of the next hour preparing for the reunion. Her mother raved about how the dress looked on Jayne. Gazing at her mirrored reflection, Jayne's astonishment was renewed. The dress was the most beautiful one she'd ever owned.

Adding the final touches to her makeup, Jayne heard her mother and father whispering in the background.

"We'd like to get some pictures of you and your young man," her father said when Jayne stepped out of her bedroom.

"Pardon me, Dad?"

"Pictures," he repeated, taking his camera from the case. "Go stand by the fireplace."

"All right." She went into the living room and stopped cold. Before her stood Riley. Tall, polished, impeccable and so incredibly good-looking in his tuxedo that she felt as though all the oxygen had escaped her lungs.

"Riley…what are you doing here?"

"Taking you to the reunion."

"But how did you know—"

"I believe your father wants to take a few pictures." Gently he took her lifeless hand in his and tucked it into his elbow.

Smiling, Dorothy and Howard Gilbert moved into the living room.

"Oh—Mom and Dad, this is Riley Chambers."

Riley came forward and shook hands with her parents. "Glad to see you again, Howard. And good to meet you, Dorothy."

Gruffly, her father motioned for the couple to stand in front of the fireplace while he took a series of photos.

"I believe these young people need a few minutes alone."

"Daddy—"

"You need to talk to your fiancé," Howard said, taking his wife by the arm and leading her into the kitchen.

Jayne didn't move and barely breathed, and she couldn't seem to speak.

"Having her father announce it isn't the most romantic way to tell the woman you love that you want to marry her," Riley said once her parents had left.

"Oh, Riley, please don't."

"Don't what? Love you? That would be impossible."

"No," she whispered miserably, hanging her head. "Don't ask me."

"But I am. Maybe it was presumptuous of me, but I bought a ring." He pulled out a jeweler's box from his inside pocket. "I don't know why you lied about inviting Mark. I don't even care. I love you, and we're going to have a marvelous life together."

"Riley." She swallowed a sob. "No, I won't marry you."

He put the jeweler's box on the mantel behind him and stared at her, his look incredulous. "Why?"

"Because I'm me. I'll never be anything other than a children's librarian. That's all I've ever wanted to be. You live life in the fast lane, while I crawl along at a snail's pace—if you'll forgive the clichés."

"But, Jayne, I'm sick of that life..."

"For how long? A year? Maybe two?"

"Jayne, I've already accepted a job—a desk job—with the Portland police. My undercover days are over."

"Riley, are you sure that's what you want?"

"I've never been more sure of anything." His eyes held a determination that few would challenge. "I've waited half my life for you, Jayne Gilbert, and I'm not taking no for an answer."

The blunt words took Jayne aback. Her lips tightened as she shook her head.

"Do you love me so little?" he asked in a voice that was so soft she could hardly hear it.

"You know I love you!" she cried.

"Then why are you fighting me?"

"I'm...afraid, Riley."

He took a step toward her, extending his hand. "Then put your hand in mine. No man could ever love you more than I do. I'm ready for everything you have to give me. I've been ready for a lot of years."

Jayne couldn't fight him anymore. Tentatively, she raised her hand and placed it in his.

"I believe we have a reunion to attend."

"It isn't necessary. You know that, don't you? All I've ever needed is you." She blinked back tears. "Now, don't make me cry. It took me ages to get this makeup right."

"You're beautiful."

She laughed and reached up to kiss him. "Thank you, but I have trouble believing that."

"After tonight, you won't. I'll be the envy of every man there."

"Then it's true," Jayne said with a trembling smile. "Love is blind."

Riley turned to retrieve the jeweler's box and offered it to her. Smiling tremulously, she let him slide the engagement ring on her finger.

"What would you say to a fall wedding?"

Before Jayne could respond, Howard and Dorothy reappeared, and Dorothy protested, "Oh, no, that's nowhere near enough time!"

"It's fine, Dorothy," Howard said. "The only thing that matters to me is whether our daughter's marrying the right man. And I'm convinced she couldn't find anyone better than Riley." He winked at his wife. "I know you, of all people, can pull off a wedding in four months."

Dorothy gave a resigned sigh. "Have fun, you two," she murmured.

"We will, Mom."

On the way down the sidewalk to Riley's parked car, Jayne gave him an odd look. "When did you talk to my father?"

"A couple of days ago when I asked his permission for his daughter's hand."

"Riley, you didn't!"

He raised his eyebrows. "I did. I told you before that I was going to do everything right with you. We're going to be married as soon as possible—in a church before God and witnesses. We're going to be very happy, Jayne."

A brilliant smile curved her lips. "I think we will, too," she said.

A half-hour later, Riley pulled into the curved driveway of the downtown Westin where the reunion was being held. He eased to a stop, and an attendant opened Jayne's door and helped her out.

They walked through the hotel lobby and took the elevator to the Grand Ballroom.

"Ready?" Riley asked as they approached.

Her breath felt tight in her lungs. "I think so."

One step into the room, and Jayne felt every eye on her. The room went silent as she turned and smiled into the warmth and love that radiated from Riley's gaze.

Whispers rose. And the girls of St. Mary's sighed.

★★★★★

FRIENDS—AND THEN SOME

1

The thick canvas sail flapped in the breeze before Jake Carson aligned the boat to catch the wind. The *Lucky Lady* responded by slicing through the choppy waters of San Francisco Bay. Satisfied, Jake leaned back and closed his eyes, content with his life and with the world.

"Do you think I'm being terribly mercenary?" Lily Morrissey asked as she stretched her legs out and crossed them at the ankles. "It sounds so coldhearted to decide to marry a man simply because he's wealthy. He doesn't have to be *that* rich." She paused to sigh expressively. Lately she'd given the matter consideration. For almost a year now she'd been playing the piano at the Wheaton. Only wealthy businessmen could afford to stay at a hotel as expensive as the Wheaton. And Lily was determined to find herself such a man. Unfortunately, no one had leaped forward, and she'd grown discouraged. Each day she told herself that she would meet someone soon. That hope was what kept Lily going back night after night.

"I'd only want someone rich enough to appreciate opera,"

she added thoughtfully. "Naturally it'd be nice if he drove a fancy car, but that isn't essential. All I really care about is his bank account. It's got to be large enough to take care of Gram and me. That doesn't sound so bad, does it?"

A faint smile tugged at the corners of Jake's mouth.

"Jake?" she repeated, slightly irritated.

"Hmm?"

"You haven't heard a word I said."

"Sure I have. You were talking about finding yourself a wealthy man."

"Yes, but that's what I always talk about. You could have guessed." Maybe she was foolish to dream of the day when a generous man would adorn her with diamonds.

"I wasn't guessing. I heard every word."

Lily studied him through narrowed eyes. "Sure you did," she mumbled under her breath.

Jake's slow, lazy smile came into play again.

Lily studied the profile of her best friend. Jake drove a taxi and they'd met the first week she worked at the Wheaton. She owed him a lot. Not only did he give her free rides back and forth to work when he was available, which was just about every day, but he'd rescued Gram and Lily from the Wheaton's manager.

Lily's starting salary had been less than what Gram had paid for an hour of piano lessons. Gram had raised Lily from the time her mother had died and her father had sought his fortune as a merchant marine. Gram had been outraged by the manager's unintended slight. And Gram, being Gram, couldn't do anything without a production. She'd shown up at the hotel in authentic witch doctor's costume and proceeded to chant a voodoo rite of retribution over the manager's head.

Luckily, Lily had gotten her grandmother out of the lobby before the police arrived. Jake had been standing next to his taxi and had witnessed the entire scene. Before everything exploded in Lily's face, Jake held open the cab door and whisked Gram and Lily away from any unpleasantness. Over the months that followed, the three had become good friends.

Jake was actually a struggling writer. He lived on his boat and worked hard enough to meet expenses by driving the taxi. He didn't seem to take anything too seriously. Not even his writing. Lily sometimes wondered how many other people he gave free rides to. Money didn't matter to Jake. But it did to Lily.

"I *am* going to meet someone," Lily continued on a serious note.

"I don't doubt it," Jake said and yawned, raising his hand to cover his mouth.

"I mean it, Jake. Tonight. I bet I meet someone tonight."

"For your sake, I hope you're right," Jake mumbled in reply.

Her words echoed in her ears several hours later when Lily pulled out the bench of the huge grand piano that dominated the central courtyard of the Wheaton. Dressed in her full-length sleeveless dress and dainty slippers, she was barely recognizable as the woman who'd spent the afternoon aboard Jake's boat.

Deftly her fingers moved over the smooth ivory keys as her upper body swayed with the melody of a Carpenters' hit.

Some days Lily felt that her smile was as artificial as her thick, curling eyelashes. After twenty-seven hundred times of hearing "Moon River," "Misty" and "Sentimental Journey," Lily was ready to take a journey herself. Maybe that was why she had talked to Jake. If she was going to meet someone, surely it would have happened by now. Sighing inwardly, she continued playing, hardly conscious of her fingers.

Five minutes later when Lily glanced up, she was surprised

to find a ruddy faced cowboy standing next to the piano, watching her.

She smiled up at him and asked, "Is there something you'd like to hear?" He had to be close to forty-five, with the beginnings of a double chin. A huge turquoise buckle dominated the slight thickening at his waist. He was a good-looking man who was already going to seed.

"Do you know 'Santa Fe Gal of Mine'?" The slight Southern drawl wasn't a surprise. His head was topped with a Stetson although he was dressed in a linen sport coat that hadn't cost a penny under five hundred dollars. A Texan, she mused; a rich Texan, probably into oil.

"'Santa Fe Gal of Mine,'" she repeated aloud. "I'm not sure that I do," she answered with a warm smile. "Hum a few bars for me." She didn't usually get requests. People were more interested in checking into the hotel or meeting their friends for a drink in the sunken cocktail lounge to care about what she was playing.

The man placed a steadying hand against the side of the piano and momentarily closed his eyes. "I can't remember the melody," he admitted sheepishly. "Sorry, I'm not much good with that sort of thing. I'm an oilman not a singer."

So he was into oil just as she suspected. Lily got a glance at his feet and recognized the shoes from an advertisement she'd seen in *Gentlemen's Quarterly.* Cowboy boots, naturally, but ones made of imported leather and inlaid with silver. Leather, Lily felt, made the difference between being dressed and well dressed. This gentleman was definitely well dressed.

"Do you know who sang the popular version?" she questioned brightly, her heart pounding so hard it felt as though it would slam right out of her chest. She'd told Jake she was going to meet someone. And that someone had appeared at last! And he wasn't wearing a wedding band either.

"Nope, I can't say that I do."

"Maybe there's another song you'd like to hear?" Without conscious thought her hands continued to play as she glanced up at the cowboy with two chins and reminded herself that looks weren't everything. But, then again, maybe he had been married and had a son her age—an heir.

"One day I'm going to find some sweet gal who knows that blasted song," he muttered. "It always was my favorite."

Already Lily's mind had shifted into overdrive. Somehow she'd locate his long-lost song and gain his everlasting gratitude. "Will you be around tomorrow?"

"I should be."

"Come back and I'll see what I can do."

He straightened and gave her a brief salute. "I'll do that, little filly."

Lily's heart was pounding so hard that by the time she finished an hour later, she felt as if she'd been doing calisthenics. Maybe he'd be so grateful he'd insist on taking her to dinner. This could be the break Lily had waited months for. It hadn't happened exactly as she'd expected, but it was just the chance she'd been wanting. Already she could picture herself sitting in an elegant restaurant, ordering almond-saffron soup and lobster in wine sauce. For dessert she'd have Italian ice cream with walnuts and caramel oozing from the sides. Her mouth watered just thinking about all the wonderful foods she'd read about but never tasted. Her Texan would probably order barbecued chicken, but she wouldn't care. He could well be her ticket to riches and a genteel life…if she played her cards right. And for the first time in a long while, Lily felt she'd been dealt a hand of aces.

Jake was in his cab, parked in front of the hotel when she stepped into the balmy summer night. Eagerly she waved and hurried across the wide circular driveway to the bright-yellow taxi.

"Jake!" she cried. "Didn't I tell you today was the day? Didn't I? The most fantastically wonderful thing has happened! I can't believe I'm so lucky." She felt like holding out her arms and twirling around and bursting into song.

With one elbow leaning against the open window, Jake studied her with serious dark eyes and a slow, measured smile that lifted one corner of his full mouth. "Obviously Daddy Warbucks introduced himself."

"Yes," she giggled. "*My* Daddy Warbucks."

Leaning across the front seat, Jake swung open the passenger door. "Climb in and you can tell me all about it on the way to your house."

Rushing around the front of the car, Lily scooted inside the cab and closed the door. Jake started the engine and pulled onto the busy street, skillfully merging with the flowing traffic. "I was so surprised, I nearly missed my chance," Lily started up again. "Suddenly, after all these months, he was there in a five-hundred-dollar sport coat, requesting a song. He called me 'little filly,' and, Jake, he's rich. Really, really rich. I can just see that Texas oil oozing from every pore." She paused long enough to inhale before continuing. "He's older, maybe forty-five or fifty, but that's not so bad. And he's nice. I can tell that about a man. Remember how I met you and instantly knew what a great person you were? That's just the kind of feeling I had tonight." She continued chattering for another full minute until she realized how quiet Jake had become. "Oh, Jake, I'm sorry, I've been talking up a storm without giving you a chance to think."

"You're talking with a drawl."

"Oh, yeah, I'm practicing. I was born in Texas, you know."

"You were?"

"No, of course not, but I thought it'd impress him."

The slow, lazy smile came into play again.

Lily studied the intense profile of her friend as he steered. Jake wasn't handsome—not in the way the models for *Gentlemen's Quarterly* were. He was tall with broad shoulders and a muscular build. But with those sea-green eyes and that dark hair, he could be attractive if he tried. Only Jake couldn't care less. Half the time he dressed in faded jeans and outdated sweaters. Lily doubted that he even owned a suit. Formal wear wasn't part of Jake's image.

As she studied Jake, Lily realized that she really didn't know much about him. Jake kept the past to himself. She knew he'd been a medic in the Army, and had an engineering degree from a prestigious college back east someplace. From tidbits of conversation here and there, she'd learned that he'd worked at every type of job imaginable. There didn't seem to be anything he hadn't tried once and—if he liked it—done again and again. In some ways Jake reminded Lily of her father who had been in the merchant marine and brought her a storehouse of treasures from around the world. Jake was the kind of man who could do anything he put his mind to. He was creative and intelligent, proud and resourceful. Lily supposed she loved him but only as a friend. He was her confidant and in many ways, her partner. Her feelings were more like those of a young girl for an endearing older brother or an adventurous sidekick. Love, real love between a man and a woman was an emotion Lily held in reserve for her husband. But first she had to convince a rich man that she would be an excellent wife.

Studying Jake now, Lily noted that something had displeased him. She could tell by the way he tucked back his chin, giving an imitation of a cobra prepared to strike. He exuded impatience and restrained anger. From past experience, Lily knew that whatever was bothering him would be divulged in his own time and in his own way.

"Well?" he snapped.

"Well, what?"

"Are you going to tell me your plan to snag this rich guy or not?"

"Are you sure you want to hear? You sound like you want to snap my head off."

"Darn it, Lily, one of these days..." He paused to inhale sharply as if the night were responsible for his wrath. Several moments passed before he spoke, and when he did his voice was as smooth as velvet, almost caressing.

Lily wasn't fooled. Jake was furious. "All right, tell me what's wrong. Did you get stiffed again? I thought you had a foolproof system for avoiding that."

"No one stiffed me."

"Then what?"

He ignored her, seeming to concentrate on the traffic. "Listen, kid, you've got to be careful."

Lily hated it when Jake called her "kid" and he knew it. "Be careful? What are you talking about? You're acting like I'm planning to handle toxic waste. Good grief, I don't even know his name."

"You could be playing with fire."

"I'm not playing anything yet. Which reminds me, have you ever heard the song 'Santa Fe Gal of Mine'?"

"'Santa Fe Gal of Mine'?" The harsh disgruntled look left his expression as a smile split his mouth. "No, I can't say that I have."

"Gram will know it," Lily said with complete confidence. Her grandmother might be a bit eccentric, but the woman was a virtual warehouse of useless information. If that wealthy Texan's favorite song was ever on the charts, Gram would know it.

Jake eased to a stop in front of the large two-story house with the wide front porch.

"Can you come in now or will you be by later?"

"Later," he answered with apparent indifference.

Lily walked toward the house and paused on the front steps, confused again. A disturbing shiver trembled through her at the cool, appraising way Jake had behaved this evening. His smooth, impenetrable green eyes resembled the dark jade Buddha her father had brought her from Hong Kong. Nothing about Jake had been the same tonight. Lily attributed it to his having had a bad day. But it shouldn't have been. They'd spent the majority of it sailing and they both loved that. But then everyone had a bad day now and again. Jake was entitled to his.

Shaking off the feelings of unease, Lily stepped inside the fifty-year-old house, pausing to pat Herbie. Herbie was her grandmother's favorite conversation piece—a shrunken head from South America. A zebra-skin rug from Africa rested in front of the fireplace.

The television blared from Gram's bedroom, but the older woman was snoring just as loudly, drowning out the sounds of the cops-and-robbers movie. With an affectionate smile, Lily turned off the set and quietly tiptoed from the darkened room. She'd talk to Gram in the morning.

After changing out of the red gown, Lily inspected her limited wardrobe, wondering what she'd wear first if the Texan asked her to dinner. Possibly the dress with the plunging neckline. No, she mentally argued with herself. That dress could give him the wrong impression. The lavender chiffon one she'd picked up at Repeaters, a secondhand store, looked good with her dark eyes and had a high neckline. Lily felt it would be best to start this relationship off right. She was sitting beside the old upright piano, sorting through Gram's sheet music that was stored in the bench when Jake returned. He let himself in, hung his jacket on the elephant tusks and picked up a discarded Glenn Miller piece from the top of the pile.

"Hi."

"Hi." At least he sounded in a better mood than earlier. "It'd be just like Gram to have that song and not even know it."

"You're determined to find it, aren't you?" Jake asked with a faint smile.

"I've got to find it," Lily shot back. "Everything will be ruined if I don't." Her sharp words bounced back without penetrating his aloof composure. "He won't be grateful if I can't find that song."

Jake sat on the arm of the sofa and idly flipped through the stack she'd already sorted. He didn't like the sounds of this Texan. He wasn't sure what he was feeling. Lily was determined to find herself a rich man and, knowing her persistence, Jake thought she probably would. When Lily wanted something, she went after it with unwavering resolve. In his life, there wasn't anything he cared that much about. Sure, there were things he wanted, but nothing that was worth abandoning the easygoing existence he had now. Lily's dark-brown eyes had sparkled with eager excitement when she'd told him about the Texan. He'd never seen anyone's eyes light up that way.

"Did you get a chance to do any writing today?"

Jake straightened the tall stack of sheet music and sat upright. "I finished that short story I was telling you about and e-mailed it off."

Lily smiled up at him, her attention diverted for the moment. Jake had talent, but he wasted it on short stories that didn't sell when he should be concentrating on a novel. That's where the real money was. "Are you going to let me read this one?" He usually gave her his work to look over, mainly for grammar and spelling errors—Jake was a "creative" speller.

"Later," he hedged, not knowing why. He preferred it when Lily had a chance to correct his blatant errors, but there was something of himself in this story that he'd held in reserve, not wishing her to see. The interesting part of being a writer was that Jake didn't always like the people inside him who appeared on paper. Some were light and witty while others were dark and dangerous. None were like him and yet each one was a part of himself.

"I know Gram's got tons more sheet music than this," Lily mumbled, thoughtfully chewing on her bottom lip. "Do you want to go to the attic with me?"

"Sure."

He followed her up the creaky stairs to the second floor, then moved in front and opened the door that led to another staircase, this one narrower and steeper. Lily tucked her index finger in Jake's belt loop as the light from the hallway dimmed. They were surrounded by the pitch-black dark, two steps into the attic.

"Where's the light?"

An eerie sensation slowly crept up Lily's arm and settled in her stomach. The air was still with a stagnant heaviness. "In the center someplace. Jake, I'll do this tomorrow. It's creepy up here."

"We're here now," he argued and half turned, bringing her to his side and loosely taking her by the hand. "Don't worry, I'll protect you."

"Yeah, that's what I'm afraid of." She tried to make light of her apprehensions, and managed to squelch the urge to turn back toward the dim hallway light. Involuntarily she shivered. "Gram's got some weird stuff up here."

"It can't be any worse than what's downstairs," he murmured, and chuckled softly as he edged their way into the black void, taking short steps as he swung his hand out in front of him to prevent a collision with some inanimate object.

Gradually, Lily's eyes adjusted to the lack of light. "I think I see the string—to your left there." She pointed for his benefit and squeezed her eyes half-closed for a better view. It didn't look exactly right, but it could be the light.

"That's a hangman's noose."

"Good grief, what's Gram doing with that?" In some ways, she'd rather not know what treasures Gram had stored up here. The attic was Gram's territory and Lily hadn't paid it a visit in years. In truth, Lily didn't really want to know what her sweet grandmother was doing with a hangman's noose.

"She told me once that her great-grandfather is said to have ridden with Jesse James. The noose might have something to do with that." As he spoke, Jake's foot collided with a box and he stumbled forward a few steps until he regained his balance.

Lily let out a sharp gasp, then held her breath. "Are you all right?"

"I'm fine."

"What was that?"

"How would I know?"

"Jake, let's go back down. Please." Her greatest fear was walking into a bat's nest or something worse.

"We already went over that. The light's got to be around here someplace."

"Sure, and in the meantime we don't know..."

"Damn."

Lily's hand tightened around his, her fingers clammy. "Now what's wrong?"

"My knee bumped into something."

"That does it. We're going back." Jake could stay up here if he wanted, but she was leaving. From the minute they'd stepped inside this tomb, Lily had felt uneasy.

"Lily," he argued.

Jerking her hand free, she turned toward the stairs and the faint beam of light. It looked as though the attic door had eased shut, cutting off what little illumination there had been from the hall. Everything was terribly dark and spooky. "I'm getting out of here," she declared, unable to keep the catch out of her voice. "This place is giving me the heebie-jeebies." More interested in making her escape than being cautious, Lily turned away and walked straight into a spider's web. A disgusted sound slid from her throat as her hands flew up to free her face from the fine, sticky threads. A prickling fear shot up her spine as she felt something scamper across her foot.

Her heart rammed against her breast like a jackhammer as the terror gripped her and she let out a bloodcurdling cry. "Jake… Jake."

He was with her in seconds, roughly pulling her into his arms. She clung to him, frantically wrapping her arms around his neck. Her face was buried in his shoulder as she trembled. His arms around her waist half lifted her from the floor. "Lily, you're all right," he whispered frantically. His hold, secure and warm, drove out the terror. "I've got you." It took all the strength she could muster just to nod.

Jake's hand brushed the wispy curls from her temple. "Lily," he repeated soothingly. "I told you I'd protect you." His warm breath fanned her face, creating an entirely new set of sensations. His scent, a combination of sweat and man, was unbelievably intoxicating. For the first time Lily became aware of how tightly pressed her body was to the rock hardness of his. Her grip slackened and she slid intimately down the length of him until her feet touched the floor. The hem of her blouse rode up, exposing her midriff so that her bare skin rubbed against the muscular wall of his chest. His hands found their place in the small of her back and seemed to hold her there, pressing her all the closer. Her breasts were flattened to his upper torso and her nerves fired to life at the merest brush of his body.

As if hypnotized, their eyes met and held in the faint light.

It was as though they were seeing each other for the first time. Her pulse fluttered wildly at his look of curious surprise as his gaze lowered to her mouth.

"Jake?" Her voice was the faintest whisper, wavering and unsure.

His eyes darkened and a thick frown formed on his face. Slowly, almost as if drawn by something other than his will, Jake lowered his mouth to hers. Warm lips met warm lips in an exploratory kiss that was as gentle as it was unhurried. "Lily." His mouth left hers and sounded oddly raspy and unsure. Her eyes remained tightly closed.

Somehow she found her voice. "That shouldn't have happened."

"Do you want an apology?"

Her arms slid from around his neck and fell to her side as he released her. "No..." she whispered. "I should be the one to apologize... I don't know what came over me."

"You're right about this place," he admitted on a harsh note. "There is something spooky about it. Let's get out of here."

By the time they'd returned to the living room, Lily had regained her equilibrium and could smile over the peculiar events in the attic.

"What's so amusing?" He didn't sound the least bit pleased by their adventure, and stalked ahead of her, sitting in the fan-back bamboo chair usually reserved for Gram.

"Honestly, Jake, can you imagine *us kissing*?"

"We just did," he reminded her soberly, his voice firm as his watchful eyes studied her. "And if we're both smart, we'll forget it ever happened."

Lily sat on the sofa, tucking her legs under her. "I suppose you're right. It's just that after being such good friends for the past year, it was a shock. Elaine would never forgive me."

"Would you lay off Elaine? I've told you a thousand times

that it's been over for months." Jake grimaced at the sound of the other woman's name. His relationship with Elaine Wittenberg had developed nicely in the beginning. She was impressed with his writing, encouraging even. Then bit by bit, with intrusive politeness, Elaine had started to reorganize his life. First came the suggestion that he change jobs. Driving a cab didn't pay that well, and with his talents he could do anything. She started introducing him to her friends, making contacts for him. The problem was that Jake liked his life exactly the way it was. Elaine had been a close call—too close. Jake had come within inches of waking up one morning living in a three-bedroom house with a white picket fence and a new car parked in the garage—a house and a car with big monthly payments. True, Lily was just as eager for the same material possessions, but at least she was honest about it.

"Well, you needn't worry," Lily told him, taking a deep breath and releasing it slowly. "Just because we kissed, it doesn't mean anything."

Her logic irritated him. "Let's not talk about it, all right? It was a mistake and it's over."

Lily arched a delicate brow and shrugged one shoulder. "Fine." His attitude didn't please her in the least. As far as she knew, Jake wasn't one to sweep things under the carpet and forget they existed. If anything, he faced life head-on.

Abruptly getting to his feet, Jake stalked to the other side of the living room. Confused, Lily watched the impatient, angry way he moved. "I'll see you tomorrow," he said on his way to the front door.

"Okay."

The door closed and Lily didn't move. What an incredibly strange night it had been. First, the golden opportunity of finding that crazy song for the Texan. Then, wilder still was Jake's kissing her in the attic. Even now she could feel the pressure of his mouth on hers, and the salty-sweet taste of him lingered on her lips. He'd held her close, his scent heightened by the stuffy air of the attic.

But, Lily realized with a start, the kiss had been a moment out of time and was never meant to be. Jake was right. They should simply put it out of their minds and forget it had happened. A single kiss should be no threat to a year of solid friendship. They knew each other too well to get caught up in a romantic relationship. Lily had seen the type of woman Jake usually went for, and she wasn't even close to it. Jake's ideal woman was Mother Theresa, Angelina Jolie and Betty Crocker all rolled into one perfect female specimen. Conversely, her ideal man was Daddy Warbucks, Bruce Willis and Mr. Goodwrench. No… Jake and she would always be friends; they'd make terrible lovers….

The next morning when Lily found her way into the kitchen, Gram was already up and about. Her bright-red hair was tightly curled into a hundred ringlets and held in place with bobby pins.

"Morning," Lily mumbled and pulled out a kitchen chair, eager to speak to her grandmother.

Gram didn't acknowledge the greeting. Instead, the older woman concentrated on opening a variety of bottles, extracting her daily quota of pills.

Lily waited until her grandmother had finished swallowing thirteen garlic tablets and a number of vitamins, and had chewed six blanched almonds. This daily ritual was Gram's protection from cancer. The world could scoff, but at seventy-four Gram was as fit as someone twenty years her junior.

"I didn't hear you come in last night."

A smile played at the edges of Lily's mouth. "I know.

Gram, have you ever heard of the song 'Santa Fe Gal of Mine'?"

The older woman's look was thoughtful and Lily nibbled nervously on her bottom lip. "It's been a lotta years since I heard that ol' song."

"You remember it?" Relief washed through Lily until she sagged against the back of the chair. Lily marveled again at her grandmother's memory.

"Play a few bars for me, girl."

Lily tensed and the silence stretched until her nerve endings screamed with it. "I don't know the song, Gram. I thought *you* did."

"I do," she insisted, shaking her bright red head. "I don't remember it offhand, is all."

Is all, Lily repeated mentally in a panic. "When do you think you'll remember it?"

"I can't rightly say. Give me a day or two."

A day or two! "Gram, I haven't got that long. Our future could depend on 'Santa Fe Gal of Mine.' Think."

Stirring the peanut butter with a knife, Gram picked up a soda cracker and dabbed a layer of chunky-style spread across the top before popping it into her mouth.

Lily wanted to scream that this wasn't a time for food, but she pressed her lips tightly shut, forcing down the panic. Gram didn't do well under pressure.

"What do you want to know for?" Gram asked after a good five minutes had lapsed. Meanwhile, she'd eaten six soda crackers, each loaded with a thick layer of peanut butter.

"A rich man requested that song last night. A very rich man who had a generous look about him," Lily explained, doing her best to keep the excitement out of her voice. "If I can come up with that song, he'd probably be willing to show his appreciation."

"We could use a little appreciation, couldn't we, girl?"

"Oh, Gram, you know we could."

"If I can't think of it, Gene Autry would know." Gram often spoke as if famous personalities were her lifelong friends and all she had to do was pick up the phone and give a jingle.

"Did Gene Autry sing the original version?"

"Now that you mention it, he might have been the one," she said, scratching the side of her head.

Lily perked up. Gram had a recording of every song Gene Autry had ever sung. "Then you have it."

"I must," she agreed. "Someplace."

"Someplace" turned out to be in the furnace room in the basement five hours later. The next few hours were spent transposing the scratchy old record into notes Lily could play on the piano.

When she sat at the grand piano at five that evening in the Wheaton lobby, 'Santa Fe Gal of Mine' was forever embedded in her brain. Each note had been agonized over. There couldn't be a worse way to memorize a song. Lily had never been able to play very well by ear.

As it worked out, the timing had been tight and consequently Lily had been unable to pay the amount of attention she would have liked to her dress and makeup.

The lobby was busy with people strolling in and out, registering for a wholesale managers' conference. At the moment the only thing Lily was interested in was one Texan with a love for an ol' Gene Autry number.

During the evening, Lily twice played the song she had come to hate more than any of the others. Her only reward was a few disgruntled stares. The lively Western piece wasn't the "elevator" style she'd been hired to play. The second go-around with 'Santa Fe Gal' and Lily caught the manager's disapproving stare. Instantly, Lily switched over to something he'd consider more appropriate: "Moon River."

As the evening progressed, Lily's plastic smile became more and more forced. She'd gone to all this trouble for nothing. Her stomach felt as if it were weighted with a lead balloon. All the hassle she'd gone through, all the work, had been for nothing. Gram would be so disappointed. Heavens, Gram nothing. Lily felt like crying.

As usual, Jake was waiting for her outside the hotel.

"How'd it go?" he asked as she approached the cab. One look at her sorrowful dark eyes and Jake climbed out of the cab. "What happened?"

"Nothing."

"Mr. Moneybags wasn't the appreciative type?"

She shook her head, half expecting Jake to scold her for being so incredibly naive. "No."

"What, then?"

"He didn't show."

Jake held open the taxi door for her. "Oh, Lily, I'm sorry."

"It's not your fault," she returned loyally. "I was the stupid one. I can't believe that I could have gotten so excited over an overweight Texan who wanted to hear a crummy song that's older than I am."

"But he was a rich Texan."

"Into oil and maybe even gold."

"Maybe," Jake repeated.

He'd walked around the front of the taxi when the captain of the bellboys came hurrying out of the hotel. "Miss Lily!" he called, flagging her down. "Someone left a message for you."

2

"A message?" Lily's gaze clashed with Jake's as excitement welled up inside her, lifting the dark shroud of depression that had settled over her earlier.

"Thanks, Henry." Lily gave the hotel's senior bellhop a brilliant smile. Two minutes before, Lily would never have believed that something as simple as an envelope could chase the clouds of doubt from her heart.

"Well, what does it say?" Jake questioned, leaning through the open car window. He appeared as anxious as Lily.

"Give me a minute to open it, for heaven's sake." She ripped apart the beige envelope bearing the Wheaton's logo. Her gaze flew over the bold pen-strokes, reading as fast as she could. "It's him."

"Daddy Warbucks?"

"Yes," she repeated, her voice quavering with anticipation. "Only his real name is Rex Flanders. He says he got hung up in a meeting and couldn't make it downstairs, but he wanted me to know he heard the song and it was just as good as he remembered. He wants to thank me." Searching for something more, Lily turned over the single sheet, thinking she must have missed or dropped it in her hastiness. Surely he meant that he wanted to thank her with more than a simple message. The least she'd expected was a dinner invitation. With hurried, anxious movements she checked her lap, scrambling to locate the envelope she'd so carelessly discarded only a moment before.

"What are you looking for?" Jake asked, perplexed.

"Nothing." Defeat caused her voice to drop half an octave. Lily couldn't take her eyes from the few scribbled lines on the single sheet of hotel stationery. Shaking her head, she hoped to clear her muddled thoughts. She'd been stupid to expect anything more than a simple thank-you. Rich men always had women chasing after them. There wasn't one thing that would make her stand out in a crowd. She wasn't strikingly beautiful, or talented, or even sophisticated. Little about her would make her attractive to a wealthy man.

"Lily?" Gently, Jake placed a hand on her forearm. His tender touch warmed her cool skin and brought feeling back to her numb fingers. "What's wrong?"

A tremulous smile briefly touched her lips. "Me. I'm wrong. Oh, Jake, I'm never going to find a rich man who'll want to marry me. And even if I caught someone's eye, they'd take one look at Gram and Herbie and start running in the opposite direction."

"I don't see why," he contradicted sharply. "I didn't."

"Yeah, but you're just as weird as we are."

"Thanks." Sarcasm coated his tongue. So Lily thought he was as eccentric as her grandmother. All right, he'd agree that he didn't show the corporate ambitions that drove so many of his college friends. He liked his life. He was perfectly content to live on a sailboat for the remainder of his days, without a care or responsibility. There wasn't anything in this world that he couldn't walk away from, and that was exactly the way he wanted it. No complications. No one to answer to. Except Gram and Lily. But even now his platonic relationship with Lily was beginning to cause problems. He admired Lily. What he liked best about her was that she had no designs on his heart and no desire to change him. She was an honest, forthright woman. She knew what she wanted and made no bones about it. Their kiss from the day before had been a fluke that wouldn't happen again. He'd make sure of that.

"I didn't mean that the way it sounded," Lily mumbled her apology. "You're the best friend I've got. I'm feeling a bit defeated at the moment. Tomorrow I'll be back to my normal self again."

Silently walking around the front of the taxi, Jake climbed into the driver's seat and started the engine with a flick of his wrist. "I can't say I blame you." And he didn't. After everything she'd gone through to find that song, she had every right to be disappointed.

"It's me I'm angry with," Lily said, breaking the silence. "I shouldn't have put such stock in a simple request."

Jake blamed himself. He should have cautioned her, but at the time he'd been so surprised that he hadn't known what he was feeling—maybe even a bit of jealousy, which had shocked the hell out of him. Later he'd discarded that notion. He wanted Lily to be as happy as she deserved, but there was something about this Texan that had troubled him from the beginning.

The moment Lily had mentioned she'd met someone, warning lights had gone off inside his head. His protective instinct, for some reason he couldn't put into words, had been aroused. That alien impulse had been the cause of the incident in the attic. He didn't regret kissing Lily, but it was just that type of thing that could ruin a good friendship. The Texan meant trouble for Lily. It'd taken him half the night to realize that was what bothered him, but he was certain. Now, after Lily's revelation, Jake could afford to be generous.

"How about if we go fishing tomorrow?"

Lily straightened, her dark eyes glowing with pleasure at the invitation. Over the past year, Jake had only taken her out on the sloop for short, limited periods of time. Lily loved sailing and was convinced that the man she married would have to own a sailboat.

"With Gram," he added, smiling. "We'll make a day of it, pack a bottle of good wine, some cheese and a loaf of freshly baked French bread, and beer for me."

"Jake, that sounds wonderful." Already her heart was lifting with anticipation. Only Jake would know that an entire day on his sailboat would cheer her up like this.

"We deserve a one-day vacation from life. I'll park the cab, shut down the laptop and take you to places you have never been."

Lily expelled a deep sigh of contentment. "It sounds great, but Thursday's Gram's bingo day. Nothing will convince her to give that up."

A smile sparked from Jake's cool jade eyes. Lily's grandmother had her own get-rich schemes going. "Then it'll have to be the two of us. Are you still game?"

"You bet." Lily pictured the brisk wind whipping her hair freely about her face as the boat sliced through the deep-green waters of San Francisco Bay.

Within ten hours, the daydream had become reality. The wind carried Lily's low laugh as she tossed back her head and the warm breeze ruffled her thick, unbound hair. The boat keeled sharply and cut a deep path through the choppy water.

Lily had climbed to the front of the boat to raise the sails and was now sitting on the bow, luxuriating in the overwhelming sense of freedom she was experiencing. She wanted to capture this utopian state of being and hug it to her breast forever. She didn't dare turn back and let Jake see her. He'd laugh at her childish spirit and tease her unmercifully. Lily wanted nothing to ruin the magnificent day.

For the first hour of their trip, Lily remained forward while Jake manned the helm. Keeping his mind to the task was difficult. He couldn't ever remember seeing Lily so carefree and happy. She was a natural sailor. He'd taken other women aboard *Lucky Lady* and always regretted it. Elaine, for one. In the beginning, she'd pretended to love his boat as much as he, but Jake hadn't been fooled. Elaine's big mistake had come when she suggested that he move off the boat and into an apartment. Pitted against his only true love, Jake decided to keep *Lady* and dump Elaine. And not a moment since had he regretted the decision.

Watching Lily produced a curious sense of pride in Jake. Laughing, she turned back and shouted something to him. The wind whirled her voice away and he hadn't a clue as to what she'd said, but the exhilaration in her flushed face wasn't something that could be manufactured. It surprised Jake how much he enjoyed watching her. She reminded him of the sea nymphs sailors of old claimed inhabited the waters.

As he watched her, Jake realized that Lily was his friend and they were fortunate to share a special kind of relationship. But it wasn't until that moment that Jake noticed just how beautiful she was. In the year he'd known her, Lily's youthful features had filled out with vivid promise. Her long hair was a rich, dark shade of mahogany and he'd rarely seen it unbound. That day, instead of piling it on top of her head the way she normally did, Lily had left it free so that it fell in gentle waves around her shoulders. Her natural gracefulness was what struck Jake most. Her walk was decidedly provocative. Jake smiled to himself with an inner pride at the interest Lily's gently rounded hips generated from the opposite sex. If that Texan had seen her walk he would have given her more than a simple thank you. But what Jake loved mainly about Lily was her eyes. Never in his life had he met anyone with eyes so dark and expressive. Some days they were like cellophane and he could read her moods as clearly as the words in a book. He could imagine what it would be like making love to her. He wouldn't need to see anything but her eyes to…

He shook his head and dispelled the disconcerting thoughts. His fingers tightened around the helm and he looked sharply out to sea.What was the matter with him? He was thinking of Lily as a prospective lover.

"How about a cup of coffee?" Lily called, standing beside the mast. The wind whipped her hair behind her like a magnificent flag and Jake sucked in his breath at the sight of her.

"I'll get it," he shouted. "Take over here for me, will you?"

A quick, tantalizing smile spread across her features as she nodded and hurried down to join him at the helm. She laughed as he gave her careful instructions. She didn't need them. She felt giddy and reckless and wonderful.

Turning away, it was all Jake could do not to kiss her again. Mumbling under his breath, he descended to the galley and sleeping area of the boat.

Lily didn't know what was troubling Jake. She'd witnessed the dark scowl on his face and been surprised. He returned a few minutes later with two steaming mugs, handing her one.

"Is something wrong?" she ventured.

"Nothing," he said, keeping his gaze from lingering on her soft, inviting mouth.

"You look like you want to bite off my head again."

"Again?" Jake was stalling for time. This foul mood was Lily's fault. She didn't know what she was doing to him, and that was his problem.

"Yes, again," she repeated. "Like you did the other night when I told you about Rex."

"I've been doing some thinking about that ungrateful Texan," he said, narrowing his eyes. "There's something about him I don't trust."

"But you've never seen him," Lily countered, confused.

"I didn't have to. Just hearing about him was enough. I don't want you to see him again."

"Jake!"

"I mean it, Lily."

Astonished, Lily sat with her jaw sagging and turned away from him, cupping the steaming mug with both hands. Jake had never asked her to do anything. It wasn't like him to suddenly order her about and make demands. She swallowed her indignation. "Will you give me a reason?"

Drawing in a deep, irritated breath, Jake looked out over the green water and wondered at his own high-handedness. The Texan had been bothering him for two days. He hadn't wanted to say anything and even now, he wasn't entirely convinced he was doing the right thing. "It's a gut feeling I have. My instincts got me out of the war alive. I can't explain it, Lily, but I'm asking you to trust me in this."

"All right," she agreed, somewhat deflated. At the rate things were progressing with Rex What's-his-name, she wouldn't have the opportunity to see him again anyway. In reality, Jake wasn't asking much. He was her friend and she trusted his judgment, albeit at the moment reluctantly.

"Someone else will come along," Jake assured her, and a lazy grin crept across his face. "If not, you'll trap one as effectively as the fish we're about to lure to our dinner plates."

"You make it sound too easy." He wasn't the one who sat at that piano night after night playing those same songs again and again and again.

"It is." He handed her a fishing pole and carefully revealed to her the finer points of casting. Luckily, Lily was a fast learner and he took pains not to touch her. Shaking off his mood, he gave her a friendly smile. "Before you know it, our meal will mosey along," he said with a distinct Southern drawl. "And who knows? It could be an oil-rich Texan bass."

Lily laughed, enjoying their light banter.

"Every woman scheming to marry money has to keep her eye out for a tightfisted shark, but then again—" he paused for emphasis "—you might stumble upon a flounder in commodities."

"A generous flounder," Lily added.

"Naturally." Cupping his hand behind his head, Jake leaned back, crossed his long legs at the ankle and closed his eyes. He felt better. He hadn't a clue why he felt so strongly about that rich Texan. He just sensed trouble.

"There's another message for you, Miss Lily," Henry informed her when she arrived at the hotel the following evening.

Lily stared at the envelope as if it were a snake about to lash out at her. "A message?" she repeated, her voice sounding like an echo.

"From the same man as before," Henry explained with ageless, questioning eyes.

Undoubtedly the elderly bellboy couldn't understand her reluctance now when only the day before she behaved as if she'd won the lottery.

"Thank you." Lily took the folded note and made her way into the grand lobby. The manager acknowledged her with a faint nod, but Lily's answering smile was forced. The message lay on the keyboard of the piano for several moments before she had the courage to open it.

> Hello, Lily—the bellhop told me your name. He also told me what time you'd be in today. I've thought about you and your music. I'm hoping that a sweet filly like you won't think it too forward of me to suggest we meet later for a drink.
> *Rex Flanders*

A drink…surely that would be harmless, especially if they stayed right here in the hotel. Jake wouldn't mind that. Her hands moved to the ivory keys and automatically began the repertoire of songs that was only a step above the canned music that played in elevators.

Although her fingers moved with practiced ease, Lily's thoughts were in turmoil. She'd promised Jake she wouldn't get involved with Rex. At the time it had seemed like a little thing. It hadn't seemed likely she'd have the chance to see him again. Now she regretted having consented to Jake's request so readily. Her big break had arrived and she was going to have to refuse probably the richest man she'd ever met. And all because Jake had some stupid *feeling.* It wasn't fair. How could anyone have a feeling about someone they hadn't even met?

Later, when she had a moment, Lily penned a note to Rex, declining his invitation. She didn't offer an excuse. It'd sound ludicrous to explain that a friend had warned her against him. *You see, my friend, Jake, who has never even met you, has decided you're bad news. He felt so strongly about it that he made me promise I wouldn't see you again.* Rex would laugh himself all the way home to Texas. No one in their right mind would blame him.

Jake was out front, standing beside his taxi when she appeared. She suddenly felt like taking the bus, but one look at the darkening sky convinced her otherwise. The night was overcast, with thick gray clouds rolling in over the bay. Lily didn't need the weather to dampen her already foul mood.

"I hope you're happy," she announced as she opened the car door.

"Relatively. What's your problem?"

"At the moment, you."

Their gazes met, a clash of befuddled emerald and blazing jet. Lily had been waiting months for this opportunity—months of built up fanciful dreams—months when she'd schemed and planned for exactly this moment. And now, because of Jake, she was walking away from the opportunity of a lifetime.

"Me!" Jake cocked his head to one side, studying her as his gaze narrowed thoughtfully. "What do you mean?" His tone told her clearly that he didn't appreciate being put on the defensive.

"Rex asked me out."

"And you refused?" Instinctively he felt the hard muscles of his shoulders tense. So Daddy Warbucks was back. Somehow Jake had known the man would return.

"I'm here, aren't I? But I'll have you know that I regret that promise and would take it back in a minute if you'd let me." She eyed him hopefully, but at the sight of the deep grooves that were forming at the sides of his mouth, Lily could tell he wouldn't relent.

Jake was conscious of an odd sensation surging through his blood. He'd experienced it only a few times in his life and always when something monumental was about to happen.

The first time had been as an eight-year-old kid. He'd been lost in the downtown area at Christmastime and frightened half out of his wits. The huge skyscrapers had seemed to close in around him until he could taste panic. Then, the feeling had come and he'd stopped, got his bearings and found his way home on his own, astonishing his mother. Later, in high school, that same feeling had struck right before he played in a football game during which he scored three touchdowns and went on to be the MVP for the season. He'd felt it again in the desert in Iraq and that time, it had saved his life. Jake had never told anyone about the feeling. It was too complex to define.

"No," he said with cold deliberation. "I'm not changing my mind."

"Jake," she moaned, feeling wretched.

"I'm asking you to trust me." He said it without looking at her, not wanting her to see the intensity of his determination. His fists were clenched so tightly at his sides that his fingers ached. Lily could bat her long eyelashes at him all she wanted and it wouldn't change how he felt. Truth be known, he wished she'd find her Daddy Warbucks and get married if that was what she wanted so badly. But this Texan wasn't the right man for Lily.

Without further discussion, Lily slid inside the cab. Disappointment caused her shoulders to droop and her head to hang so low that her chin rested against the bright-red collar of her gown. She was more tired than she could remember having been in a long time. Of all the men in the world, she trusted Jake the most. More than her father. But then it was difficult to have too much confidence in a vague childhood memory. Lily's father had died when she was twelve, but she had trouble picturing him in her mind. As far as Lily could recall, she'd only seen her father a handful of times.

In some ways Lily wished she didn't trust Jake so much; it would make things a whole lot easier.

Jake closed her door, his hands gripping the open window as he watched her through weary eyes. For half a second, he toyed with the idea of releasing her from the promise. But he entertained the idea only fleetingly. He knew better.

"Can you take me home now?"

"Sure." He hurried around the cab and climbed into the front seat beside her. A flick of the key and the engine purred. "You won't regret this," Jake said, flashing her one of his most brilliant smiles.

"I regret it already," she said and stared out the side window.

Those thoughtless words hounded Lily for the remainder of the evening. Jake was her friend—her best friend—and she was treating him like the tax man. Usually, at the end of the evening Jake would stop by the house on his way back to the dock where his sailboat was moored. But he didn't show up, although Lily waited half the night. She didn't blame him. They'd hardly said a word on the way home and when he pulled to the curb in front of Gram's rickety old house, Lily had practically jumped out of the taxi. She hadn't even bothered to say good-night.

The following morning Lily was wakened by Gram singing an African chant. Tossing aside the covers, Lily leaped from the bed and rushed into the kitchen. Gram only sang in Swahili when things were looking up.

"Gram, what happened?" she asked excitedly, rubbing the sleep from her eyes. Two steps into the large central kitchen and Lily discovered Gram clothed in full African dress. Yard upon yard of bold chartreuse printed fabric was draped around her waist with deep folds falling halfway to the floor. The shirt was made of matching material and hung from her shoulders, falling in large bell sleeves. Wisps of bright-red hair escaped the turban that was wrapped around her head. Ten thin gold bracelets dangled like charms from each wrist.

"Gram." Lily stopped cold, not knowing what to think.

The older woman made a dignified bow and hugged Lily fiercely. "*Nzuri sana,*" she greeted her, ceremoniously kissing her granddaughter on the cheek.

Lily was too bemused to react. *"Nzuri sana,"* she returned, slowly sinking into a kitchen chair. Her grandmother might behave a bit oddly on occasion, but nothing like this.

Continuing to chant in low tones, Gram turned and pulled a hundred-dollar bill from the folds of her outfit and waved it under Lily's nose.

"Gram, where did you get that?" All kinds of anxious thoughts were going through her mind. Maybe Gram was so worried over their finances that she'd done something illegal.

Hips swaying, Gram crossed the room and chuckled. The unmusical sound echoed against the walls. "Bingo," she cried, and removed four more hundred-dollar bills.

"You won at bingo!" Lily cried, jumping up from the chair and dancing around the room. Their arms circled each other's waists and they skipped around the kitchen like schoolgirls until Lily was breathless and dizzy.

"You buy yourself something special," Gram insisted when they'd settled down. "Something alluring so those rich men at the Wheaton won't be able to take their eyes off you."

Lily did her utmost to comply. She left the house and spent the rest of the morning shopping. Half the day was gone by the time she'd located the perfect outfit. It was a silky black dress with a fitted bodice that dipped provocatively in the front, granting a glimpse of cleavage and hinting at the fullness of her breasts. Studying herself in the mirror, Lily turned sideways, one hand on her hips, and rested her chin on her shoulder as she pouted her lips. It was perfect. After paying for the dress, Lily hurried home. She rushed up to her bedroom and donned her new purchase, eying her reflection in the mirror. Jake would tell her if the dress had the desired effect. Besides, she owed him an apology.

His boat was in the slip at the marina when she arrived at the marina a short time later. Lily had never visited him without an invitation and felt uneasy about doing so now.

"Jake," she called from the dock. "Are you there?" The boards rolled slightly under her heels and Lily had to brace herself. "Jake," she repeated louder, hugging the full-length coat close to her.

"Coming." His tone sounded irritated and he was frowning as he stuck his head out from below deck. He stopped when he saw it was Lily and smoothed a hand through his thick hair. "Hi." Slowly he came topside. "What are you doing here? And why in heaven's name are you wearing that ridiculous coat?"

Lily glanced down over the long wool garment that had once belonged to Gram and felt all the more silly. "Gram won five hundred dollars at bingo last night. I bought a new dress and want your opinion on it. Can I come aboard?"

"Sure." Jake didn't sound nearly as eager as she'd hoped he would.

She lifted the gray wool coat from her shoulders and let it slip down her arms. "What do you think?" she asked. "Be honest, now."

One glance at Lily in that beautiful dress, and Jake could barely take his eyes off her. She looked sensational—a knockout.

"I... I didn't know if you'd want to see me," she continued.

"Why wouldn't I?" His answer was guarded, his words quiet. Still he couldn't take his eyes from her.

"I feel terrible about yesterday."

"It's no problem." He reached out his hand in silent invitation for her to join him and Lily deftly crossed the rough wooden dock to his polished deck.

"Gram insisted I buy something new. How do you like it?"

"I like it fine," he murmured, doing his best to avoid eye contact. "You look great, actually." That had to be the understatement of the century.

"Do you honestly think so?" she asked excitedly.

Jake smiled. "You look really nice."

"That's sweet," she said softly. "Thank you."

"Think nothing of it." With a sweep of his arm, he invited her below. "Do you want a cup of coffee?"

"Sure." She paused to remove her shoes and handed them to Jake. "Would you put these someplace where I won't forget them?"

"No problem." He went down before her and waited at the base of the steps in case she needed help. One bare foot appeared on the top rung of the ladder and the side split in the skirt revealed the ivory skin of her thigh as the next foot descended. Jake felt his heart constrict. He sighed with relief as she reached the bottom rung and turned around to face him, eyes sparkling. "I'll get you a cup," he announced, disliking the close confines of his cabin for the first time. Lily seemed to fill up every inch of available space, looming over him with that alluring scent of hers.

"How's the writing going?"

"Good." It wasn't. Actually he'd faced writer's block all day, and determined that it was Lily's fault. He didn't like what was happening between them and yet seemed powerless to stop it.

"Heard any more from Rex?"

"No." Lily slid into the tight booth that served as a seat around the kitchen table. "I won't see him again," she told him. "I promised you I wouldn't."

"Someone else will come along." And soon, he hoped. The quicker Lily found herself a sugar daddy, the better it would be for him.

"I know." She smiled up at him briefly as he set the mug on the table.

He didn't join her, fearing that if he slid into the seat beside her, they might accidentally brush against one another. And touching Lily while she looked so tempting in that dress shook Jake. It would be the attic all over again and he knew he wouldn't be able to stop himself. As it was now, he could barely tear his eyes from her. She lifted her mug and blew against the edge before taking a sip. Her dewy lips drew his gaze like a magnet. Jake turned around and added some sugar to his coffee.

"I didn't know you used sugar."

"I don't," he said, turning back to her.

"You just dumped three tablespoons into your cup." She sounded as perplexed as he felt.

Jake lifted one shoulder in a halfhearted shrug. "It must be something in the air."

"Must be," Lily agreed, not knowing what he was talking about. She dropped her gaze to the dark, steaming liquid. "I've been thinking that I need lessons on how to flirt."

Jake nearly choked on his coffee and did an admirable job of containing himself. Lily was so unconsciously alluring, that he couldn't believe that any man could ignore her.

"Will you teach me, Jake?" There wasn't anyone she trusted more. Jake had been all over the world and done everything she hadn't. Lily didn't think there was a thing he didn't know. With that, he did choke on a mouthful of coffee. "Me?"

"Yes, you."

"Lily, come on. I don't know anything about feminine stuff like that."

"Sure you do," she contradicted, warming to her subject. "Every time I bat my eyelashes at a man, I'm convinced he thinks I've got a nerve disease."

"Ask Gram."

"I can't do that." She waved her hand dismissively. "Just tell me what Elaine did that made you go all weak inside."

"I don't remember."

"Something like this?" She dropped her eyes and parted her lips, giving him her most sultry look.

Jake experienced a tenderness unlike anything he'd ever known. He couldn't teach her to flirt. She was a natural. "Yeah," he murmured at last.

Discouraged, Lily straightened. Elaine had known exactly what to do to make a man notice her. For months, Jake had been so crazy over the other woman that he'd hardly ever come by for a visit. It had shocked Lily when they'd split. Maybe Jake wasn't the best person to teach her what she needed to know. But she knew he wasn't immune to a woman's wiles. The problem was he thought of her as a sister. She could probably turn up on his dock naked and he'd barely notice.

"Forget it," she mumbled. "I'll ask Gram."

3

Jake paced the small confines of his galley like a man trapped in an obligatory telephone conversation. He had to do something, and fast. Roughly he combed his fingers through his hair and caught his breath. Lily was beginning to look good to him. Real good. And that was trouble with a capital *T*. Either he found himself a woman, and quick, or…or he'd take it upon himself to find Lily a wealthy man. Both appeared formidable tasks.

If he involved himself in another relationship, it would surely end in disaster. No woman would be satisfied with his carefree lifestyle. Every woman he'd known, with the exception of Lily, had taken it upon herself to try to "save" him. The problem was, Jake didn't want to be redeemed by a woman's ambitions.

But locating a rich man for Lily wouldn't be easy either. It wasn't as if he traveled in elite circles. He had a few contacts—buddies from school—but he didn't know anyone who perfectly fit the wealthy profile Lily was after.

The only potential option was Rick, his friend from college days. From everything Jake had heard, Rick had done well for himself and was living in San Francisco. It wouldn't hurt to look him up and see if he was still single. Jake didn't like the idea, but it couldn't be helped.

Humming softly, Lily smiled at the doorman at the Wheaton and sauntered into the posh hotel as if she owned it. She was practicing for the time when she could enter a public place and cause faces to turn and whispers to fill the air. Lily felt good. The meeting with Jake hadn't turned out to be the confrontation she'd expected. Jake had every reason to be angry with her, and wasn't. If anything he'd behaved a bit weirdly. He'd seemed to go out of his way to be distant. When she was on one side of the boat, he'd stand on the other. He'd avoided eye contact as though he were guilty of something. The large bouquet of red roses on the piano was a nice surprise. A small white envelope propped against the ivory keys caused her eyes to widen, and her heart to do a tiny flip-flop. Lily knew without looking that Rex had sent the flowers. Her hands trembled noticeably as she removed the card and read the bold handwriting:

Sorry you couldn't make it, little filly. I'll see you next month on the 25th at nine.

Lily swallowed a nervous lump that clogged her throat. Next month or next year; it wouldn't make any difference. She'd given Jake her word and she wouldn't go back on it no matter how tempting. And tempting it was. Rex was interested. He must be, to send her the flowers and ask her out again.

With a heavy heart, Lily pulled out the piano bench and sat, her hands poised over the pearly keys before starting in on the same old songs.

As usual, Jake was waiting for her at the end of her shift. His gaze focused on the roses and narrowed fractionally.

"Daddy Warbucks?"

"Yeah." Lily didn't know why she felt so guilty, but she did. This was the first time in her life that anyone had sent her roses and she wasn't about to leave them at the Wheaton. "He's gone."

Jake felt a surge of relief wash over him. He wished that he felt differently about that Texan. It would have been the end of his troubles. Lily could have her rich man and he could go about his life without complications.

"He left a note with the roses, asking me out next month. Apparently he'll be back in town then."

"Are you going?"

The muscles at the side of her mouth ached as Lily compressed her lips into a tight line. "No."

"Good."

Maybe it was good for Jake, but Lily was miserable.

"Will I see you later?" she asked when he dropped her off in front of Gram's house.

"I'll be by."

Even with all his hang-ups about personal freedom and restricting schedules, Lily knew that if Jake said he'd be someplace, he'd be there eventually. Purposely waiting up for him, she sat watching the late-late show dressed in a worn terry-cloth housecoat that was tightly cinched at the waist. In an effort to stay awake, she sipped Marmite, a yeast extract, which had been stirred into hot water. Years ago while traveling in New Zealand, Gram had had her first taste of the thick, chocolate-like substance and she had grown to love it. She received the product on a regular basis from family friends now and spread it lightly over her morning toast. Lily preferred the dark extract diluted.

The movie was an old Gary Cooper one that had been filmed in the late nineteen fifties. Soon Lily was immersed in the characters and the plot and loudly blew her nose to hold back tears at a tender scene. A light knock against the front door announced Jake's arrival. She opened the door, waved him inside and sniffled as he took the seat opposite her.

Jake eyed her curiously. "You sick?"

Lily sucked in a wobbly breath and pointed to the television screen with her index finger. "No… Gary Cooper's going to be killed in a couple of minutes and I hate to see him die."

Jake scooted forward in the thickly cushioned chair and linked his hands. "I talked to an old friend today."

Lily's eyes didn't leave the black-and-white picture tube. "That's nice."

"Rick's a downtown attorney and has made quite a name for himself in the past few years."

Lily didn't know why Jake found it so important to tell her about his friend in the middle of the best scene of the movie.

Jake hated it when Lily ignored him. He couldn't imagine how she could be so engrossed in a film that made her weep like a two-year-old. "Lily," he demanded, "would you listen to me?"

"In a minute," she sobbed, wrapping a handkerchief around her nose and blowing. Tears streamed down her cheeks and she wiped them aside with the back of her hand.

Knowing that there wasn't anything he could do but wait, Jake settled back in the upholstered chair that had once belonged to a Zulu king and impatiently crossed his arms over his chest. He had terrific news to share—and she found it more important to cry over Gary Cooper than to listen to him. Ten minutes later, Lily grabbed the remote and turned off the TV. "That's a great movie."

"You cried through the whole thing," Jake admonished.

"I always cry during a Gary Cooper movie," she shot back. "You should know that by now."

Rather than argue, Jake resumed his earlier position and leaned forward in the chair toward her. "As I was saying..."

"Do you want a cup of Marmite?" Remembering her manners, Lily felt guilty about being such a poor hostess. Gram had taught her better than this.

"What I want," Jake said with forced patience, "is for you to sit down and listen to me."

Meekly lowering herself to the sofa, Lily politely folded her hands in her lap and looked at Jake expectantly. "I'm ready."

"It's about time," he muttered.

"Well. I'm waiting." Sometimes it took Jake hours to get to the point. Not that he did a lot of talking. He'd say a few words here and there and she was expected to get the gist. The problem was, Lily rarely did and he'd end up staring at her as if her head were full of holes.

"I saw Rick—my lawyer friend—this afternoon."

"The one from school?"

"Right. Anyway, Rick has become a regular socialite in the past few years and he's invited me to a cocktail party he's having Saturday night."

Lily blinked twice. She wouldn't have thought Jake would be so enthusiastic about a bunch of people standing around holding drinks and exchanging polite inanities. "That's interesting." She tried to hide a yawn and didn't succeed. Belatedly she cupped her mouth and expelled a long whiney breath.

Jake's face fell into an impatient frown. He didn't usually look that way until he was five minutes into his monologue.

"I thought you'd be thrilled," he murmured. It hadn't been easy to reach out to Rick—Mr. Success—and strike up a conversation after so many years.

"To be perfectly honest, I wouldn't have believed you'd enjoy a cocktail party."

"I won't. I'm doing it for you."

"For me?"

"There are bound to be a lot of rich men there, Lily. Undoubtedly some of them will be single and on the lookout for an attractive woman."

"What do you plan to do? Hand them my name and phone number?" she asked.

"You're going with me," he barked.

"Well, for heaven's sake, why didn't you say so?"

"Anyone with half a brain would have figured that out. You should know that I wouldn't be willing do something like this without an ulterior reason."

They stood facing each other, not more than two feet apart. The air between them was so heavy that Lily expected to see arcs of electricity spark and flash. Jake's breathing was oddly raspy. But then hers wasn't any better. They shouldn't be arguing—they were friends. Neither of them moved. Lily couldn't stop looking at him. They were so close that she could see every line in his face, every groove, every pore. Even the hairs of his brows seemed overwhelmingly interesting. Her gaze located a faint scar on his jawline that she'd never noticed before and she wondered if this was a souvenir from Iraq. He'd told her little of his experiences there.

His eyes were greener tonight than she'd remembered. Green as jade, dark as night, alive and glittering with an emotion Lily couldn't read. His mouth was relaxed and slightly parted as if beckoning her, telling her that she must make the first move. Surely she'd misinterpreted him. Jake wouldn't want to kiss her. They were friends—nothing more. What had happened in the attic had been a moment out of time and place. Still not believing what she saw, Lily raised her gaze to his and their eyes met and clashed. Jake did want to kiss her. And even more astonishing was that she wanted it, too. "Lily." He breathed heavily and turned away from her, stalking to the opposite side of the room. "I think I will have something to drink after all."

"Marmite?"

"Sure—anything."

Lily was grateful that she had something to occupy her hands and her mind. Jake didn't follow her into the kitchen, and she needed to have time to compose her thoughts. Good grief, what was happening to them? After all these months there wasn't any logical explanation why they should suddenly be physically attracted to each other. Something must be in the air—but spring was nine months away. A laugh hovered on her lips as she pictured tiny neon lights that flashed on and off across her forehead, telling Jake: *Kiss Lily.* But Lily knew it wasn't right. Jake was wonderful, but he wasn't the man for her. Thank heaven he'd had enough sense to turn away when he did.

Lily carried a steaming cup into the living room and carefully handed it to him. She wasn't so much afraid of being burned by the near-boiling water as she was fearful of her reaction if she touched him.

"I want you to attend that party with me." Jake picked up the conversation easily, pretending nothing had happened. Even though it was obvious they'd been a hair's breadth from hungrily falling into each other's arms.

"Saturday?" Her mind filled with niggling thoughts. She was scheduled to work, but she would be free at nine; she could wear her new dress. No, that was a bit too daring for a first meeting.

"Do you or don't you want to go?" Jake still hadn't taken a sip of his Marmite.

"Sure. I'll be happy to attend. Thanks for thinking of me." That sounded so stilted, Lily instantly wanted to grab back the words and tell him how pleased she was that he'd thought of her and was willing to help her out.

"I'll see you Saturday, then."

"Saturday," she echoed, and watched as Jake set aside his untouched drink and walked out of the house.

Lily didn't see Jake for two days. That wasn't as unusual as it was unsettling. It was almost as if they were afraid to see each other again.

During that time, Lily thought about Jake. She didn't know what was happening, but it had to stop. Jake was the antithesis of everything she wanted in a man. He had no real ambitions and was perfectly content to live out his days aboard his sailboat, doing nothing more than write short stories that didn't pay. Usually he received three free copies of the publication in compensation for his hundred hours of sweat and toil. Sometimes Lily wondered why Jake wrote when each word seemed so painful for him. Jake was a paradoxical sort of person. He hid behind his computer screen and revealed his soul in heart-wrenching stories no one would ever read.

While Jake was perfectly content with his life, Lily desperately wanted to improve hers. She longed to explore the world, to travel overseas and dine in the shadow of the Eiffel Tower. She yearned to see China and lazily soak up the sun on a South Pacific island. And she didn't want to ever agonize over a price tag again. Bargain basements and secondhand stores would be forever behind her. But most of all, Lily never wanted to hear "Moon River" again.

On Saturday evening Lily dressed carefully. Her dark curls were swirled high on her head and held in place with combs her father had brought her from India when she was twelve. He'd died shortly afterward and Lily had treasured this last gift, wearing them only on the most special occasions. At the end of her shift, with the thirty-ninth rendition of "Moon River" ringing in her ears, Lily stepped out of the hotel, expecting Jake to meet her. She didn't see him, and for half a second, panic filled her.

"Lily," Jake said, stepping forward.

Lily blinked and placed her hand over her heart at the sight of the tall, handsome man who stood directly in front of her. She squinted, sure she was seeing things. "Jake, is that you?"

"Who else were you expecting? Prince Charming?"

"You're wearing a suit!" A gray one that could have been lifted directly from the pages of *Gentlemen's Quarterly*, Lily realized in bemusement. The simple, understated color was perfect for Jake, emphasizing his broad shoulders and muscular build. "You look…wonderful!"

Jake ran his finger along the inside of his collar as if he needed the extra room to breathe properly. "I don't feel that way."

"But why?" She'd never seen Jake in anything dressier than slacks and a fisherman's bulky-knit sweater.

"I don't know. But knowing Rick, this party is bound to be an elaborate affair and it's best to dress the part."

Lily could hardly take her eyes from him. He looked dashing. Her gaze dropped to her own much-worn dress. "Am I overdressed? Underdressed? I don't want to give the wrong impression." Her insecurities dulled the deep brilliance of her eyes.

Jake glanced at her and shrugged. "You look all right."

All right? She'd spent half the day getting ready, fussing over each minute detail. "I hope you know you're about as charming as the underside of a toad."

"Hey, if you want romance, try Hugh Jackman. I ain't your man."

"You're telling me!" she huffed.

"Are we going to this thing or not?" He held the taxi's passenger door open for her, but didn't wait until she was inside before walking around the front of the car.

The first ten minutes of the ride down Golden Gate Avenue past the Civic Center was spent in silence.

Lily felt obligated to ease the tension. Both were on edge. "I didn't know you owned a suit."

Jake's response was little short of a grunt. The expensive suit had been Elaine's idea. She was the one who'd insisted he needed some decent clothes. She had dragged him around town to several exclusive men's stores and fussed over him like a drone over a queen bee. He'd detested every second of it, but he'd been so crazy about her that he'd stood there like a stooge and done exactly as she dictated. His weak-mindedness shocked him now. In thinking over his short but fiery relationship with Elaine, Jake was dismayed by some of the things he'd allowed her to do to him. The last party he'd attended had been with Elaine. He'd sat back and listened as she introduced him to her phony friends, telling them that Jake owned his own company and lived on a yacht. To hear her tell it, Jake was a business tycoon. In reality, he owned one taxicab that he drove himself, and his "yacht" was a ten-year-old, twenty-seven-foot, single-mast, fore-and aft-rigged sailboat that most of Elaine's colleagues could have bought with their pocket change.

"Are you going to sit there and sulk all night?" Lily questioned, growing impatient.

"Men never sulk," Jake declared, feeling smug just as Rick's house came into view. Jake parked several yards away in the closest available space. His five-year-old Chevy looked incongruous on the same street with all the fancy foreign cars, so he patted his steering wheel affectionately as if to assure his taxi that it was as good as the rest of them.

Rick's house was an ostentatious colonial-style, with thick white pillars and a well-lit front entrance. Jake swallowed nervously. Old Rick had done well for himself, even better than Jake had assumed.

"It's lovely," Lily murmured, and sighed with humble appreciation. This was exactly the kind of home she longed to own someday—one with crystal chandeliers, Persian carpets and gold fixtures.

"Lovely if you like that sort of thing," Jake grumbled under his breath.

Lily liked it just fine. "Oh, but I do. Thank you, Jake."

The genuine emotion in her voice was a surprise and he tore his gaze away from the house long enough to glance her way.

"I should have been more appreciative. I'd never thought I'd be able to attend something as wonderful as this. Oh, Jake, just think of all the wealthy men who'll be here."

"I'm thinking," he mumbled, pleased for the first time that he'd accepted Rick's invitation.

If Lily was impressed with the outside of the house, she was doubly so with the interior. She resisted the urge to run her hand over the polished mahogany woodwork and refused to marvel at the decor for too long. A maid perfunctorily accepted their coats at the front door and directed them toward a central room where drinks were being served.

"Jake, old buddy."

Lily felt Jake stiffen, but was proud of the way he disguised his uneasiness and shook hands with the short man with a receding hairline. Lily could easily picture the man as a successful attorney. She could see him pacing in front of the jury box and glancing acrimoniously toward the defendant.

"Rick," Jake said with a rare smile. "It's good to see you. Thanks for the invitation."

"Any time." Although he spoke to Jake, Rick's gaze rested on Lily. "Jake, introduce me to this sweet cream puff."

"Rick, Lily. Lily, Rick."

"I'm most pleased to make your acquaintance," Lily murmured demurely. "Jake has told me so much about you."

Briefly, Rick's enthralled gaze left Lily to glance at Jake. "Where did you find this jewel?"

Lily's gaze pleaded with Jake to not tell Rick the real story of Gram confronting the Wheaton manager in full witch doctor's costume, outraged over Lily's starting wages. "We met at the Wheaton," Jake explained and Lily reached for his hand, squeezing it as a means of thanking him.

"Are you visiting our fair city?" Rick directed the question to her.

"No, I play the piano there."

"A musician!" Rick exclaimed. "I imagine you're a woman of many talents."

Jake didn't know what Rick was implying, but he didn't like the sound of it. He bunched up his fist until he realized that Lily's fingers were linked with his and he forced his hand to relax.

"Only a few talents, I fear," Lily answered with such self-possession that Jake wanted to kiss her. "But enough to impress my friends."

"Then I'd consider it an honor to be your friend."

Lily batted her lashes. "Perhaps."

From the way Rick's eyes widened, Jake knew that Lily had impressed his old friend. A surge of pride filled Jake and he struggled not to put his arm around Lily's shoulders.

Rick reached out to take Lily's hand. "Do you mind if I steal your girl away for a few minutes?"

Jake did mind, but this was exactly why he'd brought Lily to the party. She would make more contacts here than she would during a year of playing piano at the Wheaton. "Feel free," he murmured, lifting a glass of champagne from the tray of the passing server. He didn't watch as Lily and Rick crossed the room, Lily's arm tucked securely in the crook of Rick's elbow.

The bubbling liquid in the narrow crystal glass seemed to be laughing at him and, almost angrily, Jake set it aside. He hated champagne and always had. He much preferred a hearty burgundy with some soul to it. He found an obscure corner and sat down, giving anyone who approached him a look that would discourage even the most outgoing party guest. He could hear Lily's laugh drift from another section of the house and was pleased she was enjoying herself. At least one of them was having a decent time.

Another waiter came past and Jake ordered Ouzo, a Greek drink. Gram had given him his first taste of the anise-flavored liqueur she drank regularly. Lily claimed it had made her teeth go soft, and to be honest, the licorice-tasting alcohol had curled a few of Jake's chest hairs. But he was in the mood for it tonight—something potent to remind himself that he was doing the noble thing. Now he knew how Joan of Arc must have felt as she was tied to the stake and the torches were aimed at the dry straw. No, he was being melodramatic again. What did it matter? He'd known all along that he was going to lose *his* Lily. But Lily wasn't his, had never been his. He drank down the liqueur with one swallow and felt it sear a path to his stomach. Lily was his good friend. He'd do anything for her and Gram—well, almost anything.

Jake asked for another Ouzo and drank it down with the same eagerness as the first. Another followed shortly after that. His eyes found a woman sitting on the sofa on the other side of the room, and she smiled. Hey, Jake mused, maybe this party wasn't such a loss after all. Maybe Lily wasn't the only one destined to have a good time.

He stood, surprised that a house as expensive as Rick's had a floor that swayed like a ship at sea. Suavely, he tucked one hand in his pants pocket and paused to smooth the hair along the side of his head. There wasn't any need to look like a slob.

Just when he was prepared to introduce himself to Goldilocks across the way, he heard the piano and stopped cold. "Moon River." Oh no. Rick had convinced Lily to entertain him. Jake knew how she felt about that song. Rick couldn't do that to Lily. Jake wouldn't let him. Rushing forward, he raised his hand and started to say something when the floor suddenly, unexpectedly, came rushing up to meet him.

4

Holding a small bouquet of flowers, Lily traipsed through the hospital lobby to the open elevator, stepped inside and pushed the button for the appropriate floor. She'd worried about Jake all night. He'd looked so pale against the starched white hospital sheets. Pale and confused. Lily should never have left his side, but Rick had convinced her that there wasn't any more either of them could do. Jake had been given a shot and would soon be asleep. Nonetheless, Lily had lingered outside the hall until the shot took effect, then reluctantly left.

When the heavy metal doors of the elevator parted, Lily stepped out eagerly. She had so much to tell Jake. He'd been such a dear to have taken her to the party. Everything had turned out beautifully—except for his fall, of course. Lily had met several men, all of whom had an aura of wealth. She prided herself on her ability to recognize money when she saw it. Rick had insisted on buying her a new dress since the one she'd worn to the party had gotten stained. But Lily had adamantly refused. The dress wasn't ruined. Gram had used vinegar and a few other inventively chosen ingredients to remove Jake's blood.

Lily stepped past the nurse's station and headed down the wide hall to Jake's room. The faint smell of antiseptic caused her to wrinkle her nose. Jake would be glad to get out of there.

The door to his room was open and Lily paused in the doorframe, looking at the nurse's aide who was stripping the bed of the sheets and blankets. Troubled, Lily's gaze slid to the number printed on the door for a second time to be sure she had the right room.

"Good morning," Lily murmured.

"Morning," the other woman answered flatly. "Is there something I can do for you?"

"Do you know where Jake Carson is?"

"Mr. Carson signed himself out early this morning."

Lily swallowed to relieve her voice of its shock and surprise. "Signed himself out? But why?"

"I believe Mr. Carson had several reasons, all of which were described in colorful detail."

"Oh, dear." Lily was shocked to realize she'd spoken out loud.

"I'm afraid so. He also insisted on paying his own tab and wanted the bill brought to him immediately." Impatiently, the woman jerked the bottom sheet from the raised hospital bed. "I've seen a few stubborn men in my day, but that one takes the cake."

It didn't take much imagination for Lily to picture the scene. Jake could be a terror when he wanted to be, and from the frustrated look on the nurse's flushed face, Jake had outdone himself this time. Lily was all the more convinced that she shouldn't have left him. She shouldn't have listened to Rick. Next time, she'd follow her instincts.

"Did he say where he was going?" Lily pressed.

The woman hugged the sheet to her abdomen and slowly shook her head. "No, but I'm sure the staff could give you a few suggestions about where we'd like to see him."

"I am sorry." Lily felt obliged to apologize for Jake, although she was convinced he wouldn't appreciate it. "I'm sure he didn't mean…whatever it was he said."

"He meant it," the woman growled, placing the sheet with unnecessary force inside a laundry cart at her side.

"Well, thank you, anyway," Lily stammered. "And here…" She shoved the small bouquet of daisies into the woman's hands. "Please take these." With that, Lily turned and hurried from the room.

By the time she arrived back at Gram's, Lily was more worried than before. "Gram, Jake's left the hospital."

Gram stood at the ironing board, pressing dried flowers between sheets of waxed paper. "I know."

"You know!"

"Why yes. He called earlier."

"Where is he?" Lily demanded, the wobble in her voice betraying her concern. "He shouldn't be alone…not with a head injury."

"He sounded perfectly fine," Gram contradicted, moving from the iron to the stove where she stirred the contents of a large stockpot.

"Is he at the marina? I should probably go there, don't you think? Something could happen." Not waiting for a response, Lily made a sharp about-face and headed out of the kitchen. For a panicked second, she imagined a dizzy, disoriented Jake stumbling about the sailboat. He could slip and fall overboard and no one would know.

"It'd be a waste of time."

"A waste of time? Why?" Lily paused and turned around to face Gram, her thoughts scrambled.

Humming an old Beatles tune, Gram continued stirring. "Jake's on his way over here."

"Now?"

"That's what he said."

"Why didn't you tell me that earlier?" Lily cried.

Gram turned away from the stove and studied Lily with narrowed, knowing eyes. "You seem worried, girl. Jake can take care of himself."

"I know...but he's lost a lot of blood. He had ten stitches and..."

"He's not going to appreciate it if you make a fuss over him."

Lily forced the tense muscles in her back and shoulders to relax. Gram was right. Jake would hate how concerned she was.

"What else did he say?" Trying to disguise how disquieting Lily found this entire matter, she pushed the kitchen chair under the table.

"Do you want some split-pea soup?" Gram asked as though she hadn't heard Lily's question.

"No, thanks." An involuntary grimace crossed her face. Gram loved split-pea soup, but Lily didn't know why she would be eating it in the middle of the morning.

A loud knock against the front door announced Jake's arrival. Lily battled the urge to run across the room to meet him.

Jake let himself inside. "Morning."

"Hello, Jake." Lily laced her fingers in front of her. "How are you feeling?"

"Great," he answered, breezing right past her and into the kitchen.

"Soup's ready," Lily heard her grandmother tell him.

"I appreciate it, Gram."

"When it comes to restoring a person's health, it's better than chicken noodle."

"Anything you cook is better than my futile attempts."

Shocked and a little hurt at Jake's abrupt greeting, Lily stood stiffly, halfway between the kitchen and the front door. Jake may have said only one word to her, but his eyes spoke volumes. Over the past year they'd often informed her of what he was thinking and feeling before he could say a word. They were a stormy shade of jade when he was angry, and that seemed to be happening on a regular basis lately. At other times they were a murky green, but that was generally when he was troubled about something. Then there were rare times when they sparked with what seemed a thousand tiny lights. They'd glittered like that when he'd first seen her in the dress she'd bought with Gram's bingo winnings and again later, when they'd met before Rick's party. But then they'd quickly changed to that murky shade of green. Lily didn't know what to make of that. Jake had been so easy to read in the past, but either he was changing or she was losing her ability to understand the one man she thought she knew so well.

"How are you feeling?" Lily asked for the second time, coming into the kitchen.

Jake pulled out a chair at the table, and sat drinking Gram's soup from a ceramic mug.

"Fine," he answered curtly.

"You look better." Some color had returned to his face. Yet he remained so pale that the tiny creases around his eyes were more noticeable than ever.

Gram joined Jake at the table, pouring two additional servings of soup.

"Here." She gave one to Lily who wrinkled her nose at it.

"No thanks, I prefer chicken noodle."

Jake's snort was almost imperceptible. "I'll be ready in a minute here," he added.

Lily glanced at Gram, who appeared oblivious to the comment. "Ready for what?" Lily inquired.

"Shopping."

"You're going shopping?" Good grief, he'd just been released from the hospital. "Whatever for?" If he needed anything, she'd be happy to make the trip for him.

"We're going out."

"Us?"

Jake caught Gram's eye. "You didn't tell her?"

"I didn't get a chance."

"Tell me!" Lily demanded, not liking the way Jake was ignoring her.

"Jake's taking you out to buy you a new dress," Gram informed her.

"The dress is fine," Lily protested loudly. "Didn't you tell him that?"

"I did," Gram huffed. "But he insists."

Jake's gaze bounced from Gram to Lily and back again. "Did you tell Lily that it won't do any good to argue with me on this one? I saw what I did to her dress. I'm buying her another one and that's all there is to it."

Lily sank into the chair across from Jake and boldly met his gaze. "In case you hadn't noticed, I'm standing right here. There's no need to ask Gram to tell me anything when you and I are separated by less than two feet." The words came out sharp and argumentative despite her effort to sound casual.

"If you insist." Gram chuckled. "You two remind me of Paddy and me."

Paddy was Lily's grandfather. He'd died several years before Lily was born, but the tales Gram told about him were very telling of the deep love and commitment her grandparents had shared. Lily hoped to find the same deep and lasting love with her own husband.

"You ready?" Jake asked, standing.

Lily looked at Gram for support, then back to Jake. "I hate to have you spend money on me. It isn't necessary."

"Would you like it better if Rick bought you a dress? Is that it?"

"Of course not." She hardly knew Rick and didn't want him buying her clothes.

"Then let's get this over and done with." He was halfway across the living room before Lily moved.

"Gram, what's wrong with Jake? He's not himself."

Gram shook her pin-curled head and laughed. "I can't say I rightly know, but I have my suspicions."

With Jake marching ahead, Lily had little choice but to follow him. He was sitting in the driver's seat of his taxi and glaring impatiently toward Lily as she came down the front steps.

"How'd you get your cab back?" she asked, opening the car door. They'd left it parked in front of Rick's house and Lily had wondered if Jake wanted her and Gram to pick it up for him. That was one of the things she'd planned to ask him that morning at the hospital.

"I have my ways," he grumbled, checking the side-view mirror before pulling onto the street. A heavy pause followed. "Did you have a good time last night?"

The question repeated in Lily's mind. Had she? Yes and no. The evening had been one she'd dreamed about for years. She'd met several interesting men who might be worth her time. Rick had been a gentleman, kind and considerate and genuinely concerned when Jake had fallen. He'd taken charge immediately and knew exactly what to do. Lily had been surprised at her own response to Jake's injury. She'd fallen to pieces, and Rick had been there to lend his support. "Hello? Earth to Lily," Jake said. "Did you or did you not have a good time?"

"The evening was grand. Thank you, Jake, for inviting me."

"Did you meet someone?" Anticipating her answer, his grip tightened around the steering wheel. He wanted Lily to assure him that she had found the rich man of her dreams. But in the same breath, he wanted her to tell him she'd found no one.

"Not really."

"What about Rick?"

"He was very nice."

The corner of Jake's mouth curved up sarcastically. Her word choice was comforting. "Anyone else?"

"Not really. A couple of others said they planned to visit the Wheaton to hear me play, but I don't think they'll show."

"Who?" Jake demanded.

Lily lifted one shoulder in a delicate shrug, surprised that Jake would sound angry when meeting eligible wealthy men was the reason he'd taken her to the party. "I don't remember their names."

"If they do come, I want to know about it so I can have them checked out." He was eager to know for other reasons as well—ones that weren't clearly defined in his mind. He wanted Lily married and happy and he wished to heaven that he could forget the taste of her. Every time he looked at her, he had trouble not kissing her again. He'd received a head injury, Jake told himself. One that was apparently affecting his reasoning ability. He shouldn't be thinking of Lily in that way. His only option was to set her up with Rick or one of the others—and quickly.

"Jake," Lily said softly.

"Yes?" He swallowed hard.

"Why are you insisting on buying me a dress?"

"What's the matter? Do you think Rick could afford a better one?"

"Oh, Jake, of course not."

From the soft catch in her voice, Jake knew he'd hurt her to even imply such a thing. "It's a matter of pride," he explained. "You told me Rick wanted to replace the one I ruined. My blood stained it, so I should be the one to buy you another dress."

"But Gram got the stain out."

"It doesn't matter."

"But..."

"I'm buying you the dress. Understand?"

She didn't answer.

"Understand?" he repeated forcefully.

"Repeaters is off Thirty-second."

"What?"

"The secondhand store where I usually buy my dresses." It took all of her willpower to give in to his pride. Jake had always been so reasonable, but his harsh tone told Lily she'd best concede gracefully. Either Jake would go with her or he'd buy something for her on his own.

"I'm not getting you anything secondhand."

"All right," she agreed reluctantly. "Either Sears or Penney's is fine."

"We're going to Neiman-Marcus."

"Neiman-Marcus, Jake!" Lily's jaw fell open. Jake couldn't afford to shop there.

The announcement was as much of a shock to Jake as it

was to Lily. He'd driven toward downtown, thinking they'd figure out where to shop once he'd found parking. But now that he'd spoken the words, he wouldn't back down. If he was going to buy Lily a dress, it would be one she'd remember all her life.

"I saw a dress I liked on display in Penney's." Her hands felt clammy just at the thought of spending all Jake's money on some silly dress. He worked too hard and saved so little.

"And I saw one at Neiman-Marcus," Jake countered. "You're always talking about how you want to shop there someday. I'm giving you the chance."

A hundred arguments crossed her mind as they parked and Jake escorted her through the elite department store.

"Jake," Lily pleaded.

"And nothing on sale." Jake paused in front of a mannequin. "Nice," he said to no one in particular.

"It should be," Lily informed him stiffly, reading the price tag. "This little piece of chiffon is fifteen hundred dollars."

It demanded all of his discipline for Jake to bite his tongue. Fifteen hundred dollars for a dress? He had no idea. He hesitated a second longer. "So?"

"Jake, honestly, fifteen hundred dollars would wipe you out." Lily was growing more uneasy by the minute. This whole idea was ridiculous. Pride or not, Jake had no business buying her clothes. Not here.

"May I help you?" An attentive salesclerk approached them.

"Yes," Jake insisted.

"No," Lily countered.

"Perhaps if I came back in a few minutes." The salesclerk took a step in retreat.

"My friend here would like to try on this dress," Jake said, lifting the hem of the pricey dress on the mannequin.

"Jake," Lily hissed under her breath.

"And a few more just like this," Jake continued.

The clerk gave a polite nod. "If you'll come this way."

Jake's hand on the small of Lily's back urged her forward.

"Do you have any color in mind?"

"Midnight blue, red, and maybe something white." The choices came off the top of his head. Once, a long time back, it had occurred to him that with Lily's dark hair she'd look like an angel in white.

"I have just the thing." The clerk motioned toward the dressing rooms on the other side of the spacious floor.

Like a small duckling marching after its mother, Lily walked behind the salesclerk through rows and rows of expensive dresses.

Sitting in a deep, cushioned chair outside the dressing room, Jake leaned against the padded back and crossed his legs, playing the part of a generous benefactor. This was just the type of thing Rick would relish. Jake had recognized the look in Rick's eyes the minute he laid eyes on Lily. He'd wanted her. Jake knew the feeling. He'd wanted Elaine from the first minute he'd seen her; had lusted after her and been so thoroughly infatuated with her that he couldn't think straight. But Lily was different. She wasn't Elaine—knowledgeable in the ways of the world and practiced in controlling men. No, Lily was an innocent.

Changing positions, Jake uncrossed his legs and folded his arms over his chest. He didn't know what could be taking so long—or how he was going to pay for whichever dress Lily chose. But it would be worth it to salvage his pride.

"Jake," Lily whispered, coming out of the dressing room. She wore a deep-blue dress with a scalloped collar and short sleeves. "How do you like it?"

Jake watched her walk self-consciously in front of him. It was a dress, nothing special. "What do you think?" he asked.

"The saleslady called it Spun Sapphires."

"It has a name?"

"Yes." She inserted her hand inside the thin belt. "It's a little big around the waist."

"Then try on another."

Relieved, Lily returned to the dressing room. The dress was nice, but she hated the thought of Jake spending nine hundred dollars on it. As tactfully as possible, she asked the clerk to bring dresses that were in a lower price range. Eager to please, the woman returned with a variety in the colors Jake had requested. A white crepe frock with feminine tucks and simulated pearl embellishments caught her eye.

Jake felt a little too conspicuous as he sat and waited. Since Iraq he liked to think of himself as an island, an entity unto himself. His life was comfortable. He needed no one. There were no ties to the mainland, no bridges, no sandbars. Nothing. Elaine had been the first to tug him closer to the shore. And now Lily… Just when he wanted to cast thoughts of her from his mind, he glanced up to discover her standing in front of him. She was breathtakingly beautiful in a simple, white dress. He felt the air constrict in his lungs. Without realizing what he was doing, he slowly rose to his feet. Their eyes met for an instant before Lily turned away. Jake could hardly breathe, let alone speak. He'd never seen anyone more lovely.

"What's this one called?" He swallowed and held his breath, trying to slow his racing heart. The task was impossible. Lily was a vision; she was everything that Jake had ever wanted in a woman. His fingers ached with the need to trace her cheekbones and touch the fullness of her lips.

"It's called Angel's Breath," she said.

"We'll take it," Jake informed the salesclerk, without glancing her way. Tearing his eyes away from Lily was unthinkable. He wanted to hold the memory of her in his mind and carry it with him for the remainder of his days.

"But you don't even know how much it is," Lily objected.

"The price doesn't matter." Her nose was perfect, Jake decided, with a soft sprinkling of freckles across the narrow bridge. He adored every single one.

Jake paid the salesclerk while Lily changed back into her clothes. The woman smiled warmly at him as he signed the credit card receipt for three hundred and sixty-five dollars. On Lily it would have been a bargain at twice the price.

"That dress is gorgeous on your wife," the salesclerk told him with a sincerity Jake couldn't doubt. It wasn't until they were at the car that Jake realized he hadn't corrected her. Not only was she not his wife, but he was doing everything he could to marry her off to a wealthy man so she could have everything she desired. When the time came, he'd let her go without regret. When the time came…but not today.

"Thank you, Jake," Lily told him once they were outside the store.

He looked down at her, captivated by the warmth of her smile. "Any time." He reached for her hand, linking their fingers. "Are you hungry?"

"Starved. But it's my turn to treat you. What would you like?"

"Food."

"That's what I love most about you," Lily teased. "You're so articulate." The word *love* echoed in the corners of her mind, sending a shaft of sensation racing through her to land in the pit of her stomach. They took the cable car down to Fisherman's Wharf and stood in line with hordes of tourists. Lily's favorite part of San Francisco was the waterfront. The air smelled of saltwater and deep-fried fish. The breeze off the bay was cool and refreshing. They ate their lunch on the sandy beach behind the Maritime Museum. Lily took off her sandals and stepped to the water's edge, teasing the tide and then retreating to Jake's side when the chilly water touched her toes. For his part, Jake leaned back against the sand and closed his eyes. Lily's musical laugh lulled him into a light slumber. He was content with his world, content to have Lily nearby. He thought about the characters in the short story he'd recently submitted to the *New Yorker.* Lily had claimed it was his best story yet and had encouraged him to dream big. Personally, Jake thought it was a waste of time but to appease her, he'd sent it to the prestigious publisher.

"Jake?"

"Hmm?"

Lily sat at his side, drawing up her legs so that her arms crossed her knees. "It's almost four."

"Already?" He sat up. The day had slipped past too quickly. "You're not working tonight, are you?"

Lily hesitated. "No." Jake knew her schedule as well as she did.

"Good." He settled back on the sand, folding his arms behind his head. "I'm too relaxed to move."

"Me too," Lily said with a sigh and joined him, lying back in the sand. They were in such close proximity and Jake squeezed his eyes shut at the surge of emotion that burned through him at the merest brush of her leg against his. Slow, silent seconds ticked past, but Lily didn't move and Jake hadn't the will. The summer air felt heavy with unspoken thoughts and labored heartbeats. It demanded everything within Jake not to reach for Lily's hand. He felt so close to her. His heart groaned. Lily wasn't Lily to him anymore, but a beautiful, enticing woman. "Jake?"

He rolled his head to the side and their eyes met. Her warm breath tickled his face. "Yes?"

"I've enjoyed today."

"Me, too."

"Can we do it again?"

Jake turned his head and stared into the clear blue sky. For a long minute he didn't say anything. He couldn't do this again and remain sane; having Lily this close and not touching her was the purest form of torture. But he could never be the man she wanted. "I don't know." He would be doing them both a favor if he got out of her life and moved further down the coast. That was the nice thing about owning a sailboat and driving a taxi; he didn't have a string of responsibilities tying him down.

"You're right," Lily concurred. "It's probably not a good idea."

"Why?" Something perverse within him insisted that he ask.

"Well…" Lily hedged. "Just because."

"Right," he agreed. "Just because." Standing up, Jake wiped the granules of sand from his clothes. "I think I should take you home."

"You probably should." But Lily's tone lacked enthusiasm. The day had been charmed, a gift she had never expected to receive. "Gram will wonder about us."

"We might cool her wrath if we bring a peace offering," Jake suggested.

"What do you have in mind?"

"Chinese food."

"But, Jake…"

"Gram loves it."

"I know, but—"

"No buts."

They took the cable car back to where Jake had parked his taxi. Lily tried to talk to him twice on the way through Chinatown. Jake knew his way around, popping in and out of shops, greeting friends and exchanging pleasantries along the way, and all the while ignoring Lily.

"I didn't know you spoke Chinese," Lily commented, hurrying after him.

"Only a little." He didn't mention that half of everything he'd said had been an explanation about Lily.

"Not from what I heard."

"I'm a man of many talents," he joked, loading her arms with the brown paper sacks that contained their meal.

Again on the way home, Lily tried to talk to Jake, but he sang at the top of his lungs, infecting her with his good mood. Soon Lily's sweet voice joined his. At a stoplight, their smiling eyes met briefly and the song died on his lips. Without thinking, Jake leaned over and touched his lips to hers. His hand brushed the hair from her temple and lingered in the thick dark strands.

A blaring horn behind him rudely alerted Jake of the fact that the light had changed. Forcing himself to sing again, Jake stepped on the accelerator and sped ahead.

Lily had a more difficult time recovering from the casual kiss. Had that really just happened? It somehow felt so right to have Jake claim her lips as if he'd been doing it for a lifetime. His light touch left her longing for more.

When Jake glanced at her curiously out of the corner of his eye, she forced her voice to join his, but it wasn't the same and both of them knew it.

Jake eased to a stop in front of the house. Gram was standing on the front porch, her hands riding her round hips as she paced the small area. "It's about time you got home, girl. Rick called. He's on his way over."

5

The sensation of dread went all the way through Jake. He'd known from the minute they entered Chinatown that Lily had been trying to talk to him. But in his stupidity, Jake feared that she was going to mention things he didn't want to discuss—mainly that something rare and special was happening between them. Such talk was best delayed and, if possible, ignored entirely.

"Rick's coming?" he questioned, turning to Lily and trying to disguise the raging battle that was going on inside him. Rick was better for Lily than he'd ever be. Rick could give her the world. But Jake didn't like it. Not one bit. There was something very wrong about spending the day with Lily and then watching her march off with Rick that evening. His gut instinct told him Rick was wrong for Lily, but he couldn't say anything without making a fool of himself. He'd been doing enough of that lately as it was.

"I tried to tell you earlier," she mumbled, feeling guilty. "I…we… Rick and I, that is, we're going to dinner…"

"No problem," Jake said, feigning a shrug of indifference. "Gram and I will have a good time without you." He walked ahead of Lily and took the older woman by the hand. "I guess you're stuck with me tonight."

"I'd consider it a privilege," Gram said with a smile.

Jake responded with one of his own. He led the way into the house, carrying the sacks of spicy Chinese food to the kitchen. If Lily wore the white dress he bought her, he didn't know what he'd do. She couldn't. Not after all they'd shared that day. Deep down, Jake knew she wouldn't do that to him.

Lily walked to her room with all the enthusiasm of someone going to the dentist for a root canal. She felt terrible. Everything had been so perfect today with Jake. When they'd stopped at the red light and Jake had kissed her, Lily had died a little. The kiss had felt so right—as though they were meant to be together forever. Only they weren't.

Taking her new dress from its box, Lily hung it in her closet. She wouldn't wear it for anyone but Jake. It was the most beautiful article of clothing she'd ever owned and she'd treasure it for the rest of her life.

After checking the contents of her meager closet, Lily chose a midi-length straight black skirt and matching top. She dressed hurriedly, then took a moment to freshen her makeup and run a brush through her tangled hair. She'd just finished when the doorbell chimed. A glance at her watch confirmed that he was right on time.

Gram was introducing herself to Rick when Lily appeared.

"Lily." Rick looked at her appreciatively and stepped toward her. Claiming both hands, he kissed her lightly on the cheek.

Lily had to resist wiping his touch from her face. She hadn't found it offensive, only wrong. It wasn't Jake who was kissing her and it felt unnatural. "Hello, Rick." Automatically, her gaze shifted to Jake, who had just emeged from the kitchen.

Rick's eyes followed hers. "Glad to hear you're okay after that fall, Carson."

"Yeah, thanks." Jake's reply was as abrupt as a shot.

"I'll be home early," Lily told Gram, hoping to avoid a confrontation between the two men.

Rick's hand curved around the back of Lily's neck. "But not too early."

At the front door, she turned to Jake. "Thank you for today."

He pretended not to hear her and strode back into the kitchen. He didn't like her going out with Rick, but he hadn't said a word.

"Jake doesn't mind you dating me, does he?" Rick asked when they reached his car. He drove a Mercedes convertible. Lily had often dreamed of riding in one with the top down and the wind whipping through her thick hair. Now that she was standing in front of one, she couldn't seem to muster the appropriate level of enthusiasm.

"No, he doesn't mind," she told Rick.

"I don't want to horn in on you two if you've got something going. But from what Jake said..."

"There's nothing between us," Lily said, fighting the heavy sadness that permeated her voice. "We're only friends." *And then some*, she added silently. But the *some* hadn't been defined.

"Did I tell you where we were going?" Rick asked next, politely opening the car door for her.

"No."

"The Canlis."

Her returning smile was weak. "Thanks. Sounds fantastic."

They arrived at the popular restaurant a half-hour later. From everything she'd read, Lily knew the Canlis was highly rated and extremely expensive. For the first time she'd have the opportunity to order almond-saffron soup. Funny, now that the time had arrived, she'd have given almost anything to sit at the kitchen table across from Gram and Jake and struggle with the chopsticks Jake insisted they use to eat pork-fried rice.

"You have heard much about this place?" Rick asked.

"Oh, yes. From what I understand, the food's wonderful."

"Only the best for you, Lily. Only the best."

Rick took Lily out for two evenings straight. On Sunday night, following their dinner at the Canlis, he took her to the Cliff House and ordered champagne at three hundred dollars a bottle. After years of scrimping by with Gram for the bare necessities, Lily discovered her sense of priorities was offended by seeing good money wasted on something as frivolous as overpriced champagne.

When she mentioned it to Gram later, her grandmother simply shook her head. "Did it taste better than the cheap stuff?"

"That's the problem," Lily admitted, and sighed dejectedly. "I don't know. I've had champagne that was plenty good at a fraction of the cost."

"Rick must want to impress you."

Lily's gaze fell to her lap. "I think he does." Rick wined and dined her and claimed he found her utterly refreshing. He called her his "sunbeam" and was kind and patient. Lily should have been in ecstasy to have someone like Rick interested in her. She liked him, enjoyed his company and looked forward to seeing him again; but something basic was missing in their relationship—something that Lily couldn't quite put her finger on.

On Monday evening Jake was waiting outside the Wheaton for her as usual. A warm smile lit up Lily's dark eyes as she spotted him from the lobby, standing outside his taxi.

"Hello, Jake," she said, walking toward him, her heart pounding.

"Lily." He uncrossed his long legs and slowly straightened. "How'd it go tonight?"

"Good." About as good as it ever goes, playing the same songs night after night.

"Meet any more rich Texans?" He forced the joke when the last thing he felt was cheerful.

"Not tonight."

"How did everything go with Rick?" Jake had thought of little else over the past two days. It felt good to be responsible for giving Lily what she wanted most. And wretched because it went against his instincts. But Rick was a decent sort. He'd be good to Lily.

"Rick's very nice."

"I knew you'd like him."

"I do." But not nearly as much as I like you, she added silently.

"Where'd he take you?"

"The Canlis."

"Rick always did have excellent taste." Most especially in women, Jake thought to himself. His friend wasn't going to let Lily slip away. She was a priceless gem, rare and exquisite, and it hadn't taken Rick long to covet her. Jake couldn't regret having introduced them; he'd planned it. But he hadn't expected that letting Lily go would be so difficult.

"How'd the writing go today?"

"Pretty good. I've got a story for you to read when you have the time." He reached inside the cab for a manila envelope and handed it to her.

Pleased, Lily hugged it to her breast. "Is there anything special you want me to look for?"

"The usual."

"Have you heard anything back on that one you sent to the *New Yorker*?"

Jake snickered and shook his head. "Lily, I only sent it there to please you. Trust me, the *New Yorker* isn't going to be interested in a story from me."

"Don't be such a defeatist. Who can say? That story was your best. I liked it."

The corner of his mouth edged up in a self-mocking grimace. "You like all my stories."

"You're good, Jake. I just wish..."

"What?" He opened the passenger side for her and walked around the front of the vehicle.

"I think you ought to think about novels," Lily told him, once he was seated beside her.

"Maybe someday," he grumbled.

The evening traffic was lighter than usual as Jake drove the normal route to Gram's in the Sunset district. They didn't talk much after Lily suggested Jake consider writing novels. Ideas buzzed through his mind. Maybe he ought to think about it. Almost always the characters in his stories were strong enough to carry a book-length story. Naturally it would call for more plot development, and that could be a problem, but one he could work at learning. To his surprise, he found the idea appealing.

Lily studied the man sitting on the seat beside her. His gaze was centered on the street, his dark-green eyes narrowed in concentration. Sensing Lily's gaze, Jake turned toward her.

"Are you coming in tonight?"

Mentally Jake weighed the pros and cons. He liked talking over his day with Lily and Gram. They offered him an outlet to the everyday frustrations of life. Yet, coming around every night the way he used to could mean problems. The day they'd gone shopping proved that. But did he really need to worry with Gram around? "If you don't mind?"

Lily laughed, surprised that he'd even suggest such a thing.

"Of course I don't mind. You're always welcome. You know that."

He smiled then until the emerald light sparkled in his eyes and Lily discovered she couldn't look away. "Yes, I suppose I do," he said finally.

By the time Jake returned it was after eleven. Lily sat in the living room with Gram. She'd read over Jake's short story and made several markings on the manuscript. Every time she read something of Jake's she was stirred by the powerful emotion in his stories. This one was particularly heart wrenching. The story involved a grumpy old man who lived alone. He had no women or children in his life, but he had a soft spot in his heart for animals. Late one night, the crotchety old man found a lost dog that had been frightened and had nearly drowned in a bad storm. He brought the dog, a miniature French poodle, into his home and fed it some leftovers. As he worked at drying off the dog, he complained gruffly that Miss Fifi, as he'd named her, deserved to be left out in the storm. The little dog ignored the surly voice and looked up at him adoringly with dark eyes. She was so grateful to have been rescued that she followed the old man around the house. Soon she was sleeping on the end of his bed and working her way into his crusty heart. People who saw the man with the fancy poodle were amused by the sight of them. The old man felt torn. Miss Fifi was a damn nuisance and he definitely didn't like drawing attention to himself. Yet every day, he grew more attached to the dog. At the end of the story he found her a good home and, without a second thought, went about his life as before.

Lily was sitting on the sofa with her feet tucked up under her when Jake knocked once before letting himself inside.

His gaze fell to the manila envelope. "Did you read it?"

"Yes."

Gram was swaying in her rocker, watching the news. She acknowledged Jake and returned her attention to the television set.

"Well?" He shouldn't have let her read it. Lily was frowning. The story wasn't one of his best. He should have ditched it. He sat on the end of the coffee table and leaned forward, resting his elbows on his knees.

"You're getting better and better," she hedged. "The best thing about your writing, Jake, is that you're a natural storyteller."

"But?" He could tell she was leading up to something unpleasant by the way her eyes avoided his. "But…the ending's wrong."

"What do you mean?"

"The little dog loved that lonely old man."

"He wasn't lonely."

"But he was!" Lily protested. "That's the reason the old man came to love the dog so much. He longed for companionship."

"You're thinking like a woman again. The old man liked his life. He was content. He didn't need anyone or anything."

"But he loved that fancy dog."

"And people laughed at him." His gaze centered on her breasts and he cursed himself for being so weak.

"Why should he care what people think? He didn't like them anyway. You've set him up to be so antisocial. The only friend he's got is that dog."

Smiling sadly, Jake shook his head. "That crusty old man knows that dog isn't right for him. He's doing the only thing he can by giving her to someone who will appreciate and love her."

"*He* appreciates and loves her," Lily countered hotly.

"But he isn't right for her. He loves her, but he knows he has to let her go. You missed the point of the story."

"I didn't miss it," Lily told him shortly. "It's right here, hitting me between the eyes. That old man, who you want the reader to see as strong and fiercely proud, is actually shallow and foolish."

"Shallow and foolish?" Jake spat the words back at her. "He's noble and unselfish." It astonished him that Lily, who was generally so intuitive, could be so off base in her assessment.

"Let's agree to disagree," he proposed.

"It won't sell, Jake."

"So? I've got tons of stories that'll never see a printed page."

"But this one could, if you'd change the plot around."

"I'm not changing a thing."

"That's your choice." She folded her arms over her chest and stared past him to the picture on the wall. Any other time Jake would have taken her feedback to heart. Usually he appreciated her insight and made the changes she suggested, but she was wrong about this one.

"Yes, it is my choice," he said through gritted teeth.

A heavy silence settled over them.

"Would you like a glass of Marmite?" Lily asked five minutes later, seeking some way to smooth matters over. She was uncomfortable when things weren't right between her and Jake.

"Sure." Jake followed her into the kitchen. "You disappoint me, Lily."

"I do?" She hesitated before returning the teakettle to the stove. "How?"

"With the story. You're thinking like a woman and forgetting that this is a man's story."

"Women buy the majority of magazines."

"Maybe."

"Maybe nothing—that's a fact. And what's so wrong with thinking like a woman? In case you hadn't noticed, I *am* one."

Oh, he'd noticed all right. Every time she moved in that T-shirt she was wearing, he noticed. From the instant he'd walked in the door, her breasts had enthralled him, pressed against the thin material of her shirt, round and full. Stalking to the other side of the room, Jake swallowed tightly and forced his gaze in the opposite direction.

"The fact is," Lily continued, "I don't much like the hero in your story."

"I thought we were through discussing the story."

"You were the one who brought it up."

"My mistake." Jake ground his teeth in an effort to hold her eye and not allow his gaze to drop.

"What are you two shouting about?" Gram asked, joining them.

"Jake's story."

"Nothing," Jake countered, and at her fiery gaze, he added, "I thought we agreed not to discuss it."

"Fine." Lily's arms hugged her waist.

"You two sound like snapping turtles."

"We aren't going to argue anymore, Gram," Lily promised.

"The way you two have been carrying on lately, one would think you were married. Me and Paddy sounded just like the two of you. We'd fight, but then we'd make up, too. Those were the best times," she chuckled. "Oh, yes, making up was the best part."

"We aren't fighting," Lily insisted.

"And there isn't a snowball's chance in hell that we'd ever marry," Jake barked angrily.

Involuntarily, Lily winced. She was surprised by how much his words hurt her. "You aren't exactly my idea of good husband material, either."

"Of course I'm not," Jake growled. "You're like every

other woman—you want someone who can run a four-minute mile after a fast buck."

"And what's wrong with that? A girl can dream, can't she? At least I'm honest about it." Lily battled to hold on to her temper, pausing to take several deep breaths. "Maybe it would be best if I didn't read your stories anymore, Jake."

"You're right about that," he declared, marching into the living room. He jerked the manila envelope off the coffee table with such force he nearly knocked the table over. "Damn right," he said again on his way out the front door.

The screen door slammed and Lily cringed, closing her eyes.

"More and more, the two of you sound like Paddy and me," Gram announced a second time.

Lily's answering smile was nearly nonexistent. She and Jake weren't anything like Gram and Paddy. Her grandparents shared a mutual trust and a love so true that it had spanned even death.

Unshed tears brightened Lily's eyes as she turned off the lights one by one and went to bed.

The next evening Jake wasn't outside the Wheaton when Lily was finished for the night. Standing in the lobby she looked out at the long circular driveway and she'd hoped they would have a chance to talk. But Jake was angry, probably angrier than he'd ever been with her. Lily couldn't stand it. Their friendship was too important to let something as petty as a short story stand between them.

Feeling dejected, Lily secured her purse strap over her shoulder and walked into the cool evening air. She was at the end of the long driveway when she recognized Jake's cab barreling down the street. He eased to a stop along the curb beside her.

Her heart leaped at the sight of him. Jake leaned across the front seat and opened the door. "Are you talking to me?"

"Of course."

"Climb in and I'll give you a ride home."

Lily didn't hesitate. "Jake…"

"No, let me go first. I apologize. You were right about the story. I don't know what was wrong with me."

"No," she said in a hurried breath. "I was the one who was wrong. I've felt wretched all day. We shouldn't fight."

"No, we shouldn't." He grinned at her then—that crooked, sexy grin of his that melted her insides—and reached for her hand. "Let's put it behind us," Jake suggested.

Lily smiled and felt the tension of the last twenty hours drain from her. "What did you do with the story?"

"I trashed it."

"But Jake, it was a good story. With a few changes, I know it would sell."

"Maybe. But I wasn't willing to change the ending. The best place for it was the recycling bin."

"I wish you hadn't."

"Friends?" he questioned.

"Friends." Jake may have given up on the story, but they'd learned something about each other in the process. Their friendship was important. Whatever else happened, they couldn't discard what they shared.

Her regret over the discarded story persisted as Jake drove her home, but she bid him goodnight and raced up the walk toward the house.

"Rick called," Gram told Lily when she walked in the front door.

"Okay." Lily stood at the window, watching Jake drive away. "Jake and I are friends again."

"Were you enemies before?"

"No, but we had a fight and now that's over."

"And you fretted about it most of the day."

"I was worried," Lily corrected, releasing the drape so that it fell against the window. "I don't like there to be tension between Jake and me."

"I know what you mean. I felt the same way when Paddy and I fought."

Lily remained at the window long after Jake had driven out of sight. Rick was waiting for her to phone back and Gram was walking around comparing Lily and Jake to her and Paddy. They weren't anything alike. Jake and Lily were friends…and then some, her mind echoed…and then some.

"Gram, how do I look?" Lily had swirled her hair high atop her head and put on a striking red dress.

"As pretty as a picture," Gram confirmed without looking up from the crossword puzzle she was working on.

"Gram, you didn't even look."

"But you're always pretty. You don't need me to tell you that." She yawned loudly, covering her red lips with a veined hand. "You seeing Rick or Jake tonight?"

"Rick." She hoped the lack of enthusiasm wasn't evident in her voice.

"You don't sound pleased about it."

It did show. "We're going to the opera."

"You'll love that."

Rick had managed to obtain tickets to Mozart's *Così Fan Tutte*, which was being performed by the Metropolitan Opera Company from New York. From what little Lily knew, the performance had been sold out for months. She didn't know how Rick had managed it. He'd mentioned it once in passing, much to her delight, and the next thing she knew, he had tickets.

"It's something I've always wanted to do," Lily agreed. She was fascinated by the costumes and extravagance. Rick would be the type of husband who'd take pleasure in taking his wife out and buying her huge diamonds and an expensive wardrobe. Lily forced a smile. Those things had been important to her for so long, she hated the thought of doing without them. But Rick deserved someone who would love him for who he is and not what he could provide.

The sound of footsteps pounding up the cement walkway snapped Lily out of her daydream.

"Lily!" Jake burst in the front door and grabbed her by the waist. His handsome face was flushed and his emerald eyes sparked with excitement.

"I just heard back from the *New Yorker*. They want my story!"

"Oh, Jake!" She threw her arms around his neck and gleefully tossed back her head, squealing with delight.

Jake lifted her from the carpet and whirled her around until they were both dizzy.

"Plus they're actually paying me," he added. He set her back on the carpet but kept his arms around her. Nor did her hands leave his shoulders as she smiled up at him, her eyes filled with warmth and happiness.

"I knew it would sell," she told him. "I knew it."

Jake felt he had to either let go of Lily or pull her to him and kiss her senseless. Reluctantly, he chose the former and turned to Gram who was sitting in her old rocker, swaying.

"Nzuri sana," Gram cried, resorting to the happy Swahili word to express her congratulations.

Jake bent down and kissed the older woman soundly on the cheek. "We're celebrating. All three of us. A night on the town, dinner, dancing. No more beer and television for us."

Lily's heart sank all the way to her knees. "When?"

"Right now." Jake paused, seeming to notice her dress for the first time, and sobered. "You're going somewhere." There was no question in his voice. He knew. The joy bubbling inside him quickly went flat.

"To the opera with…"

"…Rick," he finished for her. He rammed both hands into his pants pockets and gestured outwardly with his elbows. "Listen, that's not a problem. We'll do it another time."

"I don't want to do it another time."

"It works out this way sometimes," Jake announced. "Don't worry about it." He headed out the door.

"Gram?" Lily turned frustrated, unhappy eyes to her grandmother and cried. "What should I do?"

"That's up to you, girl," Gram answered obliquely.

"Jake—" Lily rushed out the door after Jake. "Wait up." The screen slammed and Lily hurried down the stairs of the porch.

Jake paused in front of his cab, keys in hand. "What?"

"Don't go," she pleaded.

"From the look of you, Rick will be here any minute."

"Yes, but I want to go with you."

"For as long as I've known you, you've talked of wanting to attend an opera. You're going. We'll celebrate another time."

"But I want to be with you."

"No."

Lily battled with herself. She couldn't wait. Jake deserved this celebration. This sale was a victory, a triumph. Ever so briefly, Jake had held her with an exhilaration that would fade in time. She wanted to be with him tonight more than anything—more than seeing an opera or sharing almond-saffron soup with Rick.

"Please, please come back in three hours," she pleaded, holding his hand. "I'll be waiting for you." Because she couldn't stop herself, Lily stood on her tiptoes and planted a warm, heartfelt kiss on the side of his mouth.

6

"Are you sure you're going to be all right?" Rick asked with such tender concern Lily thought she might cry.

In response, she pressed her palms against her stomach and leaned her head against the headrest in the luxury car. "I'm sure it's nothing serious."

"I should have known you weren't feeling well." Rick's gentle voice was tinged with self-derisive anger. "You haven't been yourself all evening."

Because Lily had felt guilty all evening!

"You've been so quiet."

It wasn't like her to deceive anyone!

"I only wish you'd said something earlier."

She couldn't. When she had asked Rick to take her home because she wasn't well, Lily had felt as if there were a neon light identifying her as a scheming liar flashing across her forehead.

When Rick parked the Mercedes in front of Gram's, Lily

automatically looked around for Jake's cab. She saw no sign of it and didn't know whether to be grateful or concerned.

Rick climbed out of the car and crossed over to her side, opening her door. He gave her his hand and studied her with worried eyes. "You're so pale. Are you sure you don't want me to stay with you?"

"No," she cried quickly, perhaps too quickly. "But thank you, Rick, for being so good to me." Her lashes fluttered against her cheek as she dismally cast her gaze to the sidewalk.

"I hope to be good to you for a very long time," Rick announced softly, slipping an arm around her waist and guiding her toward the house. "I never imagined I'd find someone like you, Lily."

The stomach ailment Lily had invented became increasingly more real. Her insides knotted. They paused on the porch and Rick tucked a finger under her chin, raising her eyes to his. Ever so gently, he brushed his mouth over her cheek. "Can I see you next week?"

Lily would have agreed to anything if it would help lessen her intense feeling of guilt. "If you'd like."

"Oh, I'd like, my sunbeam, I'd like it very much." With that he tenderly lifted the hair from her forehead and kissed her again.

Lily had the physical response of a rag doll. She didn't lift her hands to his shoulders or encourage him, but Rick didn't appear to care or notice.

"I'll call you in the morning," he promised. Within a minute, he was gone.

Like a soldier returning to camp after a long day in the field, Lily marched into the house. Gram was asleep and snoring in her rocking chair. The crossword puzzle had slipped unnoticed to the floor. Gently, Lily shook her grandmother.

"Come on, Gram, let me help you into bed."

Gram jerked awake with a start. "Oh, it's you."

"Who were you expecting?"

"Jake. You did say he was coming back, didn't you?"

"Yes…but he isn't here."

"He will be," Gram stated confidently, sitting upright. She rubbed a hand over her eyes and looked around her as though half expecting Jake to be there without either of them noticing. "Trust me, girl, he'll be here."

Lily wasn't as certain. He hadn't actually agreed to come back, but he hadn't told her he wouldn't either. Lily had been the one to convince Jake to submit it to the *New Yorker.* They should be celebrating together.

Lily changed out of her evening gown and into the white dress that Jake had bought her. A night as significant as this one demanded a dress that was just as special.

Pausing at her bedroom window, Lily parted the drapes and stared into the starlit sky. The street was empty and her heart throbbed with anticipation. If Jake didn't come, she didn't know what she'd do. Perhaps go to his boat. Tonight he wouldn't escape her.

A half-hour later, Lily sat in the still living room, staring silently at the elephant tusks that adorned the wall. The moving shadows cast by the trees outside, dancing in the moonlight, seemed to taunt her for being so foolish.

Gram's last words before heading to bed were that Jake would come. The sound of Jake's cab registered in her mind and she bolted to her feet, sucked in a calming breath and rushed to the door. He was really there. She was standing on the porch by the time he'd parked. He didn't look eager to see her and stopped the instant he realized she was wearing the dress. When he started toward her again, he trod heavily—like someone being led to a labor camp.

"Gram said you'd come." She rubbed her hands together to dispel her nervous energy.

Jake spread his fingers wide in a gesture that told her he hadn't wanted to return. But something stronger than his will had led him back to her.

"What did you tell Rick?" Jake stood on the sidewalk as if he wasn't quite sure he wanted inside.

"That I wasn't feeling well."

"And he bought that?"

"By the time we left the opera, it was true."

"And how are you feeling now?"

"Terrible." She hung her head so that her hair fell forward. "I shouldn't be here."

Why did Lily have to look so beautiful standing there in the moonlight? She was miserable and confused and it took everything in him not to reach for her and haul her into his arms and comfort her. Rick had probably wanted to do that. Involuntarily, Jake's fist clenched. The thought of Rick holding Lily produced such a rage within him that he felt like smashing his hand through a wall. "I'm glad you came back," Lily said softly.

Her intense gaze commanded his attention, and Jake knew he could refuse her nothing.

"I'm glad I did too," he admitted with reluctance, walking toward her.

"It's a little late for going out to eat. I thought...that is, if you don't mind...that we could order a pizza."

"With anchovies?"

Her eyes lit up with a smile. "Only on your half."

"Agreed." He took the stairs two at a time and paused at the darkened living room. "Where's Gram?"

"She fell asleep. I'll wake her."

"No." A hand on Lily's forearm stopped her. No, tonight was for them. "Let her rest."

"All right."

She smiled at him and Jake felt his stomach twist. If he had any sense left, he'd get out of there right away. But the ability to reason had left him the first time he'd kissed Lily that night in the attic. From that minute on he'd behaved like a fool. He'd like to blame Lily for what he was feeling, but he couldn't. With her, everything had been of his own making.

"I brought some wine." Actually he'd left it in the front seat of the cab. He hadn't been sure he'd be staying. "I'll be right back."

Lily had the wineglasses out by the time he returned. She turned to him when he walked into the kitchen and Jake found he couldn't look away from her no matter how hard he tried. "Do you want a corkscrew?"

Lily's words shook him from his trance. "Yeah, sure." He paused to clear his throat. "You look nice in that dress." That had to be the understatement of the year. She was the personification of the very name of the gown: Angel's Breath—so soft and delicate. It was the purest form of torture to be near her and not touch her.

Lily handed him the corkscrew and while he fiddled to open the wine bottle, she casually browsed a pizza flyer she grabbed from the side of the fridge. "Should we pick the pizza up ourselves or have it delivered?"

"That's up to you."

"Have it delivered." Lily didn't want to go out again or do anything that would disrupt the evening. "What toppings do you want?"

"Anchovies, pepperoni, olives, green pepper—" he paused "—and sausage. What about you?"

"Cheese," she told him, and laughed at the doubtful look

on his face. "I'm just teasing. I'll have the same except for those disgusting little fish."

The cork came out of the wine bottle with a popping sound and Jake filled both glasses. "Here."

Lily accepted the wine and took a small sip. It was excellent. "This is good."

"I wanted something special."

She touched the edge of her wineglass to his. "To Jake: a master of words, a skilled storyteller, a man of obvious talent and virtue."

"And to Lily, who lent me her support."

"Moral and immoral," she added with a small laugh.

"Mostly moral."

Together they tasted the wine and then moved into the living room to sit on the zebra skin beside the wide ottoman. Lily had a fleeting thought to suggest they light a fire in the fireplace, but the evening was warm. "Thank you, Lily, for all your encouragement."

"Thank you, Jake, for being such a talented storyteller."

"To friendship." His eyes didn't leave hers.

"To friendship," she repeated in a hushed whisper.

They each drank their first glass and Jake replenished their supply.

"Jake."

"Hmm?"

"What really happened between you and Elaine?"

The question was so unexpected that his mouth parted, searching for words. "What do you want to know for?"

She lifted one shoulder and lowered her gaze to the red liquid. "You were so close to her."

"Yeah. So?"

"And then everything blew up."

"She wanted me to be something I couldn't."

"But that's part of what's great about you, Jake. You're so versatile. You can do anything."

"But only if I want to." Jake had no qualms about his talents. He'd tried enough things in life to know what Lily said was true. He wasn't being egotistical in admitting as much, only honest.

With a lazy finger, Lily drew imaginary circles over the top of her wineglass. "Were you lovers?"

"What?" Jake sat up so quickly that the wine nearly sloshed over the sides of his glass. "What kind of question is that?"

"I just want to know." Morbid curiosity had driven her to ask.

"That's none of your business." He downed the remainder of his glass in one giant swallow. "Do you mind if we don't talk about Elaine?"

"All right." Already Lily regretted having brought up the other woman. It was a sore subject. But Lily couldn't regret that Jake had broken things off with Elaine. She wasn't nearly good enough for him.

"What about you and Rick?"

She straightened. "What about us?"

"Has he kissed you?"

Lily clamped her upper teeth over her bottom lip and hunched her shoulders. "Sort of."

"How does a man 'sort of' kiss you?"

Lily rose to her knees, planted her hands on his shoulders and slanted her mouth over Jake's. "Like this," she whispered, gently grazing his mouth with hers. Their mouths barely touched in a soft caress.

Jake nearly choked on his own breath as a shaft of desire shot through him. He broke contact and leaned back, lowering his gaze. Lily was achingly close; she smelled like summer and sunshine and everything good. He had to look away, fearing he'd feel compelled to toss aside the wineglass and pull her into his arms. "Yes, well, I see what you mean."

"You knew Rick was married before, didn't you?"

"I seem to remember something about that."

"He's been divorced less than a year."

"What happened?" Jake didn't care two cents about the breakup of Rick's marriage, but he needed the distraction. Anything to take his mind off how badly he wanted Lily.

"I'm not exactly sure, but apparently she left him for another man."

"That must've hurt." The remark was inane, but every second was torture having Lily so close.

"He's insecure and lonely."

"So are a lot of people."

Lily rotated the stem of the wineglass between her thumb and fingers. "I know."

"You like Rick, don't you?" Jake pressed. His gut feeling that Rick wasn't right for Lily persisted, but he wouldn't say anything. Not after what happened with that oil-rich Texan. Jake was beginning to doubt that anyone would ever be good enough for Lily.

"He's a nice man."

"Rich."

Softly, Lily cleared her throat. "Yes, he seems to be."

"That's what you wanted."

Lately, Lily wasn't so sure. She set the wineglass aside, got up, and moved to the window to stare into the night. The city lights obliterated the brilliance of the stars, but Lily was only pretending to look into the sky.

Jake joined her, coming to stand behind her. He raised his hands to cup the gentle curve of her shoulders and rested his cheek against the side of her head. "It's a beautiful night, isn't it?" He shouldn't be touching her like this, even in the most innocent way. Her nearness was a stimulant he didn't need. She smelled much too good for his sanity. Rick could give her all the things he'd never be able to afford. A knot of misery tightened in his chest.

"Yes, it's lovely," she mumbled. Without meaning to, she leaned back against Jake. He accepted her weight and slid his hands down the length of her arms. Desperately he wanted to hold her—to touch her without giving in to the temptation to kiss her. Lily was meant to be cherished and treasured, and he couldn't do her justice. Lily didn't move, barely breathed. The light touch of Jake's hands stirred her blood. She yearned to turn and have his arms surround her. The taste of his mouth lingered on hers unbearably.Without thinking, Jake turned his face into her hair and breathed in the fragrance of her shampoo. He lowered his face and nuzzled her ear. Lily tilted her head, luxuriating in the warm sensation that flooded through her.

"Lily," Jake breathed desperately. "I shouldn't be holding you like this."

"I like it."

"I do too. Too much."

"But I want you to hold me."

"Lily, please."

"Don't hold me then," she murmured. "Let me hold you." Without warning, she turned and slipped her arms around his waist and pressed her ear against his heart.

"Lily."

"It feels good in your arms," she purred, tightening her grip so that he couldn't break the contact. "How can it be wrong when it feels this good?"

"I don't know. Oh, Lily..." He whispered her name as he lowered his head, searching out her mouth. He touched his lips against hers, savoring her. She tasted like melting sugar, unbearably sweet and highly addictive.

Restlessly she moved against him, caught up in the moment as her passion for him took over.

"Lily," he pleaded against her mouth. "Hold still. We shouldn't let things get out of hand."

"I can't help it." She combed her fingers through his hair and looked up at him with wide, adoring eyes. "This feels so right."

"Lily..."

"Shh," she whispered and planted her mouth over his. She wound her arms around his neck and caressed his mouth with hers. "Your kiss is irresistible."

"So is yours." He paused to study the desire in her eyes. They were playing a dangerous game, which they both stood to lose. Yet he was unable to resist and he lowered his mouth to capture hers again.

Lily moaned softly, her lips moving against his. A low groan slipped from Jake's throat and he forced deeper contact, gripping the sides of her face and fusing their mouths together.

He came away from her weak, his resolve diminishing by the second. He hugged her hard, struggling deep within himself to find the willpower to release her. With a superhuman effort, he broke contact, stepping back and holding her at arm's length. "The wine went to our heads."

Her small smile contradicted his words. "We didn't have that much."

"Obviously more than we should have."

"I like what you do to me."

"Well, I don't like it," he hissed. "Tonight was a fluke and best forgotten."

"I'm not going to forget it."

"Well, I am. This isn't going to happen again. Do you understand? It's not right."

"But Jake..."

"I'm leaving. Right now,. If you have half the intelligence I credit you with, you'll forget this ever happened." He dropped his arms, and rubbed a hand over his face. "Goodnight, Lily."

She could hardly see him. Salty tears clouded her vision. "Goodnight, Jake." He was gone before she could utter another word.

"Morning." Gram greeted Lily cheerfully the following day. "I see Jake came. I told you he would."

Lily pulled out a kitchen chair and sat. After a restless, unhappy night she wasn't feeling very motivated.

"Yes, he was here."

"You coming down with a cold, girl? Your eyes are all red like you were awake half the night."

Lily blinked and offered her grandmother a feeble smile. "I think I might be."

Gram pushed a handful of vitamins and herbal supplements in Lily's direction. "You better start taking these."

"All right."

Gram gave her an odd look as Lily downed each capsule without argument. "I see you two celebrated with some wine."

Her explanation was mumbled. "Jake brought it."

"Where'd he take you for dinner?"

They had never gotten around to ordering the pizza. "We...we just had the wine."

"Ah," Gram muttered knowingly. "So you sat around and talked."

Lily pulled out the chair and stood in front of the old porcelain sink, her back to her grandmother. "Yes, we talked."

Her fingers tightened around her mug. They'd talked, and a lot more. It was the "lot more" that would be difficult to explain.

"What did Jake have to say?"

"This and that." Nervously, Lily set the mug on the long counter. "I think I'll go get dressed."

"You do that," Gram said with a knowing chuckle. "Me and Paddy used to talk about 'this and that' ourselves. Some of our best conversations were spent discussing those very things."

On Monday evening Jake wasn't parked in his usual spot outside the Wheaton when Lily finished her shift. She lingered around the lobby for an additional fifteen minutes, hoping he'd arrive and they'd have a chance to talk. He didn't. And he wasn't there the next evening, either. Lily didn't require a typed message to know that Jake was avoiding her. Maybe he felt they needed a break from each other to give ample thought to what had happened. But Lily would have felt better if Jake hadn't been playing a silly game of hide-and-seek with her.

Early Wednesday evening, Rick appeared in the lobby of the Wheaton and sat listening to Lily play. He clapped politely at the end of a series of numbers. No one applauded her playing; she was there for mood and atmosphere, not as entertainment.

When she had finished, Lily slid off the polished piano bench and Rick rose to join her.

"You're very gifted," he said, kissing her on the cheek.

"Thank you."

"Would you like a cocktail?"

Lily hesitated. She wanted to check if Jake was out front. If he was, Lily had everything she wanted to tell him worked out in her mind. She had no intention of mentioning what had happened over the wine. She'd decided that she'd play Jake's game and pretend the alcohol had dictated their uncharacteristic behavior. She planned to be witty and clever and show him that she hadn't been nearly as affected by his kiss as he seemed to believe. Playing this role was a matter of pride now. "Let me tell Jake first," Lily told Rick.

"Sure." A guiding hand at her elbow led her through the hotel and into the foyer. "Why do you need to talk to Jake?"

"He usually gives me a ride home."

"Every night?" Rick uttered a faint sound of disapproval. "I wasn't aware that you saw Jake that often."

"That's how we got to be such good friends." Lily stood between the two sets of thick glass doors, scanning the long circular driveway. Jake wasn't there. Her heart sank.

"Apparently he can't tonight."

"Apparently not."

"I'll take you home. For that matter, there isn't any reason why I can't see you home every night. I hate the thought of you having to rely on Jake's schedule for a ride home."

"I'm not relying on Jake's schedule. He's here when he can be, and not here when it's inconvenient or he's got a fare. The agreement works well for us both." Perhaps she did depend more on Jake than she should. But Jake would be as offended as she to have Rick suggest as much. "And as for you seeing me home every night, that's ridiculous."

"But I want to take care of you," Rick protested, his arm closing around her waist. "Let's go have that drink and we'll talk it over."

"There's nothing to discuss." Now Rick was irritating her. She didn't want to have a drink with him; she wanted to talk to Jake. Only Jake wasn't around and hadn't been for three days. Lily missed him. She hadn't realized how much she shared with Jake—nonsensical things about her day that only he would understand.

By Saturday afternoon, Lily was irritable and snapping at Gram. Rick had declared that he was coming to listen to her again and Jake continued to avoid her. Lily couldn't recall a time in all her years when she felt more frustrated.

"I haven't seen Jake around lately," Gram complained as Lily pulled weeds from the front flower beds. Alongside her, Gram groomed her African violets, smiling under a huge straw hat with a brightly colored bandanna wrapped around the brim.

"He's been busy." With unnecessary force, Lily jerked a weed free of the soft soil. "I haven't seen him for an entire week."

"Not since you two discussed 'this and that'?" Gram asked with a knowing glance.

"Nope." The cool earth felt good against Lily's hands. For once she didn't care if there was grit and grime under her manicured nails. Everything felt different after what has happened with Jake. "Gram, what would you say about me changing jobs?"

"Changing jobs? But I thought you liked it at the Wheaton. Or is it Jake that's worrying you?"

"Jake hasn't got anything to do with it."

"This decision seems sudden."

"Forget it, then. I'll stay at the Wheaton and play 'Moon River' for the rest of my life. I don't care if I ever see Jake again." The minute the words escaped her lips, Lily realized what she'd said, and snapped her mouth closed.

"Seems to me that you're more worried about seeing Jake than you are about playing that song."

Lily kept her mouth shut. She had already said more than she'd intended.

"Why don't you just pay him a visit?" Gram asked, undaunted.

"Should I?" Lily's first inclination was to hurry to the marina, but she had her pride to consider. Already it had taken a beating, and Lily doubted it could go another round.

"I can't see what harm it'd do."

To Lily's burdened mind it could solve several problems. To hell with her pride! "Maybe I will drop by and see how he is. Perhaps he's been ill or something."

"He could even be waiting for you to come."

Lily sat back on her haunches and brushed a stray curl from her face. A thin layer of mud smeared her cheek. "All right, I'll do it."

By the time Lily had showered and changed clothes, she had grown nervous and fidgety. Maybe going to Jake's wasn't the best idea, but Lily couldn't stand the terrible silence any longer.

On her way to the marina, she made a stop to order the pizza they hadn't gotten around to eating that other night. Carrying the thin cardboard box in both hands, Lily walked down the long, rolling dock to where his sailboat was moored.

"Jake!" Her voice trembled as she called out his name.

Below deck, Jake heard Lily calling for him and quickly closed the story he was writing on his laptop.

7

Jake's heart sped up at the sound of Lily's voice. He got up slowly, unsure of what he should do. He'd avoided her all week and with good cause. After what had happened at their "victory celebration," they needed to stay away from each other.

Besides, he reasoned, Lily didn't need him anymore; she had Rick. Jake had seen Rick's car at the Wheaton nearly every evening. He still couldn't reconcile himself to Lily's dating the guy. But he had no one else to blame. He'd introduced them. He couldn't protest at this point. He was snared in a trap of his own making. The best thing for him to do was make himself scarce.

"Jake, I know you're in there," Lily called again.

Jake's fist clenched at his side and an irritated noise slipped from deep inside his throat. If he didn't react it would be just like that stubborn woman to hop on board the *Lucky Lady* and search him out. Then he'd look like even more of a fool than he did already. Reluctantly, he climbed on deck.

"Hello, Jake," Lily began.

He tucked in his shirttails, giving the impression that he'd been preoccupied. "Lily."

"Did I catch you at a bad time? You weren't asleep, were you? Gram thought you might be sick."

His gaze just managed to avoid hers. "This is a bit of a bad moment. I'm busy."

"Oh." She dropped her gaze. "I brought a pizza. We…the other night we forgot about it."

"We didn't exactly forget it," he corrected her. "We just didn't get around to ordering it." His eyes delved into hers. Already it was happening. He couldn't help noticing how beautiful she was standing there with those huge brown eyes, looking betrayed and hurt.

"Anyway, I thought I could bring a pizza now."

Jake shifted his gaze to the flat box in her arms.

"But if you're busy, I'll understand." She didn't, not really. He must realize that coming here had cost her a lot of pride. The least he could do was make it easier on her.

Something in her voice reminded Jake that this wasn't any less difficult for Lily. It ws wrong of him to protect his ego at her expense. "It was thoughtful of you to come."

The tension eased from Lily's shoulders as Jake stretched out his hand to help her aboard. The boat rocked gently as she shifted her weight from the narrow dock to the *Lucky Lady*.

"There are anchovies on your half." She smiled up at him and Jake knew instantly that he was in trouble.

Lily drew in a long breath as though she didn't know what to say now that she was aboard the boat.

"It looks like rain, doesn't it?" she suggested, casting a discerning eye toward the thick gray clouds. "Maybe we should take this below."

Jake's chest tightened. Being alone with Lily was bad

enough, but the thought of being next to her in the close confines of the cabin was almost more than he could bear.

"Jake?"

"Yeah, sure." He led the way and Lily handed the pizza down to him before expertly maneuvering the few steps that led below deck.

"Have you been working on another story?" Lily asked as she spied his laptop. Crumpled yellow sticky notes littered the tabletop and filled what limited space there was in the dining area. "It looks like you're having a few problems. Do you want to tell me your plot? That helps, sometimes."

Setting the pizza beside the tiny sink, Jake cleared away his mess. "No," he answered starkly.

Lily was taken aback by his answer. For a minute neither spoke.

"Why not?" Lily asked, trying to sound curious instead of hurt. Jake often talked out his plot ideas with her and listened to her reactions. Invariably, he argued his point and then, more often than not, accepted her suggestions.

"Every writer comes to the time when he has to break away…"

Lily sighed and shook her head regretfully. "Why are you so angry with me?"

"I'm not." The words came quickly.

"I thought we were friends, and all of a sudden you're treating me like I'm your worst enemy."

"I'm not mad."

"I haven't seen you in a week. Friends don't avoid each other like that'."

"I've been busy." Even to his own ears, the excuse sounded lame.

"Friends are honest with each other," Lily continued.

"I haven't lied."

"Friends tell each other what's on their minds."

"Nothing's bothering me. Why can't you accept that?"

Lily made a tsking noise that sounded remarkably like Gram when she was displeased about something.

"All right," Jake countered. "You want to talk about being friends? Fine. Then maybe you should think about what's been going on between us. You may be innocent, Lily Morrissey," Jake retorted, "but you're not naive enough to believe that friends kiss the way we do." Hoping to give the appearance of nonchalance, Jake leaned against the counter and crossed his arms. "I don't like what's happening."

"Nothing's happening," Lily said, struggling to keep her voice from rising. "We aren't any different than we were six months ago."

"Oh, I beg to differ!"

"All right, I concede that our relationship has gone to a deeper level, but we're still good friends. At least that's what I'd like to think."

Jake snorted. "We're in serious trouble."

"You're being overdramatic. I… I like kissing you. You make me feel warm and tingly inside. I just don't think that's wrong."

"Not wrong; bad."

"You're only saying that because you think kissing me will lead to something more."

Jake looked nonplussed. "And it doesn't?"

"Not if we don't want it to."

"Lily." Her name came out in a rush of breath as if he were reasoning with a young child. "Kissing is only the first step. The next thing you know, we'll be in bed together and wondering how we let things go so far."

"You seem to be equating a simple friendly kiss with love and marriage. Good grief, Jake. We're friends and we just happen to like to kiss each other. It doesn't have to lead to anything."

"If we don't stop thinking like this, the next thing I know I'll be shopping for diapers."

Lily laughed. "Honestly, Jake, you make it sound far more dreadful than it is. Here, let me show you." She moved across the narrow confines of the cabin and placed her hands on his shoulders.

Jake stiffened and jerked away as if her touch burned him. "No."

"It's only a kiss, not a hand grenade."

"I don't think we should be kissing."

"But I want to prove something." Her voice was small and she couldn't keep the disappointment out of it. Before Jake had the opportunity to react, she moved her mouth against his in a soft caress.

Jake felt liquid fire seep through him. "See?" Lily announced proudly. "And I'm not humming the 'Wedding March' or anything. From everything Gram's told me, there isn't the slightest possibility of my getting pregnant from a kiss."

The thoughts Jake was having didn't have anything to do with marriage and a family. His gaze fell past her to the small area where he slept. He thought about sleeping with Lily at his side and seeing her hair spread out on his pillow. The vision of her lying there without clothes and reaching her arms out to him nearly ate a hole right through him.

"Right," he grumbled.

"To further prove the point, I think we should do it again."

"I don't know." He closed his eyes, knowing that one pleading glance from Lily and he'd give her anything she wanted. He hated his lack of self-control. It had never been like this with other women. He had always been the one calling the shots. Jake opened his eyes to discover Lily standing so close that all he had to do was lean forward and their bodies would touch. He could feel the heat radiating from her. So little would be required of him to press his thigh to hers, to feel her breasts against his chest. His senses were suddenly awake to her every curve and it was slowly driving him insane.

Unable to keep his hands away, Jake tenderly cupped her cheek. Her thick lashes fluttered closed as she turned her face into his palm. Ever so gently, she kissed the inside of his hand. The inch or so between them was eliminated before another second could pass. They stood thigh to thigh, breasts to chest, and feasted on the feel of each other. With a reverence that shocked him, Jake lowered his head and claimed Lily's mouth. Their lips met in the sweetest, most profound kiss Lily had ever experienced. Passion smoldered just beneath the surface, but this was a different kind of kiss—one that Lily didn't know how to define. Her hand crept up his chest and closed around the folds of his shirt collar as she clung to him.

When Jake lifted his mouth from hers, Lily smiled up at him and tears clouded her eyes. "That was beautiful," she whispered.

"You're beautiful." He tucked a strand of hair around her ear and traced her temple with his fingertips.

She had that dreamy look of a person in love.

Lightly, he kissed her again. "Lily, believe me when I tell you that this has to stop right now."

"Okay," she murmured. She looped her arms around his neck and buried her face in his throat. He smelled of the sea and the sun. Vital and alive. Her tongue discovered his pulse.

"Lily," he groaned, moving his hands to set her away.

"You taste good."

Already, he was wavering. He hadn't wanted her on his boat and here she was a few feet from his bed. They were in each other's arms, and from the way things were progressing, only heaven knew where they'd end up.

"I said, no more." Forcefully Jake moved away from her. Lily's expression fell into a mixture of bewilderment and hurt.

"I told you before, I want to put an end to this nonsense. You women are all alike."

"Jake—"

"It was the same thing with Elaine." It hadn't been, but Lily didn't know that and Jake was desperate to extract himself before things went any further. He had to act fast.

"I'm not anything like Elaine."

"The two of you could be sisters. You think a woman has the right to drive a ring through a man's nose and lead him around."

"That's not true." Lily struggled to swallow back her indignation.

"You women are never satisfied. There's always something that needs to be changed."

"What have I ever asked you to change?"

"My writing. At first you were content to read the short stories, but oh no, those didn't make enough money, so you started pressing me to write novels."

"But I thought…"

"The crazy part of all this is that for a time I even considered it."

Lily took a step back, staring up at Jake. She slowly shook her head, still having trouble believing that this was Jake speaking to her—the man who only minutes ago had kissed her and held her so lovingly in his arms.

"Elaine almost ruined my life and I almost let her. Thank God I saw the light in time."

"Jake..." Recklessly, Lily tried one last time to reason with him.

"You aren't any better than Elaine, worming your way into my life, using me, and then taking it upon yourself to mold me into whatever you want."

"I've never tried to change you."

"Oh that's right. You want to *save* me. Well, listen and listen good. I like my life. I don't want to be saved. Got it?"

"Would you stop shouting long enough for me to say something?" Lily demanded.

"No. Enough's been said."

"It hasn't!" she shouted. "I like you the way you are and I have no intention of saving you."

Jake snorted. "That was what Elaine said."

"I'm not Elaine!" She stabbed a finger in his direction.

"Right," he snickered.

"There's no reasoning with you when you're like this."

"Then it would be best if you left, wouldn't it?"

She didn't say anything for several seconds. "Are you kicking me off your boat?"

"I'm saying—"

"Don't say anything...it's not necessary. I get the picture. I won't bother you again...and I'll never, ever come on board the *Lucky Lady* again. You've made your point perfectly clear." She turned quickly and moved up the steps in a huff.

Jake didn't move. Above him, he heard Lily's footsteps as she hurried across the deck. Her steps were heavy and their echo cut straight into his heart. The frustrations of a lifetime of bitterness suddenly surfaced and he struggled against the urge to ram his fist through the side of the boat. He paced the tiny, enclosed area in an effort to compose himself. It was what he wanted. Lily was gone. He didn't doubt her word; she wouldn't be back. He'd driven her away for good. But Jake couldn't imagine what his life would be like without her. There were better ways of handling this situation. He could apologize, but his pride sneered at the thought. No, he'd bide his time and try to forget how deeply he cared for her. That was the only solution to avoid ruining both their lives.

By the time Lily slid into her seat at the grand piano at the Wheaton that evening, she was outwardly composed. But the inner battle continued to rage. She didn't know which had hurt the most—Jake comparing her to that horrible Elaine, or when he'd told her to get off his boat. Both had devastated her to the point that she hadn't been able to talk to Gram. Lily placed her hands over the ivory keys and her fingers moved automatically, playing from memory. Lily had learned not to involve her mind in the music. If she did, she'd have been half-crazy by now. Her smile was pasted on her mouth, curving her full lips slightly upward.

The manager strolled past her once and Lily dropped her gaze to her hands. Usually his presence meant she had done something that annoyed him. Lily no longer cared. If he fired her, she'd find another job. The monotony of playing the same songs night after night had robbed her musical gift of the natural spark she'd once possessed. She hardly ever sat at the piano to goof around anymore. And all this for what? The only wealthy man she'd met in a year's time at the hotel was Rex Flanders and that had turned out to be a bust. Even now, Jake's negative reaction to the Texan confused her. He hadn't so much as seen Rex and he'd forced Lily into promising that she wouldn't go out with the middle-aged man.

When Lily had finished the first half of the evening's set of music, she took a break. Henry, the senior bellhop, stopped her halfway across the lobby.

"Miss Lily, there's a message for you." He strolled across the carpet to hand her a beige envelope.

Lily accepted the letter and her heart flip-flopped in her chest. For one insane moment, Lily thought it might be from Jake. After a glance at the slanted strokes of the cursive script, she recognized the handwriting as Rex Flanders's.

The first genuine smile of the evening came.

Hello Lily,
I've been thinking about you lately, and about that old song you hunted down for me. As I promised, I'm back in San Francisco and I'm hoping that you'll allow me to show you my appreciation. I meant what I said about taking you to dinner. I insist. It's the least I can do to thank you.

I'll meet you in the lobby at nine-thirty. Don't disappoint me this time.
Rex

Folding the single sheet over, Lily tucked it inside the envelope. She would join Rex for dinner. Her promise to Jake had been made under duress. Besides, she owed him nothing now. He'd made that clear. He had no reason to care if she saw Rex or any other man, for that matter.

Parked outside the Wheaton, Jake leaned against the side of his cab and crossed his arms, watching the entrance. Lily was due out in another hour. He needed to talk to her so he could explain that he hadn't meant what he'd said. The anger had been a ploy to keep her out of his arms, but he hadn't meant to insult her. The apology burned in his chest. The minute she came through those doors he'd go to her and admit he was wrong. That was the very least he could do. She deserved that and a lot more.

Once he'd made his peace with Lily, Jake decided, they had to have a serious discussion about what was going on between them. They had to stop pretending their kisses didn't mean something, that they were simply friends. For his part, Jake was convinced that a serious relationship between them wouldn't work. Their life goals couldn't be more different. He wasn't going to change. And if Lily wanted a wealthy man, then she ought to look elsewhere. She was putting her schemes in jeopardy by flirting with him.

They were reasonable adults. After they'd talked this craziness out of their systems, they could go back to the way things used to be, and continue as friends. They had to acknowledge those feelings for what they were—infatuation. He was flattered that Lily found him attractive. But they could only be one or the other. They could be great friends or good lovers. Of the two, Jake sought her friendship.

Satisfied with his reasoning, Jake checked his watch again. It wouldn't be long. A crooked grin spread across his face. He felt much better now than he had that afternoon.

Lily nervously smoothed a wrinkle from the skirt of her blue dress. She glanced up to find Rex strolling toward her, his eyes alight with appreciation.

"Lily," he whispered, and collected her hands. "You're as lovely as I remember."

Rex looked even bigger and taller than she had recalled. "Thank you."

"Have you been waiting long?"

"No. Only a minute." Actually, she'd changed her mind twice. Not until she neared the huge glass doors at the Wheaton's entrance had she decided to go back and meet Rex.

"Good." His gaze claimed hers. "It doesn't seem a whole month since I first laid eyes on you."

"Time has a way of slipping past, doesn't it?" Once she'd

worried about appearing witty and attractive. Now she didn't care; she could only be herself.

"It sure does." He offered her his elbow in gentlemanly fashion. "I know a quiet little French restaurant where the food is excellent."

"That sounds lovely."

"You do like French food?"

"Oh, yes."

Smiling at her, Rex directed Lily toward the front entrance. Once outside, he stepped forward and raised his hand, calling for a taxi.

Jake was parked in the driveway, chewing on the end of a toothpick, wondering what was taking Lily so long. He had almost made up his mind to go inside and find out. As he straightened, the toothpick slipped from his mouth and fell to the ground. Lily was with that Texan. Jake was incredulous. She'd only mentioned the man a couple of times, but Jake knew instantly that the man she'd told him about was the one escorting her now. She'd promised to stay away from that pot-bellied fool. Promised. He'd been right all along. She wasn't any different from Elaine.

Stupefied, Jake watched as one of his colleagues pulled toward the front. The doorman opened the cab door and Lily climbed in the back with the Texan. Jake was so furious that he slammed his fist against the side of his taxi, momentarily paralyzing his fingers.

Well, fine, Lily could date whomever she liked. She was nothing to him. Nothing.

Inside the cab, Lily tossed a glance over her shoulder, wondering if Jake had been out front. Silently she lambasted herself for even looking. He wouldn't be there, of course, especially after a whole week of avoiding her. After what had happened that afternoon, the Wheaton would be the last place Jake would show.

Feeling agitated, Lily fiddled with her fingers. She regretted having agreed to go with Rex. She'd accepted the date for all the wrong reasons.

Rex must have sensed her uneasiness since he chatted the whole way, his deep voice filling the taxi. When she responded with only a polite word or two, he struck up a conversation with the cabdriver.

Lily wondered if the driver, who was a friend of Jake's, would mention it to him. Fervently she prayed he wouldn't, then doubted that Jake would care either way.

The restaurant, Chez Philippe, was one of the most expensive and highly rated in all of San Francisco. Famous people from all over the world were reputed to have dined there. Lily had often dreamed of sampling the excellent cuisine and catching a glimpse of a celebrity.

After arriving at the restaurant, they were seated by the maître d' and handed huge, odd-shaped menus. Lily noted that the prices weren't listed, so she was left to guess at what this dinner would cost Rex. However, she learned long ago that anyone who needed to ask about the price probably couldn't afford it.

"Do you see anything that looks good to you, little filly?"

Their eyes met over the top of the menu. "What would you suggest?" Rex listed a couple of items and Lily smiled absently. The waiter returned and filled their water glasses with expensive bottled water.

With each passing minute, Jake's anger grew until he could almost taste his fury with every breath. Slamming the door of his cab, he cursed his lack of decisive action when he'd seen Lily with the rich Texan. She'd promised him she wouldn't go out with Daddy Warbucks and with God as his witness, Jake was going to hold her to her word. As hard as it was on his patience, he waited until the cabbie who drove Lily and the Texan returned to the Wheaton.

"Where'd you take them?" Jake demanded in a tone that caused the other driver to cringe.

"Who?"

"You know who. Lily."

"Oh, yeah. That was her, wasn't it?"

"Where did you take them?" Jake demanded a second time.

The driver cleared his throat. "That fancy French place on Thirty-third."

"Chez Philippe's?"

"That's the one."

Jake breathed a quick word of thanks then rushed back to his cab, revving the engine with such force that a billow of black smoke shot from the tailpipe.

Jake's cab roared through the streets toward Chez Philippe's. He ran two red lights and prayed a cop wouldn't pull him over for speeding.

Once he was within a block of the restaurant, Jake pulled to a dead stop. What was he going to do once he arrived? To rush in and demand that Lily leave with him simply wouldn't work. He'd only end up looking like a jealous idiot. He could picture her now, looking up at him with disdain and quietly asking him to leave. He needed a plan. He parked on the street, not wanting the valet to take his cab. The fact was, Jake wasn't sure the valet *would* take it.

Hands buried deep inside his pants pockets, Jake strolled into the classy place as if he'd been dining there for years. The maître d' stepped forward expectantly.

"May I help you, *monsieur*?"

"A table for one," Jake said confidently.

"*Monsieur*, I regret that we only seat gentlemen wearing a suit and tie."

"You mean I have to have a suit and tie even before I can spend my money?"

"That is correct. I sincerely regret the inconvenience."

Jake scowled. "Do you mind if I sit and wait?" He motioned toward an empty chair.

"Sir, we aren't going to change our dress code this evening."

"That's fine, I'd just like to wait."

The stoic expression altered for the first time as the maître d' arched a skeptical brow. "As you wish."

The rush of whispers from the front of the restaurant caused Lily to glance up from her plate. As she did, her breath caught in her lungs. Jake was standing there, and from the look he tossed at her, he was furious.

8

Lily felt the blood drain from her face. Jake was looking at her as though it required every ounce of restraint he'd ever possessed not to march across the room and confront her.

"Doesn't that sound like fun?" Rex was saying.

Lily stared at him blankly. "Yes, it does." She hoped her response was appropriate.

"Good. Good," Rex continued, obviously pleased. "I thought a young filly like you would enjoy an evening on the town."

The first time she'd met Rex, Lily had torn Gram's house apart looking for that crazy song on the chance he'd suggest spending an evening with her. A lavish date with a rich man had been Lily's dream for many years. She was a fool if she was going to allow Jake's foul temper to ruin tonight. She forced her chin up a notch. Jake had made his views of her plain, and she wasn't going to let him wreck her evening.

"Where would you like to start?" She planted her elbows

on the white linen tablecloth and rested her chin atop her folded hands, staring at him expectantly.

"There's a small dance floor at the St. Francis."

"That sounds grand," Lily simpered.

"We could have our after-dinner drink there as well, if you like."

"That would be wonderful."

From the corner of her eye, Lily noted that Jake was pacing the small area in front of the maître d's desk. A smile tugged at the edges of her mouth. She certainly hoped he got an eyeful. The memory of the insults he'd hurled at her earlier was enough to encourage Lily. She wasn't much of a flirt but with Rex sitting across from her and Jake just waiting for the opportunity to pounce on her, Lily gave it all she had.

Jake had claimed she was a schemer; she was only proving him right. Once he saw the way she behaved with Rex, he would get the message and leave.

The waiter approached their table with the bill. While Rex dealt with it, Lily took the opportunity to glance in Jake's direction. The shock of seeing him had faded and was being replaced by indignation. Jake had a lot of nerve.

"Are you ready?" Rex asked.

"Yes." Lily's heart constricted as Rex pulled out her chair and she stood.

Her wealthy escort placed a hand on the small of her back, urging her forward. Lily looked up at him with adoring eyes, ignoring Jake. She held her breath as they approached the front desk, wondering if Jake would cause a scene. Indecision showed in his eyes and she quickly glanced away.

For his part, Jake battled with uncertainty. He'd been a fool to have followed her there. He felt he ought to punch the lights out of that oil-rich Texan and grab Lily while he had the chance. But he couldn't do that. Lily would never forgive him and he already owed her one apology.

The hem of her skirt brushed his leg as she scooted past him and Jake jumped back as though he'd been burned. His eyes demanded that she look at him, but Lily refused. She tucked her hand in the crook of the Texan's elbow and glanced up at him adoringly.

Unsure of what he should do, Jake stood where he was for an entire minute, silently cursing. If he had any sense left, which he was sincerely beginning to doubt, he'd go back to the marina and forget that Lily had broken her promise.

Once outside, Jake's feet felt as though they were weighted with concrete blocks. He gave a companionable salute to the valet as he passed.

Lily and the Texan were in the backseat of another cab, pulling out of the circular driveway and Jake stepped back as they sped away.

As he returned to his taxi he increased his pace. He couldn't ignore the gut feeling that something was wrong with Lily and Rex. The *feeling* had always perplexed him. He hadn't *felt* right about Lily and Rick either, but this time the sensation was far stronger. If anything happened to Lily, he'd never be able to forgive himself. Foolish pride no longer dictated his actions; he was driven by something far stronger: fear.

His hand slapped the side of the taxi and he jumped inside and revved the engine. It only took a minute to locate the other cab driving Lily and Rex. Jake stayed a fair distance behind them, fearing that the other driver would suspect that he was following him.

When they entered the downtown core, Jake relaxed. The other cab was in his territory now and Jake wove in and out of traffic without a problem. The driver dropped Lily and the Texan off at the St. Francis Hotel. Jake couldn't fault the man's taste. He rounded the corner and was lucky enough to locate a parking space.

The doorman opened the tall glass door as Jake approached the hotel entrance. Music from the piano bar filtered into the lobby from the cocktail lounge and he headed toward it. Although his gait was casual, his eyes carefully scanned the darkened area for Lily. When he spotted her sitting at a tiny table in the middle of the room, he heaved a sigh of relief.

As inconspicuously as possible, he took a seat at the far corner of the bar so he could keep an eye on her without being seen.

"Can I help you?" The bartender spoke and Jake swiveled in his seat to face him.

"A beer," he replied. "Any kind. It doesn't matter."

"Right away."

Sitting sideways, Jake propped an elbow against the edge of the bar and centered his attention on Lily. She really was lovely. Jake couldn't blame Rex for being interested. Jake recalled the day he'd taken her out on the *Lucky Lady* and the way she'd sat perched on the bow, laughing. The wind had tossed her hair in every direction, making her resemble a sea nymph, soaking in the early summer sun. Something had happened to him that day—something so significant that he had yet to determine its meaning. From that moment on, Jake concluded, his life had been in a tailspin.

The bartender delivered his beer and Jake absently placed a bill on the counter. Holding the thick glass with one hand, he took a long sip. It felt cool and soothing against his parched throat. He set the glass back on the bar.

Glancing in Lily's direction again, Jake noted that Rex had reached for her hand and held it in his own as he leaned across the small table, talking intimately with her. From this distance Jake couldn't read Lily's reaction.

Without thinking, Jake slid off the bar stool and stood. His fist knotted, but he managed to control his immediate outrage. Another man was touching Lily and although it appeared innocent enough, Jake didn't like it. He didn't like it one bit. Furthermore, he trusted that overweight Texan about as much as he did a rattlesnake.

Several couples were gliding around on a small dance floor on the other side of the lounge and Jake watched as Rex stood and helped Lily to her feet. Jake downed the remainder of his beer when the Texan escorted Lily to join the dancing couples, bringing her into his arms. Holding hands was one thing, but dancing was another. There was nothing more Jake could do, but act. He ate up the distance to the dance floor in three huge strides.

Lily wished she hadn't agreed to come to the bar with Rex. She felt like a fraud. She had no desire to share a drink and conversation and had even less enthusiasm for dancing. Rex's hands felt warm and clammy against her back and she resisted the subtle pressure of his arms to bring her closer.

They'd already circled around the small dance area once when Lily glanced up and noticed Jake coming toward her with abrupt, angry strides. She knew she should be furious, but her heart responded with a wild leap of pleasure. After her behavior in the restaurant, Lily had been disappointed in herself. Rex was a nice man. He didn't deserve to be used. Jake tapped Rex's shoulder. "I'm cutting in." He didn't ask, but simply announced it.

Rex looked stunned. "Lily?"

"That's fine," she murmured, dropping her gaze. "I… I know him. This is Jake Carson."

Jake took Lily by the waist, pressing her to him as he whirled her away.

"Jake—"

"No, you listen to me. What kind of game are you playing?" He pushed the words through clenched teeth. He was being unreasonable but he didn't care. He wanted answers.

"I'm not playing..."

"You assured me that you wouldn't be seeing Daddy Warbucks."

"That was before."

"Before what?"

"Before you *assured me* that I was a nuisance and asked me to leave your precious boat."

"Consequently your promise doesn't mean anything?"

"No," she cried, then changed her mind. "Yes."

"Dinner was bad enough, but did you have to come here as well? What's the matter? Didn't that fancy restaurant give you ample opportunity to flaunt yourself?"

Lily was too outraged to answer. "Let me go."

"No. I'm taking you home."

"Rex will take me home."

"No way. You promised me you wouldn't be seeing that rich bullfrog, and I'm holding you to your word."

"You can't make me do anything." Lily didn't understand why she was fighting Jake when the very sight of him made her heart race. If only he'd stop behaving like an arrogant fool, she'd tell him that she longed for him to take her home.

"I don't have much taste for making a scene, but I won't back away from one if that's what you want."

"You're acting crazy."

"Perhaps."

"There's no question about it. You're bossy, stubborn and unreasonable."

"Great. Now that you've named my personality traits, we can leave."

"Not without saying something to Rex."

Jake relaxed his hold. "I'll do the talking."

"That's hardly necessary."

He didn't answer as he gripped her hand in his and led the way off the dance floor. The other couples cleared a path for them and Lily wondered how much of their heated conversation had been overheard. Embarrassment brought a flush of color to her cheeks.

Rex stood as they approached the small table.

"I'm taking Lily home," Jake informed the older man.

"Lily, is that what you want?" Rex eyed her seriously. His brows formed into a sharp frown as he waited for her to respond.

"Jake's an old friend," she said, trying to explain.

"I see," Rex said slowly.

"I hope you do," Jake added. His hand continued to grip hers as he headed out of the cocktail lounge, half pulling Lily as he went.

In her heels she had difficulty keeping up with his wide strides and paused momentarily to toss an apologetic look over her shoulder, wanting Rex to know she was sorry for everything.

"Are you happy?" she asked, once they hit the sidewalk.

"Very." He thrust his face toward her. "Don't ever pull that trick on me again."

Recalling all lessons on ladylike behavior Gram had drilled into her over the years, Lily battled to keep her temper. She only partially succeeded. "And don't you *ever* do that to me again."

"Keep your promises and I won't," Jake barked.

They didn't say another word until they were inside the cab, headed home.

The anger was slowly dissolving inside Lily. Everything had changed in the past few weeks and she didn't know if it was for the better. A year ago, she'd started playing piano at the Wheaton with so many expectations. In that time she'd dated two wealthy men and met Jake. Rick and Rex weren't anything like she'd dreamed. Jake was Jake: proud, stubborn, and so very good to her and Gram. She'd ached over the loss of something precious and wonderful—her relationship with Jake—and prayed it wasn't too late to salvage it.

"I thought you didn't care anymore what I did," she murmured, longing to explain why she'd accepted Rex's invitation.

"Believe me, it wasn't by choice." His hands tightened on the steering wheel.

"Then why did you..."

"I couldn't care less who you date," he lied smoothly. "But you'd given your word about that Texan and I was determined to see that you kept it."

"That's why you followed me tonight?" Her voice was little more than a whisper.

"Right."

"I see." She clasped her hands together tightly in her lap. She'd hoped that he'd admit that he cared for her and had been concerned about her welfare. But that was clearly too much to expect in his present frame of mind.

Jake dropped her off in front of Gram's and drove away as soon as she closed the car door. Once inside the house she struggled to maintain her composure. Gram was asleep and Lily was grateful for that. She would have had trouble recounting the events of this evening. Nothing had gone right, starting with accepting Rex's invitation to dinner.

Knowing that any effort to sleep would be useless, Lily wandered into the kitchen and set the kettle on the burner to boil. When it whistled, she poured the boiling water into a mug before adding a tea bag. A loud knock at the front door surprised her and her heart rocketed to her throat. She didn't have time to react when Jake burst in.

"We need to talk," he announced, coming toward her.

Lily couldn't have moved if her life depended on it.

"Well?" he demanded.

"Would you like a cup of tea?" Lily noticed that his defenses relaxed at the offer.

"Yes."

She busied herself bringing down another cup from the cupboard and adding a tea bag to the steaming water. The action gave her a moment to compose her thoughts. Her head buzzed with all the things she longed to say. As much as she tried, she couldn't keep her gaze off the man who filled the doorway, staring at her.

She gestured toward a chair, indicating that Jake should take a seat. She found it bewildering that only minutes before they had been shouting at each other and now they were behaving like polite strangers.

She set the second steaming mug on the tabletop across from her own and sat facing Jake. She gripped her mug and stared down into the black liquid.

The silence grew heavy and Lily was unsure if she should be the first one to wade into it.

But then they spoke simultaneously.

"Lily—"

"Jake—"

"You first," Jake said and motioned toward her with his hand.

"No…you go first."

"All right." Another lengthy pause followed. "I'm here to apologize."

"For what?"

"Come on, Lily, don't play dumb," He accused.

"I'm not." Her own temper flared. "Are you apologizing for this afternoon or for what happened this evening?"

Jake raked his fingers through his hair. The kitchen suddenly felt small and Jake seemed so large, filling every corner. Despite everything she longed to feel his arms around her again, comforting and gentle.

"I see," Jake said finally. "I guess I do owe you an apology for both." His finger fiddled with the handle of the mug. As yet he hadn't tasted the tea, but then neither had Lily.

"I owe you one myself. I don't know what possessed me to go out with Rex. I shouldn't have. I don't know why I did." Her voice was husky. "That's not exactly true. I went with him because I wanted to get back at you for this afternoon."

"I didn't mean what I said." A telltale muscle twitched along his jaw.

Lily raised her eyes to meet Jake's, unsure that she had understood him correctly.

"Those things I said on the boat were spoken in desperation."

"But why?"

"Come on, Lily, surely you've figured it out by now." He pushed back the chair and stood, taking his tea with him. He marched to the sink and then turned back to her, leaning against the counter as he finally took a sip from his mug.

"You mean because we were kissing again?"

"Bingo."

"But I like kissing you."

"That's the problem, kid."

Lily winced at the use of the childish term. "All right, well, we don't ever have to touch each other again."

It wasn't what Jake wanted, but for his peace of mind and for the sake of a treasured relationship, he had little choice but to agree. "That would be best."

"The kissing was just the result of my own curiosity."

"So you said."

Lily's heart was hammering in her throat. She was forced to admit how much she'd come to enjoy Jake's touch and the thought of them never kissing again filled her with regret. She took a sip of her tea, which had grown lukewarm.

Jake followed suit. There didn't seem to be anything more to say but he wasn't ready to leave, so he searched for an excuse to linger. "You were right about me being unreasonable this evening."

She released a short, audible breath that told of her own remorse. "Going out with Rex and flaunting it in your face like that was childish of me."

"So you knew I was waiting tonight."

"No." Her stare found his. She'd hoped, of course, but she hadn't guessed that he'd be there after their confrontation on the sailboat. "My feelings were hurt and I didn't think you'd care one way or the other if I saw Rex—especially after today—so I agreed to dinner. I regretted it from the minute we left the hotel."

"You seemed to be enjoying your meal." His jaw clenched at the memory of Lily in that fancy French restaurant.

Lily swallowed at the lump of pride that constricted her throat. She'd come this far. "That was an act for your benefit. It's stupid, I know, but at the time it made sense."

A crooked grin lifted one corner of his mouth. "You're

lucky that me making a scene in that restaurant *didn't* make sense."

"I guess I am." She returned his smile, wondering if there would ever be a time when his expressive eyes wouldn't affect her.

Jake glanced at his watch. "I suppose I should think about heading home." A few more nights like this one and he'd have trouble paying his bills.

"It is late." Lily couldn't disagree with that, but she didn't want him to leave. She never did.

He took one last swallow of the tea and placed the mug in the sink. "I'm glad we were able to resolve our differences."

"We were both wrong."

"Are you working tomorrow?" He already knew she wasn't, but asking delayed his departure.

"No."

"How about an afternoon on the boat?" It was the least he could do.

Instantly, her dark eyes brightened. Lily loved the *Lucky Lady*, and the thought of spending a carefree afternoon with Jake was an opportunity she couldn't refuse. "You're sure?"

No, he wasn't. Spending the day beside her without being able to touch her would be pure torture for him. But he knew it would make her happy.

"Jake?"

"I invited you, didn't I?"

"Then I'd love to."

"It's a date then. Meet me around noon?"

"I'll be there." She followed him through the living room to the front door. "Jake."

He turned, his brow knit with doubts over the sailing invitation. "Yeah?"

"Thank you for coming back. I wouldn't have been able to sleep if you hadn't."

His body relaxed. "Me neither." With that he was gone.

The following morning Lily was humming as she worked around the kitchen. She had a lemon meringue pie baking in the oven and was assembling some pastrami sandwiches when Gram returned from the garden nursery. The older woman carted in a full tray of potted plants.

At Lily's dubious look, Gram explained, "They were on sale."

Continuing to pack the sandwiches, Lily commented, "But aren't you the one who insists that we don't save money by spending money?"

"Good grief, no."

"Are you sure?" Lily tried unsuccessfully to hide a smile.

"Of course I'm sure. I may be seventy-four, but my mind is still good. I'm the one who says that when the going gets tough, the tough go shopping."

Lily burst out laughing. "I love you, Gram. I don't think I let you know that nearly often enough."

"Sure you do, girl."

Lily hugged her grandmother. Gram might be a bit eccentric, but she had given Lily a good life, taking her in and raising her in a home full of love. "I've got some news for you."

"What?" Gram leafed through the mail, tossing the junk mail without a second glance. The rest she stuffed into an overflowing basket on the kitchen counter.

"I'm giving the Wheaton my two-week notice."

Gram looked doubtful. "Now why would you do that?"

"I don't like it there. This morning I saw a job posting for a music director at a daycare center. I already called and booked an interview."

"And you'd enjoy that?" Gram regarded her skeptically.

"I'm sure I would. You know how much I like children."

"That you do. You're as natural with them as you are with us old folks."

Opening the refrigerator, Lily scouted its contents, taking out two red apples.

"You going somewhere?"

"Jake and I are taking out the *Lucky Lady*."

Gram sank into a kitchen chair and propped her feet up on the one across from it. "Rick phoned last night. I forgot to tell you."

"What did he want?"

"Just to remind you that he was taking you to dinner tonight."

Lily bit into her bottom lip. "Darn." She'd forgotten about that. "Did he say what time he'd be by?"

"Seven. He didn't seem too happy when I told him you were going out with that fellow from Texas."

Hands on her hips, Lily swiveled around. She'd phoned Gram during her break to explain why she'd be late. "You told him?"

"Had to, girl. He'd mentioned swinging by the hotel to see you."

"Great," Lily grumbled. On second thought it was probably just as well. Rick seemed to want to get too serious too quickly, but Rick was nice and deserved someone who would appreciate him.

"How much do you like this Rick fellow?" Gram wanted to know.

"He's all right."

"Seems to be well off."

"He's got money, if that's what you mean."

"That's what you've been wanting."

The words had a brittle edge to them. Lily opened her mouth to argue that Gram made her sound calculating and shallow, but she found she had no ground. That was exactly the way she'd been in the past. Her ambition to marry rich had made her so narrow-minded that it was little wonder she'd been disappointed with both Rick and Rex.

"I'm not so sure anymore," Lily murmured, tucking the lunch supplies into the bottom of a wicker basket. "I've been doing some thinking lately and I feel that there are certain things in life more valuable than a fat bank account."

"Oh?" Gram gave her a look of mock surprise.

"Money's nice, but it isn't everything."

"The next time house taxes are due I'll tell that to the county clerk."

"We've always managed in the past; we'll do so again."

Gram mumbled something under her breath, but she was smiling and Lily wondered what her game was.

"So you're going to spend the day with Jake? I take it you two have resolved your differences?"

"We're working on it," Lily hedged. They'd taken one step forward, but at the moment it seemed a small one. There was so much she wanted to share with Jake and feared she couldn't. Her job at the Wheaton was coming to an end, but she wouldn't tell Jake until she had another one to replace it. Otherwise he might worry. He cared for Gram and her. Lily only wished he cared a little bit more.

9

Jake placed the jib sail on the bow of the *Lucky Lady*. He was nervous about this excursion with Lily and regretted having suggested it. However, he realized that Lily loved being on the water and that the invitation to sail would go a long way toward repairing their friendship.

Strolling down the long dock that led to Jake's boat, Lily saw him working on the bow. She paused to admire him. Her heart fluttered at the sight of his lean, brawny figure. He was all man, rugged and so completely different from Rick that it was difficult to picture them as friends. Jake possessed an indomitable spirit and a fierce pride. Of the two men, Rick was the more urbane and sophisticated, but there was a purity of character in Jake. He was true to himself and his beliefs. Rick was too easily influenced by those around him. He considered it important to flow with the tide. Jake was the type of man who *moved* the tide.

"Morning," she called, standing on the pier and waving at him.

"Good morning." Jake straightened and Lily noted he wasn't smiling. Wasn't he pleased to be sailing today? Was he only doing this for her? Hoping to turn things around, she held up the picnic basket enthusiastically. "I packed us a lunch."

"Good thinking." He climbed down from the bow. "Are you ready to cast off?"

"Aye, aye, captain." She saluted and handed him the basket before climbing aboard. While he fiddled with the ropes, Lily took off her light summer jacket. She'd worn jeans and a sleeveless top, hoping to catch a bit of a tan on her arms. She didn't hold out much hope for this day, but desperately yearned to smooth over the rough edges of their relationship. Jake had been such a good friend. There were things in her life that only Jake knew. She could tell him anything without fear of being criticized or harshly judged. Anyone else would have called her hard-hearted and callous to set her sights on a wealthy man. Not Jake. He'd even gone so far as to introduce her to Rick and try to help her fulfill her ambitions. And she had helped him. Jake longed to be a successful author. He could do it, too. The *New Yorker* wouldn't buy a short story from someone without talent.

"We're going to have nice weather," Jake said, looking to the blue sky.

"Yes, we are." They were tiptoeing around each other, Lily realized, each afraid of the other's response. "Can I raise the sails again?"

"If you want." He kept his sights straight ahead, manning the helm.

Feeling self-conscious and a little unsteady on her feet, Lily climbed to the bow and prepared to raise the sails. She waited until they were clear of the waterway that led from the marina to the deep, greenish waters of San Francisco Bay before hoisting the sails and tying them off. The boat instantly keeled and sliced through the rolling waves.

Holding on to the mast, Lily threw back her head and raised her closed eyes to the warm rays of the summer sun. A sense of exhilaration filled her. Her unbound hair blew behind her head like a flag waving in the breeze. She loved this. Her skin tingled with the force of the wind and the spray of saltwater. "This is great," she called down to Jake a moment later. Finding a comfortable spot, she sat and wrapped her arms around her bent knees. She felt marvelous—better than she had in weeks; giddy with happiness. She looked at Jake and their eyes met. Lily's cheeks grew warm as he studied her. His eyes became serious and seemed to linger on her mouth. She smiled at him. He responded with a short, almost involuntary, grin.

Jake found himself incapable of looking away. Lily was so lovely that the picture of her at this moment, her dark hair wind-tossed and free, would be forever seared in his mind. He yearned to go to her, kneel at her feet, and promise her the world.

He felt as though he'd been punched in the gut. The emotion he felt for her went far beyond friendship. He was in love. All this time he'd *been* in love with her and hadn't been able to admit it—not even to himself. A frown drove deep grooves in his brow. What was he supposed to do now? He'd always cared for her. Recognizing his feelings couldn't make a difference. There were things that Lily wanted that he could never give her. Fancy parties, diamonds and expensive clothes. From the pittance he earned driving a taxi and writing stories, it was unlikely that he could ever afford those things. He might love her, but he wouldn't let that love destroy her dreams.

Lily studied Jake and noted that he was brooding. She couldn't recall a time when he'd been more withdrawn.

Concerned, she cupped her hands around her mouth and called out: "Are you hungry?"

Jake stared out across the water before answering. "I could eat something." Actually, he was ravenous but he wasn't sure he was ready for Lily to join him on deck. Now that he'd acknowledged his feelings, it would be ten times more difficult to keep her out of his arms.

Lily hadn't eaten since early morning. "I'm starving." Watching her step, she worked her way toward the opposite end of the sailboat to join him.

Jake watched her as she approached. The sun glittered through her hair, giving it an almost heavenly shine. Her lips were pink and so inviting that the muscles in his abdomen tightened. Each step she took emphasized the lovely lines of her neck and shoulders and the curve of her breasts… Jake's thoughts came to an abrupt halt.

This type of thinking wouldn't do either of them any good. He could fantasize until doomsday about making love to Lily and it wouldn't change anything. She was going to marry some rich man and Jake was going to let her.

Lily glanced up from the picnic basket to find Jake watching her, clearly amused. "Is something funny?"

"No." His gaze shot past her to the water, but when he turned back to her, he smiled, his face relaxing and his eyes growing gentle and warm.

Lily experienced the effects of being near Jake almost immediately. She was so tempted to just reach out and touch him. She sat as far away as she dared without being obvious. Yet she was drawn to him like a homing pigeon to its place of rest.

"What did you pack?" Jake asked.

"Pastrami sandwiches and homemade lemon meringue pie." She removed the cellophane and handed him a sandwich.

"Mustard?" He cocked one dark brow with the question.

"Your wish is my command."

"Your memory impresses me."

I'm glad something does, she mumbled to herself, suddenly feeling gloomy. She didn't dare get close to Jake, even in the most innocent way. Lily was tired, having slept only a few hours the previous night. She yearned to curl up in his arms and nestle her head against his chest. She looked away, fearing he would take one look at her and know what she was thinking.

"Aren't you going to eat something?" Jake asked. "I thought you said you were hungry."

"I am," she answered, somewhat defensively. Reaching inside the basket, she withdrew another sandwich, unwrapped it and took a bite. "There's cold beer if you want one," she told him.

"Sure." Lily grabbed one for him and another for herself.

"I didn't know you liked beer. I thought you preferred wine."

"I do sometimes. Beer's good too. It's an acquired taste. Gram says it's good for what ails you."

Jake downed a large swallow and wiped his mouth off with the back of his hand. "Gram's right."

Lily took a more delicate swig. The liquid felt cold all the way to her stomach. She took another bite of the sandwich. "My dad was a big beer drinker."

"You've never spoken much of your father."

"He died when I was young." Lily looked at the sails as they billowed in the wind, avoiding eye contact with Jake.

"What about your mother?"

"I don't remember her," she said, her voice growing soft. "The pictures Gram gave me of her make me wish I had. She was really beautiful. But she died of complications following surgery."

"You must have been very young."

"Three. Gram took me in then because Dad traveled so much. I don't think Dad ever recovered from losing my mother. Gram says they loved each other like no two people she'd ever known, except her and Paddy. Yet my parents were nothing alike. Mom was delicate. From her pictures, she looks like a fragile princess. And Dad was this big hulk of guy—a lumberjack sort of fellow. I have wonderful memories of him. Whenever he'd come home it was like Christmas; he brought Gram and me the most marvelous gifts. I saved every one. Mom and Dad's picture sits on my dresser. I'll show it to you sometime if you'd like."

The smile in Jake's eyes widened and spread to his mouth. "You must resemble her."

"Me?" Lily laughed. "No, I'm more like my dad. I've got this big nose and fat cheeks and ears that tend to stick out."

"You're lovely."

"Why, Jake, what a nice thing to say." She laughed and took another swallow of the beer. "When was the last time you had your eyes examined?" It felt good to tease him again. "What about your parents?"

"There's not much to tell. They're both still alive. I don't see them often. I'm kind of the black sheep of the family. My two brothers are successful. One's a bank executive and the other's a physician."

"And you're the almost famous writer." Lily was obliged to defend him. This past month when Lily had been seeing Rick and Rex had taught her how unfair it was to judge people by their bank balance.

"No, I'm a cabdriver and a failure. After all, they paid for four years of college for me that have completely gone to waste."

"It hasn't been wasted."

"In their eyes it has."

"You're a strong and solid man and if your parents don't see that, then I pity them." Jake was earthy and intelligent. A man of character and grit. He may have chosen a different path than his brothers, but that didn't make him any less a success.

"My mother would like you." His voice was oddly gruff. "She'd see you as just the type who could reform me."

"But you don't want to be saved. Remember?"

"You're right about that." But if anyone could ever do it, it would be Lily. A house, family and responsibilities wouldn't be half bad if he shared his life with her. The change wouldn't come easy, but he would be more prone to consider it with her.

They finished their beer and sandwiches and Jake ate a thick slice of pie, praising her efforts.

The sun shone brightly against the horizon and the boat plowed smoothly ahead through the choppy waters. Gradually, Lily's head began to droop. The beer had added to her sleepiness, and now she fought to keep her eyes open.

Intent on his duties, Jake didn't seem to notice until Lily started to slouch against his side. Instinctively he reached for her, looping an arm around her shoulders and pressing her weight to his side. The sheer pleasure of holding her was overwhelming. And yet it felt so natural. Pressing his face into her hair, he breathed in the fresh scent of her. She reminded him of summer wine.

Closing his eyes, Jake took in another deep breath and held it. He'd never told another living soul about his parents' disappointment in him. His love for Lily surged at the way she'd wanted to defend him. Her eyes had sparked with fiery indignation. A lazy smile spread over his features. The wind changed directions and he expertly manipulated the canvas sails around to catch the power of the moving air.

Relaxed now, he stretched out his legs and crossed them at the ankles. A man could get accustomed to this. The woman he loved was in his arms and the sea was at his command.

Lily stirred, feeling secure and warm. Slowly she opened her eyes and realized the cause of this incredible relaxed sensation. Suspecting that any sudden movement would destroy the moment, Lily gradually raised her face to Jake. His serious eyes met hers.

The sails flapped in the breeze and still Jake didn't move. Lily remained motionless and the moment stretched out until she lost all concept of time. It could have been seconds or even minutes, she didn't know. Jake's face was so close to hers that she could see every line etched in his face. Jake smiled. Then, a fraction of an inch at a time, his mouth edged toward hers.

Lily closed her eyes, surrendering to him. Ever so gradually, his mouth eased onto hers. Lily felt her heart melt, but resisted the urge to lock her arms around his neck. Although she yearned for more, she was unwilling to invite it. Only the day before, Jake had ardently claimed he hadn't wanted this. Yet here he was, holding her, kissing her and looking as though it would take all the forces of heaven and hell to drive them apart.

The kiss lindered for what seemed like a lifetime. When he finally dragged his mouth from hers, Lily didn't protest. Her response had to be careful. It would be tragic to destroy this moment. She kept her eyes closed and savored the feel of his breath as it continued to fan her lips. She could tell that Jake was as affected by the kiss as she.

"Oh, Lily," he whispered. Jake bent his index finger and gently pressed it to her lips. "Did you enjoy your nap?"

Her response was a faint nod.

"Good."

Unhurriedly, as if moving in slow motion, Jake lifted his arm from her shoulders. Lily shifted her weight and stretched. Sitting up straight, she smoothed her hands over her jean-clad thighs, searching for something to say.

"We're doing it again and we said we wouldn't," Jake said.

Lily cast her gaze to the deck. "You're right."

"We should think about heading back. It's been a full afternoon."

Lily felt hurt and cheated. Why did Jake find it so objectionable to kiss her? Every time he did, it was wonderful. "Okay," she mumbled. "If that's what you want."

"Don't you?"

"No. Yes. I don't know anymore. What's wrong with kissing me?" she asked him bluntly.

"Plenty. I'm not right for you." His brow narrowed into a heavy frown. "I'd never make you happy."

"I'm happy with you now," she cried, her voice breaking.

"Sure you are, but it won't last, Lily. I'm saving us both a lot of heartache, understand?"

"No, I don't."

His mouth hardened and he stared straight ahead, effectively closing her out. Lily had seen that look often enough to realize that she might as well argue with a brick wall, for all the good it would do her.

A sudden chill went all the way to her bones. She reached for her jacket. Jake was freezing her out again; but somehow it hurt more this time.

As they neared the marina, Jake momentarily gave her the helm and moved forward to lower the sails. The lump in the back of her throat had grown so large she could barely swallow. Even breathing was difficult. Today should have been special. And now it was ruined.

"Lily, listen. I'm doing this for your own good."

"Stop it, Jake," she all but shouted. "Why can't you be honest, for once? I don't know what you're trying to prove. I couldn't even begin to guess. I'm tired of playing your games."

The *Lucky Lady* glided smoothly into her berth. Lily waited just long enough for the boat to steady before leaping onto the dock.

"Lily, wait." Jake jumped after her, pausing to secure the vessel. "Don't leave like this. We need to talk this out." He didn't know what he could say, but seeing Lily this upset was more than he could bear. He had to find some way to reason with her.

She turned to face him squarely. "Sorry, no time. I've got a date with Rick."

The words hit Jake with all the force of a freight train. She had a date? Jake held her gaze and a muscle flexed convulsively in his jaw. Apparently it didn't bother her to go from one man's arms to another's. "Then what's keeping you?"

"You certainly wouldn't be interested in keeping me, would you?" Maybe it was cruel of her but she wanted him to experience just a little of what she was feeling. "Rick likes me. He isn't hot and cold."

Sadly she shook her head. "Goodbye, Jake." She turned and walked up the narrow dock. Every step took her farther from Jake and somehow Lily felt she'd never be coming back.

Jake watched her go, his fist knotted at his side. Half of him demanded that he race after her, but the other commanded that he stay exactly where he was. Against all good sense, he'd done it again. He'd kissed her and regretted it, punishing Lily for his own weakness. It wasn't Lily's fault he couldn't control himself around her. Nor was it her problem that he'd fallen in love with her. But something had to be done. And quickly.

In the past, he'd toyed with the idea of packing up and moving down the coast. They couldn't continue on this way. They were confusing one another, fighting their feelings, denying what they yearned for most. He had to get out of her life completely. There was no help for it. He had to leave.

Jumping back on the deck of his boat, Jake moved with determined strides. Now that he'd made up his mind, he felt better.

Belowdecks, he reached for the sea maps, charting his course down the California coast. He was a free man, no ties, no bonds. He could go without a backward glance. Except…

Jake paused. *Except.*

He slumped against the counter. He couldn't leave Lily. It would be like leaving a part of himself behind. Who was he trying to fool? He loved her. Loved her enough to give up the precious freedom he'd struggled to maintain all these years.

He'd sell the boat before he'd lose Lily. The thought nearly paralyzed him. He'd meant it. Lily was worth ten thousand *Lucky Lady*'s.

When a man felt that strongly for a woman there was only one option: marriage. He waited for the natural aversion to overtake him. It didn't. The startling fact was that it actually sounded quite appealing.

His mind conjured up a house with a white picket fence around it. He could see Lily in the front yard planting flowers, pregnant.

That, too, had a nice feel to it. Jake hadn't thought of it

much, but he'd like to have a son. And a daughter would be a joy if she looked anything like Lily.

Marriage, a family, responsibilities, a regular job—those were all the things he'd despised over the years. Jake had claimed they weren't for him. But they would be if he had Lily at his side. All this time he'd had the gut feeling that Rex and Rick were wrong for her. Of course they were. *He* was the one meant for Lily. In time, Jake would give her the fancy things she wanted. He even looked forward to doing it.

Shuffling through his closet, Jake took out his best clothes. He'd shower and shave first so he'd look halfway decent. A man didn't ask a woman to be his wife every day of the week.

"Hi, Gram." Lily walked in the front door and tried to put on a happy face.

Rocking in her chair, Gram glanced away from the TV show she was watching. "You've been crying."

"It…just looks that way. I've got something in my eye."

"Like tears," Gram scoffed, slowly getting to her feet. "What happened?"

"Nothing." Lily's could feel her control slipping. "Jake kissed…me," she finally said.

"Why, that's no reason to cry, child." Gram gave her a perplexed look as if she couldn't comprehend why Lily would find Jake's kiss so repulsive.

"I—I…know…but…he…doesn't…want…me."

"He'd hardly be kissing you if it wasn't what he wanted."

"You don't understand." She wiped the tears from her face. "I'm so in love with him, Gram. But you know Jake. He doesn't want a woman in his life. Loving him has ruined everything. We've lost him."

Gram's look was thoughtful as she slipped her arm around Lily's waist and hugged her close. "Dry those tears. You and I have weathered worse over the years. And as for losing Jake, we can't lose something we never had. Let Jake sort this out for himself. He's a smart man."

"I don't ever want to see him again."

The older woman smiled. "You don't mean that. But I know how you feel. Paddy and me had some pretty good fights in our time."

"We didn't fight," Lily insisted. In some ways she wished they had. An argument would have cleared the air. It might even have brought out the truth and helped them find a solution—if there was one.

Slowly Gram walked into the kitchen and put on the kettle. "I'll make you a cup of Marmite."

"Thanks, Gram," she said solemnly. She'd spent so much time trying to find herself a wealthy man that she'd allowed herself to be blind to the treasures she already possessed.

The last thing Lily felt like doing was getting ready for her date with Rick. She had to end things. She'd been using him and that couldn't continue.

The doorbell chimed just when Lily was touching up her makeup. The telltale redness around her eyes had faded and she looked reasonably attractive.

Lily stuck her head around the corner to be sure that Gram had answered the door. With the television blaring, Gram often didn't hear the bell. It had gotten so bad that Jake had become accustomed to knocking once and letting himself in. At the thought of Jake, a tiny shudder went all the way through her.

Rick stood awkwardly in the living room and Lily offered him her brightest smile. She wasn't looking forward to this evening. "I'll be with you in a minute."

"Take your time," he said, smiling back at her.

Tonight wouldn't be easy, but she wasn't going to be maudlin.

After grabbing her purse and a light wrap, she rejoined Gram and Rick in the living room, forcing herself to smile.

Knowing Lily would be out with Rick, Jake waited for what he considered a reasonable amount of time before heading over to Gram's. Content now that he'd made his decision, he climbed inside his faithful taxi and absently ran his hand along the empty seat. He'd sell the cab. That would be the first thing to go. While waiting, he'd scanned the newspaper. Finding a decent job shouldn't be too difficult. Engineers seemed to be in demand, and although his degree had several years' dust on it, he'd been a good student. An employer would recognize that soon enough.

On impulse, Jake stopped at a corner market and picked up a small bouquet of flowers. He didn't know what kind they were; flowers were Lily and Gram's department. Humming, he eased to a stop in front of Gram's house, climbed out of the car and slapped his hand across the hood as he ventured past. He felt good. Once everything was straightened out with Lily, he'd be on cloud nine.

Gram answered his knock and he proudly shoved the flowers in her direction. "Is Lily home yet?"

"Are these for me or her?"

"Both."

"I'd say you're a bit late."

It wasn't like Gram to snap or grumble. Jake glanced at his watch. "It's barely ten."

"That's not the late I'm talking about."

"Is Lily home or not?" His own patience was running short.

"Not. I don't know what's come over you, but Lily came home from her time with you in tears."

Shifting his weight from one foot to the other, Jake cleared his throat. He hadn't expected the third degree from Gram. "I came to apologize for that."

"And I'm telling you, you're too late."

A sudden chill went all the way through Jake. "What do you mean?"

"Rick was here earlier."

"I know." All evening he'd been haunted by the image of Rick kissing Lily. He'd considered intercepting their date, but he'd done that before and had promised himself he wouldn't again.

"Only this time Rick didn't come alone."

Confused, Jake shook his head, not understanding Lily's grandmother. "How do you mean?"

"Rick came a-courting with a two-karat diamond ring in his pocket," Gram explained. "He's requested my permission to ask for Lily's hand."

10

"I see," Jake said slowly. The words went sour on his tongue. He did indeed understand. Lily had finally achieved her goal. She'd landed herself a wealthy man. Swallowing back the angry denial that trembled at the end of his tongue, Jake buried his hands deep inside his pants pockets. "I imagine Lily was thrilled?" He raised expectant eyes to Gram. The happy, carefree feeling that had been with him from the moment he'd decided to ask Lily to marry him slowly shriveled up and died.

"I can't rightly say. Rick planned on asking her at dinner this evening."

"Lily will accept." She'd be a fool not to, Jake knew.

"It's the best offer she's likely to get," Gram asserted, eyeing Jake in his best clothes. "But I'll tell her you were by."

"Don't." The lone word burst forcefully from his lips. "It wasn't anything important." He took a step back and bumped into the front door. Abruptly he turned around and gripped the doorknob, needing a moment to gather his thoughts. "Actually," he said, turning back to Gram. "On second thought you can mention that I was here. Tell Lily that I wish her and Rick every happiness."

"Do you want me to tell her anything else?" Gram encouraged with her usual astuteness. "You didn't bring these flowers for an old woman."

Jake's gaze fell on the elephant tusks mounted on the wall and the zebra-skin rug spread in front of the fireplace. Herbie, the shrunken head who Gram claimed was their spiritual protector, sat on the end table in its place of honor. Jake would miss all of it, and Gram with her African chants and wise old eyes.

"No," he murmured sadly. There was nothing left to say. Lily's dreams had come true, and his nightmares were of his own making.

The following morning, Lily sat down at the kitchen table with a mug of hot coffee. She needed the caffeine. The evening with Rick had been a disaster from the start. After he'd learned that she'd gone out with Rex, Rick had panicked and come to her with a huge diamond ring and a marriage proposal. She didn't want to hurt him, but she couldn't marry him either.

The morning paper was spread across the table and Lily mindlessly read the headlines. Gram pulled out a chair to join her. "Where'd the flowers come from?" Lily asked, noting the colorful bouquet in the middle of the table.

Gram glanced up from the comic-strip section of the newspaper and grinned. "A secret admirer."

"Oh?" Gram had attracted more than one man. But to the best of her knowledge, Lily had never known her grandmother to see or talk of anyone except her beloved Paddy.

"Only my secret admirer couldn't decide if the gift was meant for me or you. He finally decided on me."

"And who could this indecisive fellow be? Tom the butcher? Or that new man who's been eyeing you at bingo?"

"Nope. It was Jake."

"Jake!" Lily did her utmost to disguise the wild happiness that shot through her. "Jake was here? When?"

Idly, Gram folded the newspaper to the crossword section and scrunched up her brow as she studied the fine print. "Late last night. It must have been close to ten."

Nearly too overwhelmed to speak, Lily stumbled over her words. "Why didn't you… What did he… Flowers?" She clenched the soft bathrobe at her throat. Jake. Here. Why, oh why, hadn't Gram said anything sooner?

"I don't know what he wanted. He was acting oddly."

Lily jumped to her feet. "I'm going to get dressed. Did he stay long?"

"Five minutes or so. Not long." Gram didn't look up as her pencil worked furiously across the newspaper, filling in the words. "Just remember what I told you the first time we met Jake: you and he were meant for each other."

There was a gleam in Gram's eye that hinted at something more, something she wasn't saying.

"Since Jake came by here, it would only be polite to return the visit. Right?" She didn't wait for Gram to answer her. "He obviously had something on his mind or he wouldn't have come. I mean, it isn't like Jake to stop by unexpectedly." He did exactly that three or four times a week but Lily was grateful her grandmother didn't point it out.

Hardly caring what she wore, Lily dug through her drawer and found a pair of white linen pants and a floral print top. A quick run of the brush through her hair left it looking shimmering and healthy.

At the marina, the first thing Lily noticed was Jake's taxi with a For Sale sign propped against the dashboard. Lily stared at it with disbelief. The money from the short story sale to the *New Yorker* had been good, but not enough to live on. Jake would never sell his source of income.

Hurrying now, she half-ran down the wooden dock that led to his slip. She spotted him immediately, working on the deck, coiling a large section of rope around his arm. Her pace slowed. Now that she was here, there didn't seem to be anything particular to say. Although he was facing her, he didn't acknowledge her approach or give any indication that he'd seen her.

"Morning, Jake." She stood with her hands clenched together in front of her.

He ignored her, continuing to wind the thick rope around his arm, using his elbow as a guide.

"There's a For Sale sign on the cab."

"I know."

"But why?"

"It's for sale." His voice held no welcome.

Lily could see that this topic wasn't going anywhere. "Gram said you were by the house last night."

"I was."

If he didn't stop with that stupid rope and look at her soon, she was going to rip it out of his arms. "The flowers are lovely."

Jake's mouth tightened. "Consider them a goodbye present."

Her heart pounded wildly in her ears. "Goodbye?"

"Yeah, I'm moving down the coast."

"This is all rather sudden, isn't it?"

"I've been thinking about it for some time."

Lily set her hands on her hips. "You'd move just to spite me, wouldn't you?"

For the first time, he halted and glanced up at her, his eyes a brilliant green. His feet were braced slightly apart as if anticipating a fight. "You're not making any sense. I'm moving because..."

"Because you're afraid."

Jake snorted. Inwardly, he admitted that she was probably right. He couldn't be around Lily without wanting her and the best thing for them both was to remove the temptation. "I've fought in Iraq, tangled with drunks who couldn't afford to pay their fare, and listened to your grandmother sing an African chant over my head. I'd say you have little reason to accuse me of cowardice." That, too, was a half-truth. Just being close to Lily caused him to tremble. What had made perfect sense the day before seemed like utter stupidity now. He loved her, yes. But that didn't mean they should get married.

"You're going away because of me."

"Yes!" Jake shouted, feeling angry and unreasonable. "I have this particular quirk about being seen with a married woman."

"I'm not married."

"Not yet, but you will be. Gram told me about Rick's proposal."

She held up her bare left hand, fanning her fingers. "I turned him down."

"That wasn't a smart move."

"I don't love Rick."

"That's your problem, Lily. You've got too much conscience. Loving him isn't necessary. Rick can give you all the fancy things you want."

"He can't give me what I want the very most."

"Give him time."

"Even that won't work," she assured him.

"And what is it that you want so badly?"

"You."

His dark eyes found hers, stunned and staring. "You don't mean that."

"I love you, Jake Carson."

"I don't have the money to buy you a fat diamond."

"A simple gold band will do." For every argument Jake presented, she would find a solution. She hadn't come this far to let him slip away.

"My home is right here. There isn't going to be any fancy house." *Except maybe one with a white picket fence and a row of flowers at the front.*

"In case you hadn't noticed, I love the *Lucky Lady*. We'll live right here."

"And what about kids? There's no room for children here." He gestured casually at the confines of the sailboat.

"Then we'll buy a bigger boat."

"I told you before that I can't give you the things Rick could." He didn't know why he continued to argue. He loved her.

"No, you probably can't. But I've learned how meaningless diamonds are. I love you, Jake, and if you love me back, I'd consider myself the wealthiest ex-piano player in town."

Jake's defenses relaxed as he let the rope fall to the deck. He held out a hand to Lily, guiding her safely aboard the *Lucky Lady*'s and into his arms. He buried his face in her hair and held her for several minutes, just breathing in the fresh fragrance of her. "I love you so much that part of me would have died to stand by and watch you marry Rick."

"Then why would you have let me?" Even now she couldn't understand his reasoning.

"Because I wanted to give you all those material things you deserved. But in order to do that, I had to let you go."

Lovingly, Lily cupped his face. His strong, proud features seemed to intensify with each word.

Lily sighed as relief washed over her. "The only thing I'll ever want is you."

"I'm already yours. I have been since that night in the attic and probably long before then, only I refused to acknowledge it." His strong arms held her closer as if he feared she would escape him.

Lily's eyes gleamed with happiness. "Gram was right."

"About what?"

"Before I left this morning, she told me that you and I were destined to be together."

Unable to resist any longer, Jake tenderly kissed the corner of her mouth. "How could she be so sure of that?"

Lily's hands toyed with the hair at the back of his neck. "Remember the day we met in front of the Wheaton when Gram chanted over you?"

His mouth found her cheek. "I'm not likely to forget it."

"Gram was sealing our fate. That was a fertility rite. We're doomed to live a long, happy life. And from what Gram said, we're going to need a very large boat in the years to come."

Jake chuckled. "I can live with that," he told her, and then he kissed her, certain that this time he'd never let go.

★ ★ ★ ★ ★